Please Return to
George Carthay
402-291-3105

D0107936

KALLISTE

a novel

ROGER DELL

Kalliste Copyright © 2019 by Roger Dell

Alla Salute Press

All rights reserved. No portion of this book may be reproduced — mechanically, electronically, or by any other means, including photocopying — without written permission of the Publisher.

ISBN 978-0-9963950-2-1

First Edition

Editors Paula Jacobson & Sheilah Kaufman of Cookbook Construction Crew

Cover illustration Ken Hendricksen

Cover design artwork Reid Ogden

Cover layout & interior design Amy Wilder Files of wilderbydesign

Maps & chapter icon Annie Bailey

IN MEMORIAM

My Parents

THE DEEP BLUE SEA
(MEDITERRANEAN SEA)

THESSALY

AEGEAN SEA

TROY

IONIAN
SEA

DELPHI

ATTICA

ACHAEA

ATHENS

MYCENAE
TIRYNS

PELOPONNESUS

AEGINA

KEA

ASTERIE

SPARTA

MINOA

NAXOS

PYLOS

SIFNOS

ASTIPALAEA

CYCLADES

MILOS

KYTHERA

KALLISTE
(SEE DETAILED MAP)

ANALFI

MEDITERRANEAN SEA

CRETE

(SEE DETAILED MAP)

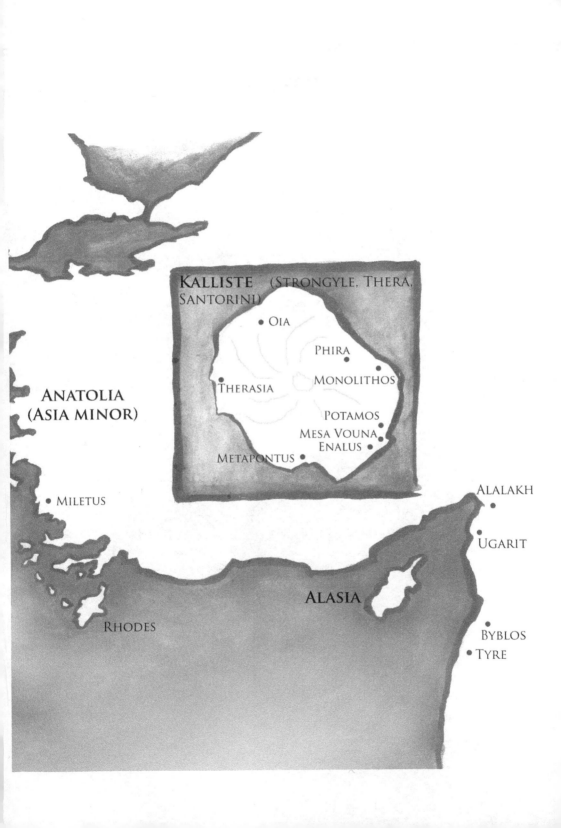

KALLISTE (STRONGYLE, THERA, SANTORINI)

- OIA
PHIRA
MONOLITHOS
THERASIA
POTAMOS
MESA VOUNA
ENALUS
METAPONTUS

ANATOLIA
(ASIA MINOR)

- MILETUS

ALALAKH

UGARIT

ALASIA

RHODES

BYBLOS
- TYRE

CRETE

MEDITERRANEAN SEA

KYDONIA •

WHITE MOUNTAINS

MOUNT IDA •

LIBYAN SEA

TIMBAKI —

MATALA —

SNOW CRYSTAL

PHAISTOS

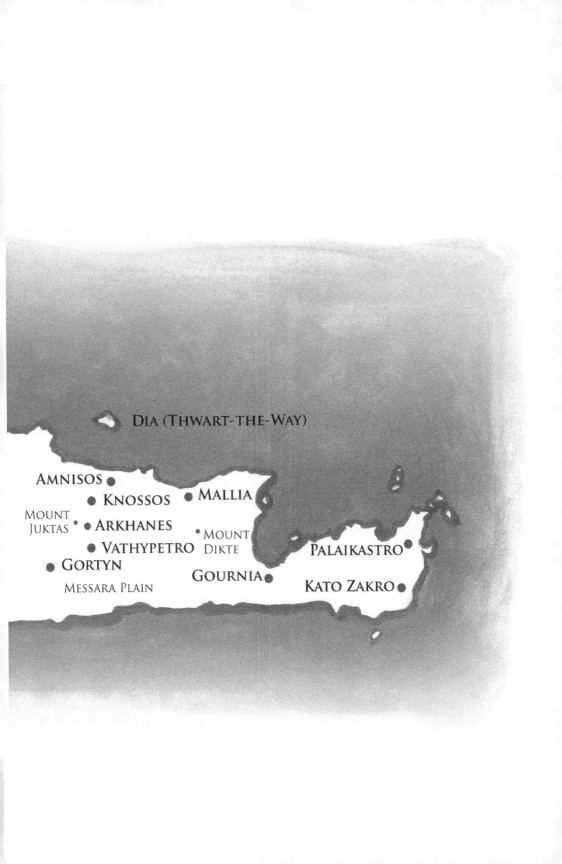

DIA (THWART-THE-WAY)

AMNISOS •
• KNOSSOS   • MALLIA
MOUNT
JUKTAS • • ARKHANES
• MOUNT
• VATHYPETRO   DIKTE
• GORTYN
PALAIKASTRO •
MESSARA PLAIN
GOURNIA •
KATO ZAKRO •

CAST OF CHARACTERS

Gods & Goddesses

Apollo	Achaean God of the Sun; divinity of light, reason, fine arts, and music
Ares	Achaean God of War
Britomartis	Cretan/Cycladic Goddess of Wild Life; divinity of hunters
Diktynna	Cretan/Cycladic Goddess of Seas and Seafarers
Eileithyia	Achaean/Cretan/Cycladic Goddess of Childbirth
Great Mother Goddess	Cretan/Cycladic Divine Protectress of Earth, Nature, the Underworld, and Souls
Poseidon	Achaean God of the Sea
Zeus	Chief of the Achaean gods

Main Characters on Crete

Androgeus	Son of King Minos and Queen Pasiphae
Aphaea	Handmaiden to Princess Biadice of Phaistos
Ariadne	Daughter of King Minos and Queen Pasiphae
Biadice	Princess of Phaistos
Catreus	Son of King Minos and Queen Pasiphae
Daedalus	Master artist at Knossos and builder of the Labyrinth
Glaukus	Wise man; guest at Snow Crystal
Minos	Dynastic King of Crete; husband of Queen Pasiphae
Pasiphae	Queen of Crete; wife of King Minos
Rhadamanthys	Prince of Phaistos

Main Characters on Kalliste

Andrus	Prince of Potamos
Althaemenes	Scribe; brother of first lieutenant and pilot Phanus at Phira
Cretheus	Father of Idomeneus at Phira
Henithea	Mother of Idomeneus at Phira
Himera	Daughter of Sarpedon at Metapontus; betrothed to Idomeneus
Idomeneus	Prince of Phira
Lacinius	Prince of Therasia
Miletus	Yeoman of Idomeneus
Oenopion	Prince of Oia
Phanus	First lieutenant under Idomeneus; pilot of boat, the Dove; brother of Althaemenes
Sarpedon	Prince of Metapontus
Thoas	Prince of Enalus

Main Characters in Achaea

Aegeus	King of Athens; father of Theseus
Jason	Leader of the Argonauts
Theseus	Prince of Athens; son of Aegeus

Main Characters from the Near East & Beyond

Ananda	Wise man from India; guest at Snow Crystal on Crete
Rib-Addi	Merchant from the Levant; resident in Knossos-town on Crete
Ta-ch'ih	Wise man from China; guest at Snow Crystal on Crete

saluting the distant island from which we had cast off early that morning, my home, jewel-like Kalliste.

The chariot ride to the capital was a bumpy one. As I was jostled back and forth, I dreamed about past pleasures within the halls and suites of the palace. Before my eyes danced images of the fabulous items that could be found in the spacious palatial marketplace: gold and silver jewelry, bolts of expensive purple linen and wool, finely worked alabaster, statuettes in metal and ivory, and countless other treasures. I knew that at the stalls' delectable foods, spices, and many fine wines — though none as fine as rich-soiled Kalliste's — asked to be sampled. Dried fruits, covered with the gold made by Cretan bees, begged to be eaten. All these delights, fit for the goddesses, were available to us mortals. My mind reeled at the thought of the deep-waisted women who adorned the apartments of the capital; they were as plentiful as exotic birds in Libya. From all around The Deep Blue, the women were sent to King Minos as presents, tributes, or prizes. Not being niggardly, the king shared them.

Such images quickened my heart, but others stilled it, coming in the form of questions. Would I find the capital sad and somber after the recent earthquake? Had Minos decreed a period of silence prior to the festival, putting a ban on revelry? While they repaired their earthquake-damaged apartments, would the citizens be too busy to play? Had gay music and dance been replaced by dirge and prayer? And would this greatest of cities now look like a jumble of firewood, with beams and columns scattered everywhere like so many broken twigs and branches?

Before I knew it, the roofs of the palatial apartments rose before me. Jumping out of the chariot, I thanked my driver and told him that I wanted to walk the rest of the way. When my foot stepped upon the first stone of the Sacred Way, my fears about the damage to the palace and the city began to subside; simply feeling that large slab beneath my foot gave me a sense of well-being. It was the oldest and longest road in the world, representing the permanence of Minos's rule, and as long as its stones remained in place, I believed that the kingdom would continue to expand and prosper. Over the past few decades, we people of Minos had come under attack from the northern barbarians for being overconfident, lazy, and weak. Such sniping was natural from the Achaeans who lived inland, north of us; but others, such as those war-loving Easterners, the Hittites, were joining in. Maybe the charges were partly true. But as I walked along the Sacred Way, it seemed to me that we were relaxed because we sat upon the shoulders of a thousand years of glory. The pavement stones were the solid footprints of our forefathers.

When I came to the first palatial structure, I found it perfectly intact. Next to it lay three upper-story columns, badly split during the earthquake, but their replacements, freshly painted vibrant red, were already carrying their weight. If each structure had suffered so little, I thought to myself, it would not be a serious rebuilding project after all. But when I turned to continue, my eyes met a woeful sight. On the north side of the Sacred Way lay a totally demolished house: first, second, and third story walls had collapsed inward, and the ceilings and the roof had fallen on top. As my heart sank, my mind raced, recalling the words of the Cretan messenger who, a month before, had brought the news of the quake to us on Kalliste. He had said that only one building suffered major damage to its foundation. Later, I found out that this house was indeed the one singled out by the messenger and that it had collapsed shortly after the messenger had shoved off for Kalliste.

I began to run along the road, looking at every structure for damage. I was relieved to discover that each building had about the same amount of damage as the first one and repairs were either underway or completed. Overall, the palace looked to be in fairly good condition, but I could not be completely convinced until I stood in the central court.

As usual, the theater and customs house were jammed. I quickly moved through the crowds of musicians, acrobats, orators, dancers, and magicians and made my way to the northern passageway. Hastily returning the salutes of the guards, I glanced up at the open portico to see if the magnificent fresco was intact. It looked fine, no noticeable cracks in the rampant red bull, its captors, or the fragile olive sprays on the ocher background. At last, I entered the central court. Turning, I could see most of the important apartments and assess their damage. The Cretan messenger had reported accurately, I thanked the Great Mother Goddess, Steerer of All Things. The de-

ONE

WE SET SAIL for Crete at dawn, two days before the Spring Festival. My men and I were as lighthearted as children for it was the Moon of Sailing and our first long voyage since winter. We became intoxicated by the pungent smell of the sea and the salty taste of the fine spray.

By the time the sun reached its zenith, our boat, the Dove, had covered half the distance from our home island, Kalliste, to Crete. Nothing unusual marked the passage. Suddenly, the sea-people appeared. It was the largest school of dolphins any of us had ever encountered. There must have been over a hundred eager creatures leaping and diving and skimming alongside the Dove. Even more amazing than their number was their dogged insistence on talking to us; with their clicking, chirping, and squeaking, they were clearly trying to communicate.

During our many years at sea, my men and I had often heard dolphins conversing among themselves. But that time as we sailed to Crete, the dolphins were directing their chatter at us! They wanted to alert us to something, and whatever it was, it was urgent. In pairs, they darted up to the prow, twisting their glistening heads toward the deck and staring intensely at us with large eyes, all the time increasing the volume and pitch of their cries. After one pair finished and swam on, a new pair replaced it, squeaking what sounded like the same warning. Incredible! The helmsman threw out the remains of his lunch: a crust of bread, a half-eaten mackerel, and pieces of squid—which dolphins love—but, amazingly, the food was ignored.

The curious scene went on for some time. Then the dolphins broke off, diving together into the dark blue sea. Dumbfounded, we turned and stared at one another. The dolphins' behavior was surely an omen—an emphatic one. But an omen of what? It couldn't have been the weather, which was perfect and showed no signs of changing, nor did the gentle sea. We had no seer aboard, so for the remainder of the voyage, we tried to interpret the sign for ourselves. Some said it meant that the fishing would be bad that year. Others thought that the recent earthquake on Crete had disturbed the sea as well as the land, leaving the dolphins troubled and confused. As it turned out, no one came close to the omen's true meaning.

When we passed Dia, the small island lying just north of the port of Amnisos and which sailors call Thwart-the-Way, earth-smelling air filled our nostrils, and our interest in solving the riddle of the dolphins began to fade. Soon we drew close enough to see people strolling along the wide dock. No matter how many times we had done it before, it was always a thrill to approach the capital of our empire, Knossos, and to anchor at Amnisos. In the marketplace and wine shops, sailors, merchants, courtiers, ambassadors, and every other kind of traveler from every land under the Four Pillars of the World could be found milling about, chatting, and calling.

After tying up the Dove, we were greeted by an official welcoming party, and I was ushered through the crowd to a waiting chariot. Once I climbed into the chariot, I turned back to wave goodbye to my crew. Already, every man was over the gunwale, all agog, racing down the dock; like sailors anywhere, they knew what to do when they made land. I started to lower my arm—knowing the last thing they were thinking about was their good captain—when I spotted a dark speck on the horizon. Smiling to myself, I brought the back of my clenched fist to my forehead, struction had been to the upper stories primarily, and, by the time I arrived, the damaged crossbeams and columns had been carted off. With architects, carpenters, and craftsmen hard at work, the palace was a beehive. As their subjects lovingly reshaped the hive, the queen bee and her king were being catered to somewhere deep within the complex of apartments.

When I saw the apartments and the rebuilding activity, I breathed a deep sigh of relief; Knossos was rebounding as only it could. I chuckled, glad that I had all day tomorrow to enjoy myself in the palace before the Spring Festival started.

The next day, I satiated my appetites and thirsts in that city of cities. That evening, I shuffled along slowly, as I made my way through the puzzle of streets towards the apartments that housed the visiting royalty. My mind, however, was not totally blunted. I thought about the upcoming events. Everybody was looking forward to the bull-leaping, especially the first contest, for a new team from the City of the Rock, Athens, was scheduled to perform; it was only the third Athenian team in history to be sent to Knossos. Unlike others from around the world who sent their teams to honor our King, the Athenians bitterly resented sending their team. Eighteen years ago, Androgeus, a son of Minos and Queen Pasiphae, was ambushed and slain by henchmen of King Aegeus of Athens. In his fury, Minos waged war on Athens. While he was at it, the king punished several other cities in the north, those that had not been paying him tribute. Pasiphae, as High Priestess, helped her husband, by convincing the Mother Goddess, to set aside Her role as averter of earthquakes. Thus, ruinous earthquakes shook Athens and all of Achaea. Finally, the Athenians and the other Achaeans consulted their oracle at Delphi and were told to pay whatever penalty Minos proposed — and quickly. The negligent cities began paying tribute at once. At the end of every Great Year — that is, every ninth year — Athens, because of its king's despicable deed, was forced to send seven maidens and seven youths to compete in the dangerous bull-leaping contests. While other teams, like those from Egypt and Alasia, the Copper Island, came respectfully to display their prowess, the Athenians came reluctantly. Oddly, despite this, it turned out that many of the best leapers came from Athens.

As I neared the royal apartments, I passed a row of food stalls and wine shops. I spotted, within one of the wine shops, a short elderly man dressed in a tattered Levantine robe. He was a strange-looking man, stoop-shouldered and long-limbed. His nose, big as a parrot's, looked as though it had been broken four or five times. Slouched on a rickety wooden bench, the old man was haranguing two very drunken Knossosans.

"Let their damn mummies rot. Who cares? They need us, we don't need them! If King Minos — bless his imperial soul — and his trade advisors would only listen to me…I know how to deal with these pyramid builders. I'm telling you, you can't give in to them; you have to keep on pressing. I know how their minds work. Remember, I traded with them for over thirty years! Oh, they're a crafty lot, all right. And smooth. But see here, just follow my reasoning." The old man's request seemed entirely out of the question, for his two young listeners had slumped to the floor, their eyes barely open. Unconcerned, the speaker went on, "You know that they use our Cretan honey for embalming their mummies, right? Fine. I say, let's continue shipping them as much as they need. I mean, if the whole population of Egypt needs to be dipped in honey tomorrow, we have enough!

"But for all those earthenware pithoi full of honey, let's get something decent in exchange! You must agree we get nothing in return from these people except perfume, hairy little monkeys, and ostrich eggs. Sure, they also send us little statues and trinkets, some made of pretty stone and faience. But what can you do with 'em, huh? There are only so many Egyptian baubles an apartment can take! Even though our marketplace is loaded with such things, the Egyptians continue to send us more. Why don't they send us some useful things?" In a conspiratorial tone, the old man asked, "Do you know that in Egypt they have horses with humps on their backs for storing water? Those beasts don't need a drink but once a month. And do you know that in Egypt they have scrawny-necked birds that give birth every day? Fresh eggs every day. Let them send some of those creatures over here to Crete.

"So, they send us some lovely ivory," the old man replied to an imaginary rebuttal. "It in no way equals our sweet honey in value." He paused for a moment, scratched his curly head and swigged some wine. "What about our cypress and pine," he said, having found his thread again. "We send Egypt forests of trees because the earth over there is nothing but sand!"

Knowing he could talk a donkey's hind leg off and feeling sorry for his two bleary-eyed companions, I entered the shop, "Come on, Rib-Addi, be fair," I said. "What about all the gold and gems the Egyptians send us? Not to mention those Kushites for our royal guard."

Rib-Addi turned slowly toward the door and, even before our eyes met, said, "Ah, good Prince Idomeneus, I had heard you were in our battered city." Then he rose, and we embraced each other warmly. I ordered a refill of wine for my friend and a cup for myself. As we sat down, I begged Rib-Addi to drop the old Egyptian controversy and fill me in on the earthquake and other news about Knossos.

My father, the noble Cretheus, had made but one voyage to the distant East, and it was then that he met Rib-Addi in the port of Byblos. Rib-Addi had been born to one of those innumerable tribes that make their homes in the inhospitable Canaanite land of hills and dunes. He had seen the great Nile in the south, the well-walled city of Troy in the north, and everything in between. Rib-Addi's enormous knowledge of the world proved to be quite a boon to my father, and for many years they sailed together. When my father died at sea, five years ago, the Easterner moved to Crete, having decided to live in Knossos instead of returning to his homeland. He lived off the wealth he had garnered from his hard work with my father.

"Will you be wrestling in the games, Excellency?" Rib-Addi asked.

"No, I think not, my friend. I haven't practiced much in the last six months. It's been too cold to roll around the courtyard in a loincloth!"

"Ah, yes. Do you still offer five sheep to any subject who can defeat you, my lord?"

"It's up to ten now. As you know, Rib-Addi, these prizes are the only way I can get any honest competition. Even though my subjects know me well, they still feel uneasy about wrestling against their prince, hesitating to give me a good throw. Thus, the prize if they should defeat me and the assurance that there would be no retaliation."

"This prize goes to any islander, Sire, not only those from your town, Phira?"

"Yes, of course."

"What about visitors to Kalliste?"

"Yes, all comers are welcome to try their skill."

Rid-Addi smiled, his eyes glinting. "And how many succulent animals have been cut from your flock, Prince Idomeneus?"

"Not a one."

"My lord, you must compete at this year's festival," cried Rib-Addi, clapping his hands together. "A barbarian inlander who claims that he is the greatest wrestler in the world will be entering! He claims to have invented new holds and throws! Can you imagine this arrogant savage suggesting that the traditional techniques need improving? Inventing new holds, ha! Is there no end to the insolence of these people?"

"I guess it's possible to introduce something new every now and then," I said dryly, "but, as you know, only minor variations are accepted in our arenas. Wrestlers of Minos must always employ the standard sacred moves and obey the time-honored rules — it's been this way for generations."

"Aye, you can't expect an Achaean to understand the subtlety of wrestling, let alone the sanctity of it."

"No, he doesn't comprehend how the athletes compete representing pairs of elements: earth and sky, light and dark, water and fire, male and female. He doesn't appreciate how each match represents the struggle and reconciliation between these elements, nor how the athlete who is victorious is so because the Bright-Eyed Goddess Britomartis, Lady of Strife, gave Her blessing to that athlete's element, not to the athlete himself.

"Though Achaean wrestlers don't seem to comprehend these things — or don't wish to — I must admit they are quite good. I guess I have competed against a half dozen of them over the years. They have tremendous strength and endurance, and they brave pain exceedingly well."

"This is no surprise," said Rib-Addi. "They are always warring against each other, and what they learn on the battlefields they bring to the arena."

"True. When you lock up with one of them, it's like tangling with a wild but crafty boar. An Achaean's power can be awesome, spellbinding. It's hard to put into words, but you become awed by the sheer animal strength of your opponent. Many a good wrestler has lost a match because of this strange spell. And no Achaean I have ever grappled with was above cheating."

"Aye," said Rib-Addi. "I understand that when their backs are to the referee, they'll scratch and bite like big cats."

"'Tis true. But a good Cretan or Kallistean wrestler can turn this zeal for victory to his advantage."

Rib-Addi nodded his head. "Well, Prince Idomeneus, at the bull-leaping contests in two days, you can scout out this braggart for yourself."

"You mean he's one of the Athenian leapers?"

"Aye, and a good one, too, or at least that's what the boys who have been watching the practice sessions are saying. You'll be able to see his quickness and dexterity for yourself, and if you like what you see and think him a worthy opponent, you can challenge him. That's if the Athenian survives the bull, of course. The wrestling matches are going to be held the day after the bull-leaping."

"It might be interesting, Rib-Addi, for I have never wrestled a bull-leaper before."

Rib-Addi looked tired and was feeling his wine, so we decided to head for our respective apartments. As we started to get up, he froze and grabbed my arm. "Sire, I must be getting old, or maybe I'm just drunk, but I forgot to tell you the juiciest detail about this Athenian, a detail that will flavor this year's festival more than a boatload of Tyrian harlots! The wrestler volunteered to come here."

"Incredible! That's unheard of for an Athenian."

"Even more incredible, he's the son of King Aegeus of Athens!"

"What? The king let his own son volunteer for such a mission? I can't believe it! Are you sure?"

"Yes, it's true, my lord," replied Rib-Addi, swallowing his spittle. "Knossos has been buzzing about it ever since the Athenians arrived. King Minos will watch this bull-leaping contest more keenly than usual, that's for sure! It would certainly be sweet revenge for Minos if this braggart died on the horns of the bull." Rib-Addi stopped and tugged at his beard. "But then you wouldn't have the chance to snap his barbarian neck. That would be a pity."

"So be it," I said without thinking, for I was wondering about the foolish Athenian. To consent to come to the capital, the son of Aegeus must be without his senses, for he faces certain death, either in the arena on a bull's horns or in his quarters on an assassin's dagger. Silently, I prayed that the Athenian would survive the bull, and that any would-be assassin would stay his hand. I knew I had to wrestle the barbarian. If he was not a fool, he possessed a kind of bravery I had never encountered. "What name does this Athenian go by?" I asked Rib-Addi.

"His teammates call him Theseus."

TWO

ON THE OPENING DAY of the Spring Festival, all the princes from throughout the kingdom were awakened early and escorted to the throne room for an audience with the king. In earlier years, we used to wait patiently for the king's arrival while sitting comfortably on the stone benches lining the walls of the antechamber. Our numbers, however, had mushroomed with the addition of so many new colonies that we filled the antechamber and spilled out into the central court. Each colony had been founded by a son of King Minos: this practice began with the first king and was continued by his successors, right down to the present king, Minos the Thirtieth. Someone commented that, in the future, the audience itself would have to be held in the court.

Before entering the throne room, each prince filed past the basin in the middle of the antechamber and purified himself by rinsing his hands in the clean cool water. We all managed to fit into the throne room, while leaving an aisle clear. Soon trumpets blared, proclaiming the arrival of the king. Minos strode regally down the aisle, returning our salutes. He mounted his exquisitely carved alabaster throne, which had an undulating back that perfectly matched the flowing fresco on the wall; the fresco depicted slender lilies on a rocky outcropping, painted in alternating bands of red and ochre.

Besides his sixty-odd years, the only things which distinguished Minos from most other men were the incredibly dark rings around his eyes and the livid whiteness of his skin. Being secluded in his palatial quarters, he rarely saw the light of day, and his complexion was fairer than a woman's.

Throughout the entire audience, the wide-ruling king did not utter a word. In fact, as I think about it, during all the audiences and public appearances I saw him at over the years, I never heard him say anything! His only means of communication at those functions were solemn salutes to those gathered and occasional quick gestures to his retainers. He could have been mute for all I know.

Before the official business of assigning new ports began, a slab-sided, skinny-legged priest led us in prayer. We thanked the Mother Goddess for accepting our offerings and putting aside Her wrath, which was obvious in the earthquake She allowed to take place on Crete last month. Then the high minister and eldest son of Minos, Prince Catreus, stepped forward to read off the list of port assignments.

Catreus was short and slight of build and had the fine features of Cretan nobility; the only discordant thing about his looks was an ugly scar that ran down his left cheek. He read off the new port assignments in a soft melodious voice. Some of those present did not receive ports because they were princes of landlocked cities or towns and did not trade on The Deep Blue. They were interested, nevertheless, in who got what. My town, Phira, was assigned Asterie as its additional port of call. Though a tiny island that would not increase our exports by much, Asterie was just north of Minoa, making our new circuit only a little bit longer. I was happy not to have to sail to some far-off port; my confidant within the palace had gotten me the assignment I had wanted.

After the ports were assigned, clear-voiced Catreus detailed the agenda for the entire Spring Festival. Then King Minos was escorted out, and all the princes were dismissed. Stepping out into the central court, we saw teams of workers busily constructing temporary gates at the entrances to the court and barricading the doors and windows of the ground floor rooms. The court was being transformed into a huge arena, with facades, barricades, and hurdles acting as retaining walls, all in preparation for the following day's bull-leaping contest.

For most of the day, I met with Prince Rhesus of Asterie and other princes to discuss business. Later on, I enjoyed myself in the palace's entertainment spots, finishing up by soaking in one of the splendidly appointed baths. All the rebuilding after the damage of the quake had stopped for the festival, and the palace and city were neat and, for the most part, complete. The Knossosans were in good spirits, gladly casting off the sorrow brought by the quake.

On the second day of the festival, thousands of people sat around the central court waiting for the start of the first bull-leaping contest. To be sure, there was no more exciting nor more colorful place in the world than the great court during the contests. Dignitaries from afar lounged in splendor in the second and, where possible, third stories of the palace; none of them seemed to mind the slight inconveniences resulting from unfinished repair work on the balconies.

Moving from story to story and balcony to balcony, the vendors shouted at the top of their voices, "Honey cakes! Roasted almonds! Candied fruit! Dried figs! Sweet wine for the drinking!" The ladies of the palace were perched on their special temporary stands. All painted, perfumed, and coiffured, the beauties were festooned with glittering gold, rock crystals, precious gems, and ivory. As the Great Goddess directed, again and again I turned my attention to those stands.

The stirring of strings, horns, and drums replaced the clamor of the crowd as King Minos and Queen Pasiphae entered the royal box on the second story and took their seats. Their magnificent thrones, which had been removed from their rooms and placed in the box, commanded the entire area. Before long Prince Catreus and his sister Princess Ariadne joined their parents, taking seats on the king's left side. Behind the royal family stood a small army of guards, servants, and advisors waiting to carry out any request.

Directly across the court from the king's box, a special section had been roped off for the nobles from the colonies. We had a perfect vantage point for observing action in the middle and at both ends of the court and any activity in the box. As I glanced down the aisle, I saw Prince Sarpedon, most covetous of men, coolly staring over at the king. Sarpedon, who must have been in his fifties, was a generation older than I and most of the other princes in the section and was a head taller than most men. Though he spent as much time indoors as Minos, he had a swarthy complexion that startlingly set off the whites of his eyes and his jet-black irises. As ruler of the city of Metapontus, Sarpedon was the most powerful and richest man on Kalliste. But he wanted a wider arena: Crete. He believed that if anyone from the colonies could become the next king, it would be he. Since his daughter, the lovely faced Himera, was betrothed to me, I should have been happy for the advantageous position Sarpedon had connived his way into — but I wasn't. I hated the man. I remember that day at Knossos wondering if, during all the games he attended at the capital, Sarpedon had ever taken his eyes off the king's throne?

Trumpet blasts announced the team from Athens, as a temporary but sturdy gate in front of the northern passageway opened. In single file, the seven maidens entered the arena. Completely unadorned, the young girls were naked except for very skimpy, tight-fitting loincloths. Unlike leapers from other cities, Athenians never wore jewelry that could snag on a rising horn. Most of the girls had even cropped their hair short like men to prevent it from flying in their eyes and temporarily blinding them. That could prove fatal.

Following closely on the heels of the maidens, the youths from Athens marched into the arena and, like the maidens, they wore only loincloths. From a distance, the only distinguishing features between the sexes were the breasts and white skin of the girls. Even from my second story seat, I could tell that the athletes were barbarians from inland. They were all rawboned and had long angular noses. When they walked, it was in unison, as if they had been marching since childhood. A dozen or more Cretans marching together would certainly make a mess of it. Even our soldiers would fall all over each other! Northerners seem to be marching all the time; a two-day forced march is nothing for them. And the Spear-Carrying Goddess Britomartis, Lady of Strife knows, I have seen enough Achaeans, specifically Athenians, on maneuvers, their boar tusk helmets glistening in the sun.

I tried to guess which Athenian was Prince Theseus. I finally chose the biggest of the lot — a strong-limbed youth with a large head and a bushy brow.

As they halted in the middle of the arena, the barbaric athletes looked toward the west and then up at the royal box, and, at first, refused to salute our king and queen. Catcalls rained down on the athletes. Finally, they acknowledged Minos and Pasiphae, then turned and perfunctorily saluted the northern, eastern, and southern sides of the arena. I watched their expressions carefully, especially those of the youth whom I took to be Theseus, the wrestler. From their blank stares, it was clear that the Athenians did not comprehend nor care about the significance of the holy contest in which they were to play a major role. They did not understand that the Mother Goddess was about to be honored as well as humans could honor Her, bull-leaping being the ultimate dance to our Creatress. I could see from their cold stares that the foreigners who had cast their lot with their sky god, Zeus, were thinking only about their moves and signals. After all is said and done, I suppose it was for the best that they were concentrating on their performance, for, since they did not pray to our Goddess, they had only their training and guile to shield them from bloody death.

The tail end of the dedication prayer given by Queen Pasiphae was drowned out by the snorting and stomping of the bull. Goaded into the narrow passageway at the southeastern corner of the court, the beast was eager to exit. The athletes—so cool and unruffled before—began to twitch their shoulders and shuffle their feet. When the opening ceremony ended, the athletes broke into their initial formation, a large egg-shaped ring spanning about half the court. In the middle, two young men positioned themselves about ten arm's lengths apart. The atmosphere in the arena fairly quivered with excitement.

All eyes turned toward the king. In one slow, even movement, Minos brought his right fist up to his chest, and when flesh touched flesh, the bull was sprung. He charged out with head held high and nostrils flaring, as if he wanted to inhale the entire arena and all the spectators. The huge beast was black all over. He had a block-like head with a perfect set of horns, a broad back, and several generous rolls of fat under his neck and stomach. Centuries before, when the contests first began, the high death toll of leapers proved without a doubt that fit bulls had to be burdened somehow. Today, bulls earmarked for the contests are carefully tended and given excessive amounts of feed; they are bred to be overweight and slow.

As the bull advanced into the human ring, the two youths inside the ring began to spin and dance feverishly. The bull took notice of the pesky distractors and charged one. Neatly and swiftly sidestepping the charge, the youth circled to the rear of the animal and slipped into the formation behind him. The bull did not turn to pursue him. Instead the beast went capering wildly across the court, headed for the northern part of the ring. Above the screaming crowd, I heard the command from the unit leader nearest the action. The two Athenians closest to the onrushing bull jumped out of the ring and sprinted in opposite directions. In hopes of picking off one or the other, the bull lunged first to his left and then to his right. He was going so fast, he missed both athletes and lost his balance, the front legs buckling underneath the massive body. Bellowing furiously, the beast came skidding to a halt just shy of the northern facade, his front legs torn and bloodied.

As if in one voice, thousands of people gasped. The incident may sound humorous, a big bovine clumsily falling down after missing two targets, but seasoned contest watchers found nothing to laugh at. Bulls sacred to Britomartis, Mistress of Hunters and Animals, were treated with respect at all times: while they were being raised, during the contests, and, afterwards, when they were sacrificed. To those of us who knew the sport, the incident was an ominous beginning.

On the arena floor, however, the Athenian athletes danced for joy, believing, no doubt, that the bull's spill was a sign of an easy opponent. But there was little time to savor their first success. The bull fitfully stood up, and the team hastily reformed the ring. The beast charged with fire in his eyes. Once again, he missed the targets, though he remained on all four. Clearly, the athletes from Athens had been well drilled; they performed their difficult and dangerous escapes with fluid grace.

After a dozen futile charges, the bull stopped, refusing to be coaxed into the shifting ring any longer. He had not even come close to nicking one of the darting dancers. In quick staccato fashion, the captain of the team shouted out an order, and his teammates quickly jumped into a new formation. The captain, recognizable by the directions he gave, was a wiry man with finer features than the others—male or female. He looked a little older than his teammates. The new formation was fan-like, composed of three rows, about twenty feet apart, one behind the other. The row closest to the bull consisted of three athletes, the next of five, and the last of six.

Near the southern entrance, the bull stood motionless. With his head cocked to one side, he glared at the new alignment, and if it were possible to see a bull smile, I swear I saw it on that day. From up high, it looked to me as if clay dolls had been neatly set up in rows, and a naughty child was about to stomp them into a thousand pieces. The bull must have had a similar vision.

Attacking with head lowered and with renewed confidence, the bull streaked toward the first row of humans. When they were within killing range, the two athletes closest to danger spun toward each other with arms outstretched and hands opened. The moment their hands met they pushed off with all their might, just as the black blur arrived. The maneuver propelled the athletes in opposite directions and the speed at which they fled from their positions made it seem as if a single person had been split in two. But we all knew better. So did the bull.

To my knowledge, the remarkably brave maneuver, which required absolute perfect timing, had never been attempted before at Knossos. Pandemonium engulfed the stands—people screamed uproariously and pounded one another on the back. The bull was quickly into the second row, then the third. In each row two teammates performed the same maneuver. In the matter of a few moments, the bull had sliced through three rows, missing six seemingly stationary targets. He arrived at the northern end of the arena only to look up and see a wave of delirious spectators perched in safety. In order to vent his frustration and to strike something—anything—the bull rammed the temporary gate, knocking several oak boards loose.

The second formation was good for twice as long as the first. Eventually the beast refused to react to the second formation, and another one was introduced. All in all, the team from Athens used five different ones that day, each to perfection.

Finally disenchanted, the bull came to a halt in the center of the court. His head lolled, and his breathing was labored. He slobbered profusely on the flagstones. The athletes had befuddled him. For all his charging, he had gored only the athlete I took to be the wrestler. It was when the wrestler was switching from the fourth formation into the fifth; he was not fast enough to dodge the bull's wildly swinging horns. One horn caught the athlete on the thigh. Although it bled quite a bit, the wound did not stop him from continuing.

During a bull-leaping contest, my loyalty was oddly torn. On the one hand, I wished for the best possible performance by the athletes: one of pure dance, composed of speed, agility, and daring. For my taste, bloodshed during a contest was unnecessary. The blood on the altar was quite enough. On the other hand, I always felt for a defeated, sulking bull. Regal, massive, powerful beyond human comprehension and sacred to Britomartis, a bull, it seemed to me, was brought pitifully low when it met failure in the ring. As I said, I did not wish to see anyone gored, yet a majestic creature weighing over forty talents striking wooden barriers out of frustration was a sorry sight.

During the first part of the contest, the Athenians had made their adversary look incredibly awkward and stupid. But the preliminary action, no matter how risky, was not the ultimate test of an athlete. Bull-leaping was. There was a world of difference between sidestepping a bull and somersaulting over his back.

The played-out bull stood at mid court as the young girls drifted toward the north and formed a single file facing south. All around me in the princely section and those adjacent to it, the betting became heavy. You see, not everyone felt as I did about the contests. Many Knossosans and visitors who swarmed round the central court did so only to bet on the athletes' chances of injury or death. On every wager laid, one out of the two gamblers hoped for blood; gamblers were not interested in grace or beauty, let alone holy significance. Wagering was a gruesome appendage, but my father once told me that it had been a part of the sacred contests as long as anyone could remember. Bets were laid on the injury likely to result from a leap, the extent of the injury, and whether it would stop a participant from continuing. The athletes were identified by the color and design of their loincloths. When the action was fast and furious, the wagering was, too.

To no one's surprise, my "wrestler" had become the gamblers' odds-on-favorite to bite the arena dust first, as he was the only one to have been gored. The wound on the man's thigh, which he had received because of his slowness, was a sure sign that he would perish.

The single file composed of maidens, the first to leap, directly faced the bull. The youths, the first to catch, formed a loose loop behind the beast. On the captain's command, the girl at the head of the line stepped forward and began a slow, methodical dance; she looked like a long-legged bird stepping very cautiously around a tricky snare. As she moved in delicately controlled stops and starts, she created an intricate zig-zag pattern across the arena floor. In our section, we could not recall ever seeing the dance, but we agreed it represented one's movement through the famous mazy passages of the palace. We also agreed that the foreigners were putting on a wonderfully original performance. Whether they knew it or not, they were pleasing Britomartis with their skill and inventiveness.

One by one, the other girls followed in the footsteps of the first, as if the first had painted them on the flat stones. When finished, they were once again in line, with the lead girl staring in the bull's eyes from about twenty feet away—dangerously close. She took a deep breath, then sprinted at the woebegone beast. Too tired to return the charge, he simply took a few plodding steps and lowered his big head in an attempt to skewer the maiden. From about a body's length away, the leaper sprang for the horns, grabbing them halfway down from the tips. Feeling the sudden downward thrust on his head and neck, the bull tossed his head up and back. The action shot the leaper over the beast's back in a midair somersault, and, for a brief moment, the broad back of the bull and the thin back of the maiden were parallel. The girl attempted to land feet first on the animal's rump, but the powerful toss had been too much. Realizing she was overshooting her target, she swiftly altered her landing and aimed for the pavement. Unfortunately, she was descending at too low an angle; she would have tangled in the bull's legs or been kicked in the back of the head had not the youths come to her rescue. Inches from the bull's sharp hooves, two young men caught the maiden in the air and feathered her down to a safe landing. The maiden's calm and the youths' preparedness and bravery brought a healthy applause. As usual, a few gamblers moaned. Because of the landing, the leap was not technically correct. Nevertheless, the Athenian team had demonstrated its finesse and courage once again.

The next acrobat managed to hit the bull's back with her feet, but she was too far to one side and slipped off, toppling to the unforgiving stones with a smack. The youths scrambled to her side and swept her away before the bull noticed her predicament. No doubt, she would awake stiff and bruised the following day. But she had lived to leap again.

The remaining five girls made it over the treacherous hurdle safely. The last girl's leap was nearly perfect. The golden-haired maiden struck the bull's rump firmly with her feet, then dove into her companions' arms. In our section, we had difficulty remembering the last time the first half of a team had vaulted without a death, let alone without bloodshed.

Next it was the young men's turn to leap. Having exchanged places with the triumphant girls, the youths lined up, then began their approach dance. It was the same as the girls' but performed with more vigor. When the last youth came to a halt, the bull took notice.

By that time in the contest, it seemed as if a bond had been forged between the beast and the Athenians; the athletes were getting all the cooperation they could have possibly asked for. Some gamblers who had lost big vented their anger on the beast, accusing him of not being a beast at all but rather two large barbarians disguised in a bullock hide. Others charged that the bull must have danced with the Athenians before, claiming that he had been born and bred on some farm in Attica, the province that included Athens, and had been brought over with the athletes. One boisterous faction, made up of exceedingly drunk merchants, argued that the creature had been bribed! Before the contest, the Athenians had allowed the bull to couple with all seven girls, ranted the drunkards, claiming that the bull's friendly behavior was his part in the deal. The lewd story provided the merchants with an arsenal of foul words, shouted first at the bull, then at the girls, and, finally, at the youths.

The truth of the matter, of course, was neither obscene nor preposterous; the bull was docile because it was exhausted. The bull had presented his body to the maidens as if it were a training model, like the ones all leapers practiced on. Even as a child, I had heard tales of how Daedalus had fashioned wonderful models out of wood, bronze, and bovine hide and horns.

When the young men were ready, the hulking bull did appear, indeed, to be a stuffed copy of himself, standing dumb and motionless in the arena. Every seasoned spectator knew better though. If there is one thing certain about a bull — any bull — it is that he is unpredictable.

At the head of the line was the "wrestler," strengthening my opinion that he was Theseus; surely the son of a king would want to be first. In my heart, I felt certain I would never wrestle the youth. How could he possibly survive a vault, bloodstained from the goring as he was already? I remembered Rib-Addi's words about King Minos's sweet revenge. Looking across the court, I searched for a hint of satisfaction in the king's face. There was none. His expression was as blank and cold as ever. His eyes said nothing.

The Athenian took a deep breath. Then another. Then another. Sensing that he was stalling and that his spirit had taken flight, the people in the audience began to taunt him. Some tossed rotten fruit and bits of leftover sweets at his feet. The tension in the arena was palpable. I stiffened; my palms were moist.

Suddenly the leaper broke and ran forward, reaching the bull just as he lowered his dangerous head. The youth leapt, and as his hands were about to grasp the horns, the bull jerked his head violently to its left. The right horn shot up and the left dropped down, striking the ground and splintering the tip. Trying to react to the unexpected movement, the youth managed to catch the right horn with his hand. But he missed the left horn. Clinging on to the bull's head for his life, he frantically grabbed a clump of matted hair and yanked it out. The athlete's body arced downward, following the plunge of his arms and head. He resembled a person tucked in a dive about to enter the water. But the central court was not a pond. With a sickening thud, the back of his head struck the bull's snout, and his neck and shoulders rammed the bull's forehead. After that whip-like action, the athlete slumped to the ground. I believe he died on contact, his neck snapping like a twig.

At last the bull had someone who could not run away, and he proceeded to spear the fallen Athenian in the neck and groin at the same time. As the bull pushed the lifeless bundle before him, lurid blood streaked the white limestone floor. Though they must have known it was too late, the horror-stricken Athenians encircled the bull, trying their best to distract him and pull their comrade away. The bull took no notice.

A long time passed before the beast tired of the sport. Finally, he bounded over the scarlet body and trotted away with head held high, victorious and defiant, like some battle-brave hero. Two pallid Athenians slipped over to the body and dragged it to the northern entrance where an attendant opened the gate just enough to pull it in.

An atmosphere of restlessness descended on the arena. My throat was parched, my skin as bumpy as an Egyptian crocodile's. The remaining leapers were faced with the almost impossible task of blotting from their minds the picture of their fallen companion. It was clear that the Athenians had trained long and hard with the first male leaper; he may have been a relative, a close friend or a lover to one or several of them. In the brightness of day, the young man had died a gory death before thousands of gawking, jeering strangers. Despite that, the survivors had to regroup.

The scent of blood wafted across the central court.

With their captain's prodding, the Athenians managed to pull themselves together. The next leaper up, a slender youth, slowly moved forward. Without thinking, he rather immodestly pulled at his checkered loincloth, as if to summon up all of his manhood. To the audience's surprise, he did not linger at the head of the line, but made his approach run at once.

The bull was bloated with confidence. Instead of standing still or shuffling forward a few feet as before, he charged. All morning he had not moved so quickly. As beast and human approached each other, the athlete's spirit took flight; the youth decided that he wanted no part of the confrontation. Breaking off his approach run, he skidded to a halt and veered to his right. The soles of his feet and his backside paid the price for that decision. That was the least of his problems. When the spirit flees, the mind clouds over. The leaper should have remembered that his teammate was undone by the bull's sudden twist—to its left. If the second leaper had veered the other way, things might have been different. Going at full speed, the bull lunged to its left, hooking the young player under the right arm with the jagged-tipped horn. The beast's mighty head rammed into the Athenian and with a powerful neck jerk threw him into the air, about fifteen feet out in front. In two long strides, the rampaging bull was upon the body, stomping and goring it ravenously. Instead of making a move to intervene, the other players ran away pell-mell in terror.

As the Athenians scrambled wildly over the arena floor, a shameful side of Minos's people showed itself. Knossosans and other citizens from around the kingdom yelled for blood, challenging the Athenians, urging them to jump to the last man. It was an ugly scene, and one that took place only when Athenians were performing. They brought out the worst in us. Braying like a bronze trumpet, the captain shouted above the unruly crowd, desperately trying to regroup his teammates. First, he rebuked them for their cowardice; when that didn't work, he exhorted them to behave bravely or perish.

Two maidens sidled over to join him, but I doubted whether the valiant captain could turn the tide. I got up to leave. I didn't want to see more blood. After inching my way down the aisle, I turned to walk up the stairs when suddenly a frail bag of bones bumped into me. It was Rib-Addi, drunk as a sailor on the town. He reeked from head to foot, his breath sour from wine and his clothes stained with carnelian-red blotches. Several princes, seeing our collision, quickly switched their abuse from the Athenians to Rib-Addi.

"What are you doing here, you oily merchant?"

"Get out of our section! Go back to the wilds of Canaan, old man."

"I asked him to join me to watch the contest," I shouted to my peers.

Their eyebrows climbed their foreheads, but they sealed their lips.

Spinning Rib-Addi down onto the nearest bench, I demanded, "What on earth are you doing in the princes' section, you old fool?"

"Your Highness," He paused for a loud belch. "Your Highness," he continued, slurring his words, "I came to see what you thought of Theseus the wr...wr...wrestler. With all the action, I got so excited, I guess I forgot where I was, or where you was, or—"

"All right, Rib-Addi, all right." I laughed inwardly at Rib-Addi's condition despite myself. "You know, it shows a mean heart to make light of the wrestler's performance now," I chided.

"Why, my lord?" he croaked, gazing at me with a befuddled look.

"Because if you had had your nose out of the cup for a moment, you would've seen that the wrestler was taken by Britomartis. He was the first youth to leap."

Rib-Addi twisted away from me with a grunt and squinted toward the arena floor. His head swiveled back like some exotic bird's, and he wailed in winey triumph, "But, Sire, Prince Theseus is still alive! He's rallying his frightened chicks around him right now—look see!"

Lest he pitch off the bench, I kept both hands on Rib-Addi while I glanced over my shoulder. In the center of the arena, the maidens were busily distracting the bull, while at the northern end, the remaining youths were listening to the captain. Shouting out instructions, he grabbed the youths by the forearms one by one and shook them vigorously. I could see that he was breathing new confidence into his men. "The brave captain is Theseus?" I asked the slumping Rib-Addi.

"Why yes, Sire," he said, "didn't you know?"

"No. I took the husky leaper, the one who fell first, for Theseus. Since one's station in life means nothing among bull dancers, I didn't even consider the team captain. But now, thanks to you, Rib-Addi, I see that this captain is princely, indeed. A true leader." Rib-Addi winked and nodded his head. I continued, "Regardless of his physical size, if Prince Theseus is able to save his team at this late stage, then, without doubt, he's a very big man." Again Rib-Addi nodded knowingly, but this time his chin dropped so far down that it bounced off his bony chest. We both turned toward the court to see what would happen next.

Theseus lined up his male charges facing the bull. The maidens were poised behind the beast ready to act as catchers. Yelling last-moment instructions to the front, Theseus knelt on one knee alongside his men. Then he rose to his feet and ran to the back of the line. After what seemed like an eternity, but was probably no more than a few moments, the first youth broke into a lope, then sprinted for the bull. With head lowered and horns flashing, the bull eagerly returned the youth's charge. With perfect timing, the Athenian leapt into the air. Instead of grabbing the horns, his hands hit the bull's broad head and pushed off precisely when the thrust came. The force shot the youth over the beast's back, and, just like the first girl, he never touched the rump, landing feet first on the stones where he curled himself up and rolled like a ball.

By not grabbing the horns, the leaper violated the first and most important rule of bull-leaping, but I could tell that the Athenians couldn't have cared less about the violation. They were too busy hopping off the ground and cheering their comrade for having leapt and lived.

The next four acrobats attempted the same spring off the bull's head, and though they received minor scrapes and bruises, they survived. That was all Theseus had wanted. Cleverly, he had ordered his vaulters to aim for the head, a larger target, much easier to connect with than the slender, tapering horns. The crowd did not like the use of the head-spring vault and yelled their displeasure. Yet, I could not help marvel at how Theseus had brought his teammates back from the brink of disaster. After the two deaths, I thought it certain that the remaining youths would perish.

At the southern end of the court, the eleven successful vaulters danced around the bull, distracting him by feinting charges and leaps. At the northern end, Theseus stood perfectly still, head tilted back, eyes raised toward heaven. It appeared to me as if he was meditating, or praying to some god or other, asking for a blessing. Suddenly, in a deep voice, he bellowed at the bull. The beast withdrew his attention from the others and wheeled round to meet his adversary. For an eerie moment, bull and man stared deeply into each other's eyes. Then, without warning, they broke, rushing headlong at each other.

On the dead run, the bull twitched its massive head first to its left then to its right, but Theseus, not fooled, leapt, caught the horns, arced like a rainbow, and struck the bull's rump firmly with his feet. He sprang off, sailing high into the air, waving away his would-be catchers and landing with his left leg forward, right leg back, and knees slightly bent. Perfect!

"Aahs" and "oohs" poured out of the stands. Acknowledging the flawless vault, the partisan crowd gave the leaper a fine applause. Had he not been the son of Aegeus, Theseus would have been sprinkled with flowers and drowned in an earsplitting ovation.

One who didn't hold back was Rib-Addi. He was off the bench cheering, once again drawing the ire of the nearby princes. "Sire, this is a most formidable man! Look…do you see? He isn't even winded! What about that landing? He didn't move a muscle. Amazing! I would happily give a mina of gold — if I had one — to see him wrestle you, my lord."

"If the Goddess so desires, Rib-Addi, you'll see it tomorrow — free of charge."

THREE

AFTER THE SPECTACULAR vault by Theseus, the Athenians were bedecked with garlands and ushered from the arena. They were replaced by a dozen muscular slaves who carried on their shoulders a huge net, woven of rope two-fingers thick. They ringed the bull and cast the net over him. He put up a halfhearted struggle, lurching at one or two of the slaves, but before long he was completely played out; he was no opponent for the fresh and powerful men.

Soon the southern gate swung open and in trooped a small army of priestesses and priests, led by musicians. Bringing up the rear, a team of dusty-gray donkeys pulled a small wagon, upon which sat a colorful altar made of limestone slabs covered with plaster. Every surface of the altar was filled with scenes painted in blue, russet, and white depicting the very ceremony we were about to witness. Six slaves strained as they lifted the altar off the wagon and placed it in the exact center of the court. The setting-up of the altar was not a procedure done in other arenas, such as Mallia where a permanent sacrificial altar stood in the central court, giving the acrobats a decided advantage — several times I had seen them use the altar as a lifesaving screen. Frightened acrobats even cowered on top of it. Knossosans sneered; they would never allow any such prop to destroy the purity of their contests.

After the altar was in place, all twelve slaves pinned the bull down and quickly bound his forelegs then his hind legs. Binding both pairs of legs together, the well-coordinated team bent down, shoulder to shoulder, and reached under the animal. Standing up with a loud "humph," they lifted the beast with them, placing the massive hulk on the altar with surprising gentleness.

The musicians began playing an ancient song on their pipes and seven-string lyres. Carried aloft in sedan chairs, the king and queen came down the western stairway. The rulers wore headdresses fitted with gilt horns: the horns on Minos's headdress were from a bull, those on Pasiphae's from a cow. After the king and queen dismounted, Pasiphae stepped forward and blessed the Four Pillars and all the spectators around the central court. Then she broke into a lovely paean to Britomartis, the background music accenting the sacred words.

After the paean, a priest, heavy with years, shuffled over to the bull and anointed his head with perfumed oil. Next, two priestesses sprinkled the bull's head with barley and wheat from the previous season. A strong-limbed priest standing by the cart removed the beautiful cloth, purple with sea dye, that was covering a large golden double axe. The holy weapon was actually made of hard bronze, gilded, for even heavily alloyed gold would fail the job. As if at a funeral, in slow measured steps, the priest, axe in hand, made his way over to the bull. The priest stood by the creature's head as the last grains fell and stuck to his curly forelock.

At this point, all attention shifted to High Priestess Pasiphae. Slowly moving her arms, she began to tell the story—in mime—of the very first bull-leaping contest. The bull's capture, the making of Daedalus's model, the training of the acrobats, and, finally, the contest were told to the accompaniment of the lyres.

When she finished, Pasiphae dropped her left arm to her side, but kept her right arm, cocked at the elbow, in front of her body. Ever so slowly, the priest raised the double axe high into the air. He stood as still as he could but trembled slightly; the sun's rays blinked off of the sharp blades of the axe. Suddenly Pasiphae brought her clenched fist to her forehead. The priest flexed his knees and sprang upward, balancing on his tiptoes. The sacred axe came down swiftly.

Blood gushed forth from a gaping wound in the bull's neck and was collected in metal vases by the priestesses to later sprinkle on the many altars of the palace, the city, and the nearby towns. On these same altars, The Great Mother, Mistress of Animals, also received Her share of the sacred flesh. The remainder of the sacrifice appeared at the king's feast, held that evening in the grand banquet hall. During the feast, princes, courtiers, magistrates, and foreign dignitaries were required to partake of the bull. I usually enjoyed a well-cooked side of beef, but I could not stomach that particular meal. Out of all the king's feasts I attended, I never once allowed a morsel of the sacrifice to pass my lips, always stealthily passing my share on to a waiting palace dog. I did not object to the sacrifice, but felt, having come to know the bull during the contest, I just could not eat his flesh.

After the sacrifice was completed in the central court, the king and queen made their departure. Then, with the nobility leading the way, the spectators streamed out of the stands to invade the entertainment spots of Knossos. Later, they would return for the afternoon bull-leaping contests.

That evening, I left the feast early and, as usual, a bit hungry. I took some figs with me and ate them on the way to the athletes' apartments. As I walked through the narrow streets, the awful sight of the bull mashing and piercing the first and second male leapers stuck in my mind. At that moment, it was not difficult to understand why the people of Athens had concocted the fable that told how their athletes were brought to the bull-leaping contests not to perform, but to be eaten!

From what I could piece together, the fable went like this: The twice-seven athletes — who were labeled sacrifices — were chosen by lot after every Great Year, shipped from Athens to Knossos, dedicated to some goddess or other by King Minos and Queen Pasiphae, and fed to a voracious monster, half-bull and half-man, called the Minotaur. Supposedly, this hybrid monster was kept somewhere beneath the palace in a secret underground pit, which could only be reached after negotiating a tortuous section of passages, which the Athenians call the Labyrinth. You see, they simply borrowed the holy title for the palace of Knossos, Labyrinth, meaning "House of the Double Axes," and applied it to a special maze within the palace. Growing for hundreds of years, the palace was indeed a maze, new passageways joining and crisscrossing old ones in every possible direction. Admittedly it could be confusing, especially to foreigners used to one-room huts. So, it was not surprising that foreigners had chosen one aspect of our capital, condensed it, and come up with the mysterious "Labyrinth."

When I arrived at the apartments that housed the athletes, I dropped my somber thoughts and asked a Kushite guard where the captive Athenian leapers were quartered. Before the black man could speak, a woeful dirge answered for him. Walking toward the moaning at the end of a colonnade, I peered through a doorway to discover the Athenians scattered about a long room. The garlands of lilies, which had been presented to the leapers after their impressive performance, were heaped in the middle of the room, either crushed by hand or stomped under foot. Two young men were sprawled on couches, while two were sitting on the floor with their backs to the wall. The seven maidens, who were at the far end of the room mourning their comrades, were producing the sad lamentation I had heard outside. As they wailed, they pounded their fists against their chests and yanked out strands of hair from their swaying heads.

Suddenly I was face to face with Theseus. He had been standing behind the door, acting as a sentinel—though clearly not a very good one. As he darted in front of me, the swift-footed Theseus did not make a sound, but the others—so well trained—sensed his movement and spun round. Only once before in my life, when I cornered a vicious boar in a thicket, had I been stared at with such hate.

Defiantly, Theseus tried to block a view I really didn't want. "May I help you, sir?" he asked with a surprising fluidity in our language. I knew that the polite greeting was not the one he really wanted to give me; I gave him credit for his princely restraint.

"Yes, you may, Prince Theseus. Sorry, but I would like a word with you." He nodded and stepped out into the moonlit colonnade, closing the door behind him. The guards were all eyes and ears, but they kept their distance. It was only then, as he walked alongside me, that I noticed Theseus was limping badly. The question I came to ask was moot. And I felt even worse for being there. "I offer my condolences for your teammates who died today, Prince Theseus. But I also came here to praise your performance, so my visit is bittersweet."

"Thank you. Our performance was indeed a mixed blessing from Poseidon, The Earth Shaker." He stared unflinchingly into my eyes, knowing that the mention in our kingdom of one of his gods was blasphemy. There was a tense pause. He went on, "Since you know my name, sir, may I know yours?"

"Your name flew quickly through the capital, Prince Theseus. As for me, I am the son of Cretheus and Henithea. I am called Idomeneus, the Prince of well-founded Phira on Kalliste."

"Ah yes, the wrestler-prince. I learnt of your fame when I first arrived in this...this place. If I remember correctly, it was that little Easterner and his cronies who were singing your praise." (Rib-Addi, I thought to myself.) "I must admit, though, I think they were trying to scare me. No offense, Prince Idomeneus, but they exaggerated your feats so that even Hercules would have found them impossible."

"As you know, a tipsy source is sometimes worse than none," I said with a thin smile. Theseus smiled, too, exposing for the first time a kink in his bronze nature. "I do enjoy wrestling," I continued, "and, in fact, I came here to challenge you to a match tomorrow."

"Well—"

"But your limp made answer for you."

"Yes, to be sure. It was a stupid injury. It happened at the end of the contest. Since you were there, you may recall my unassisted dismount?"

"It was the highlight of the contest."

"Maybe...but not very smart. You see, when I hit the pavement, I pulled or tore a muscle," he said rubbing his upper left leg. "Instead of rolling, or, better yet, allowing myself to be caught, I wanted to land without bending my knees. I wanted to stay standing, head held high." He fell silent and stared again. Without saying it in so many words, Theseus had made his point; the gritty dismount was a defiant gesture to every Cretan and islander in the arena.

"Well," I muttered, "twas a brilliant dismount, though I'm sorry—for both you and me—that you were injured. Maybe in the future we can wrestle each other, when you're healed. Once again, I am sorry to have interrupted your mourning."

Theseus hesitated, staring at me again, but in a different way than before. Finally, he replied, "Prince Idomeneus, I must say that your compassion for me and my people surprises me. You see, my experience in the arena today just confirmed my opinion of the Cretans—which I will not utter. And I assumed that the colonists, like yourself, were cut from the same bolt of cloth. But you seem…different.

I had to admire the man's pluck.

"Prince Theseus, I could tell you that the abuse flung at your team was caused by too much wine, or the moon's phase, or the earthquake's curse. But I am sure you would see through these veils for what they are; thin excuses. So, I will simply say that the behavior you saw today occurs only when teams from Athens perform, no others. Need I go into the reason?"

"No, don't. I know it well, though it varies from place to place."

Ignoring his sarcasm, I said, "As you meet more and more of King Minos's people—away from the arena—your opinion of us may change."

"I have already met the king himself." he snapped.

"Oh? When?"

"Your king came down to the port under the pretense of inspecting the new crop of victims. But it was clear from the first that Minos really came to harass me, the son of King Aegeus, supposed murderer of Androgeus."

"Supposed?"

"Aye, supposed! Listen, when Androgeus died, I wasn't even born. All I have to go on is my father's word, and he says he had nothing to do with it. That's good enough for me. I'm sure you take your father's word as truth?" I nodded in agreement without commenting. "Anyway," he continued, "King Minos goaded me into a confrontation. It was something about one of our girls, the blonde, Eriboea. Tossing a gaudy signet ring into some deep water, your king challenged me to retrieve it. When I did, he stormed off in his sedan chair, his face flushed with anger. Needless to say, he was hoping I would stay down with the fishes, but he chose the wrong place to pitch his ring. Poseidon rules the sea and I am his son." Theseus did not elaborate on the mysterious statement. His face was somber, his eyes like burning coals. "Prince Idomeneus, since that incident at the port, my teammates have been preparing all of my meals with their own hands."

I turned away from Theseus and glanced down the colonnade, searching for nearby guards. They were out of earshot. I turned back only to see hovering before my eyes the glowering face of my father, enveloped in a luminous vapor. My father had always distrusted Athenians — all Achaeans, for that matter — and had warned me never to befriend them. Startled, I shook my head, and the apparition disappeared.

"Are you all right?" queried Theseus.

"Uh, yes…yes, I'm all right." Though I shivered like a newborn calf, I leaned forward and said, measuring each word, "While you're in the Labyrinth, I suggest you have one of your men guard your back at all times."

FOUR

EARLY THE NEXT DAY, I was a spectator once again in the great arena: boxing and wrestling were the sports. I saw Rib-Addi at one of the intermissions and explained that my match with Theseus would have to wait. "Damn," he croaked, stomping the ground. But the newsmonger promised to fill the stands whenever we did wrestle, claiming that there were hundreds of people dying to see the prince from Athens and me pitted against one another.

I left my seat before the last wrestling match was over because I wanted to go to bed early; I needed my rest for the following day's journey. As I was leaving the arena, I spoke briefly to my friend Rhadamanthys, Prince of Phaistos. He had to stay on for meetings in the capital but had arranged for my accommodations in his palace and would join me there within a few days. In order to make Phaistos in a day, I had to leave Knossos before the sun rose. Therefore, I awoke the next morning just as the Lion faded on the west horizon. As I glanced at the constellation, I remembered that the night before the Great Bull had bounded across the sky. I thought of how the spirit of the sacrificed bull was watching over the earth, and I wondered how many bovine spirits made up the Great Bull, considering the long history of the contests.

That morning, I enjoyed the peace and silence of being the only guest in the banquet hall. The servants, alerted of my early departure, had prepared a hearty breakfast of toasted cereal with goat's milk, honey, and fresh fruit. At the royal stables, I was generously outfitted for my trip with one of the latest gifts to King Minos from Zidantash the Second, King of the Hittites: a handsome chariot, very popular in Anatolia and Syria. Panels of ivory, stained purple and cunningly set into a wooden frame, were carved with detailed scenes, depicting an Eastern sovereign and several heroes taking part in a bull and lion hunt. Inside the chariot, there was room for two men and their weapons kits.

With bronze fittings and long and short strips of tanned leather, the stable boys hitched up a pair of black horses, also gifts from Zidantash, who had sent them when they were just foals. A Cretan driver named Evanus was assigned to me for my trip to Phaistos and my stay there. The royal family at Knossos had been very generous to me. I felt a tinge of guilt about my seditious comment to Prince Theseus. But it soon passed.

After leaving the palace, we headed south and took a neatly paved cobblestone road that ran under the main aqueduct. The road snaked through the countryside and, as we approached the first small town, the cobblestones gave way to dirt. Over the cobblestones, our teeth had chattered as if it were winter, but when we reached the dirt road, the ride was smoother. If one had surveyed the region, one would have seen a land settled for many generations, for far and wide, the stiff forests of pine and cypress had been thinned for fuel and timber. All of the dwellings in the nearby towns and villages and all of the upper stories at Knossos were in debt to those forests.

Occasionally the road narrowed into a finger's-breadth lane, was washed out, or was etched with crisscrossing wagon wheel ruts. At times, we had to get out and walk the chariot around fallen trees. Going south, we passed the thriving city of Arkhanes, where Minos had his summer palace. A little bit farther on, we stopped for water at the country villa of Vathypetro, where all around wild almond trees were in full bloom, accenting the green countryside with flashes of pink and white.

When the sun was halfway to its zenith, we reached the magnificent valley known as the Messara. Stretching as far as the eye could
see, the rich Messara followed the sweet running waters of the river
called Gero. The valley was a patchwork of vibrant colors: the dark
greens of the pine, cedar, and cypress forests; the golden fields laden
with wheat and barley; the silver olive groves; and the yellow, green,
and purple vineyards. Alongside the large crops were lovely orchards
of apples, pomegranates, and figs. Smaller fields of various green spices and plots of onions highlighted the outskirts of the villages. Circular
granaries dotted the valley floor like so many pithoi. Even from a
distance, you could spot the tidy rows of beehives running up the
slopes of the north mountain range. White specks blanketed the
foothills, and if you watched hard and long enough, they would move:
they were grazing goats and sheep.

Handsome Cretan houses sat nestled under shade trees. Besides
farmers' homes, there were stately manor houses and country villas,
owned by wealthy merchants or government officials, who occupied
them only at certain times of the year.

The Messara, most fruitful of valleys, was the envy of the kingdom—in fact, of the entire world! Egypt coveted its honey, olive oil,
and aromatic flowers. And an Egyptian burial would not have been
the same without the Messara's trees. Egyptian carpenters used wood
from the cedars and resin from the pines to construct lavish coffins.
Egyptian embalmers extracted a moss resin from the lichen clinging
to the oaks and used the resin as an aromatic filling for mummies.

All around The Deep Blue, people depended on the surplus
wheat grown in the Messara for their bread; the Cyclades and the
barbarous inland were especially dependent on Cretan wheat.

The Messara, sweet-spaced horn of plenty, was under the direct
control of Phaistos. As one might expect, there was an intense rivalry
between that city and the mighty capital, Knossos. Every Minos in
history had been jealous of the abundant wealth of the valley and
Phaistos's commanding position at its west end. Unfortunately for
every Minos, the Messara was too far away to administer from the
Labyrinth. Thus, by default, Phaistos became the main caretaker of
the valley, with Gortyn to the north administering only a small portion. Over the years, Phaistos had evolved into an almost autonomous

power, though it still paid taxes to the capital in the form of produce, and Prince Rhadamanthys gave way to Minos on points of law. But in all other spheres, Rhadamanthys, my good friend, and Phaistos went their own way.

Staying to a hard-packed dirt road that was scarred with ruts, we sped through the valley and followed the westward sun. The road was a major east-west passage, and, indeed, we saw countless wagons filled to overflowing, heading for either the market at Phaistos or its port, Timbaki.

Late afternoon, the proud head of Phaistos palace appeared before us, soaring high upon its large hill. To my mind, it was the most magnificent palace in all the world—more awe-inspiring than even Knossos. The setting was unsurpassed. Perched on the east shoulder of the hill, the palace commanded the valley. The northern, eastern, and southern apartments overlooked a sheer drop of over two hundred feet. To the west, protecting the palace from the mighty Zephyrus, the crest of the hill rose sharply, looking like a beehive. If you stood on top of the hive and looked westward, you could see the wash of the breakers. To the north, famous Mount Ida watched over Rhadamanthys's peaceful home. The feeling of the palace was stately, soft, distinctly feminine. Though the palace had taken shape over centuries, the architects and artisans had been able to keep all the parts in harmony. It is true that both Knossos and Kalliste were blessed with many lovely things; however, the Mother Goddess's gifts to Phaistos were a thousand and one, which was why it was the gem of the kingdom.

I ordered Evanus, rather brusquely, to make haste; the approach to the palace always made my heart race. We sped along the winding road climbing up the side of the hill. Once on top, we regained a wonderful view of the lovely Messara, spreading out and away from us like an open palm leaf. When we arrived at the palace, we were cordially welcomed by a handful of courtiers, all of whom knew me well. I instructed Evanus to stable the team and dismissed him for five days. I told him that if I used the chariot at all in that time, I would drive it myself. Pressing a gold ingot in his hand, I bade him have a good time in the city below. Thanking me profusely, he broke into a toothy smile and skipped off in the direction of the nearest wine shop.

The courtiers led me to a royal apartment that Prince Rhadamanthys had set aside for my use. The last apartment in the southeastern complex, it stood breathtakingly balanced high above the city. Two servants brought me food and drink served in elegant dishes, pitchers, and cups that had been potted at least three hundred years ago. The cup that I drank from was eggshell thin and covered with a fanciful light-on-dark design. A vessel that especially caught my eye was a fruit stand decorated with white spirals on a blue ground, accented with red teardrops. The spirals had sawtooth borders, which were echoed in the carefully scalloped rim and foot of the vessel. I doubt if that exquisite piece exists anymore.

I had time to visit the alabaster baths before my audience with Rhadamanthys's lovely wife, the deep-waisted Princess Biadice. But I could not relax in the warm water and when time for my audience came around, I could scarcely keep from running to the princess's throne room. I had to keep checking my gait, for, after all, a prince must be dignified.

In the throne room, I stood gazing at the colorful frescoes covering the walls. Serene landscapes and seascapes of red, ochre, and blue undulated over the plaster, with lilies, sea-daffodils, papyri, and fantastic hybrid plants sprouting up in the most unexpected places. Strange but gentle beasts roamed the brown and red mountains as birds swooped and cavorted in the cream-colored sky.

The princess did not keep me waiting long. She entered with her dazzling entourage of three bright-eyed handmaidens, each in full bloom. I pretended to take no notice of them as I exchanged royal salutations with the princess. I assured her that Rhadamanthys had been fine when I saw him in Knossos and that he sent his love. I told her briefly about the Spring Festival. I thought I was concealing the true subject of my mind, but wise Biadice saw the dilemma I was in; she kept the audience to a minimum. After my abbreviated description of the bull-leaping contest, she politely excused herself and was escorted out by her lovely ladies, while I was left alone in the room, staring at the paintings, but not seeing them. The scenes blurred into blotches of light and dark colors, as if a rainbow had melted onto an artist's palette.

After what seemed like an eternity, but must only have been a short time, I heard a noise. It meant only one thing. My eyes were riveted to a section of the fresco just left of the throne that depicted a

row of large pyramid-shaped mountains. One of the mountains began to tremble slightly, as if the Goddess was moving the earth once
more. With a creaking sound, the mountain slowly swung away from
the wall, followed by a small white hand. Out of the dark secret passageway, my love gingerly emerged into the warm glow of the throne
room. We raced into each others' arms.

Aphaea seemed to be even more ravishing than the last time I
had seen her, but I felt the same way every time I saw her! My love
was well-favored by the High Goddess, She with doves and flower
buds in Her hair. Aphaea's wavy black hair enfolded a delicate face,
like a mother cradling a new babe; her large, almond-shaped eyes
were the bluish-violet of an sapphire; her petite nose turned up ever
so slightly at the tip; the soft outline of her lips was filled in with a
wine red; her neck was perfectly formed as if it had come from a
master-potter's wheel; and her body was comely and graceful. The
faintest hint of incense enveloped her for Aphaea spent many hours
at the altar each day.

After being locked in a long kiss, we slowly parted. "I could have
screamed," Aphaea sighed. "Standing there so close to you, but not
being able to kiss you, or touch you, or even speak to you!"

"Well, you should have," I teased. "I wouldn't have minded...
though it might have disrupted the audience. Biadice wouldn't have
blinked an eye, but I bet your two companions would have fainted
away! They must have an inkling, no?"

"No, I don't think so, my dear. Our love is known only to
Princess Biadice and Prince Rhadamanthys. Our secret is safe with
them. Every day I thank the Goddess for the strong friendship between the prince and you."

"Yes, our bond goes way back. We have like minds on many
things...just as long as that doesn't include you," I teased, stealing a
kiss, "he and I will stay good friends."

Feigning resistance, Aphaea said, "Oh, you're mean-hearted
Idomeneus! You know how Prince Rhadamanthys has treated me
with exceeding kindness during my tenure."

"Ah, ha!"

"Oh, stop that, you know what I mean! It's because of your love
for me that I am so favored in the palace. And don't think the other

girls don't notice the partiality shown me. They just can't understand why. Well, that's all right—I don't let it bother me."

"Good! But if we stay here embracing any longer, someone will discover us for sure. Then the others will really have something to gossip about." I stole another kiss. "Will Biadice grant you some time this afternoon and this evening?"

"Yes, I'm sure…now that you're here."

"Excellent! When the afternoon prayers are completed, meet me at the apple orchard by the junction of South and Matala roads. There you will find me high upon my ivory throne."

"Whatever do you mean?"

"You'll see—it's a surprise!"

"A surprise? A Hittite army couldn't keep me away!"

We kissed one more time, then Aphaea entered the secret passageway, closing behind her the door-concealing mountain. In a flash, I was away from the throne room, preparing for our tryst.

Later that afternoon, I awaited Aphaea, the sweet scent of the fruit filling my head. The day was wonderfully clear and bright, and a gentle north breeze rustled the leaves ever so slightly. I thought to myself how blessed I was: The woman I loved would soon be at my side, and we would drive through the richly flowered Messara in a magnificent chariot, powered by two noble steeds. All that, plus the fact that I was the much-admired Prince of Phira on Kalliste, made me thank the Goddess Steerer profusely.

Suddenly, I spied a wisp of a form gliding down the road. As my soft-stepping Aphaea approached the orchard, I held the horses as still as possible, imploring them to be silent. Soon Aphaea stood before the row of trees in which I was concealed. A look of consternation crept across her beautiful face; it was so disturbing that I could not wait out the long concealment I had planned. With a snap of the reins, the high-necked horses pranced forward, separating the leaves. Though she stepped back startled, Aphaea managed to remain unruffled, for she had learned from Biadice to be calm at all times.

To shield herself from the sun, Aphaea held an ivory parasol aloft. As I smiled down at her from the chariot, she looked as delicate as a narcissus. I helped her into the chariot, and we broke into laughter. Taking the south road, we descended into the wide-spaced valley, with happiness and love in our hearts.

Stopping at three secluded spots we had discovered on previous outings, we walked and talked, laughed and kissed. The last spot was at the curved bay called Matala, where we strolled hand-in-hand along the golden beach. We stopped now and then to admire the pattern etched into the sand by the receding water, or to collect some shells, or to track a sand crab.

During our stroll, Aphaea spotted a motley seashell off to our right—about eight paces away. When she left my side to examine it, I knew the chance I had been waiting for all day had come. When her back was to me, I went a few feet, bent down, and carefully placed her gift into the moist, tightly packed sand, leaving it partially exposed. Just before she turned around and started back, I returned to the spot where she had left me. When she reached my side, she explained that the shell was still occupied, but not by its original owner; a crab had decided it would make a splendid villa and had claimed it. Aphaea left the proud new resident undisturbed.

As we walked on, I could scarcely conceal my eagerness; a telltale smile crept across my face, but Aphaea did not notice it because she was too busy wondering who had made the fresh footprints we came upon. Then she saw the brilliant flash in the sand. "Idomeneus, look! I let her run ahead to gather up her treasure. When I reached her side, she was holding in her quivering palm the golden pendant. She stared silently, almost reverently at her discovery, her brow knit in disbelief, her lips parted in surprise. The pendant was in the shape of two handsome honeybees facing each other. As Aphaea examined the pendant more closely, she saw that the bees were cleverly working together to deposit one large drop of honey into a circular comb, which they held between them in their slender legs.

The eyes and stripes of the bees, the rims of the disks, and the comb were decorated with minute grains of gold, painstakingly attached to a gold sheet, a technique our craftsmen learned many years ago from the East. Over the bees' heads, a bead was suspended in a filigree cage, above which was a loop for a chain.

Aphaea looked down at the footprints in the sand, looked back at the pendant, then looked up at my smiling face. I gave her a kiss and pressed a delicate golden chain into her hand. Before she could speak, I said, "While these bees are busily at work, they are whispering that Aphaea will become Idomeneus's shining bride."

With tears welling in her violet eyes, Aphaea said, "Oh, Idomeneus, my love…do you really mean it?"

"Yes, my darling. No more delays, no more worrying about what this person or that person will say or do. I've spent much too much time away from your arms. I shall have everything taken care of. I've already spoken with Rhadamanthys. He and Biadice are the only ones who know about us. Well, and now these bees know!

"Rhadamanthys feels certain that Biadice, while being very sad to lose you, will set you free with her blessing. Before I leave Phaistos, I will speak to her. In three moons, By-our-Lady, you will be my wife, Princess of Phira!"

"Idomeneus, I know I'm not dreaming because I'm clutching this pendant in my hand," Aphaea murmured. Suddenly her tears of joy became tears of fear, "I'm worried about your being foresworn to Princess Himera. What will Prince Sarpedon—"

"Don't worry, Aphaea," I interrupted. I spoke to her with winged words. "Nothing can stand in our way: not princely pledges, nor the word of the king himself. Nothing!"

"Sarpedon will never release you from your father's pledge. Never! He has a foothold in Phira—and everywhere else on Kalliste—and he won't just cast it away. He'll try everything in his power to stop you. He'd rather see you dead."

She was right.

"Spit! Why did my father agree to this marriage between Himera and me?"

"Back then, I'm sure he thought that it was best for your town," Aphaea said bitterly, "You know, an alliance between Phira and Metapontus, the family tie between you and Sarpedon's daughter."

"Goddess, Steerer of All Things, help us!"

Hand-in-hand we walked along the beach. "Dear, before you speak to Biadice," Aphaea said, "please go back to Kalliste and talk to Sarpedon."

"Why?"

"Maybe he could be convinced, with gold, to release you from your father's pledge."

"No. He has more gold than he needs. There's nothing I can give him that he doesn't already have — except me. And he can't have me!

"Listen, for two years, you and I have been meeting secretly and I'm sick of it. We must begin our life together. Now! Never mind the difference in our ranks or the enmity our marriage will cause."

"Yes, but before announcing our plans here on Crete, you should tell Sarpedon. And Himera, too. She deserves that. You may not care for her, but she may for you. Does she?"

"I don't know. I never see her. Himera was pledged to me when she was born. That was eight-and-ten years ago: I was only nine. We have no feelings for each other; we don't even know each other."

"Still, she deserves an explanation."

"All right. I'll hold off speaking to Biadice. I'll go to Metapontus when I return home. But, no matter Sarpedon's or Himera's reaction, we will be married in the month when artichokes are ripe."

"The Goddess willing."

Within the great honey-colored headland commanding the north end of Matala bay, there were scores of caves of all sizes, and in our bittersweet mood, we decided to visit them. There were ancient objects — tools and weapons — to be found in those caves, but, even though Aphaea and I visited several, we found nothing. In order to watch the gilt sun sink into the sea, we climbed to the highest cave of all. I had packed a fluffy woolen blanket in the chariot, which I laid on the hard-packed cave floor. We stretched out on the blanket, and, as the golden beams of the setting sun bathed the cave, the Mother Goddess, Lady of Love, cast Her invisible inescapable net over us, kindling our desire. We lost ourselves in each others' arms. When I remember the soft delights we shared, my body aches.

For several days after our trip to Matala, Princess Biadice allowed Aphaea to slip away as often as possible; I was always there waiting with open arms. Thus, for a short time at least, we were together, out visiting our favorite places in the swift chariot, far from inquisitive eyes.

One night, after smuggling Aphaea back into the princesses' apartment complex, I found a note waiting for me in my room. Prince Rhadamanthys had returned from Knossos and wished for me to meet with him in a room off of his large apartment. Rhadamanthys was more than a good friend to me. He was a distant cousin; our great-great-grandfathers had been brothers. While Rhadamanthys's ancestor stayed on in Crete to become the twentieth ruler of Phaistos, mine went to Kalliste to become the founder and first prince of a new colony, Phira. More than once, the native Kallisteans tried to run my great-great-grandfather out; during his lifetime, Phira was burned to the ground twice. Over the years on Kalliste, however, the kings of Crete planted more and more colonies, including Metapontus, so that within a century, the natives were subdued, many being taken on as palace servants or vassals.

"I would much rather have been here with you," said Rhadamanthys when he greeted me, "than at those meetings back at Knossos. Nothing ever gets accomplished. The only interesting thing was the stir in the palace caused by the bull-leaping heroics of the Athenians. Especially Prince Theseus."

" Were the palace officials upset?"

"Well, you can imagine the bind Minos's people were in. They had to condemn Theseus and his teammates for their insolent ways, yet praise them for one of the bravest displays in arena history. Ha! The citizens, and even some palace grandees, have placed this Theseus on high."

"Yes, but his instant fame may be just as quickly snuffed out. Say by an assassin's blade."

"Hmmm. No, I don't think so. At least, not right away. The king is too shrewd, too calculating to rob the masses of their meteoric hero solely to avenge a loved one. Minos is a patient old fox. And meteors have a way of burning out."

For the remainder of the evening, we went on to discuss the Achaean threat to Minos's empire. Rhadamanthys and I agreed that although the bronze-shirted Achaeans were growing in ambition, they were many decades from mounting a coordinated attack against our kingdom. Our fleet covered the heaving sea like a blanket. Our colonies on strategic islands, such as Kea, Aegina, and Kythera, encircled the north inland like a noose. Though the Achaeans were great warriors on land, their navies were nothing to speak of. Moreover, if the Achaeans were to pose any kind of threat at all, their numerous well-walled cities would have to stop warring among themselves and form a pact against us — that was highly unlikely.

Rhadamanthys promised me that he would talk with the princes of Crete about how to discourage any barbarian thoughts of expansion. I told him that after returning to Knossos, I would speak to my confidant about the matter. Half-jokingly, my friend declared that it was too bad I didn't get to wrestle Theseus and didn't snap the Athenian's neck; then we would have had one fewer barbarian to worry about.

On the morning I was due to leave Phaistos, I heard a gentle tattooing on my door. When I opened it, soft-stepping Aphaea slipped by me. "How did you sneak away?" I exclaimed.

"Shhh...I just had to say goodbye. Who knows when we'll see each other again."

"We'll see each other as soon as I officially cancel my betrothal to Himera, and as soon as my mother sets the most auspicious day for our wedding. Then, I'll sail back to Crete and speak to Biadice." Aphaea turned from me and walked slowly to the window. "What is it, dear?"

"It's a big step to marry out of the royal family. In fact, I'm not sure it's ever been done before."

"Neither am I, but it doesn't matter to me, Aphaea."

"There are those who will call for your crown — Sarpedon for one. As the oldest prince on Kalliste and ruler of Metapontus, he might be able to convince Minos that you should step down."

"Aphaea, my love," I said, holding her slender wrists. "If it came to that, if I had to step down, I would, gladly, to be with you."

"Oh, Idomeneus —"

"But wait, don't worry; it won't come to that. I have friends at the capital who will take our side. Trust me. You just start making plans to be on Kalliste this summer — in your wedding gown."

Ambrosial dawn was soon sending shafts of golden light through the window. Though it hurt, I had to tear myself away from Aphaea's white arms in order to meet Evanus, the charioteer, at the stables. My love and I said goodbye with a tender kiss.

FIVE

THE EVENING that I had returned to Knossos, I had a cheery dinner with some Knossosan friends. After dinner, while a loud drinking game was in progress, I excused myself and made it, unnoticed, to the king's apartment complex. The guard who was supposed to escort me through the complex was waiting at the appointed spot. He led me to a large bronze-studded door, deep within the palace, and knocked rhythmically. A familiar voice commanded us to enter. We stepped into a huge room and saluted Prince Catreus, King Minos's oldest son. He rose from a chair behind a papyrus-laden desk and returned our salutes, dismissing the guard at once. Unknown to anyone, except Rhadamanthys, Catreus was my influential friend within the Labyrinth. More well-placed he could not have been, unless, of course, he sat on the king's throne himself.

It was only the year before that Catreus and I had become fast friends. I saved his life. He had been visiting Kalliste on official business, and, as a break, I invited him to go up the great mountain with me in search of boar. In a shady draw, we cornered a big one, heavy with ivory. I stood by while Catreus went in for the kill, brandishing his long spear. As the prince tried to drive it home, the spear snapped in half. If I had not jumped in to finish the job, King Minos would have lost not only his son but also his most trusted advisor.

As Minos got on in years, he shifted more and more responsibility to his able son, and, before long, Catreus was involved in every major trade, military, and political decision in the kingdom. Thus, when it came to things like port assignments, my bond with Catreus was as good as gold, forged as it was with a brave deed and some boar's blood.

Since I knew Catreus was always busy with one thing or another, I got right to the heart of the matter. I told him about my marriage plans and the probable stir it would cause on Kalliste. After listening attentively, Catreus smiled, sat back in his chair, and said, "I see no problem at all. Understand that my father and his spies have kept a close eye on Sarpedon for some time. That accursed man has been trying to spread his tentacles over all Kalliste. The prospect of Phira being added to the towns already under Sarpedon's sway is alarming."

"Indeed," I agreed.

"Whatever the reason, Idomeneus, the king would not be upset if you canceled your wedding to Princess Himera. In fact, I'll thank you officially for him, right now." Catreus poured us some wine, and we drank a toast to my Aphaea of the lovely tresses.

At one point in our discussion, I casually asked what was to become of the Athenian athletes. "As is the custom," Catreus said, "the barbarians will be required to leap two more times, at the summer and autumn contests. The survivors will be sent back to Athens. No Athenian, however, has ever lived through three bull-leaping contests," Catreus reminded me with relish. He was the kingdom's most outspoken critic of further relations with the Athenians and the other Achaeans; policy meetings within the Labyrinth were memorable for Catreus's acrimonious tirades against the inland barbarians.

You can imagine how Catreus was all ears when I told him about the fears Rhadamanthys and I had about the barbarians one day taking the field against us. "Idomeneus, the Achaeans presence—Athenian and Mycenaean mostly—in Syria and Canaan is dangerous," Catreus claimed. "It's critical that we find ways to block their inroads over there. I'm looking into it right now." He didn't elaborate. All he said was that, at least for the present, all we can do is keep our guard up.

After another cup of wine, I said goodbye to Catreus and left his study, elated by his words of support for my marriage to Aphaea. Although I would soon be returning home and facing the inevitable bitter confrontation with Sarpedon, at least that night, I felt both confident and defiant, knowing I would have the king and his court behind me.

Next morning at the port, I found my crew milling around the Dove. The pilot, Phanus, who was also my first lieutenant, reported that all hands were present, and the Dove was ready to make for home. The crew gave me an enthusiastic welcome; I accepted their warm greeting with a smile. I climbed aboard and entered the compact cabin on the stern, where I donned my captain's helmet.

Amnisos Harbor was stiff with masts like a donkey's bristling back, but Phanus and the helmsman took us neatly through and the oarsmen rowed us swiftly along. About a quarter of the royal navy was anchored that day. The remainder was probably spread out over The Deep Blue: some warships escorting Minos's trading convoys and some, with colors unfurled and weapons gleaming, cruising in and out of faraway ports to remind subjects and foreigners alike of the might of Minos.

Once the warships were cleared, we upped oars, hoisted the sail, and, as Diktynna, Protectress of Sailors, willed, caught a strong Notus. Far to the northeast, below a mackerel sky, a small cone could be spied on the horizon—Mount Kalliste.

Knifing through the waves as easy as you please, the Dove made excellent time and, by late afternoon, skirted the cape that lay southeast of Metapontus. When sailors approached from the south, coming from Crete or Libya, the cape was the first Kallistean landfall they made. In a moment of playful abandon, the Mother Goddess had gouged out countless caves and tunnels along the cape. Though some were not deep, others were endless; no man had ever crawled more than a couple hundred feet into them.

A flock of seagulls gathering in the sky caught Phanus's eye, and he called my attention to them. I ordered him to bring the Dove under the birds. I was struck by the absence of the cries, incessant and piercing, those scavengers make when they discover flotsam or dead fish. All that could be heard was the rattle of the Dove's rigging and the thud of her bow as it bounced over the waves.

Phanus spotted it first, directing our attention to a body about ten boat-lengths off our bowsprit. Long and smooth, the white form slowly bobbed and turned. The crew strained to make it out, but not until we came alongside and saw the jug-shaped head did we recognize it as one of the sea-people, floating on its back, dead.

Seeing the dolphin like that was unsettling, its underbelly high above the blue water, its tail and flippers stilled, its big intelligent eyes shut tight. For a moment or two, we stared in silence.

Suddenly we realized that the fish was not floating, nor was it alone. Six dolphins swam beneath it, gently paddling in a circle, each one using its strong snout to buoy the lifeless body.

We didn't know what to make of such a sight. Had the dolphins brought a severely sick companion to the surface to help it breathe, all to no avail? Was it some kind of wake before a watery burial, which no man had ever witnessed before? Did this encounter with the dolphins have anything to do with the earlier one we had on our way to the Spring Festival on Crete? We asked these questions in hushed voices, but no one could supply the answers.

In order to breathe, the dolphins parted the surface with their shining heads. Unlike the first encounter, there was no chatter, no urgent cries, no coming up to the Dove. Instead, each dolphin glanced at us, then produced a short eerie whine reminiscent of the bereaved female Athenian bull-leapers in the room at the palace. With the sail slackened, we stayed alongside the unnatural scene, feeling confused and helpless. Without warning, the white underbelly sank into the blue and was lost. Along with it went the living bier.

In a somber mood, we continued our passage, gaining the east side of the cape. There, Phanus spotted another flock of seagulls hovering over a brightly painted boat that drifted in the shallow water close to the beach-break. The kind of boat used by our fishermen. It was unmanned, and there was no one in sight on shore. With dread in our hearts, we headed for the craft.

As we came alongside her, we found nothing floating along her seaward side, nor did we find anything amiss when we warily peeked into her hull. Alas, when Phanus and I boarded her and peered over the gunwale facing Kalliste, our eyes met a woeful sight: a body fouled in a fishing net that had snagged on a thole and was floating in the water. The bloated corpse was not that of a fish but of an old man. Slowly, we hauled in the heartrending catch. There were no cuts or bruises on the fisherman, no indications of a struggle in his boat. It appeared as if Diktynna, Inventor of Nets, had taken the fisherman in the same way he had taken countless fish of Hers. Phanus recognized the man as belonging to the little village of Potamos, which lay up the coast and around the headland called Mesa Vouna. On the rolling waves along the cape, our joy of returning home vanished like a dragonfly in the night.

We brought the old fisherman to his home in Potamos for the last time. Friends of the grief-stricken family told us that he had been amazingly healthy and spry for someone his age—over threescore years. When he pushed off that morning, he had been fine. We told them about the dolphin, but the folks at Potamos could not find a connection between the death of the old man and the death of the fish, except that each had died mysteriously and bloodlessly in their element. We left the wailing village with both incidents weighing heavily upon us. When we tied up at Phira's little wharf, we had come no closer to understanding their causes nor their meanings.

I pondered the riddle of those two deaths for much of the Sheep Shearing Moon. As did everyone else, for the stories flew around the island with the inevitable exaggerations and embroideries taking place. Since the trading season was approaching, however, other things, less mysterious, began to occupy our thoughts. During my absence, Miletus, my trusty steward, initiated a number of projects necessary for an early run up the Cyclades. He oversaw the repair work on our three trading vessels: the patching of sails, the mending of rigging, and the painting of hulls. He also began the important preparatory work in our storerooms, ordering the keepers to select the proper numbers of wine vintages to be exported that summer and ensuring that the scribes kept accurate tablets of every pithos. Miletus also kept an eagle eye on the careful pruning of that season's vines, vegetables, and fruits. Thanks to trusty Miletus, in little more than a month after my return from Crete, we were ready to sail to the Cycladic ports, including Asterie.

Before sailing, I wanted to meet with Prince Sarpedon and to break the news of my upcoming marriage to Aphaea. I told Miletus and my mother about my new wedding plans, and their reactions were what I expected. Since he had seen Aphaea a number of times at Phaistos, Miletus enthusiastically concurred with my choice. As strange as it sounds, I spied a little jealousy in the old goat when we spoke of her beauty. Nevertheless, Miletus brought up, as tactfully as possible, the impropriety of my marrying anyone other than Himera. He was concerned not only with the possible repercussions at Metapontus, he explained, but also with those at Knossos. Marriage agreements between royalty were never dissolved except, of course, upon the death of one of those to be wed.

While I carefully spelled out the change to my wedding plans to her, my mother remained silent. When I finished, she asked, "Who are her parents?"

"Her father is Tereus, the head cook at the palace. And her mother is Nephele, a leading seamstress in Phaistos."

"How long has Aphaea been in the palace?"

"Since she was ten-and-four, ten years now."

"Does she want children?"

"Oh, yes, of course. Maybe three or four." As we talked, the intensity of my love for Aphaea shone through. That was all my mother needed to see. Before long, she granted me her blessing with a big hug and a kiss.

"If there are snags—political or otherwise—I'll leave them in your capable hands," she said. "But, as the head priestess of Phira, I will pray to the Mother, Dove Goddess of Love, Fertility, and the Hearth, for your marriage."

"Don't worry mother. I have a powerful friend in Knossos who will help me in this."

"I will pray anyway. It is with the Goddess."

That morning I went to see Prince Sarpedon and Himera at Metapontus; I did not expect kind understanding from them. I met with the prince in the throne room and told him, simply and frankly, my feelings and plans. Sarpedon took a few moments to compose himself, deciding how to deal with such a serious blow to his grand design. When his tense face went slack and a crooked little smile appeared on his thin lips, I knew he would try to treat me like a son in need of counseling.

"My dear Idomeneus," he said, "I see the dilemma you're in, and how, being of noble heart, you want to make the righteous decision. I know you don't want to bring shame on yourself or on your father's good name." He said the last part with his head cocked to one side. "So, you propose to wed one and not the other. But your strong blood has blinded you to the fact that the solution is even simpler than choosing this one or that one. Because of your birthright, you have the prerogative to take both! One as princess, the other as mistress. And I'm sure I don't have to add which would be which. Idomeneus, I am surprised that you're overlooking this common practice." Sarpedon said with a lecherous grin. "It's found in every palace, you know."

"Yes, I'm aware of the practice, but it's not what I want for Phira. I'm determined to have just one woman as my palace companion, and that woman is Aphaea."

The twinkle in Sarpedon's eye faded, along with his paternal posture. Trying to keep his rage under rein, he gave me a dark and rolling eye from under his bushy brow. "What about your father's word? Remember," he growled. "I have it in writing, you know, with his seal. What are we to do with it, eh? Go on, tell me! Toss it aside? Piss on it? Cast it into the sea? Oh, Cretheus, thank Goddess you are not here to see your only child defile your honor! And for what? Lust for a woman. A common woman, at that. It's too unbelievable!"

"Believe it, Sarpedon," I shot back. "I regret breaking my father's vow, but I know he would've forgiven me. And as for Himera, she is young and beautiful. You'll marry her off to another prince with little trouble, I'm sure."

"You're sure. You're sure," he mimicked sarcastically. "I want her at Phira—you insolent upstart! This has always been my desire—"

"I know all about your desires, your political desires, your motives. That's all you ever think about, but that's no concern of mine!"

"Minos shall hear of this…oh yes he shall. We'll see what royal favors and easy port assignments you get from now on!" After the threats, I could see by his raised eyebrows that he had hit upon a new point. "Who put you up to this?"

"What in the world are you talking about?"

"This wench of yours…from Phaistos you say, right? Rhadamanthys! Yes, that's it. That black cur! He would just love to get one of his kind enthroned on Kalliste. Yes, I can see it now. He probably sired this bitch on some palace tart, and, after the wedding, he plans on stepping forward and proclaiming his fatherhood. He would have his big foot on our land, then."

That was too much! If I had had my dagger, I don't know what would have happened. "You're mad, Sarpedon, mad," I yelled. "You see plots everywhere! You forget, not everyone has your foul mind and black—"

At that moment the door flew open, and Sarpedon's bodyguards burst into the chamber with swords drawn. Clearly, the swell and tone of my voice had carried through the thick door into the hallway. Sarpedon played the scene beautifully, allowing the guards to stay longer than they needed to, then dismissed them with swaggering assurances.

"Listen, Sarpedon, there is nothing more to be said. Just let me see Himera for a moment for I'd like to tell her myself."

"Impossible! What gall!"

"Never mind, I'll get word to her somehow." I cursed him roundly as I stormed out of Sarpedon's chamber. A man will utter hateful things when his blood is boiling. The thought of Himera hearing the news from Sarpedon's venomous tongue made my skin crawl. Before I left Metapontus, I left a message for her with a friend of my mother's, giving the woman instructions to deliver it at once, for there was a chance that Sarpedon would not tell his daughter immediately and that my message might reach her first.

On the way home, I felt as if a heavy load had been lifted from my shoulders.

SIX

THE GREAT GODDESS, Mother of the Mountains, had blessed Kalliste with abundant natural wealth and beauty. Its name, in fact, means "most beautiful one." Long, gently-sloping ridges and narrow valleys radiated out from the great mountain like spokes from a hub. The loamy soil broke easily beneath the plow, and the carefully tilled terraces formed a bewildering maze on the island. An ancient song described how—long before man walked the earth—the Mother had prepared the soil of Kalliste in a huge oven. Tenderly adding the proper ingredients in just the right amounts, the Goddess baked them for a thousand years, creating our rich red soil.

What grew in that soil were her gifts to us. Our olives, artichokes, onions, pomegranates, figs, apples, and cherries were as good as those anywhere in the empire. And our grapes were unrivaled! Visitors from across the waves were always fascinated by the unique way we grew them. Because the wind swirled around Mount Kalliste and spun down its slopes with such force, our ancestors devised a way of protecting the tender fruit. The earliest farmers invented the technique of using twine to force the vines to grow in circles, making them look like huge baskets or nests. Shielded from the battering wind, the grapes matured slowly on the inside of the "nests." The countryside was dotted with these nests, as if some giant bird had built them for its growing family. From these perfect grapes, we Kallisteans created perfect wines, both white and red. Despite the fact that the other islands produced their own wine, we supplied our much sought-after Kallistean wine to many of them.

One day, Miletus and I were inspecting the vines around Phira when we spotted a messenger on the south road; by his speed, we knew he was bringing some urgent news. Miletus recognized him as one of Sarpedon's men. Before the messenger reached the vineyard, he was shouting, "People are sick and dying along the coast! We need help! We need to bring the sick to Metapontus! Can you bring your wagons, Prince Idomeneus?"

"What is happening, man?" I demanded.

"We're not sure, Sire," he gasped, skidding to a halt. Taking a deep breath, he leaned on his herald's staff and continued, "Early this morning, scores of villagers from the south shore began arriving in the city. They were sick, very sick. Some died right there in our streets! Many kept saying that the air was poisoned, that some evil was let loose amongst them, that the island was doomed! They begged to know why the Great Goddess would allow it!"

"How can we help?" I asked.

"Prince Sarpedon entreats you to put aside your anger with him. He requests that you take some wagons along the south coast as far as you can, evacuate the sick, and bring them to Metapontus."

"We'll start right away."

"Bless you, Your Grace. Now I must run, carrying my message up the island. Farewell, Sire." He dashed up the road, heading for Oia.

Swiftly Miletus and I rounded up oxen from the pasture and assigned field hands the task of driving our farm wagons—twelve in all. Soon we were on the road, dark questions and heart-clawing fear abounding.

The sun was high overhead when we reached sandy Potamos. As we rolled into the village square, it looked as if the population had increased tenfold. Before we could get down from the wagons, we were engulfed by a sea of wide-eyed people, each person screaming his version of the incredible story. The townsfolk of Enalus, which lay just around rocky Mesa Vouno to the south, had abandoned their homes and fled to Potamos. Prince Thoas of Enalus was there to meet me as I scrambled down from my wagon.

"It's an evil day on Kalliste, Idomeneus," he cried. "An evil day. Woe to the people of Enalus. We must have committed some terrible sin. What about Phira? Was your air poisoned too?"

"No. When we left, the air was sweet and fresh. Thoas, what in Goddess's name is going on?"

"As close as I can figure," he said, "a current of poisonous vapor is passing over the south tip of the island. The vapor has the strength to kill all in its path: plants, birds, animals, and people."

"From what I heard, Metapontus has been spared. No poisonous vapor was reported there."

"Oh? Well at Enalus we received a strong dose. It sent us running. Some of my people swooned, some had spasms and headaches. Many were sick to their stomachs. But none were lost to us...at least not in town...I don't know how many of our people were in the fields or on the road. I had the entire town, including our livestock, evacuated. When we reached the Potamos side of Mesa Vouna, we discovered that the villagers here were ignorant of the contamination."

"Thoas, what was the evil vapor like? Can you describe it?"

"Yes, By-our-Lady, for I still have its odious taste in my mouth. When the vapor reached Enalus, the town reeked, as if a thousand seagull eggs had been smashed and allowed to rot in the sun. We wanted to pinch our noses closed; yet, at the same time, we were forced to gasp for breath." The townsfolk from Enalus, pressing hard on Thoas and me, agreed with the vivid and nauseating description of the vapor.

"But where could such a thing have come from," I wondered aloud.

"That's the question, Idomeneus," replied Thoas. "Just now, as you arrived, I was trying to get a small party up. I want to go around the headland to see if the wind has blown the poison away. My people, however, are reluctant to go, and I can't blame them." Though Thoas spoke without a trace of scorn or reproach, his people shrank back like scolded dogs. "Before they return to their homes," Thoas continued, "the Enalusans want our priestesses' assurance that the air has been purged. At this very moment, I have them petitioning the Great Mother on our behalf. How long it will take the Goddess to respond is anyone's guess."

I pulled Thoas to one side, away from the throng, and whispered, "If you want to find out if the plague's left Enalus and try to discover its source, I'll go with you, friend."

"Good! I knew I could count on you, Idomeneus. I'll have my stable boys bring two mules — they're swifter than donkeys. And just in case we have to flee for our lives, I think it better to ride on their backs than have them pull us in a wagon. Have you ever been on the back of one of these beasts, Idomeneus?"

"Aye, twice on Crete." My reply was true, but I didn't bother explaining that both times I was thrown no sooner had I mounted. A cross between a donkey and a horse, the mule was new to our kingdom, used mostly for hauling and field work. There were only four on Kalliste: two at Metapontus, two at Enalus. At Phira, no one except me had ever tried to ride one.

As the boys brought the mules, an ashen-faced Miletus tapped me on the shoulder and asked, "Is this wise, Your Grace?"

"Miletus, my trusted companion, I've got to find out about this vile vapor. You know how we've been beset by a series of inexplicable tragedies. And now this. Maybe the answers lie around that headland," I said, pointing to Mesa Vouna. I slapped Miletus on the shoulder and climbed aboard my mule.

After a few last-moment instructions to his people, Thoas mounted his mule, and we both shouted "Yaw haw!" The obstinate mules did not budge; it took our insistent rods to get them moving and keep them moving. Heading out, we waved goodbye to a worried crowd of Kallisteans.

The path around Mesa Vouna was as narrow as a needle; as we rode along it, gray salt water licked the legs of the mules. Reaching the south side of the headland, I could feel my entire body pound like a child's drum. I peeked at Thoas. He was breathing quickly and sweating hard. Getting his attention, I gave him a nod and a weak smile. We prodded our mules with new urgency.

From the headland to Enalus, the air was pure and brisk, no whiff of the awful odor Thoas had described. As we rode through the town, I asked him, "Could you see the killing vapor against the sky? I mean, did it have form or color?"

"No. No form, no color," he replied. "It was just there."

The streets of the town were eerie, devoid of the living sounds of people and animals. Thoas and I decided to explore farther down the coast, thinking there might be farmers or fishermen in need of help and that maybe we could find the source of the vapor.

For a long stretch, the road was deserted, but eventually we came across a grisly sight: an abandoned wagon with its ox team lying stiff before it. We continued on, shaken and even more wary.

When we reached a slight bend in the coast, we spotted a dozen contorted corpses scattered along the road, farmers who had attempted to flee to Enalus. It was heartrending. Most of those Goddess-forsaken men had their hands around their throats. If Thoas and I had not known of the airborne poison, we would have thought that death by self-strangulation had taken place. Instead, it was clear that the farmers had been clutching their throats in order to aid the flow of air, but the air was lethal. There was nothing to be done but stare in bewilderment at the twisted bodies; the burials would take place later.

As we continued along, the air was still sweet. The sun shone brightly in a blue cloudless sky. Thoas tried to keep in mind the names of the dead he had recognized, but the farther we went, the more difficult his task became. The road was strewn with farmers, fishermen, tradesmen, and itinerant merchants who had been going about their business when death struck them down. The entire area looked like a battlefield littered with heavy losses. But there were no spears, swords, shields, or blood.

"Right out there," I said, pointing to a spot off shore, "was where we found the old fisherman and his boat."

Suddenly Thoas reined in his mule and turned toward me with a jerk. As if we were surrounded by spies, he whispered, "There. Did you smell it?"

"No. I smelled nothing. Was it the vapor?"

"I'm not sure. For a moment there, I thought I got a whiff of it, but it's gone now."

We continued...slowly. The only sounds were the clip-clop of the hooves and the lapping of the waves.

About a quarter of a league from the headland, Thoas came to a halt. I immediately knew why. A scent, accurately described by Thoas as rotten egg, wafted under our noses. Though unpleasant, the odor was so faint that it didn't make us ill. We agreed to go on, hoping to locate its source.

On the rocky shore along the cape, the bodies of several fishermen lay twisted and lifeless. Their nets, which had been cast over the water before the calamity, were buoyed by dead fish. All around the nets, however, more fortunate fish darted about. How had they escaped both the fishermen and the vapor? I pointed out to Thoas the approximate point on the horizon where the Dove came upon the mourning dolphins.

Moving across the cape, Thoas and I scouted both land and sea for the source of the vapor. As we approached some caves, the odor intensified. We constantly checked back and forth to see if either of us was feeling ill.

Suddenly, I reined in my mule with one hand and with the other reached over and grabbed Thoas by the arm. "Over there...on the right...the ground-level cave. Do you see it?" I exclaimed. A continuous stream of yellowish gas spewed forth from a cave that was half the height of a man. After spiraling out from the cave about forty feet, the gas mixed with the air and became colorless.

Kalliste, our beloved home, was producing a hideous poison that was killing us. The riddle was solved. The old fisherman and the dolphin — a fish that breathes like a man — had been the first victims. They must have been hit with a blast, which then quickly subsided, only to resume again with greater force, spreading mass death across the cape.

Knowing that at any time a Zephyrus could kick up, blowing the poison in our faces, Thoas and I proceeded with great care. We got within five paces of the cave, carefully observing the deadly opening, the sallow gusts of gas, and the surrounding area. As if the sun had burned it, the sparse vegetation along the shore was withered and jaundiced for a hundred feet in either direction.

Without apparent reason, the obnoxious jet began to slacken. Soon it was reduced to a series of weak puffs. Finally, the puffs stopped, but when we tried to approach the mouth of the cave, the lingering stench drove us back, for it clung to every nearby rock and plant. Though we waited a while, we still could not get close enough to look inside the cave. There was nothing more to be done and our light was fading, so we mounted our mules and headed back.

At Potamos, we gave our sad report to the grief-stricken towns-people and villagers of Enalus; everyone's heart ached. Thoas and I tried to lessen the shock by assuring the people that, with our own eyes, we had seen the vapor die. Just in case, Thoas decided to camp his people right on Potamos's beach for the night; the next day, if the air remained clear, he planned to take his people back to Enalus. He sent runners to Metapontus and beyond to inform the anxious island-ers of what we had seen. As I led my empty wagons out of the little square, poor Thoas was besieged by his people, all desiring to hear if he had seen their loved ones, or, rather, hoping to hear that he hadn't. For if their kith and kin had not been spotted, there was a chance that they had escaped up the great mountain.

As the month passed, the air around the island remained pure. It appeared that the Goddess had spared us Kallisteans more pain. Be that as it may, guards were posted at the mouth of the cave, and a network of runners was set up in order to give us early warning in case the lethal gas was turned loose again. Enalus was reoccupied, and Thoas and his people had the lamentable task of gathering up their dead. Mass burials were held all along the south shore, as the pungent smell of Egyptian myrrh replaced the odious vapor. All told, five-and-forty people had perished, and ten people went blind.

All the sacrificial altars on Kalliste ran red with blood, laden as they were with crooked-horned sheep and fat oxen. The priests and priestesses slept very little, for they were in almost constant prayer. Many islanders joined them. A messenger from Metapontus was dis-patched over the open sea. We awaited advice from Minos on addi-tional rituals and the order to begin our trading voyages, which had been postponed when the Goddess for some unfathomable reason, permitted our own land to expel the noxious gas. I sent my own per-sonal messenger to Phaistos, but what happened next no wise man, priestess, nor king could have prepared us for.

It was the beginning of the Grain Harvest Moon. The air was mild and lightly scented with the blending of sweet rush and mint.

Along with the palace retainers and scribes, Miletus and I had just finished our dinner and were lounging in the dining hall on couches, cracking delicious nuts, and sipping some of Phira's fine red wine, as red as rabbit's blood. I remember Miletus loudly defending me against the vicious rumors that were seeping out of Metapontus and spreading across the island. His face was as red as the wine. "Can you believe these lackeys of Prince Sarpedon's spreading such nonsense? They're serpent-tongued toads; that's what they are! At this time of woe, we should all be pulling together, not trying to divide the Kallisteans." He quaffed a cup of wine in one go and continued. "But they won't get very far with such a preposterous tale. Who's going to believe that our Sweet Earth Mistress poisoned Kalliste simply because Prince Idomeneus chose to marry one woman and not another? One would have to be maggotty-headed to fall for such a shallow invention."

A grave scribe named Althaemenes, brother of Phanus, my first lieutenant, warned, "The people are shaken by what has transpired, Miletus. They've had their brains rattled by fear."

"Ah, the good folks of Kalliste are made of sterner stuff than that, my friend," Miletus broke in. "They're no fools. They're not going to believe that She, Protectress of Nature—being unhappy with Prince Idomeneus—sacrificed scores of people on the south shore, leaving Phira untouched. It just doesn't add up."

The calumnies against me were nothing new. A few days after the cave incident, Sarpedon began to blacken my name, intensifying his attack when our trading voyages were postponed because of the tragedy.

That night in the dining hall, I reached for my cup and noticed a rippling effect on the surface of the wine, as if a pebble had been dropped into a still pond. Having had my share of wine, that life-giving medicine against despair, I didn't trouble my mind about why the ripples were there. Instead, I sat numbly admiring their delicate pattern.

A few moments later the high-pitched cry of a lark pierced the still night air. The conversation in the room stopped, everyone pricking up their ears. The lark is the herald of sunrise; for it to cry at nighttime was unheard of.

Presently there were more cries. I heard a dove and a raven. Soon everyone in the room heard them, too. Before long, an ear-splitting cacophony created by larks, doves, ravens, owls, swallows—every kind of bird—echoed throughout the palace and all of Phira. Our feeling of bewilderment rapidly turned to alarm. The others in the palace felt the same way; they poured into the corridors, urgently asking each other what was going on.

As if the awful screeching, cawing, and hooting of the birds wasn't enough, the town dogs began howling, the sheep began bleating, and the beasts of burden began bellowing and braying.

As I went to push away from the table in front of me, I looked down to see the wine lapping against the inside of my cup, like so many stormy waves pounding the shore. Then the foot of the cup began to tremble, creating a pitter-patter on the table top, which was picked up by all the other cups on all the other tables. Then the cups rattled across the tops of the tables as if they were huge drums and the cups were dancing to the common beat.

I looked at Miletus who was already at the door, his eyes transfixed on my table. He looked up and said, simply, "Earthquake."

The faces of the retainers and scribes blanched—I'm sure mine did too—and we froze, panic-stricken, for one horrible moment, until the shrill screams in the palace jarred us into action. Miletus shouted out a quick order, "Get everyone out!"

As we sprinted from the hall, we heard the ceramic vessels breaking and the metal vessels bouncing on the stone floor. We elbowed through the corridors, shouting to those who glutted them to move outside into the central court. We banged our fists on closed doors so that all got the word.

I fought my way to my mother's suite, searching her bedroom, dressing room, toilette, and bath without finding her. My blood ran cold. Racing through the deserted corridors, I shouted her name, kicking in locked doors.

Suddenly, I stopped in my tracks and thumped my forehead with the heel of my hand. "Stupid," I said aloud. Reversing direction, I flew through the western sector of the palace, quickly arriving at the main shrine on the second story. There, assisted by two sobbing priestesses, my mother softly prayed before the altar, as miniature horns of consecration and double axes jiggled along the top. I ushered her and her assistants unceremoniously out of the shrine, through the corridors, and into the court. The assistants breathed a sigh of relief, but my mother was quiet, passive. She displayed not the slightest trace of fear.

We were the last ones to make it into the central court. The four of us joined the other palace residents huddled in darkness as the cacophony created by the birds and beasts reached a feverish pitch. Though no one spoke, we knew that everyone was waiting for the groaning of the earth which, we had always been told, accompanied earthquakes and was the most dreadful sound in the world.

Gradually the racket of the animals and the sounds of falling objects subsided. The palace and all of Phira became quiet, unnaturally quiet. Before long we heard a child begin to sob somewhere in town, then wail uncontrollably. It was the humans' turn. Soon children from every home and those cowering in the court began crying. Women picked up and increased the bitter lamentation, which became as loud as the alarm that the animals had given us.

After speaking with my mother and Miletus, I climbed onto the balcony of a second story apartment, while the men quieted down the women and children. "My people listen; listen to your Prince," I shouted. "Look! Look around you! The Holy Mother has spared us. Our palace and town still stand. No one is injured. What we felt was a warning, just a warning. The Loud Thundering Goddess has told us that She is not appeased yet. She wants more sacrifice, more prayer from the people of Kalliste. So, for the rest of this night, until the sun rises, we'll give Her great offerings and prayers—right here in the court—together. My mother, Princess Henithea, and her priestesses will guide us. Surely the Great Goddess shall listen to us and be pleased with Her children."

I climbed down as my mother began the prayers. With the help of some men, I began a small fire in the center of the court, far from the apartments. Miletus organized and dispatched a party to go through the palace making sure all the lamps were out and collecting blankets and water.

Accompanied by a priest and two retainers, I went as fast as my feet could carry me to the main square in town, leaving my mother and Miletus in charge of the palace. The square was overrun with townsfolk and nearby farmers, and I delivered the same message to them that I had given to the courtiers. I returned to the palace, leaving the priest to conduct the sacrifices and prayers and the retainers to keep an eye on things. That night, I moved back and forth between the palace court and the main square surveying the damage.

The next day, we discovered that every town and village on Kalliste had felt the earth shake. The damage in other places was similar to the damage at Phira: broken pots, cracked plaster, and a few split beams. Nobody on the island was seriously injured—just a few bumps and bruises received while people pushed and shoved to get to safety.

But the blow was devastating. A few Cycladic islands, like Milos and Sifnos, were sometimes jostled by quakes. Never Kalliste. Our wisest bards could not remember a single verse mentioning the Goddess's displeasure with us. No old-timer could recall the slightest tremor. Lofty Kalliste had been Her favorite. Now that was all over.

Two days after the earthquake, the messenger who had been sent to Knossos to report on the lethal vapor arrived home. No sooner had he reported to Sarpedon than the messenger was sent back over the swell of the waters with the latest loathsome news. He returned from Crete within two days, carrying a long list of atoning sacrifices we were to make in order to avoid further and more serious quakes. The mysterious vapor had baffled the Cretans; they offered us no solutions. But earthquakes were another matter, for the Cretans had experienced more of them than any other people and knew how to quell the Earth Mistress's wrath.

Unfortunately, the prescriptions we received from the Knossosan priestesses did not work, or, rather, worked only partially, because for the next couple of weeks Kalliste was subject to a series of tremors, equal to or slightly less than the first. Damage was minimal, but despair and worry engulfed the people. Our love for our special island was tarnished, our faith in Our Lady shaken.

In the light of the latest crisis, I knew that the people of Phira, including some in the palace itself, were listening closer to Sarpedon's allegations against me. More then once, a heated discussion stopped abruptly as I approached. Invariably, one of the men would launch into a monologue about the harvest, or the postponed trading voyage, or some other topic. I kept asking myself—as Miletus had said aloud that night of the first tremor—how can they possibly believe that

insidious lie, knowing it originated in Metapontus. Nevertheless, I
was troubled enough by all the whispering to seek out my mother's
sensible opinion. Once again, I interrupted her at the altar, but I was
more composed the second time. She saw the worry in my face and
stopped her prayers at once. We walked down to the small garden, her
favorite, which faced the great mountain. A sacred stone pillar and a
miniature tree of life stood in that brightly flowering garden. There, I
poured out my concerns about the rumors against me.

When I finished, my mother put her hand on my arm. "My noble son," she said, "when first I heard these calumnies against you,
despite their ominous implications and despite the troubles we had, I
actually laughed. Yes, laughed! Even my priestesses who relayed these
rumors to me joined in, for we who are close to the Blessed Goddess
realize that She would not act in such a petty, humanlike manner."
My mother paused, clearing her throat. "But then, Idomeneus, the
holy earth shook. That had never happened on Kalliste before. And
now…now, I'm not sure what She is thinking,"

My mother looked around her to make certain we were still
alone, then said in a gentling tone, "My son, shepherd of men, you are
the rightful and wise Prince of Phira, and even I, your mother, High
Priestess of Phira, would not presume to tell you what to do. But let
me ask you this. Wouldn't it be wise to cancel…" She stopped short
and held my arm tightly, for she saw that within me coals were being
fanned. She quickly added, "Or at least can't you postpone the wedding until we determine if the Great Mother is angry with you, so
angry that She would ravage this island and kill its people for spite?"

So long had I waited for Aphaea to be by my side, I exploded at
the mere suggestion. "Thundering Goddess, these awful things have
nothing to do with us. You saw how the king sent Sarpedon's messenger back home without the slightest mention of my plans to marry
Aphaea. No order to drop the plans. No censure. No admonishment.
And you can bet Sarpedon was hoping for all these."

"You speak of the affairs and concerns of men, Idomeneus. I
speak of the Immortal Goddess."

"Why should evil come to a man who carefully attends the
Goddess? Why should I fall out of Her favor? Over the years I've
made the altars groan under countless offerings. I've burnt frankin-

cense on every outdoor altar and in every chapel on this island. Right here, before this pillar and tree, I've whispered or chanted a thousand prayers—with you at my side. Every winter when the Mother Goddess's Young Consort departs in His sacred boat, I mourn; and every spring when he sails back, I celebrate. Don't these things mean anything? Just because I've decided to marry a different girl, will the Goddess forget all I've done?"

"No, Idomeneus. She'll remember your worshipful acts for eternity. But now, you've broken a sacred vow, the vow of marriage, one that the Holy Mother, Protectress of Love, Fertility, and the Hearth, holds dear. She may be warning you."

"Mother, what kind of deity would kill innocent people—not even Phirans to warn me?"

"Don't talk that way, son. It's not given to us mortals to know the Goddess's mind. She alone has woven our lives, and only She knows the warp and the weft. It's fruitless, and blasphemous, to question Her motives. All we can do—all the priestesses can do—is pay attention to the omens, see how they're connected, what they're telling us, and act accordingly."

"So, we're powerless, then."

"No. With sacrifice, proper sacrifice, and prayer, prayer from the heart, we can gain Her beneficence."

So, Her favors can be bought. I didn't say that to my mother, of course, but I was thinking it. I was beginning to believe that the very act of offering sacrifices and prayers was a salve, that's all. By simply participating in timeworn and trusted rituals, people allayed their own fears and doubts about the future. The All-Powerful Goddess was unmoved by such mortal rites and rituals, if She was aware of them at all. Regardless, She went about steering the world as She wished.

I don't think my mother read my thoughts, but after the pause she said, "Son, if the Goddess's actions don't touch you, what about the feelings of your subjects. When they, your friends and your neighbors, hear these charges against you, back-eddying thoughts enter their minds. My heart is eaten with grief when I see how they turn against you."

"Mother, they're suffering because of the evil that has befallen us, and they're looking for someone to blame."

"You could remove the doubts of everyone on Kalliste," she said gently.

With the back of my finger, I touched her beautiful cheek. "Well, in this time of crisis, I'll do what you ask. I'll postpone the wedding." The bright radiance of my mother's face made me think it was the right decision. "I'll postpone it only until the Moon of New Wine, though," I added. "Before then, I want to see a proclamation, in plain words, from the High Priestess of Knossos, Pasiphae herself, clearing Aphaea and me of any wrongdoing."

SEVEN

WORD OF THE POSTPONEMENT of my wedding flew on the wings of the wind; all Kalliste knew of it in no time. The spectre of Sarpedon's crooked smile haunted my dreams, and I could only imagine what use he would make of the news. Therefore, to make sure her hopes were not rekindled, I sent a special message to Princess Himera, explaining that I had not altered my decision to marry soft-eyed Aphaea. The postponement was simply a concession I made to the uneasy disposition of my people.

Those people, the folks of Phira, greeted the news with such glee that they would have broken into dance had not the priestesses at Knossos expressly forbidden any sort of celebration during the crisis. I had clearly underestimated how much Sarpedon's insidious lie had poisoned the minds of my subjects, for the grave and troubled eyes that had avoided me before were now gay and shining. It was almost as if the terrible things—the vapor and quakes—had never taken place on our island. Or as if the people simply refused to believe anything else would befall them. After all, their prince had put off the ill-advised union with the unknown Cretan; thus, everything would return to normal and the Goddess's beneficence would be restored — so they thought.

The Phirans were as simple as children, and their understanding stumbled on the jagged falsehood Sarpedon had sown on Kalliste. Not one among them had the faintest notion of the way The Web was woven, and I had not the heart to teach them. The fact is that when I saw the look of relief in the faces of my people, I grew bitter. Their faces reminded me of how I had allowed myself to be squeezed into the cowardly decision of delaying the wedding. Before long, I began to loathe the sight of my own people, despising them for the sacrifice I had made and the hurt I had brought to Aphaea.

Yes, poor Aphaea. Before the news reached Crete, I sailed the Dove to Timbaki, the port of Phaistos. A person may have thought that my telling Aphaea of the postponement would have been extremely difficult. Not at all. It seems that people on Crete had been discussing constantly what they called the "Kalliste Question," and possible answers; Aphaea heard Biadice and her priestesses discussing it every day. In fact, Aphaea said she concurred that maybe a delay in our wedding until the strange phenomena on Kalliste subsided was the best course. I was of two minds: first, I was glad, of course, that Aphaea took the postponement so well, and second, I was infuriated that she and I were put into such a situation.

I composed a message and gave it to a retainer with instructions to rush it to Knossos. There he was to hand it over to a certain palace guard. The retainer must have been curious about the message; he couldn't have known that the guard would secretly pass it on to Catreus. I wanted to know from my confidant why his mother hadn't come out in my behalf concerning the Kallistean disasters. I wanted Catreus to press Queen Pasiphae to make her proclamation of my innocence — now. I wanted the Phirans to realize the truth.

Rhadamanthys saw how angry and perplexed I was and suggested that we leave the palace at Phaistos and take a walk to Snow Crystal. The path we took snaked around the south side of the hill, and as we reached the west slope, the broad Gulf of Messara came into view. Soon we were at Snow Crystal — an unusual name for a summer palace, to say the least. Keen-witted Rhadamanthys enjoyed playing with words. When you caught sight of his superb

Snow Crystal, you knew there could be no other name for it. The tiny palace was completely paneled with thin sheets of snow-white alabaster. They sparkled and glittered when struck by the sun's rays, as if the palace were one gigantic snowflake. The residence and the attendant buildings were completely encircled by a stand of cypress trees, a perfect counterpoint.

In the springtime, the little palace was staffed by a few servants who kept up the premises and looked after the few guests. When the warm months arrived, Rhadamanthys moved the entire royal household from the main palace to Snow Crystal, taking advantage of the cool sea breeze. Then Snow Crystal was as busy as an anthill. Personally, I liked it just the way it was on that late spring day: quiet, slow, practically deserted.

As Rhadamanthys and I started down the stairway that descended from the road, the servants, alerted to our visit, rushed out to greet us. The stairway ended at the intersection of the two wings of the palace. The northern wing contained the numerous workshops for Rhadamanthys's artisans, some of the most talented in the kingdom, who fashioned wonderful things for him and those around him. Situated diagonally across a small court from the northern wing, the western wing was composed of the living quarters: suites, studies, small halls, and dining rooms. Snow Crystal was an eloquent Cretan palace in miniature.

We made our way through the western wing, arriving before a solid oak door with shining bronze studs. Rhadamanthys knocked twice, showing respect a prince usually reserved for the king. "Please enter, Sire," said a voice in a strange accent. Rhadamanthys pulled open the heavy door, and we entered a sunlit study. Every time I visited it over the years, the study looked the same: the four large windows flooded with soft light, the mottled stone benches arranged around the perimeter, the lovely paintings of fish and other marine life on the walls, and the large cedar table inlaid with pieces of pear wood and encircled by cushioned benches. But the rest of the room looked as if it had been hit by an avalanche. Faded and yellowed with age, thick rolls of papyrus were strewn all over, each document partially unrolled. Inscribed clay tablets and torn scraps of palm leaves were intermingled with the papyri. The documents were written in

Egyptian, Akkadian, Hittite, and occasionally, the new script used by the Achaeans. Odds and ends littered the floor, laying partly hidden under the documents, like snakes under rocks. There were small balls made of opaque alabaster or fiery amber, copper tubes twisted into weird shapes, stone vessels of different sizes, and crystal magnifying lenses. Visitors had to tread carefully.

While Rhadamanthys and I picked our way across the debris, two old men slowly began to rise from their seats at the table. They twittered at the same time, apologizing for not having greeted us formally at the stairs, apologizing for the condition of the study, apologizing for their unkempt robes. The greeting was their usual one and a refreshing change for Rhadamanthys and me — no one ever forgot when princes were to arrive except the wise men of Snow Crystal. Rhadamanthys and I returned each other's wink. "Gentlemen, please," Rhadamanthys exclaimed, "it is we who should apologize for catching you unawares. Please remain seated." A little theatrically, the two breathed a sign of relief. With the princes standing and the commoners sitting, we exchanged greetings.

"Our good friend, Prince Idomeneus," said Ananda. "We have missed your razor-sharp mind!" Rhadamanthys and Ta-ch'ih concurred, but, embarrassingly, it took me a few moments to understand what Ananda had said! Each time I saw him, I had to become reacquainted with his odd accent. And I had to do the same with Ta-ch'ih's because his was even thicker.

After the awkward pause, I replied, "You are most kind. All of you. You know if it were possible, I would be here at Snow Crystal every month!" Ananda and Ta-ch'ih smiled and clapped their hands at the idea of my having monthly visits, but then they remembered the troubles on Kalliste and offered their sincere condolences. I thanked them.

You could not envision three more unlikely friends than Rhadamanthys and the two sages. Ananda was the same height as Rhadamanthys, about five and a half feet, but there the similarity ended. Ananda's skin was the color of a ripe black olive, though his features were small, unlike the prominent features of a Kushite or a Libyan. Long and silvery, his luxuriant beard reached all the way down to the neckline of his yellowed robe. The threadbare garment was fastened in such a way that it exposed the right shoulder while hiding the left.

With a twinkle in his eye, Ananda loved to say that he came from a part of the earth beyond the Four Pillars. To men of Minos, of course, it was ridiculous to say such a thing, for we believed the Pillars cast their shadows across the entire earth. And Ananda enjoyed seeing us grapple with the statement, always adding that his home was so far east — so much farther than what we called The East — that his people considered the fabled city of Babylon as part of The West! Before he came to us, we had no knowledge of Ananda's people, and they, Ananda swore, had no knowledge of us. That was hard for us to believe. How could people living anywhere be ignorant of the greatest sea power in the world? After all, our kingdom had ruled The Deep Blue for centuries, cleared it of ruinous pirates, and established trade routes over the water that rivaled Egypt's landlocked trade routes. Broad-minded Ananda tried to lessen our incredulity and smooth our injured pride by insisting that his people were impartial. They had only the slightest knowledge of the Egyptians!

According to Ananda, his incredibly out-of-touch people lived in a fortified, mud-brick city called Hari-Yupuya. The spot from which the city sprang was holy, having been occupied since the beginning of time and favored by a great goddess. Crops grew well because they were nourished by a sacred river, the Indus. Burgeoning trade with the East (their West) made the people prosper and the city flourish.

About fifty years ago, fair-skinned raiders from the north began to infiltrate the river valley. The raiders worshiped a war god who was referred to as Puramdara, meaning Fort Destroyer, and whose name was Indra. One by one, the cities in the valley fell to the raiders from the north. Eventually Hari-Yupuya was besieged. Many of the citizens sneaked out, fleeing to the south. Many stayed on and fought — and died. Believing resistance was useless against the fierce invaders, Ananda, then a young acolyte to the priesthood, fled. He did not go south with the others but headed west for Babylon. After many tribulations, he reached that timeworn city and was taken in by priests.

After spending almost a decade in Babylon and absorbing much wisdom, Ananda grew restless and wanted to return to his homeland, even though he knew it meant certain death. But the King of the Kassites, rulers of Babylon for over a century, placed him and three Babylonian priests on a caravan headed for Ugarit in northern Syria, wishing them to learn about the religion of the people there. The caravan was ambushed by bandits and only two people escaped death, Ananda and a muleteer. For months they wandered, drifting south and eventually winding up in the ancient city of Jericho, where they parted company.

Traveling widely throughout Canaan, Ananda attached himself to several sovereigns, learned the ways of many tribes, resided in many cities, and lost all hope of ever returning home. He decided to go down the sea-flowing Nile, and it was in the Egyptian cities along that murmuring river that Ananda heard of the Keiftu, Rulers of the Isles of the Great Green, which is how the Egyptians referred to the people of Minos. Burning with a desire to see the kingdom of the Keiftu, Ananda, after two years of trying, finally managed to get passage on a Cretan merchantman. That was ten years ago.

Ananda was quick to meet with the priestesses and priests of Knossos and engage them in lively discussion concerning goddesses and gods, and how they were understood by the different peoples throughout the world. Though they could see that he was well traveled, no one in the capital believed Ananda's story about his far away homeland. The Knossosans thought that he had come from some no-name hill tribe, and that he had concocted his goddess-favored city just to impress everyone.

For a while, Ananda's views on religion were politely listened to and tolerated because he was a foreigner. Eventually, the priests became annoyed. Ananda asked too many unanswerable questions. His contrary arguments were galling. Soon a conspiracy against him sprang up. Before long, Ananda was faced with banishment or death. Fortunately, Rhadamanthys stepped in and received Minos's permission for Ananda to live in Phaistos. Minos was wary of any sort of conspiracy—regardless the target—and was more than happy to be rid of the nuisance. It was then that Ananda, the man from the other side of the earth, became the first permanent resident of Snow Crystal.

Rhadamanthys and I sat down next to the wise men. Rhadamanthys motioned toward the middle of the table and said, "So

I see my stones have been up for discussion." He was referring to a row of a dozen crudely worked stone objects, which, over the years, Rhadamanthys had discovered in the caves at Matala.

"Yes, Your Highness," Ananda concurred. "They are excellent supports for the contemplation of mankind. In fact, yesterday, we debated your brilliant theory about their origin. When Glaukus returns from his walk, we would like to discuss it with you."

"Yes, I was wondering where the old dreamer was when we arrived," I said.

Ta-ch'ih took my comment for criticism, though I did not mean it as such. "Oh, we told him that you would be here today, Sire," Ta-ch'ih volunteered.

"I'm sure he'll be back shortly…probably just went for one of his little daydreaming jaunts. Maybe he stopped to collect some of those vile little mushrooms he eats. I certainly wouldn't let one of them pass my lips, growing under cow dung as they do."

We rocked with laughter. Ta-ch'ih was satisfied that he had circumvented what he took to be my displeasure with Glaukus. Ta-ch'ih was about five years younger than Ananda, or about three-and-sixty. His face was so like a wrinkled raisin that you could hardly pick out his features. Only on close scrutiny, you could see that Ta-ch'ih's eyes were charcoal-black dots floating in tiny yellow pools. His eyes were not the eyes of a Cretan, big and almond shaped, but, instead, they resembled the narrow and pointy leaves of the mountain climber plant. His complexion was a dull burnt orange, like no one else's I had ever seen. His scraggly little gray beard hung like a goat's but was not as full. Stooped and frail, Ta-ch'ih looked like a twig that had been bent unmercifully by the north wind but refused to snap.

Just like Ananda, Ta-ch'ih had been a thorn in the side of the Knossosans. Unlike Ananda, though, it was not what Ta-ch'ih preached or how he questioned people that brought him into danger, but what he left unsaid or craftily implied. He was subtle like a mosquito, which lands unnoticed on your arm, dines, then departs; soon you have a harmless-looking pimple that becomes a burning welt. The functionaries at the capital, whom Ta-ch'ih bothered the most, had the same reaction after engaging Ta-ch'ih in discussion.

For example, say the royal pig keeper got into a mild argument with Ta-ch'ih about the distribution of wealth in the kingdom, a common enough topic. When the two parted, the pig keeper might believe he had had the upper hand during the exchange; he might even believe he had taught the foreigner a thing or two. But because Ta-ch'ih was so barbarous tongued, his little figures of speech, allusions, and parables took time to sink in. Belatedly, Ta-ch'ih's message would become intelligible, then it would drop like an anchor! "Did that old snake really say that?" our pig keeper might cry. "That's pure sedition! He can't get away with that!"

Needle-witted Ta-ch'ih never avoided such encounters, and, what made it worse, he arrived at Knossos less than one year after Ananda had been extracted by Rhadamanthys. Minos's palace was in no mood for another irksome storyteller. Thankfully, Rhadamanthys had learned of Ta-ch'ih's clever rhetoric and exotic past. Snow Crystal opened its doors to its second resident.

In the capital, Ta-ch'ih's reports of his homeland were dismissed as lies, just as Ananda's had been. That was not surprising since Ta-ch'ih's stories were even more unbelievable! He declared that his people had never heard of Ananda's because they lived too far to the west! In turn, Ananda claimed that his people had never heard of Ta-ch'ih's, believing that theirs was the last major city to the east.

Over the years at Snow Crystal, Ta-ch'ih had given us many vivid accounts of life in his native city Hsiao. Capital of a fair-sized kingdom, Hsiao lay just south of a swirling river known as Huang He, the Yellow River, named for the mud it carried along. The city, the nearby towns, and the spacious hinterland were controlled by a swaggering king, Chung Ting, who held his subjects' lives in the palm of his hand. He lived in a magnificent palace, guarded by spearbrave warriors who drove bronze chariots. Within the palace walls, gangs of craftsmen—men who chewed on slavery's bread—created bronze cauldrons and fine stone carvings. Keeping the royal accounts, a host of scribes lived comfortably, though precariously, within the palace compound. Ta-ch'ih was one such scribe.

If you traveled due east from Hsiao for one moon, you could reach the end of land and look out onto a great expanse of water. There, each day, you could watch the gold-gleaming sun being born, rising in all its glory above the sea swells. Unlike our sea, which also had glorious sunrises but ended at the Canaan coast, his sea went on forever. When still a young man, he had made the journey to watch that amazing sunrise, and he cried when he saw it, believing it to be the most sublime sight in the world.

Managing to stay on the good side of his powerful king, Ta-ch'ih thought he would finish out his life as a well-respected senior scribe. That was not to be. One night, suddenly, the ruler died. Some suspected poison. Charges were brought, but none was ever proven.

As was the custom, an extravagant burial was planned for the ruler. It took weeks to prepare. An elaborate tomb was dug and stocked with provisions and items that the deceased would need in the Time Afterdeath. Ta-ch'ih's description sounded like the incredible stories we had heard of the pharoah's burial, though the part about the chariot and live horses accompanying the king into his tomb sounded more like an Achaean practice. But the burial of Ta-ch'ih's king did the Achaean's one better. When the king was lowered into the ground, he was accompanied by his living and breathing wives, servants, slaves, and a host of other courtiers—including the scribes! Though aware of the ancient custom, Ta-ch'ih had never worried about it; the ruler was in his prime, healthy, feared by all, well-guarded in his unassailable palace.

So, with proper solemnity, the scribes were lowered into the tomb. Or so Ta-ch'ih surmised. He had long fled. Throughout the western provinces, he and three other runaways were pursued by a full squadron, eventually losing the soldiers in the towering mountains. For a while, the runaways felt ashamed, despising what they saw as their lack of duty to their master, the king. One even tried to take his own life. But time healed their feelings of self-hate. With the warm sun on their necks and the mountain air—so full of freedom—in their nostrils, the four men were glad to be alive.

Since they knew they could never return to the Yellow River Valley, they decided to continue west. Their journey lasted an incredible six years. Along the way, they stopped and lived for months in different places. They lived mostly among desert people, whom they thought very sociable. During that time, two of the scribes died of disease. Eventually Ta-ch'ih and the other survivor reached the city of Alalakh in Syria.

By that time, our friend had assumed the name we knew him by, Ta-ch'ih, which meant "Old Fool." He felt it was only proper that an old fool who had seen where the sun rises should see where it sets. Merchants in west Anatolia had told Ta-ch'ih that if he stood on a Cretan beach that faced westward, he would be at land's end, and, from there, he could see the sun sink into a limitless body of water. As soon as he could, the wanderer caught a ride to Crete on a merchant ship. Since arriving at Snow Crystal, late every afternoon Ta-ch'ih would stroll down to a nearby beach and watch the sun die.

EIGHT

"HERE COMES GLAUKUS," hooted Ananda.

Ta-ch'ih rose and joined Ananda at the window. "The dreamer is crawling along at his usual pace," commented Ta-ch'ih. "I've never seen anybody move as slowly as he."

"Nor have I," added Rhadamanthys thoughtfully. "That time I almost died, Glaukus sure took his sweet time coming to my aid. My illness had baffled all the priests here and at Knossos; wizened old Glaukus was my last hope. The grandees in the Labyrinth thought him mad, but I knew he was divinely inspired by the Great Goddess, in Her manifestation of Mistress of Doves and Poppies: he could read Her divine mind. As you all remember, he performed the cure without potions, without cutting, and without the burning of pungent plants. He started by jiggling some quartz rocks in his hands, while wailing an eerie song, like some dog yelping at the moon. Then he numbed me with a poppy potion. But really it was his magic hands that did the trick, extracting a black clump of flesh from my gut without drawing blood. You saw the repulsive clump with your own eyes, right, Ananda?"

"To be sure. It was most hideous and foul smelling, Your Grace."

"I feared it would be agonizing, I must admit," said Rhadamanthys, "yet, I believed in that eccentric old man, putting myself in his hands. You know, throughout the entire removal of that thing I didn't feel a twinge of pain. That was…ah…about four years ago, now."

"I think it was a miracle you were able to carry Glaukus off to Snow Crystal after he performed such a feat," I said.

"Yes, one would think that such abduction would be checked by the king," Rhadamanthys concurred with a grin, "but on the contrary, Minos gladly presented Glaukus to me to keep, even though they were blood related. You see, Idomeneus, anybody who doesn't prostrate himself to the king and his officials cannot survive long at Knossos. Ananda and Ta-ch'ih can attest to that. The priests believed that Glaukus's miraculous cures, visions, and dreams were undermining their power. And, of course, the old seer refused to have his prophesies censored; if he saw something, good or bad, he felt compelled to pronounce it. But these so-called holy men wanted to make public only certain prophesies, while withholding others. Eventually the priests began spreading lies about Glaukus's powers. As preposterous as it sounds, they claimed that Glaukus predicted mishaps and disasters so unerringly because…because he somehow caused them!" The grin had left Rhadamanthys's face, and he was beginning to boil. "How Glaukus was able to manifest his predictions and why Diktynna, Britomartis, or especially the Great Mother would allow him to do so was never explained by those toadying liars." Rhadamanthys was flushed. "If I ruled Knossos, the first thing I would do would be to expel any poison-tongued priests hiding behind holy vestments. As it stands now, these evil priests have usurped the power of Knossos's time-honored priestesses! The priests have Minos wrapped around their little fingers."

As Rhadamanthys's words bounced off the alabaster walls, the oak door slowly creaked open and Rhadamanthys and I stood up. In wobbled the time-ravaged Glaukus. His body had felt the millstone of over eighty years, some said five-and eighty, but nobody, not even Glaukus, knew for sure. The man was pure Cretan through and through. His eyes were large and dark, his complexion ruddy, his silver beard luxuriant, and his aquiline nose perched like some regal emblem on his perfectly chiseled face. He did have royal blood coursing through his veins, being one of the sons of Minos the Twenty Eighth, making him uncle to the reigning Minos.

Slowly, Glaukus became aware of the presence of four instead of two in the study, and he muttered, "What? What's this? Visitors? Ah, Your Highness, how good of you to stop by. And young Prince Idomeneus, Bless-our-Lady, it's you! What a wonderful surprise! Ah, but your excellencies should have sent word ahead." Out of the corner of my eye, I saw Ta-ch'ih shrug his shoulders. "I would have had these fuzzy-minded layabouts tidy up a bit," Glaukus said, shaking a scrawny finger at Ta-ch'ih and Ananda.

I could not make out what Ta-ch'ih or Ananda said in rebuttal, for they were jabbering at the same time. By and by, Glaukus called for silence. Then, not content to leave well enough alone, Glaukus added, "Well, at least you two could have offered our guests a seat. Haven't you learnt that simple custom yet in all the years you have lived amongst us?"

"They *were* seated until a crotchety old tortoise arrived," Ananda retorted.

Pretending not to have heard, Glaukus bade us be seated around the table. He turned toward the open door and barked out an order for some refreshments. By the time he ambled over to the table and got settled down beside us, we could hear the servants' feet slapping on the limestone; two boys brought trays laden with food and drink. The refreshments were served in matching bowls and cups, thrown about fifty or sixty years ago. Though not as old as the pieces I had used earlier at Phaistos, they were equally as handsome, covered as they were with plants and flowers painted in subdued earthen hues.

As the five of us helped ourselves to the selection of cheeses and honey cakes, the sages got off a few more harmless barbs between mouthfuls. "Well, Glaukus," Rhadamanthys said, "I understand you've been discussing the stones I discovered at Matala. What do you think?"

"I must tell you, my lord, of a wonderous dream I had last night. It concerned stones just like these," Glaukus exclaimed, pointing his wavering hand toward the strange objects on the table.

"Wait. Before you went to sleep, did you finish off your cache of mushrooms?" asked Rhadamanthys with a smile.

Producing two filth-covered objects from a sleeve in his robe, Glaukus said admiringly, "I found these beauties this morning! And there'll be more out there as the days grow warmer. But, to answer your question, no, Your Grace, I didn't eat any last night. Other 'fruits' of the bountiful earth—these very stones you found at Matala, Sire—inspired my dream.

"Yesterday," Glaukus continued, "my cronies here and I were discussing these curious stones in light of your theory, Prince Rhadamanthys. Last night, I retired early but could not fall asleep. As I said, I did not have a single mushroom, nor a cup of wine. Not a thing! I just lay down in bed, and, as Ananda has taught us, breathed deeply from right below the belly and thought of nothing.

"All of a sudden, the tranquil cloud I was enjoying lifted! I saw myself entering a dark, forbidding cave in the side of a cliff—now mind you, earlier I had been unable to sleep, therefore, I cannot say for sure if I was awake or asleep when my 'dream' occurred. Very sheer was that cliff. And the same color as the headland at Matala when it is struck by the rays of the dying sun. But for sure, I wasn't at Matala; the only water around was a sparkling stream, weaving gently through the valley. Towering trees of a type I had never seen before sprang up on either side of the stream. The entrance to the cave was small. It appeared to be carved by the Goddess's hand, so perfectly round was it. Cautiously, I took a few steps inside and was immediately surrounded by the darkness one finds on a moonless night. Be that as it may, I needed no lamp, for I could see perfectly."

I remember Rhadamanthys's telling me once that Glaukus could walk around Snow Crystal or through a cypress forest in total darkness, never stumbling or losing his way. In the early morning, when the lamps were not yet lighted, sometimes the old man would visit the kitchen and prepare himself some food. Then he would silently return to his bedroom, all without the aid of an oil lamp!

Bubbling with excitement, Glaukus rattled on about his dream. "After I had gone…oh…thirty feet or so, I noticed a glow ahead of me. The cave opened up into a high chamber, and I was bathed in a warm yellow light. Hundreds, no, more like thousands of limestone spikes appeared to be dripping from the ceiling, spikes like the ones you find in Our Lady Diktynna's cave above the Lasithi, but sharper. On the floor in the middle of the chamber, seven people huddled around a well-fed fire.

"At that moment, I felt the presence of another being on my left, slightly behind me. I turned to see standing there...you, Idomeneus!" As he said the last sentence, Glaukus glanced at me, holding my eyes in his penetrating stare. He continued, "In my dream — or vision — I was not startled by your presence, Prince Idomeneus. We seemed to belong there, together. Like me, you wore a white robe.

"Soon we knew — though how I don't know — that these people comprised a family. In all those stories you've told me, Ananda and Ta-ch'ih, you never came close to describing people so bizarre. Each one was extremely stoop-shouldered and short, but each had a big head with big features. Thundering Goddess, they would have made a barbarian look like a gorgeous lily!

"Each one wore a tattered animal skin. At first glance, the garb seemed to cover the limbs as well as the body; something like what our shepherds wear in the cruel winter. On closer examination, though, Prince Idomeneus and I discovered that the matted dark hair on these people's arms and legs never belonged to any other creature! They would have put our prize sheep to shame, so thick was their wool! And a good thing, too, because away from the fire the cave was bitter cold. Prince Idomeneus and I inched closer and closer to the warmth.

"It was odd, but throughout our entire stay with the family, we were never noticed, as if we were two flies on the ceiling, our wings stilled, just watching.

"Before long, Prince Idomeneus and I understood the relationships of the family members. The younger man and woman were mates and parents of the children. The woman sat intently sewing an animal skin draped over her knees. We could not make out what kind of beast the skin came from, but it must have been gigantic, twice as big as the biggest Cretan bull! The older woman, whom we took to be the mother of the young woman, assisted. With eyes as big as pomegranates, the little girl watched her mother and grandmother work the piece.

"On the other side of the fire, the two boys were busily striking pointed black stones against chunks of limestone. Right before our eyes, they each created one of these." At which point, Glaukus reached over and picked up one of the stone objects Rhadamanthys had found at Matala. The prince believed it to be a crude lamp. Looking into Rhadamanthys's eyes, Glaukus said, "Yes, my lord, they were similar to this one here, though a little cruder."

A smile ran across Rhadamanthys's face, and he encouraged the seer, "Please go on, tell us more."

"As you wish, Excellency." said Glaukus. "Well, these little urchins filled the hollows of their lamps with melted animal fat, not olive oil. Then they added strings of twisted fiber, which curled to the bottoms of the lamps, absorbing the liquid. The boys pulled up an end of each string and lighted the wicks with twigs from the fire. Then they sat back and marveled at the ingenious objects they had made. Soon they began to bicker about whose was the more handsome, held more oil, gave off more light. Suddenly, the father ended the argument with a loud grunt.

"All the time the women and boys were working, the father and the elderly man, the grandfather, were doing the same. Each held a blunted piece of black stone in one hand—like the boys—and in the other balanced a chunk of flint. With sparks flying, they struck the flints with short measured strokes, causing flakes to drop off. On the ground before each man was a considerable flake pile. With admiration, Prince Idomeneus and I watched as they created several of these spearheads." Unfolding his gnarled fingers, Glaukus displayed in his palm one of Rhadamanthys's spear heads. "On the ground between them," the sage continued, "they had a selection of spear heads to show for their days work. Propped against a pillar of limestone which rose from the cave floor, two crude but dangerous looking spears were at the ready. Each was over six feet long. At the end of each spear, a notch and a fuzzy cord held the point in place—"

"Aha, you see, I knew it," interrupted a rapt Rhadamanthys, unable to contain himself, his voice hoarse with excitement. "Could you tell, my wise and good wizard, how long ago these people lived on the earth? And where they lived? If not on Crete, did they live inland? To the east? To the west? And what did they call themselves?"

"Alas, Your Highness, I don't have answers to these important questions," Glaukus sighed. "I have a feeling, though, that these peo-

ple lived a long, long time ago—way before the palaces of Knossos or
Phaistos were even envisioned by our ancestors, even before the great
pyramids of Egypt were built!

"I also have a feeling, in the pit of my stomach, that their home
was nearer to where the sun sets than ours." Ta-ch'ih's ears pricked up
like a donkey's at that last part.

"Do you have any idea why I accompanied you into the cave,"
I asked.

"No. You see, it is extremely difficult to make sense out of each part
of a dream. You can say something broad about a dream, but if you try
to get too specific you can get into trouble. Believe me, I know. In that
priest-ridden capital of ours, it happened to me more than once."

When he said that, the old bitterness could be read in Glaukus's
face. "But Prince Idomeneus, do listen to the rest of my strange dream.
Maybe you'll discover for yourself why you chose to make an appearance," Glaukus said cryptically. I was delighted to hear him say that
because I thought he was through. Glaukus continued, "Prince
Idomeneus and I watched the family for an inestimable amount of
time, trying to absorb all that we witnessed. As if our very lives depended on understanding these people, we listened intently to their
conversational gabble. The odd thing was that we had no knowledge of their savage language of grunts, humphs, and yelps—Ananda
and Ta-ch'ih, after such gibberish, when you slip back into your
strange tongues, I will no longer make fun of you—Yet, miraculously, what these people were uttering was intelligible to us! Why?
Only the Great Mother knows.

"After a while, we left the family and their warm fire and entered
a long narrow tunnel, which twisted and turned like a fast-moving
snake. We knew we were going deeper and deeper into the bowels of
the earth. Salty water dripped from the ceiling, now and then splashing on our heads and shoulders. Prince Idomeneus clutched the back
of my robe, for it was pitch dark, yet I could see like an owl.

"We had to walk hunched over with our shoulders tucked in because the tunnel got lower and narrower. My head pounded. I thought
we would never escape from the black chasm, that we would have to
spend eternity there. Mercifully, my thoughts on that dismal prospect
were interrupted by you, Prince Idomeneus. Your free hand had felt

some scratches on the wall. You pulled me to a halt and asked if I could see the scratches. I could, but, at first, they appeared to be wild scribbles without any meaning. Then, slowly, I focused on one jumble of lines, which seemed to stand out more than the others. As if a veil had been lifted from these old eyes, I beheld a wonderful little engraving of an animal. A deer! Well, I reckoned it was a deer. With those huge horns and exaggerated proportions, it was meant to represent some deer-like creature.

"The creature was incomplete, for the forequarter, back, and underbelly were the only parts shown. Nevertheless, the carving was a masterpiece, accomplished with delicately controlled incisions; the creature seemed to breathe the very air we did. I tried to describe it to Prince Idomeneus, but even running his hand over the engraving did not clarify it for him.

"The deer's head was pointing in the direction we had been going, and, after a time, we moved on. I looked back at the deer, only to find that it had disappeared into the confused scribbles on the wall. Soon I began to notice other beasts lightly etched into the walls and ceiling: bulls, cows, horses, rams, boars, wolves, lionesses, and different types of deer-like creatures.

"Besides those, I also saw many fantastic or imaginary animals rendered in the tunnel. There was one that had the shape of an ox, but had a large hump on its back, long shaggy hair under its chin and neck, and short horns, which, instead of projecting out the sides of the head like an ox's, curved upward and back. Another had the same shape as the elephants I've seen drawn on Egyptian and Syrian papyri. But the brute on the wall had lines carved into its body that clearly were meant to show hair. From its huge head to its gigantic toes, this creature was covered with long stringy hair.

"There was one bizarre creature that I don't think has a counterpart in all the world. It looked a little like an overstuffed boar, but it was clearly not. The thing had an enormous hump on its back and a long block-like head, which drooped to its feet. On its unsightly snout, above its thick upper lip, two dangerous looking sword-like horns were mounted. Shaggy hair covered its body. Oddly, all the creatures portrayed wore a mantle of fur, even the ones I recognized from our own pastures and forests that don't have long hair. While examining the engravings on the walls, I was reminded of the hairy members of the family we had just left.

"Poor Prince Idomeneus could not see these marvelous animals. Soon, however, he got to see an even greater display. As we crouched in the black tunnel—I gazing enraptured at the walls and he squinting to no avail—someone glided by us. It was the grandfather from the savage family. I say glided because I did not see his legs move, and, somehow, he squeezed between us and the wall without touching us. He was like a ghost. Though shivers ran up our backs, we were strangely compelled to follow the grandfather through the tunnel toward a beckoning light.

"The tunnel gave way to a lighted chamber, larger than the first one we had seen. Instead of a crackling fire, the chamber was lighted by hundreds of flickering lamps, covering most of the ground. Our eyes were dazzled by the magnificent colors on the ceiling and walls, for everywhere on the rocky surfaces, brilliantly painted animals galloped and gamboled. Some were enormous, the size of carts. They circled around rocky outgrowths, merged with bumps, and slinked into shallow holes. They were all rendered in profile, the outlines filled in with black, red, yellow, and ochre. For the longest time, Prince Idomeneus and I stared dumbstruck at these extraordinary paintings.

"Suddenly, I felt the hair on my neck stand straight up, like that on a hedgehog's bristling back. There was someone or something standing directly behind us. Prince Idomeneus sensed the presence too, for we both wheeled round at the same moment. Then, like startled children, we lurched backward. Before us stood an imposing deer—a real one, not one painted on rock! It loomed over us, standing on its back legs like a human and holding its front legs before its body like a rabbit. The deer's big round eyes, veiled by a silvery film, gazed over our heads, looking at... nothing. Shadows from the creature's gigantic antlers danced on the ceiling and down the wall.

"After a moment or two, the deer spoke. It spoke in the same savage tongue as the family. Though the words should have been incomprehensible, once again, we understood. 'You humans have come from a distant land. And a distant time in the future. Fear nothing from this place, nor from me,' the deer said, assuring and commanding in one breath. 'No harm will come to you here. Once again you will breathe the earth's air above, unlike the beings you see painted on these walls. Their days on earth ended long ago, long before the days of your ancestors. Yet, their generations were as many as the leaves, many more than your generations have been or will be. They were greater fighters than your people. Greater hunters. Greater runners. Greater travelers. They had more strength than your people. More courage. More endurance. More perseverance.

"'No matter their powers, though, they were taken from the sunlight. Their spirits pass the endless day in a brighter light now. But they left a rearguard on earth to observe your passage; that is why you recognize some of their forms. This rearguard observes you humans who now reign, who now fight, who now hunt, who now build lairs. And who will one day pass into the bright light.'"

"Suddenly, right behind us, a blast of cold air exploded out of the tunnel, causing our clothes to billow like sails. All but a handful of the lamps were extinguished. The deer was gone. Out of the smoky atmosphere, a form emerged. It was the grandfather. In his misshapen barbaric face, I spied traces of resignation and sorrow: dewy teardrops hung from his thick lower eyelashes.

"Slowly, as if I were a weather-beaten bucket being raised from a well, I began to come to. The chamber, the paintings, and Prince Idomeneus faded into nothingness. Like some relic of the past, though, the grandfather's face, savage but sage, stayed with me throughout the ascent. It, too, disappeared when I became aware of the bedroom ceiling above me."

Everyone dreams. After awakening, though, how many people act upon their dreams, leading their lives according to the signposts they encountered during sleep? Old Glaukus was one who did. Not only did he follow his dreams but also his daytime phantasms and visions. When Glaukus began to wonder aloud about the meaning of his cave dream, we paid close attention.

"The meaning of the first part is clear to me," Glaukus stated. "Recently, we had been speculating about the relics discovered at Matala and about Prince Rhadamanthys's ideas about their uses. In my dream, as I explained, similar objects were created by the boys and men. There is no doubt in my mind that the dream confirms your theory, Prince," the seer averred, turning to Rhadamanthys. "It can safely be said that the ancient songs told the truth: in the earliest days, the Mother Goddess placed our ancestors in the caves at Matala, and there they began our glorious civilization, living by their wits with the aid of stone tools. Right now, we would probably be living like those ancient people if She, in Her infinite wisdom, had not taught us to prepare hard bronze."

Rhadamanthys nodded knowingly. For years he had been telling anyone who would listen that the relics he found at Matala proved that the earliest inhabitants of Crete had settled in the Messara. Of course, the grandees at the capital scoffed at his theory. They claimed that Rhadamanthys instructed his lapidaries to carve the objects, hoping to fool the people into believing that the objects were authentic and that the Messara, and by association Phaistos, not Knossos, was the cradle of Cretan civilization. The Knossosans boiled at the thought of it.

"The fact that these relics lying before us on the table are finer than the ones that I saw in my dream may be explained by any number of reasons. Maybe these objects were made by craftsmen instead of boys and untrained men. Maybe in those bygone days, the most talented hands belonged to the men of Crete. Maybe these objects were hewn in a later era, when men took more care in doing such things. Or maybe the kind of rock had something to do with the differences in the shapes and finishes. Be that as it may, it is clear that before copper and tin were brought together to make bronze, early Cretans and other people survived by shaping stones they found around them.

"The second part of the dream is much more difficult to interpret," Glaukus sighed, tugging at his beard. I slid anxiously to the edge of the bench; the sage seldom had trouble understanding his dreams and visions. "If one is to believe the strange deer, then the fantastic creatures painted on the cave walls actually represented animals that once walked the blessed earth. Britomartis, Mistress of Wild Beasts, must have placed them here ages ago. Then swept them away. They must have been the shaggy ancestors of the animals now dwelling under the Four Pillars, for that is what the deer meant when it spoke of a 'rearguard' left behind to observe us. But I wonder why the more bizarre beasts did not leave descendants?"

"They may have," Ananda piped up. "The large boar-like creature with the swords on his snout sounds like an animal that still lives in my homeland. But instead of hair, this animal has thick plates of hide on its body."

"Yes, that beast is known back at Hsiao, too," added Ta-ch'ih. "Its horn is prized for its magical powers."

"Then maybe all the animals from that bygone era did leave descendants," Glaukus mused. Wrinkling his brow, he said, "The big question—the one that really gnaws at me—is what was the deer trying to tell us? Ever since I had the dream last night, my head has ached over this. My walk didn't clarify things in the slightest. First, we were contrasted with the beasts represented in the paintings."

"In a very unfavorable light," Ananda added. "It seems they did everything better than we do."

"Yes," said Glaukus. "Nevertheless, they were taken from the light of day."

"That last sentence...the one about our passing into the bright light...what does that mean?" I asked.

"Maybe the bright light is the sublime radiance that shines from Elysium, the Isles of the Blest," said Rhadamanthys. "If so, it is reassuring to hear, since we believe that in the Time Afterdeath we abide on those Isles. Could the deer simply have been confirming our belief?"

"I don't know," said Glaukus. "The deer used the phrase 'your people.' I'm not clear on what it meant by that. Did it mean my people, the Cretans; or Prince Idomeneus's people, the Kallisteans; or all the people in the kingdom; or—if all men are brothers—all the people on earth? If I am right in believing that the grandfather's expression was in reaction to the deer's message, then it portends something dark."

That was the first time we had ever seen Glaukus unsure of the meaning of one of his dreams and, consequently, unable to predict future events. His uncertainty made us a bit jumpy. Clearly Rhadamanthys's relics had instigated the dream, but was there a deeper cause for it? Rhadamanthys brought up the recent earthquake at Knossos, and we agreed that it could have had something to do with it. But the quake had occurred months before, and, immediately afterwards, the earth was stilled. Besides, the priestesses and priests assured us that Britomartis, Averter of Earthquakes, was satisfied with our prayers and abundant sacrifices of sheep and red-backed oxen.

I told my friends about the tremors on Kalliste, the poison gas, and the dolphins we had encountered to and from Crete. "What's the connection?" Rhadamanthys asked after I finished.

"I'm not sure if there is one but look at the similarity. The dolphins attempted to communicate with men, but, in the end, just like the deer, left them confused."

We mused over these riddles, getting nowhere. Suddenly Rhadamanthys brought up a third. "What about the unusual events at the bull-leaping contest?" he said turning toward me. "Why, in their first contest ever, had the seven maidens been allowed to leap without a mishap? Then, afterwards, why had the bull swiftly killed the two youths, only later to be conquered by the last five?"

"And why did Britomartis, Lady of Strife, permit Theseus's perfect leap?" I asked.

Glaukus pondered our words for a while. "The bull is the symbol of our people," he said, "the people of Minos. The leapers from Athens stand for all the barbarians who live beyond the lap of the waters. Though Minos now extracts a penalty from these inland barbarians for an old injury, it is small indeed compared to what they might extract from us. We must be careful, or they could leap over us, ruling where we now rule."

As if it were a white thunderbolt hurled down from Mount Ida, the ominous warning ignited the air in the study. Quicker than we had ever seen him move before, Ta-ch'ih jumped up and rushed over to a pile of tortoise shells and ox bones lying in a corner. Carefully, he selected a shoulder blade from the pile, like some charm-fashioner deciding on just the right gem for a setting. Knowing what Ta-ch'ih would need next, Ananda yelled out the door for fire, then cleared a place on the table for Ta-ch'ih to work.

Sitting down with the fair-sized bone balanced in his lap and propped against the edge of the table, Ta-ch'ih searched for a bronze poker under a disarray of scrolls. After fumbling about, he found one. A quick-stepping servant came with a torch and handed it to Ta-ch'ih, who placed the point of the poker into the flame. While he waited, Ta-ch'ih turned the bone around, revealing numerous rows of small pits previously gouged out by a chisel.

When the point of the poker glowed a brilliant red, the old man pulled it out of the flame and thrust it into several of the pits. "Did the events at the bull-leaping contest mean that one day the Achaeans would master the men of Minos," he asked an unspecified god. Like a snake, the bone hissed, the pungent smoke drifting up to the ceiling. Soon tiny irregular cracks began to appear on the other side of the bone. Ta-ch'ih withdrew the poker and doused it in his wine cup. He then patiently examined each crack on the bone.

Finally, he looked up and matter-of-factly said, "Glaukus is right. The action at the bull-leaping contest signified that, if things continue as they are going, a barbarian will one day wear Minos's crown." Picking up a knife, Ta-ch'ih inscribed the question and answer on the bone in his strange picture writing.

For the rest of the day, we discussed Glaukus's prophesy and Ta-ch'ih's oracle. Theories and ideas were proposed, defended, defeated, and dropped. We took our dinner in the study and continued to talk. It was late at night when fatigue overcame Rhadamanthys and me. The three wise men, however, could have carried the discussion into the early morning.

Tired and baffled, Rhadamanthys and I got up from the table and started to go. But Ta-ch'ih had one last thing to say. "Heaven above and earth below are but parts of one great, unending net. This net can be likened to a spider's web: beautifully woven, wonderfully intricate, swaying with every breeze, no matter how mild. A tiny insect lands on a single thread of the web, far from the center, out on an edge. And yet the spider in the center knows. Everything that occurs on the threads, no matter where or how insignificant, sends a quiver through the whole web.

"My friends, each event we discussed today occurred on a different thread of The Web: the dream with its bizarre people and animals, the earthquake, the dolphins, the strange phenomena on Kalliste, the bull-leaping contest. The vibrations created by these events, however, seem to converge, to overlap in some mysterious way. For now, we cannot know why this overlapping took place. But only a fool would be blind to such a portentous event."

NINE

STRANGE INDEED is the working of the universe. Not long after my return to Kalliste, the earth stopped shaking. The cessation of the tremors proved to the Phirans, beyond a shadow of a doubt, that they were right in believing the charges against me. When they passed me in the streets, I saw the smug faces. The breach between them and me widened even more. Though it sounds evil, I wanted the earth to shake some more, thinking that it would show them how my personal life, and especially my proposed wedding to Aphaea, had nothing whatsoever to do with the Goddess's angry mood.

On an overcast morning in the middle of the Artichoke Month—the month when Aphaea and I were supposed to wed—I became restless and edgy. I knew I had to get away from all the courtiers and the palace hubbub. I felt compelled to flee Phira altogether. I hastily gathered together some nets and curtly told Miletus to watch over things because I was going to snare some partridges. Miletus gave me a sideways look but said nothing. He knew I never went in for bird-catching, because I disliked wringing their scrawny necks. I guess my face told Miletus it would be better for everybody if I got away for a while.

I allowed two palace hounds, Deino and Taras, to accompany me on my stroll. They were unmistakable signs to anyone who saw me that I really had no intention of catching birds; those two monsters would start yapping at the sight of a grasshopper.

When I started out, my body felt as tense as if it were about to explode, like an acorn thrown into a fire. I relaxed on the walk, though, realizing that it was the first time in many moons that I had had a chance to be alone—my four-legged companions notwithstanding. Many thoughts danced through my head, but none weighed me down; I was able to let them flow by. I thought about my good friends at Phaistos, wondering if they had had any breakthroughs concerning the strange phenomena that had visited Kalliste. I wondered how Theseus and his comrades had made out at the summer festival, for it had taken place at Knossos only a few days before. Ordinarily, I would have been there.

Time after time, my mind came back to Aphaea.

As I walked along, I tossed a small olive branch ahead for Deino and Taras. They chased after it in a frenzy, constantly overrunning it, scrambling back and falling over each other in a wild attempt to be the first to snatch it up. Prancing like a prize steed, the victor would bring it back to me triumphantly, while the loser would relentlessly try to steal it away. Neither of them knew enough to drop it on command; in order to throw it each time, I had to wrest it from a slobbering mouth.

We passed the huge outcropping of rock that commanded part of the coast and from which the beach received its name: Monolithos. Soon the dogs and I were frolicking along the shore. I collapsed in the soft sand as the dogs splashed in the shallow, blue-green water. Now and again, the sun peeked through a cloud's dark sheathing. I was content just sitting there listening to the tune of the lapping waves and watching the playful hounds. The thoughts in my head slowed down. Then ceased. The idle bird nets made a soft cushion. I rested in peace.

While not breaking the serenity that surrounded me, two cavorting swallows caught my attention. Ever since that terrible night two months earlier, birds carried a new meaning for us Kallisteans. But the swallows did not make a peep. I looked on as

Deino and Taras made deranged leaps at the low-flying birds. It was a ridiculous sight.

"Ah ha, you're playful and free-spirited, now," I said to the swallows. "But if I were a true hunter, you'd soon be entangled in my nets. Enjoy your freedom little ones. For tonight, at least, you'll not be part of anyone's pie."

The dogs continued their uproarious yelping and baying, which I thought was overdone, even for them. My shouts did not silence them.

When I craned my neck skyward again, the birds were gone. Glancing out to sea, I spied them skimming over the waves, headed in the direction of Astipalaea, lying far to the east. Birds don't go east when they depart here, I said to myself, wondering if the poor things were sick and if they would ever find their way to land.

Before long, some ravens flew overhead, their wings flapping so vigorously that they were blurs. The dogs began their racket again. I tossed a harmless pebble in their direction and turned around toward Mount Kalliste to see if any more birds were heading our way. To my amazement, the beclouded sky was darker yet, for it was filled with great flocks of every kind of bird imaginable. Tiny ones. Broad-winged ones. Drab ones. Brilliant ones. It looked like the mass exodus that takes place every year during the Strong Wind Moon. Except then, the birds head south, toward Libya, not east, toward Astipalaea.

Suddenly the pit of my stomach turned. My whole being shivered like a newborn colt. I sprang to my feet and was confronted with a bizarre scene: Below the winged tribes, every sort of walking, crawling, and creeping creature that the red earth feeds was scrambling over the terraced fields. Rabbits, foxes, boars, goats, oxen, mules, and cats were running helter-skelter, running away from the mountain and kicking up a dust storm. Dozens of four-legged beasts, winded and wide-eyed, arrived at the long beach where I stood. If I had held open my nets, I could have snared enough game for two winters!

As the animals reached the shorebreak, it looked as if they would not stop there, but, instead, dive right into the foaming sea. And some did! But realizing that they didn't know how to move through the water-world, those landlubbers quickly turned back, streaming onto the beach, soaked and shivering. There were two, however, that appeared as if they would never turn back. Deino and Taras. Wildly paddling, the dogs followed their escorts, the birds, toward distant Astipalaea. It was madness!

I did not attempt to rescue my companions. Instead I raced up the beach, heading for the trail that led from Monolithos back to Phira. The only thought in my mind was to get home quickly! Running as fast as my feet could carry me, I reached the trail and turned up it. All kinds of living things, screeching dementedly, galloped or flew by me. As the only creature heading for the mountain, I ran the gauntlet, putting my head down and racing as fast as I could.

After a short distance, something deep within me told me to look up. When I did, my vision was blurred, and the great green mountain before me did not have its usual sharp outline, always so striking against the sky. From its lofty pinnacle to the bottom of its slopes, Mount Kalliste appeared fuzzy, out of focus. Even after shaking my head to clear it, the mountain still looked the same. With a sinking feeling, I realized that my eyes were not playing tricks on me. By-the-Goddess, I wished they had been. Alas, it was the great mountain, itself, shaking like some colossal kettle about to boil over.

I came to a halt, my eyes straining to open further than they could. All around me, trees began to blur as their trunks, branches, and leaves shook violently. My legs felt like swaying palms. I scanned the length of the island, discovering that Kalliste was trembling from mountain to shore.

Then, from the bowels of the earth, that terrible sound—the one we Kallisteans had only heard about—came forth. It was a deep groan, a rumble that went deeper and deeper, louder and louder, ten times louder than the loudest thunderclap. My hands shot to my ears. My knees buckled, partly because of the swaying earth, partly because of fear. I felt the ground shifting and grinding beneath me.

I was knocked down by a tremendous jolt, as if I had been thrown by a mighty wrestler, one whom I could hear but not see. I lay sprawled on my stomach as two more jolts in rapid succession lifted me a hand's width off the ground and slammed me down. My whole body rattled. My ears filled with ringing, like bronze bells. A fine red dust rose up, concealing everything.

Then, all of a sudden, nothing. No noise. No movement. Just the choking red dust, so thick that I could not make out the great mountain in front of me; for a moment, I thought it was gone. Slowly, a shaft of sunlight pierced the clouds and dust, striking the green head of Mount Kalliste. It had survived the powerful quake. But what hadn't?

Gazing at the lofty peak and sky above, I made my pledge: "Almighty Goddess, I pray that my Phira has survived your wrath. Please, please let it be so! I'll sacrifice to you ten oxen, never broken, red-coated and fat, if it be so!"

Warily I rose, spitting the dirt and dust from my mouth. Though my legs were shaky and my stomach felt as on a stormy sea, I began to trot up the trail. Soon I was running.

I passed a farmhouse totally in ruin; it looked as if a gigantic hand had simply pushed it over. The farmer and his family stood before it, wailing, tears streaming from their eyes. In their sorrow they didn't notice me go by.

All along the east slope of the island, farmhouses were flattened. I remember thinking that the farmers' dwellings were made of resilient wood. The buildings in Phira, including the palace apartments, were built with mostly stubborn stone. Could they have survived if the farmers' dwellings had not?

The air was filled with the terrified bleating of goats and sheep and the crazed braying of donkeys. Unlike the others, those beasts had not reached the shore because they were either tethered or hobbled. Slowly and valiantly, the hobbled ones staggered and stumbled toward the shore. How pitiful it was to see the animals abuse themselves so — all to no avail.

Halfway to Phira, two young boys saw me coming up the trail and ran out to intercept me. Before I reached them, I screamed, "Please! I mustn't stop! I have to go straight to Phira!"

"Oh please, my lord, please," shouted the older of the two. "Please help us! Our father is trapped under the barn roof!"

I clenched my fists so tightly that the fingernails almost pierced the skin. My mind was reeling. Without breaking stride, I turned into the tiny farmyard, reaching the collapsed barn with the boys right on my heels. Their father was alive but pinned under the large ridgepole. When the roof caved in, its planks and rafters were knocked free, so we had no problem reaching the man. No matter how hard we strained, though, the three of us could not roll away the heavy beam. "I will give this man a few moments more. If by then he is not free, I will fly off," I said to myself.

Ordering the boys to find two strong poles or branches, I frantically searched for a likely spot underneath the ridgepole. It took two trips to carry them, but the boys brought me long logs from the wood pile. I wedged one end of each under the ridgepole, and, with the boys on one and me on the other, we managed to roll the crushing weight off the farmer. He lived but would never walk again; his two boys became the men of the house that day.

As fast as I could go, I resumed my dash up the trail. At one point, I was almost trampled by a lumbering ox. The dumb beast tried to avoid me as I tried to avoid it, but each way I moved, it moved. During that close call, I was glad the ox was hobbled.

As I neared town, about a quarter of a league in front of me, I saw a mysterious sight. It looked as if someone, or something, had constructed a wall right across the trail! The closer I got, the larger the wall loomed. I came to an abrupt halt. If I hadn't, I would have pitched into a crack, a huge crack in the earth. I gasped when I peered down into the dark chasm, for it was bottomless.

On the other side of the chasm, the red earthen wall rose six feet high. It had not been built by the hand of man nor giant; the very earth itself had been thrust upward during the quake. After that day, it became clear to us on Kalliste that the side where I had been standing had actually dropped down and that the other side was at its normal height. At the time, though, it didn't matter. All that mattered was that I was faced with an incredible obstacle, one which the Goddess had thrown in my path, and I had to figure out some way to overcome it.

From where I stood, the chasm was much too wide to leap over. Looking along it toward the northeast, I saw that it got wider and deeper. So, I raced along the edge in the opposite direction.

At a few spots, it seemed that I might be able to jump over the dark abyss. But each time I tried, I balked, breaking off my approach run and skidding to a halt precariously close to the edge. I knew that I wouldn't have made it. I continued along the ragged crack, looking for just the right spot.

As I went farther south, the grotesque wound in the earth appeared to have almost healed itself or knitted itself together, for the chasm was much narrower. What seemed like a wall to me on the other side became lower and lower. This is it, I thought. I moved back from the edge, about thirty paces, turned around, took a deep breath, then sprinted toward the abyss. Springing high, I flew over the yawning gap, stretching my body out toward the red wall. My chest smacked the stony edge as my arms reached over the top. My hands clutched the loose soil. I began to slip backwards, my fingers acting as bent plowshares, digging long, desperate furrows in the dirt; I knew I was done for if I couldn't anchor my fingers. None too soon, I stopped my fall, and, with all the strength I could muster, I pulled myself up and over the edge. In a moment, I was dashing over the fields, picking up the trail once more.

At last, I reached the north-south road. Black smoke was billowing up over Phira. My heart plummeted. In a flash, I decided to slip off the road and race through an apple orchard, working my way around Phira; if I wanted to reach the palace at all, I would have to avoid the chaos in town. I splashed through the stream and came up by the western entrance of the palace. Through the fine dust settling everywhere, I saw that, at least in the western sector, most of the walls were still standing. But several apartments were belching smoke, and water was flooding the corridors. Lamps and braziers had been overturned; water mains had shattered.

The palace seemed deserted. Then, through the smoke and dust, I caught a glimpse of some phantom-like forms moving down a corridor. I ran toward them, calling out as I went. Two courtiers were helping an injured man. It was Miletus.

"I'm all right, I'm all right," insisted Miletus. But the blood spurting from his forehead and the way he slurred his words said otherwise.

"He was struck by falling plaster, Your Grace," exclaimed an exhausted Althaemenes. "We're taking him to the central court!"

"Aye, bandage him well. Is there anyone else in the palace?" I asked. The other man, a cook, supporting Miletus turned away, but Althaemenes looked straight into my eyes, searching them for a long time. Too long.

"Althaemenes," I cried, reaching out toward him.

"My lord, Princess Henithea…no one has seen her. I'm afraid—"

"No," I shouted, brushing away Althaemenes's imploring hand and bolting.

I streaked down the corridor, heading for the main shrine. It had withstood the devastating jolts, for the walls, though scarred, were still standing. But upon entering, I saw that it was just a cruel illusion. Overhead was the discolored sky; the roof had come crashing straight down, scraping the plaster off the walls. Big raindrops splashed on the broken remains of the roof and ceiling.

Trying to banish the thought that no one could have survived under that mass of rubble, I feverishly began tossing aside large chunks of plaster and sections of broken beams, working close to where the altar should have been.

After clearing a small portion of the debris, I was startled by a sharp cry directly behind me. It was Althaemenes, screaming for me to get out of the shrine because the northern wall was about to topple over. I spun around and leapt for the doorway, diving into Althaemenes's arms just as the wall came crashing down.

In as calm a voice as he could muster, Althaemenes said, "You will not find your noble mother under there, my lord." I stared at him begging to hear, yet not really wanting to. "She was just found in your study. She is at rest. She has joined the Immortal Goddess."

I turned toward the corridor wall, my head tucked in the crook of my arm. I cried unbridled tears. Everything hit me at that moment: the earthquake, the destruction, and the final horrible blow. I wanted the earth to swallow me up.

After awhile, I mumbled through my tears, "Take me to her."

With his arm around me, Althaemenes led me through the battered palace as if I were a blind man. We stepped out into the central court, and there, in a neat row, were several bodies covered with cloaks, rush mats, whatever had been at hand. Those who had lost loved ones stood over the cruel scene, wailing and pounding their breasts. I knew which body was my mother's, for her two priestesses knelt on either side, screaming and tearing out their hair. Two servants had discovered her beneath the debris of my study and had carried her out to the court. They stood by sobbing.

Althaemenes brought me over to my mother, honored lady of Kalliste. I dropped to my knees, embracing her for the last time. Though her spirit abided in Elysium, her form was still warm. Scarlet ichor issued from her wounds.

Raindrops mixed with teardrops as I turned my face toward the sky and harangued the Death-Dealing One: "Oh, you wicked Goddess! Now you've taken the purest of us all. Our prayers and sacrifices weren't enough for you? Well, topple the Four Pillars! Bring down the sky! But you won't squeeze a tear from our eyes after this. We'll drain them all, here, on this sweet flesh…"

TEN

THE WRATH of the Goddess reached our neighbors across the loud sea; the islanders of Milos, Sifnos, and Minoa felt their land shake beneath them. Even on spacious Crete, from one tip to the other, a trembling was felt. There was little damage on those islands and no lives lost.

Alas, on sad Kalliste, we had to roll aside the huge stones sealing the entrances to the round tombs. The bones of those long departed had to be stacked high to make room for their kinsmen whose lives had been blotted out during the terrible earthquake and its aftermath. Kalliste's death toll was appalling: Phira lost eighteen, Metapontus one score and three, Enalus one score, Oia ten. And, so it went around our shores.

After the catastrophe, people on the island began to say that those who had perished were fortunate. At least their eyes were closed before they had to witness even more tragedy, which, no doubt, would befall us. Many predicted we would all find a place in those cold dank tombs before long.

I had to admit I felt the same way. It seemed as though we were on an ill-fated thread of The Web, and it appeared certain we were headed for a time of unimaginable sorrow. Our immediate period of despair was oddly shortened by the task of caring for the injured; it made us forget ourselves and the uncertain days ahead.

Though a bitter herb, I went ahead and made the sacrifice I had promised the Goddess Steerer after the earth stopped moving. For She had allowed Phira to survive, crippled as it was. Besides, the meat from the animals we had slain helped to feed my people in those desperate days. Farmers who had lost everything streamed into town, and we put them up as best we could. The rebuilding of their dwellings, barns, and granaries would be a priority.

Shortly after the aroma of funerary frankincense and myrrh had been carried away by the breeze, a convoy from Knossos reached Kalliste. Minos had sent provisions, supplies—including logs dressed for use—master builders, artisans, and a company of well-armed Kushite guards. All of that was necessary to help us pull our lives back together—except the last. Why had the king sent the black guards in all their war gear, we asked? We were told that the capital wanted to prevent looting on the island. Looting? What! Kallisteans stealing from their neighbors in the wake of the cruel blow we had all suffered together? Kallisteans behaving like freebooters? Preposterous! It was an insult we did not take lightly. Maybe that kind of behavior happened in other parts of the kingdom, but not on our island, we said. The princes of Kalliste parleyed, then sent a joint message to the king, asking for the removal of the troops. He refused.

A short while later, lo and behold, a half-dozen looters were caught. One at Enalus, five at Metapontus. They were executed on the spot! We were dumbfounded, crushed to learn of the abominations, and we drank the deep cup of humiliation to the bitter dregs.

After the great earthquake, the worst thing would have been to allow us to wallow in our grief, therefore, the wide-ruling Minos was right in his insistence that we Kallisteans begin rebuilding as soon as possible. The men and supplies he sent got us back on our feet, raising our ebbing spirits. Of course, the farmsteads were attended to first. Next came the shrines, then the palaces and towns. The palaces and their respective towns were the distribution centers for the island, and, as long as they were not functioning as such, usual activity had ceased. Lastly, villages and hamlets were restored and even improved. Slowly, with the backing of the capital's treasury, we began to clear the rubble of what was once our homes and to start anew.

In addition to the aid from Minos, the good Rhadamanthys sent me a shipload of his renowned artisans to help me rebuild Phira. Later I learned that he had had a problem persuading Aphaea that it was better if she stayed at Phaistos, instead of rushing to my side. Though I longed to hold my beloved Aphaea and weep in her bosom, Rhadamanthys was right, of course. It was better that I was alone during the reconstruction, for I had no time for anything or anyone else.

During the laborious planning and overseeing of the reconstruction, stouthearted Miletus was invaluable to me. He had recovered nicely from that awful blow to the head that he had suffered during the quake, though a long telltale scar stayed with him from then on. We spent long days together working out each detail of the rebuilding projects for the town and palace. We wanted them to be even more beautiful than before as a tribute to my mother. We vowed that a new and greater Phira, like a splendid lotus, would rise from the black ashes, its roots nourished by the earth in which my mother rested, along with so many other good Phirans recently taken from us.

In the palace, the most visible sign of the earthquake was an angry gash that ran through a row of storehouses, across the western court, through several apartments, and into the domestic quarters. The gash was half the height of a man and as thick. Like a thunderflash, it took a zigzag path, disfiguring paved corridors, thick walls, drainage pipes, everything. Gazing into the crooked crevice, we were reminded of the awesome power of the earthquake, which had twisted foundation stones that were impossible for ten men to budge, popped large cobblestones out of alignment, and shattered others into thousands of pieces. Some walls, like the one in the main shrine on the second story, made of thick mud brick and solid wooden crossbeams, had toppled over.

I decided to knock the shrine's three remaining walls down and build a larger, more splendid shrine. Two thick cypress trees, inverted and carved into tapering column shafts, were placed on new bases. The shafts were painted black, with a thin band of vibrant red around their bottoms.

Bulging black capitals rested upon the shafts. The walls were erected in the usual way, using sun-dried mud bricks framed with half-timbers, except that we added more timbers than in the past. That was on the recommendation of our Cretan advisors who explained that the beams would give more flexibility to the walls, saving them if the earth shook again. We took their recommendation seriously.

Before long, the new walls were covered with frescoes depicting priestesses performing various duties, such as collecting crocuses, pouring libations, leading processions, and praying before altars. The ceiling of the shrine was covered with a spiral design created in raised stucco. Red, yellow, and blue rosettes were painted between the spirals. The heavy marble altar, the one my dear mother spent so much of her life before, was kept in its original place, and the sacred objects that had survived, the ones made of metal, were reverently returned to the altar.

While the shrine was being resurrected, workmen were busily repairing or replacing the damaged stones in the corridors and courts. Earthquake-buckled walls of apartments and workshops had to be repaired. Most required only patch work, but a few required new limestone blocks and bricks; all around the palace grounds mud bricks were drying in their wooden forms.

Five apartments had been gutted by fires, and, of course, they had to be completely torn down and rebuilt. The worst of the fires had hit our storerooms. The center one contained olive oil and burned violently, spreading its intense heat to three magazines on either side. Each one of them held ten large pithoi containing much of our grain and spices. They were totally engulfed by flames. Lost was half of our winter's supply of wheat, barley, and lentils, and all of our spice stock. Without sesame, mint, coriander, safflower, and the like, our food was uninspiring for a long time afterwards.

Farther north in the palace another magazine, constructed out of thick unyielding stone, had been stacked to the ceiling with expensive ox, pig, goat, and deer hides. The magazine acted as one big oven, and all of the hides burned to crisps. One of the first things we did was clear the magazine, burying the smoldering skins. In spite of that, an occasional whiff of their repulsive smell drifted over the palace, overpowering the rather pleasant scent of the charred spices. Since we drew our water off the ever-flowing stream, one of the first things we had to do was to seal off our shattered pipes to stop the flooding. For several weeks, the repair work on the plumbing and drainage system inconvenienced everyone as pipes, gutters, and cisterns had to be patched or torn up and replaced. Huge, newly molded clay conduits lay drying in the courts. After what seemed like an eternity, sweet mountain water was once again flowing through the pipes of the palace, while refuse and waste were being carried away.

Lying east of the royal residence, the town of Phira had not been hit as badly, but Miletus and I tried to keep its rebuilding on the same schedule as the palace's so that the two would come back to life at the same time. Second-story fires had destroyed about a tenth of the town's total living quarters and that, coupled with the fact that many refugees from the farmlands sought shelter, caused a severe housing shortage. But the generous people of Phira opened their doors to the farmers and their families; no one slept under the stars.

Before long, the town and palace of Phira began to resemble the condition they had been in before the great quake, as did the other towns and palaces around the island. In fact, they looked even better than before. It was hard to believe that such a disastrous event could have yielded any good results.

I would sometimes walk along the trail that led to Monolithos, as far as the great chasm. Sometimes I brought Deino and Taras along. Yes, they had survived. I guess they had thought better of challenging the sea swells and swimming to Astipalaea; they must have turned back soon after I left the beach. They showed up at the palace a few days later, hungry and noisy as ever. About a month after the earthquake, the winged creatures also returned to Kalliste.

At one time or another, everyone on the island came to examine the horrible rent in Kalliste's red earth. A bridge was built so people could cross, and a small altar was erected nearby; it was never without fruit and flowers. After making my offering, I would stand over the chasm and gaze down into its blackness. Sometimes I would toss a rock in and count to five or six before I heard its distant report.

The Plowing Moon was waning by the time most of the major rebuilding was done. In their newly rebuilt homes, our people, exhausted from their miseries and hard work, huddled around fires. Peace was upon the land.

Just when we thought our time of healing had come, the relentless Mother Goddess presented us with yet another disaster. Near Oia, at the north tip of the island, a fisherman discovered a patch of strangely discolored water: Alternating streaks of black, white, jaundiced yellow, and blood red lapped and stained a secluded sandy beach. Sometimes the colors mingled, but mostly they remained separate and distinct. And, oh, yes, the dappled water had a putrid odor, the fisherman recalled, like rotten eggs. Even before the story was confirmed, Sarpedon placed the guards back on the cave at the south cape and reestablished the network of early-warning runners.

When Prince Oenopion of Oia went down to the shore to collect a sample of the discolored water, the fisherman's report was sadly confirmed. To his horror, Oenopion discovered that the unnatural water had spread along the coastline, filtering into every little nook and inlet, extending well beyond the beach where the fisherman had spotted it. In fewer than seven days, all of Kalliste was ringed by a rainbow of colors.

To an approaching sailor, it would have appeared that the Earth Mistress had placed a garish garland around the island, perhaps to show the world She was through plaguing it. But the colors of the garland were not those of summertime flowers, and, upon reaching the shore, the sailor would have discovered washed-up fish, their scaly bodies stained in bizarre hues.

As soon as word of the baffling phenomenon reached Crete, King Minos sent Catreus to Kalliste; it was Catreus who had first mentioned the garland effect. The day Catreus arrived at Metapontus, small puffs of toxic gas were spotted at the cave, so he was able to witness that for himself. The alternating winds, Boreas and Zephyrus, pushed the gas out over the waves and soon it dissipated. Nevertheless, the south cape was placed off limits to everyone except the guards.

Overnight, the dappled band of water around Kalliste changed its appearance. No longer were the separate colors visible, for they had been replaced by shades of yellow: gold, copper, ochre, agate, and amber. Just as suddenly the water changed again. The yellows vanished and were replaced by an unbroken band of milky white. What meager offerings we could spare were placed on the altars. We prayed day and night.

Two days after his arrival on Kalliste, Catreus stood in my study. "Your island is a puzzle to the entire kingdom, Idomeneus," he said. "Now this discolored water that keeps switching hues—who knows what to make of it?"

"Well, one thing is for sure, I've nothing to do with it," I said brusquely.

"Yes, I'm sorry it's been so late in coming, my friend, but I have with me the proclamation clearing your name. Here." He handed me a scroll with the Queen's seal.

"You know, those insane charges against me spread over the entire island. Even my own people in Phira believed them. What took Pasiphae so long in declaring my innocence?"

"It was the doing of those damn priests in the Labyrinth. They couldn't fathom the reason for the poison vapor no matter how many times they entreated the Mother Goddess. They couldn't admit that they couldn't solve the riddle, because if they did, they'd lose face."

"So, they chose to believe Sarpedon's lies?"

"I don't think they actually believed them, but you—thanks to Sarpedon—were a convenient scapegoat...at least until they figured out why Kalliste was poisoned."

"They never did, though."

"No. But after the earthquakes here and on some of the other islands, like Sifnos and Minoa, and then, finally, on Crete, they had to abandon the lame excuse of your betrothal to Aphaea causing the disasters. Excuse me, but one would have to be an ass, and wine-befuddled, to believe a small-town prince on Kalliste could enrage the Great Mother Goddess so that She would rattle the whole empire."

"Well, thank you, I think. I hope you made Sarpedon read the proclamation."

"Idomeneus, that's the reason I came to Kalliste. I made him read it to his assembled court and had it posted around the city of Metapontus. Copies went to the four other towns—Oia, Enalus, Potamos and Therasia—and you have yours for Phira."

"Thank you, my friend. I'm sure that without you on my side, my innocence would still be in the balance."

Catreus gave me a weak smile and said, "I must tell you that my mother and father are deeply concerned about your Kalliste. They keep on talking about what happened on Crete, two hundred years ago, when earthquakes devastated the island. You've heard the stories?"

"Who hasn't? It's said that when the palaces on Crete were leveled, chaos surged across the kingdom. In the islands, commoners — both colonists who came from Crete and people who were born here — tried to topple their princes. A dark, sinister side of our people was exposed to the world. The revolts, however, were total failures. And the ringleaders quickly felt cold bronze axes on their necks."

"Yes," averred Catreus. 'But, nonetheless, the revolts occurred. The king and queen hope none spring up on Kalliste."

Remembering the looting that took place after the big quake, I could not assure Catreus that a revolt was impossible on my island.

ELEVEN

EACH NIGHT, the New Wine Moon was losing more and more of its radiance, as if its light were being bled out. That was the month in which I had planned to marry Aphaea. As things stood, with the disastrous quake and all the deaths so fresh in everyone's memory and the concern over the white water encircling Kalliste, a wedding was out of the question. Once again, I would have to postpone it. And once again, I would tell Aphaea in person. The day after Catreus left Kalliste for Crete, I did the same, but instead of heading for Knossos as he did, I sailed for Phaistos. Miletus stayed back to help put the finishing touches on the various rebuilding projects, and I took a skeleton crew along on the Dove. After we got beyond the wind shadow cast by Mount Kalliste, we made excellent time to Crete.

Princess Biadice arranged for Aphaea and me to meet in a small apartment in the southeastern corner of the palace. As my love and I embraced, I was never so happy to see anyone in my life. "My heart has been weeping for you these long months, Idomeneus," Aphaea said in a gentling voice. "What things you've suffered through. I'm so sorry about your mother."

"She was the cornerstone of Phira—and my life. Things will never be the same without her. Why did the Goddess take her from us?" Aphaea stroked my hair softly, trying to comfort me. "My mother spent her life in devotion to the Goddess. Offering sacrifice, burning incense, praying. Always praying. Her life was the last life the Goddess should have snuffed out."

Aphaea surveyed me thoughtfully. "Maybe that is why She took her," she said, a sweet smile on her lips. "The Goddess, Mistress of Souls, wants and needs Her best adorants at Her right-hand side in Elysium. And, you can be sure, that's where your mother is, now."

"And what about us here on this miserable earth? We grieve, tearing our hair out, never to see my mother's lovely face again. I tell you it's a wound that never heals. My father, the noble Cretheus, died at sea five years ago and still my heart is pierced with severe pain."

"But, Idomeneus, now your mother and father are together again, residing with the Goddess, walking in that shining land, the Elysian Fields. That place, so full of divinity, is where all of us wish to be. You should set aside your brooding and rejoice, for the souls of your parents are together." I closed my weary eyes and held Aphaea tightly; try as she might, she could not ease the overmastering grief I felt.

After I had my fill of weeping, I gave Aphaea the proclamation by Queen Pasiphae and explained how Catreus had hand delivered it. As she took it, she said, "Yes, I know it word for word; it was posted all around Crete."

"Dear, as you know, the New Wine Moon is rapidly fading…I, ah…I don't think…"

"I know, love. The wedding must be postponed once more. I thought as much after the terrible earthquake wreaked havoc on Kalliste. It's all right; we can wait. We have our whole lives ahead of us."

"Oh, I wish we could just get married now, right here at Phaistos—in secrecy."

"That would never work."

"Alas. How could I get you back to Kalliste to live with me without anybody knowing?"

"Not only that. I was thinking more of the Steerer of All Things."

"What about Her?"

"Well, we might be able to fool people for awhile, but never the

Goddess. No one can keep a secret from Her. She knows all."

"Perhaps, but does She care. I mean, why should She care when we get married? Queen Pasiphae, the Goddess's surrogate on earth, has proclaimed our innocence in all that happened on Kalliste. We're free to wed, now."

"Yes, but what about this new phenomenon...this strange-colored water around your island."

"You mean, you've heard news of it, already?"

"Indeed. It's on the tongue of every Cretan. What is it?"

"I don't know. I've brought samples of the water in jars to show the wise men. Maybe they can figure it out. Anyway," I said, regaining my thread of thought, "what does the water have to do with our wedding?"

"Don't you see? It's a sign that the Goddess is still upset. And until we can discover why, and until She is appeased, any ceremony, especially a happy one like a wedding—even a secret wedding—would be ill-timed. The marriage would be doomed."

"Well, tomorrow, I'm going to meet with the wise men and Rhadamanthys. I've been reporting to them about all that's transpired on Kalliste. Maybe they have some answers. Because, all I know is that, whether or not the Goddess is involved, the ominous events on Kalliste have kept us apart." We spent the rest of the day and night in the tiny apartment, trying to make up for lost time.

The following morning, I went to Snow Crystal with Rhadamanthys in search of answers. Ananda, Ta-ch'ih, and Glaukus took the jars of water from me as if they were gifts of precious gold. I had had samples of the water collected as soon as the phenomenon appeared and then after each change. The wise men carefully observed, alternately, the rainbow-colored water, the orange, and the milky white. They poured the water into vials and held them up to the light. They added drops of foul-smelling unguents, then shook the solution and recorded the color changes. They dipped papyrus and linen strips into the water and observed the staining patterns. Using heavy bronze cauldrons, they boiled the water and collected the residue. They even took a gulp of water from each jar, swilled it around in their mouths, and spat it out.

The testing went on for the better part of the morning. Rhadamanthys and I watched on anxiously, though in silence; we did not want to plague the sages with a flood of questions.

At last, the sages laid down the jars and vials. They huddled in a corner of the study, speaking in hushed voices. My heart pounded like a drum.

After what seemed like an eternity, the three wise men shambled over to the table around which Rhadamanthys and I sat. Ta-ch'ih and Ananda prodded Glaukus to speak. "My dear lords, what I say now, I do not say lightly. For months we have been carefully studying the reports Prince Idomeneus has been sending us and, now, we have this new evidence, the strange water." The sage cleared his throat.

"When I was a little boy, those many years ago, I was told tales about giants who lived on earth. One of these tales ran thus: To the northwest, far across the unharvested sea, four giants lived in peace, being well-disposed to the nearby people. Most of the time these colossi just slept. They slept so much, in fact, that eventually the people forgot that they were even there. Indeed, they forgot to sing the giants' praise in their songs or celebrate their towering magnificence in their poems. One day the giants awoke and were incensed by the people's lack of respect. Bitter suffering ensued. They shook the ground and stirred up the waters. They spit large boulders at passing ships, toppling the masts and cracking the hollow hulls. Scores of ships took the sea plunge. The neglectful people choked on foul smelling fumes exhaled by the giants. If they became really enraged, the giants pierced their own skin, and thick, red hot blood gushed forth, flooding and burning the barley-laden fields. These evil deeds made the giants so hot that smoke rose from their lofty heads.

"Now," Glaukus continued, "do you remember, Rhadamanthys, when you were a little boy, how swift ships from our colony on Kythera reached that inhospitable land where these ruinous giants lived?" Rhadamanthys and I nodded. "And how the sailors on those ships discovered that these giants were really—"

"Mountains," a wide-eyed Rhadamanthys declared, not realizing he had broken in.

"Mountains, yes! Huge mountains that behaved like the evil giants in the legends. They are the evil giants! The inland barbarians call them Vesuvius, Aetna, Stromboli, and—"

"Vulcano," I said.

"Yes, and they sometimes use this last name for any one of these mountains. I think," Glaukus said solemnly to me, "that your great mountain is just like them."

"What the hell are you saying, old man." That was the first time I ever used the Achaean curse.

"You live on a land-ravaging, man-destroying volcano."

"No, Glaukus, no!"

"Yes, my son, I'm afraid it's true. And these sages," Glaukus said, pointing to Ta-ch'ih and Ananda, "agree with me. The samples of water you brought today convinced us. Along with the reports you sent us on the other phenomena, these samples show that Kalliste is an awakening giant."

My chest was tight with fear. I wanted to scream but couldn't.

"Here, look at this." Glaukus picked up a tattered yellow scroll and unrolled it.

"So what," I said, my voice cracking. "It's a sketch of Kalliste, seen from, I think, the west."

"No, it's not, Idomeneus. We just uncovered this the other day. This is a copy of a long-lost scroll showing the volcano-island Stromboli. You see, in profile it looks just like Kalliste."

"That doesn't prove anything," I snapped.

"No, not in itself. But combined with the putrid water and the poisonous gas, it tells us that Kalliste is a sea-girt volcano ready to erupt."

"And the earthquakes, never before known on your island, are clear signs," added Ananda.

I turned to Rhadamanthys for help. He was in shock; his grief-darkened eyes stared at me vacantly. "I can't believe it," I muttered.

"It claws my heart to tell you this, Idomeneus," said Glaukus. "There is nothing for you to do but warn your people of the awful dangers that can begin at any moment."

"How can I? How can I tell them that their island, which has sustained them their whole lives, has now turned on them? That their mountain—symbol of their homeland—will try to kill them?"

"You might save their lives if you tell them now," declared Ananda, "for, in time, Mount Kalliste will speak for itself."

I turned to the old diviner, Glaukus. "Does this mean that the Kallisteans were the people mentioned in your dream?" I quavered.

"Are my people, all my people, going to be sent to the Elysian Fields like those who died—including my honored mother?"

With a shrug of his shoulders he said, "I do not know."

The voyage home seemed like the longest of my life. I spent it in my cabin, thinking about the wise men's revelation. Believing it one moment, not believing it the next. When we rounded the south cape, I went outside and stood on the prow, staring at my island. Kalliste: most beautiful. Could it be true?

Once at Phira, I remained in my suite of rooms for two days: I had all my meals sent in, and I spoke to no one. My mind was reeling over everything that had happened. At sunrise on the third day, I was startled from my bed by an urgent banging on the door. Before I got the word "enter" out of my mouth, the door flew open and in leapt a servant, crying, "Come quickly, my lord, the mountain is burning!"

Outracing the servant to the western court, I arrived to find an anxious group of Phirans gazing skyward. When I looked up, my eyes beheld a ribbon of smoke, spiraling above the great mountain and mingling with the fluffy clouds. The smoke came from only one spot on the mountain: the very top. No flames were visible. Nevertheless, my subjects believed that they were witnessing a distant forest fire. One moment's reflection, though, would have told them that was unlikely; the summit of the mountain was the wettest spot on the island, due to the fact that the clouds always struck it and thus released their rains. How could the trees way up there burn?

I knew the answer.

A delicate fire flickered under my skin and sweat rolled down my face. A trembling seized me all over. My ears were filled with high-pitched maddening sounds, and it seemed I was close to death. I wanted to blurt out what I knew, for if I didn't, if I kept it within my breast, I would burst. My hands shot to my mouth, stifling my scream, which would have caused panic in the court and throughout the palace.

Other early risers began to stream in and soon the court was packed. For the longest time, I was unaware that Miletus was standing by my side. It wasn't until he asked, "A fire, my lord?" that I turned and saw my trusty steward. Without uttering a word, I grabbed him by the wrist and gruffly pulled him away from the throng. We huddled against a wall that abutted the southern side of the court.

"What is it, Your Grace?" exclaimed Miletus.

"Sh! Not so loud, Miletus!" I took several deep breaths as I attempted to pull myself together. Putting my two hands on his shoulders, I stared deep into Miletus's confused eyes. I began. "Listen very carefully, my friend. Listen to everything I have to say."

"My lord, I will."

"That is not a fire up there."

"It isn't?"

"No. The top of the mountain has split asunder and the smoke is issuing forth from inside."

"What?"

"I know it sounds unbelievable, Miletus. But just think what's happened in the last four or five months: first the poison vapor; then the earthquakes; then the ugly water choking our bays; now this. It's said that these are the very things that accompany those giant mountains in the distant west across the sea. These are the signs of a...a volcano. Kalliste is a volcano, Miletus."

"No. That's impossible. That's a lie."

"It's the truth, and it's well-rounded, though my heart aches to utter such words."

Miletus shook his silvery head. 'But I've lived here my whole life. No, it's just not possible. Look, we've been plagued by these unnatural phenomena for less than half a year. In the past, why didn't—"

"Because the giant was asleep. It has been sleeping all these long years, ever since the first man set foot on this rock. This year the giant awoke."

Wounded and angry, Miletus fell silent, keeping his eyes riveted on the smoking summit above us. Slowly, the truth of my words overturned his resistant heart. His face grew as pale as summer-burnt grass. He began to tremble as I had when the light of truth had shone on me, and his eyes filled with tears. When I saw that, mine did too.

After a few moments, he spoke. "These sad eyes have seen enough. Death-Wielding Snake Goddess of Souls, if ever I put roof to a shrine that delighted you, or if ever I burnt in your honor the fat thighs of bulls and goats, fulfill this wish of mine: Strike me here and now with a rapid-fire thunderflash."

Brushing aside my tears, I held him firmly in my arms and whispered softly, "My dear Miletus, I don't know what all this will come to. Tomorrow—nay, the next moment—is uncertain. For now, though, we must shepherd these people. Soon they too will recall the legends of the giants and remember the Kytherans discovery of the four volcanoes in the far west. And they'll learn the lamentable truth. To avoid panic, I think it best if we broke it to them now."

Miletus was in a stupor as he turned toward me but snapped out of it when his vacant eyes met mine. "Aye, Sire, you're right," he said. "No doubt they'll put all the parts together. They're not fools."

"I'll tell them I suspect that Mount Kalliste is a volcano, that until someone goes to the top, it can't be confirmed. That might ease the blow a little, plus give us some time to plan how to deal with this latest disaster."

"I once heard," Miletus said, "from an old salt who had visited the land of the giant volcanoes that sometimes they smoke and nothing more. And, within time, the smoke stops."

"Good. Yes, that's good. I'll tell our people that, too. It should help."

As we walked back to the center of the court, Miletus stopped and pulled me aside. "Sire, do you suppose the smoke above is filled with the same kind of gas that issued from the cave?"

"I don't know, but I wouldn't be surprised."

"Because if that smoke is poisoned, Sire, and if it is carried by the winds over all Kalliste, then released—"

"Goddess forbid, you're right."

"That Boreas is blowing south. Phira's safe for now."

"Aye, but what about Metapontus?"

We went to the low wall separating the court from the western garden and looked south. We could not see the city from there, of course, but it looked as if the clouds were racing south.

I said to Miletus in a hushed voice, "All we can pray for now is that the wind remains constant and strong, carrying any poison out to sea."

Cautiously, Miletus replied, "Yes, Your Grace, but then what of Crete?"

Like a stone anchor, my heart dropped. Aphaea! Rhadamanthys! The sages at Snow Crystal!

"Surely," I gasped, "the poison will be thinned out, diluted before it travels that far! It'll be harmless."

To comfort me, Miletus nodded in agreement. But neither of us knew for sure. We walked over to the center of the court, where I broke the devastating news about Mount Kalliste to my people.

That afternoon, Sarpedon sent an expedition to the top of the mountain. The members of the expedition, brave men all, reported back that the smoke mixed with steam spewing forth from a long fissure in the center of a depression two hundred feet long and twenty to thirty feet wide. With a great rushing noise, the steam was being shot up, engorging the clouds above. I cannot express how relieved we were when, later, we heard that the poison-laden smoke and steam never reached Crete.

Alas, what the wise men had discovered, and what I had told my subjects that morning in the western court, was confirmed. Mount Kalliste—which meant just about all of Kalliste—was one big volcano.

One can imagine how the awful sight of our mountain coughing up envenomed steam and smoke affected us. There was no enemy to blame for our woes except the very land we cherished. At that time of sorrow, I wished that I alone indeed had been the reason for all the troubles. At least then my people could have banished me, and maybe prevented The Web from tearing or unraveling even further.

There was some talk about abandoning Kalliste. Such talk would have been inconceivable a year before. Even after the vile vapor killed so many of us, and the disastrous earthquake shattered our lives, and the deadly sea water choked our ports and bays, no one dared propose such a thing. Leave our home? Our lands? Our island? To go where? To do what?

After it became clear that Kalliste was a smoldering furnace, people began thinking the unthinkable, fearing that the awakened giant would find even more terrible ways to kill its children.

Though I felt awful doing it, I assigned guards to our wharf to keep an eye on the vessels. The other princes did the same. It was difficult, because the people had been shaken to the core, but we princes tried to discourage talk of fleeing, pointing out that no one had perished since the earthquake, even though we had been surrounded by ominous warnings. Possibly, just possibly, we argued, that, after Knossos sent along new orders and we faithfully carried out the sacrifices, the angry Mother of Mountains would be appeased.

The orders from the capital didn't arrive as soon as we had been led to believe they would. Our argument did not stem the tide; some islanders, we learned, were sorting out their belongings, deciding which items they would take with them when they fled. Who could have known that the orders from Knossos would be as loathsome to us princes as the heartrending news about Kalliste itself?"

TWELVE

WHILE WE AWAITED the envoy who was to bring the king's orders, conditions on the island changed little. The steam that rose from the summit of Mount Kalliste mingled with the billowing clouds above, then was driven south by the constant wind. Occasionally, there was a lull, then the steam would spiral up again.

The unbroken band of white water around the island, to which we had grown accustomed by then, disappeared and was replaced by large pools of vibrant greens and purples. As if the sea were a huge pot of swirling paints, the two colors warred against each other, roiling wildly.

As the Knossosans tried to unravel the mystery of the Earth Mistress's displeasure, I wondered how many fat sheep and shambling, crooked-horned oxen from Phira would feel the cold blade on their necks. When Minos's envoy finally landed at Metapontus, Sarpedon sent a runner who, I expected, would be clutching a long papyrus in his hands. I assumed the scroll would enumerate the longest list of sacrifices ever required of generous Phira. But the runner carried nothing except his herald's staff. He explained that the princes of the five towns were to come to Metapontus at once, for there, Minos's envoy would read aloud the prescribed hecatomb. We were not to be accompanied by a single priestess, steward, or servant; the message was only for the ears of the nobles. Such secrecy was unusual, but we princes, anxious to hear the remedy for our ordeal, had no other choice but to obey.

Arriving at the city, we were led into the rebuilt palace throne room. There we confronted a sulking Sarpedon seated on his throne and a dour-faced envoy standing stiffly at the back of the room. The envoy was an important magistrate from the southeastern sector of Knossos's domain—not your usual messenger. It appeared to me that, before we arrived, Sarpedon had pressed the Cretan to unroll the scroll so that Sarpedon would have been the first to know the particulars of the hecatomb. The Cretan had refused, and, even as we princes from the five towns entered the room, he clutched the scroll close to his bosom. The envoy-magistrate, a man of honor, was obeying his orders. The air between him and Sarpedon was as tense as in any arena.

As we warily eyed the two antagonists, the massive bronze-studded door slammed behind us. Rising abruptly, Sarpedon turned toward the still motionless Cretan and spoke to him in a harsh tone. "There! Now all the good princes of Kalliste are assembled. Let us learn what no other ears must hear." Sarpedon did not introduce the man, and the Cretan, for his part, did not even act surprised. Instead he quickly stepped forward and began to slice through the clay seals on the scroll with a crystal-handled dagger. The impressions on the seals were large and could have been made by only one signet ring, that of Minos.

With one more seal to go, the envoy paused and looked up. "My noble lords," he said, "you realize I was only following—"

"Yes, yes, just proceed," Sarpedon coldly interrupted.

The envoy's head dropped quickly, but I saw that his lips pressed tightly together, his eyes narrowed. He cut through the last seal with a flourish, then twirled his dagger in the air and rammed it into its gilt sheath. Holding the top edge of the scroll with two fingers, he allowed the ivory rod upon which the papyrus was wound to drop, and the document unrolled itself with a snap. Clearing his voice, the Cretan read aloud, "Praise be to the Immortal Goddess, the Much-Punishing Steerer of All, She of the Bow-Glory, with eyes that shine frighteningly.

"Illustrious Princes of towering Kalliste, I, Minos, King of the islands that span The Deep Blue, am sorely grieved to learn of your troubles. One disaster follows hard upon another, and—try as we may in the capital—we cannot fathom why you and your followers have fallen out of favor with the Almighty Goddess. Thus, we do what we can, which is to prescribe the appropriate hecatomb that will unlock the heart of the Earth Mistress.

"Your king, by whose pleasure you rule your lands and subjects, commands that you make a great hecatomb. When you place the sacrifices on your altars, you are to free their spirits from their flesh in the usual manner. Let the blood stain the altars but allow no fire to touch the portions that you usually cook for the delight of the Goddess. Instead, carry those portions up Mount Kalliste, and there, with proper prayers, cast them into the steaming crevice. In distant lands, we have learned, people who live with mountains like yours practice this manner of offering. Upon returning to your respective palaces, you must hold great feasts with the remaining parts of the animal sacrifices. This will please the Great Goddess.

"Now hear what your king demands you offer up to the Loud-Thundering Goddess. Each town, plus the city of Metapontus, will sacrifice ten suckling pigs; five faultless she-goats; five full-horned rams; two unbroken red-backed oxen, thick with fat; and one…"

As if he had forgotten how to read, the envoy stopped in mid sentence, staring dumbfoundedly at the scroll. His jaw dropped as he squinted at what was written next.

We all grew impatient, but it was Sarpedon who demanded that the shaken Cretan either continue reading or hand over the document. The envoy gripped the scroll tightly in his trembling hands and in a tense voice resumed. "A-a-a-a, two unbroken red-backed oxen thick with fat, and one…one youth and one maiden—"

"What?" I exclaimed.

"Let me see that," Sarpedon barked, tearing the scroll out of the man's hands. Sarpedon read silently down the scroll, then read aloud, "Red-backed oxen, thick with fat, and one youth and one maiden, both chaste. Each prince must choose the youth and maiden from his own subjects. Those chosen to end the rancor of the Great Mother Goddess, thus saving Kalliste, shall not be dispatched by axe, like the bestial offerings, but by knife. And their consecrated bodies shall not be divided but placed whole into the steaming rift.

"Ever-obedient Princes of Kalliste, I, Minos, your long-ruling King, expect this royal command to be carried out in all its particulars. I realize these sacrifices will be offensive to your loving natures, but we at Knossos have proof that these very sacrifices will tip the scales of the wise Mother in your favor. Now, without delay, obey, and spare your island further disasters. Glory be to the Goddess Steerer-of-All."

Sarpedon looked down at the bottom of the scroll, then said, "And here in red wax is an impression of the king's seal?"

For a few moments, the throne room was silent, as if all those within had gone mute. Then, like a shower of hailstones, we blurted out our feelings. "What's going on in the capital?" shouted Thoas, brave Prince of Enalus.

"Are those priests and priestesses crazy advising the king of such a… such a… crime?" Oenopion of Oia said.

"Good Goddess!" I cried, "Haven't our people suffered enough from these plagues? Why should their leaders slaughter their young?" I thought for a moment, then said, "I'm sorry, king's decree or not, I for one will not obey."

"I wonder what the King is thinking when he says there is proof that the sacrifices work?" asked Thoas.

"Good question," said Andrus of Potamos.

"Wait," said Thoas, "don't those barbarians offer up their own children, virgins every one, during times of disaster?"

"Yes," cried Andrus, "you're right! I've heard the same thing! The incense-smelling priests and priestesses at Knossos must be basing this hecatomb on what barbarians do."

"Barbarians, yes," I declared, "for don't the warlike Achaeans sacrifice peasants to gain a favorable oracle?"

"Aye," answered Thoas. "For that matter, the Hittites, lashers of horses, will cut a throat or two to please their skygod. And don't the Egyptians bury scores of retainers alive when a pharoah takes the Boat of the Dead?"

"And the same is done at Hsiao," I said without thinking.

"Where on earth is that," asked Thoas.

"Ah, never mind. It's not important. What is important is that now our king is convinced that we too should make such grisly offerings."

"Yes, of course, here on Kalliste," said Lacinius of Therasia, "but I would like to see Minos tell Cretan princes to sacrifice their innocent subjects. Ha, never! I go along with Idomeneus; the animals I will slay, not my citizens."

"I also," said Oenopion.

"And I," said Thoas and Andrus.

There was an uneasy silence as we waited to hear Sarpedon's gruff voice. At last we turned toward him and stared, forcing the cur to speak. "Friends, my fellow Princes, is it wise to blatantly ignore a plain-worded decree from King Minos? Remember when he sent the black guards to discourage looting after the earthquake? Remember how we reacted, and remember how ridiculous we looked when it was quickly proven that we did need their help?"

Thoas and Oenopion were caught off guard by Sarpedon's comment. Andrus and Lacinius were under Sarpedon's thumb. All four pondered in silence. Not I.

"That was different, Sarpedon," I snapped.

"How so," he said challengingly, knitting his brow. I could see he remembered our last confrontation.

"Because the King and his people know a lot about the unrest caused by earthquakes. And they were right about Kalliste. But what does Minos or anyone at Knossos—anyone in our whole kingdom, for that matter—know about appeasing the Earth Mistress when Her wrath spews forth from a volcano? Nothing! Nothing except some hearsay about savages who live in some Goddess-forsaken lands."

"Idomeneus is right," said Thoas.

"Well, this hearsay is good enough for the King," barked Sarpedon. "Here is his decree." He shook the scroll in my face.

"I think the King was severely ill-advised," I retorted, pushing his hand away.

"Oh, you think so? Well, I think something must be done to break this chain of disasters. And if that something is sacrificing a youth and a maiden—and the king says to do it—we must do it."

"I care not a straw for what you think, Sarpedon," I said. "You thought the breaking of my betrothal to your daughter caused the poison vapor. Ha!"

"You dog! How dare you bring that up in my home."

"Well, the Queen made it clear in her proclamation that that was a wicked lie."

"Please, you two," Thoas broke in, "Lay all that to rest. It's this vile act of human sacrifice that concerns us here."

Sarpedon's face blanched, and he stared daggers at me.

"I think our people would panic," said Thoas, "if we turned our hand against them, slaying their children."

"I think they'd rebel," I averred. "What do you think Andrus? Lacinius?" They both glanced at Sarpedon. But not even the intense glare from the most powerful man on the island could make them disagree with Thoas and me.

Finally, Lacinius said, "Yes, I don't see how, after what has transpired, we can do this to our citizens. The timing couldn't be worse." Andrus nodded in agreement.

During our heated words, we had forgotten all about the Cretan envoy. After Sarpedon had snatched the scroll from him, he had faded into the background, like some distant figure in a fresco. As if with a single mind, we princes realized that the man had overheard every word we had said. In unison, we turned toward the envoy. The man stepped from the corner into the middle of the room and spoke. "Famed princes of Kalliste, I know what you're thinking. Allow me to say that after hearing what the king wants done, I am as disturbed as you. As far as I know, in our whole history, we men of Minos have never even contemplated such vile acts. What would our forefathers think of us if word of this somehow reached the Elysian Fields, and they learnt that we even mentioned such things? What would our children and our children's children think of us in the years ahead?

"I praise you, princes of Kalliste, for your stand against this odious part of the king's decree. As far as what was spoken here today, and by whom, no one on Crete nor anywhere else will ever learn from me, Goddess forefend. You have my solemn word."

The envoy's brave speech and manner convinced us all of the truth of his words. We set the huge hecatomb to take place the next day.

As soon as I arrived home that evening, I conferred with Miletus and the priestesses, instructing them to alert everybody in the palace and in the town about the following day's ceremonies. We sent word to the shepherds, goatherds, pig keepers, and cattlemen to cut out the required number of beasts, then, long into the night, we worked preparing things in the central court.

I told no one—not even Miletus—about the other sacrifices that King Minos had wanted us to make; the princes had sworn to keep the call for human sacrifices a secret among us. When he heard the incomplete list, Miletus exclaimed, "Well, that's not as bad as I thought it was going to be." I gazed at him, shielding my feelings.

Early the next morning, the palace was filled to overflowing. A circle, a dozen people thick, ringed the main court. Courtiers and townsfolk glutted the corridors, filling every window and door space. The roofs of the royal apartments were lined with precariously balanced citizens eager to see the ceremony. As always, the backdrop for our ritual was the great mountain—looming larger than ever.

My dear mother would have been proud of her two lovely-faced assistants; they and a young priest who wielded the double-axe were then the only surrogates of the Goddess in Phira. After the animals were dispatched and the Goddess's portions were removed from the bodies, a team of servants quickly carried away the remainders to the kitchen. If the meat was to be well-prepared by that evening, the cooks had to begin at once to roast it on the long spits.

The Goddess's portions were mounted on strong poles and secured with ropes. On my command, a servant standing at either end of each pole hoisted the consecrated meat onto his shoulder. Snaking its way out of the palace, the long procession, which I headed, made its way to the ravine gouged out by our largest stream. We moved along the north bank of the stream, slowly ascending the volcano.

In my years at sea, when wild waves climbed the mast, I had had to lift up the spirits of many young sailors by exclaiming that Diktynna, Protectress of Seafarers, would save us. But never was my leadership tried more than on the day I led those trembling courtiers up the volcano. For it was as if they had received wind of Minos's call for human sacrifices and they were afraid of being selected once we reached the steamy fissure. I had to prod them continuously with assurances that we would stay only a short time. While I spoke to them, their eyes were fixed on the spiraling column of steam overhead. All along the way, one person or another was praying for the Mother of Mountains to protect him. If a single person would have broken and run, I am sure the others would have been on his heels.

The two priestesses marched up front with heads held high and breasts thrust out, their long skirts and dark tresses flying behind them. Though they were not used to such a difficult trek, they made the ascent with an air of grandeur and calm. Before long, their confidence infected all those behind them. If my words of encouragement were useless that day, the example set by those two young women was not; our party was the second to reach the summit, arriving at midday.

Scanning the head of the mountain, I observed at once the awesome changes. Prior to the time the volcano awoke, its head was fairly level and green, crowned with fragrant cypresses like a fertile plateau. But on the day of our climb, we saw that the center of the summit had caved in, resembling an enormous coffin. Running through the coffin, from east to west, the ugly fissure had swallowed the shrine that had been dedicated to the Great Mother Goddess hundreds of years ago. With enormous force, the volcano spewed out a roaring monstrous column of yellowish-white steam.

Though it was difficult to divert my eyes from such an astonishing spectacle, I quickly led the Phirans around the rim to the northmost point, where Prince Oenopion was waiting with his courtiers from Oia. The four-and-ten-day period when the Wind Sleeps was nearly upon us, but there was still a fair northerly. On the spot where the Oians and Phirans were standing, we could hardly smell the putrid odor.

Before long, the representatives from the three other towns joined us. Then Sarpedon appeared with his people. He had wisely led them around the west side of the mountain, avoiding the contaminated fumes drifting over the southern rim.

There must have been a hundred Kallisteans from the five towns and Metapontus standing on the rim. As we huddled together for warmth, the priestesses led us in prayer. Then we princes took the lead, escorting our groups to the closest edge of the long fissure. We approached cautiously, trembling with fear as we went. Standing over the horrible wound in the summit, we couldn't see down more than ten feet, so thick was the rising steam. Swiftly we ordered the bearers of the sacrifices to deposit their loads, and so they did, hastily dumping poles and all into the steamy abyss.

We all—princes, priestesses, and retainers—moved back from the rim. All, that is, but those in the party from Metapontus. Like the people of the five towns, the Metapontusians had dumped their sacrifices into the crevice. Sarpedon stood before his people saying something, as two of his retainers slipped behind the party. Suddenly, each grabbed a flower-bearer—one a boy and one a girl—and dragged the surprised children in front of Sarpedon. At the fiend's command, his henchmen slit the children's throats and cast their lifeless bodies into the fiery pit.

Everyone stood in shock for one terrible moment. Then a din rose up from those of us from the five towns that almost drowned out the volcano. As if not to be outdone, the volcano shot off a great blast of steam with an unearthly "whoosh" We started to edge backwards, as did Sarpedon and his people. Slowly the ground started to tremble, then shake.

Everyone on the summit turned and ran. As we made our descent, each prince herding his people down a different path, large raindrops fell, accompanied by distant thunder. All the way back to Phira, the rain drowned our tears of fear and outrage.

When we arrived home that evening, the news of Sarpedon's foul deed spread like wild fire throughout the palace and town. To avert a panic, I told my people the truth: how King Minos had called for human sacrifices, how the five princes of the towns had refused to carry out the order, how accursed Sarpedon decided on his own to slay two of his people. I promised them, on my mother's tomb, that not one hair of one of their children would be offered up to the volcano.

That night the roasted meat, cheese, honey, bread, and fruit went to waste. But I made sure the pitchers kept coming; everyone wanted the red nectar to keep them numb, to make them forget what had happened that day on the mountain.

The next morning, I awoke to a sound I had almost forgotten: the laughter of little children. They were playing a game in the small court outside my chamber. My heart was buoyed. I threw a robe over my shoulders and headed for the court for I wanted to see the source of such happy noise. As I walked briskly down the corridor, the court appeared before me, and I spied three children, a daughter of Althaemenes and two sons of the palace vintner. The children were gathering large snowflakes as they drifted down to earth. The entire court and the evergreen shrubs surrounding it wore a thin white mantle.

I recalled my early days and how I loved those rare occasions when snow reached all the way down to Phira. Stepping out from under the roof of the colonnade, I opened my palm to snatch some snow, wanting to wet my parched lips. The flakes that touched my flesh were not wet. In fact, they were just the opposite. They piled up in tiny molehills, like grains of sand, then slipped through my fingers. Bewildered, I brought my hand to my mouth and cautiously stuck out my tongue to taste...ash. Burnt, dry, gritty ash! Though it was strangely cool. I spat it out in disgust, then tilted my head upward and stared at the only possible source of such a cruel joke.

Since the wind had died, the steam rose straight as an arrow, feeding the immense cloud hanging over the rim of the summit and overshadowing the east slope. The steam and cloud formed a monstrous yellowish-white pine tree composed of ash and mist.

Our spirits ebbed even lower. Once more, we had failed to appease the Mother of Mountains. Once more our offerings—including the unspeakable ones—were rejected; She told us so by incinerating the hecatomb and sprinkling its ashes on our heads.

We on Kalliste had a new thing to contend with: ash falling from the sky.

At first the ash was just a nuisance; several times a day the servants had to sweep it away, for it drifted through the palace, seeking out nooks and crannies. But after a couple of days, we noticed that the limbs of trees were drooping due to the accumulation of ash. Farmers had to go through their orchards and groves, shaking their prize fruit-bearers to rid them of the ash.

In time, every four-legged creature on the island was a dingy white, the color of an obstinate donkey when it takes its dust bath. Before they were allowed into our rooms, Deino and Taras and the other palace dogs had to be brushed thoroughly. As if we had aged over night, we Kallisteans turned gray. We went around shaking our dark locks and brushing off our shoulders, as if our scalps had dried up. And even though we squinted, our eyes turned as red as a mad dog's.

The rain of ash marked the beginning of a series of disastrous events that made our earlier miseries seem slight. Since the first misunderstood sign, the poisonous vapor, the giant had been awakening from its long sleep, slowly, over many moons, and in strange fits. But the ash signaled that the giant was fully awakened and ready to show the world its true strength.

When the Dog Star scampered up from the east and the brightest of the Wanderers floated by, we knew that the coldest season was upon us. The season brought the shortest days of the year and that, coupled with the fact that the cloud of steam and ash was growing, kept us in almost constant gloom. Our lamps burned day and night, depleting our oil supply. What worried me more than the levels in our pithoi was what would happen if the island shook again and those lamps were sent crashing to the floors. But what else could we do? We had to see.

The ash presented more and more of a problem as it piled high on our flat roofs. Several newly rebuilt farmhouses collapsed under the weight; five Kallisteans were injured, but none was lost to us. We princes sent word to all the farmsteads that any buildup over three fingers in thickness was cause for alarm, and we ordered the farmers to keep their buildings as free from ash as possible. In the palaces and towns, we had small armies of workmen shoveling and sweeping off the roofs.

The time had come for us to think the unthinkable.

I called a meeting to be held at Phira to discuss our possible exodus from Kalliste. After all, we were not in the same situation as those people who lived inland around the base of, say, Vesuvius. When that giant was on a rampage, the people could pick up and leave, walking or running. We Kallisteans were more like the inhabitants of Stromboli, an island-volcano that rose from the sea. When their giant was upset with them, the Strombolians had to flee across the waves to the mainland or the large island of the Sicels. If things got worse on Kalliste, we would have to do likewise, sailing south to Crete. How could we manage such an enormous exodus? There were not nearly enough ships to move everybody at once, not to mention their possessions and livestock. Some unfortunate islanders would have to stay back, waiting for the ships to return from

Crete. Who would stay back? Who would choose them? There must be a better solution, I thought to myself.

The meeting lasted a long time. Sarpedon sent one of his yeomen, Crito, in his stead. Feelings ran high, although in the end we agreed that the best way to avoid panic was to begin sending our people to Crete in small waves, starting immediately. To carry out the evacuation in stages, we would need, of course, the complete cooperation of the Cretans. Their fabled hospitality would be sorely tested; they would have to shelter and feed us until the volcano became idle and we could return to Kalliste. I suggested that perhaps the royal fleet could be used to help shuttle our people over the sea swells. The following morning, a messenger carrying a report of the deteriorating conditions on the island, our proposal to evacuate, and our request for assistance, was dispatched to the capital on Crete.

Late one night, about ten days later, Miletus and I were up planning the evacuation of Phira; we were not going to wait to hear from the king before starting the crucial work. The pale handles of the waxing moon must have circled high above us, though, due to the cloud, we could not see them. Miletus and I were listing the materials that the courtiers would carry with them when they fled, and the scribes were busily scratching everything down. We gave priority to the sacred objects used throughout the palace. Then came the official documents and the heavy treasure boxes. Items made of precious gold, silver, and bronze, such as tableware and weapons, were certainly not to be left behind. Even though the voyage to spacious Crete would take only a day, we decided to bring as much food as we could carry, for we had not heard yet from Crete and had no idea what to expect once we landed. Since we wanted to take many of our most beautiful local and imported ceramic pieces anyway, it would simply be a matter of filling them with food stuff. We would bring with us only the very oldest and very newest pots. The latter were decorated with sea creatures, the style that was then the rage of the capital, and, in fact, the pots had come from Knossos only last summer. Strange, we thought, that after such a short stay on Kalliste the pots would be returning to the land where they were made.

As we were finishing our work, Miletus, the scribes, and I were startled by a noise. It was not like the terrible groan the earth produced when the Goddess shook it. But rather, it was a boom, resembling a low thunder roll cut abruptly short. And yet it was different, somehow more ominous. After a few moments, we heard it again. Then again. Each one was slightly louder than the previous.

Spilling into the courts, the palace people ran to observe the mountain, which stood dark and vigilant over Phira, showering us with even more ash than before. We stood shivering in the courts for a long time before the giant spoke again. A few moments before the noise was heard, the top of the mountain flared a brilliant orange. A short while later, a heavier dose of ash came down and mingled with it were olive-size pebbles made of compacted ash, which could be easily crushed between finger and thumb. My people and I kept an all-night vigil during which we heard the fearsome boom twice more. Prior to each boom, the brow of the mountain flashed, and afterwards the downpour of ash was heavier, the pebbles larger.

Kalliste became a beacon in the night—we later learned—for the flashes on the mountain could be seen from other islands, including Crete. But from our dangerous position, it appeared to us Kallisteans as if an enormous oven had been lit on the summit, and it was fully stoked.

The next morning when the darkness was somewhat diluted, I sent my fastest runner to Metapontus with a simple message: if you have not done so already, Sarpedon, send another messenger to Crete. When the runner arrived, he discovered that Minos's envoy had finally come—Catreus himself. My confidant in the capital carried with him an elaborate plan of evacuation and resettlement that obviously had taken much time to prepare. The princes of the five towns had begun to think that the delay was our punishment for disobeying Minos's call for human sacrifices. But when we saw the particulars of the many-scrolled plan, we realized why we had not heard from the capital sooner. The entire scheme had Catreus's unmistakable touch. He would remain at Metapontus until the volcano either ceased its activity or became so threatening that Kalliste had to be abandoned immediately. Catreus alone would decide the next step.

If and when that decision to abandon the island was made, we would sail to Crete at once, instead of going in stages as we had proposed. About three-quarters of the royal fleet, composed of warships and merchantmen, was moored at Amnisos and at other ports along the north coast, and would come for us when Catreus sent word. Upon receiving its order, each squadron would hurry to its town of responsibility. When the squadron arrived at the wharf, the sailors would help load people and property onto both Kallistean and Cretan vessels. The sailors and islanders would put as much aboard as they could, and the things which did not fit would be left behind. Then the convoy would set sail, hiving off from Kalliste and heading directly for a city on Crete. There the Kallisteans would disembark and be absorbed into the local population.

Only the grand island of Minos could accomplish such a feat and not disrupt the fabric of its society. The people of Metapontus would be resettled at Knossos. The farmers under Sarpedon's jurisdiction would be placed on farmsteads just outside Knossos, where they and their families would live and work until Kalliste was habitable once more. Those who had lived within the city of Metapontus would move in with the citizens of Knossos. Sarpedon's court would be installed in the famous Little Palace, northwest of the Labyrinth. Clearly, the shrewd Minos did not want his scheming guest right under his roof; at the Little Palace, he could keep Sarpedon at arm's length, while keeping a wary eye on him.

It was decided in Knossos that the other Kallisteans would be relocated as follows: the townsfolk of Oia to Palaikastro, Enalus to Kato Zakro, Potamos to Mallia, and Therasia to Kydonia. Temporary wooden shelters were being thrown up in all of the Cretan cities to supplement the available apartments.

The ships that transported my people from Phira would have the longest voyage of all; they would have to sail from the east coast of Kalliste all the way around the west tip of Crete, then halfway along the south coast. To my mind, it was worth it, because the Phirans would resettle in a city I knew and loved—Phaistos. Rhadamanthys was already generously preparing Snow Crystal for my entourage.

What a cruel paradox: if my island home became uninhabitable, forcing me to flee, I would then be united with my love, Aphaea of the lovely locks. The design of the Goddess Steerer is shrouded in darkness and unintelligible to earth-born beings, except a few. Before

I left Snow Crystal, Glaukus had said to me that he felt that he and I would be spending more time together before too long. At Snow Crystal, I would be with those I loved the most.

Catreus's plan was well received by all on Kalliste. And it came none too soon. Around the island, the baleful phenomena that had plagued us grew worse and worse. The ring of two-colored water strangling our shores widened, rising and falling in fits. The noxious vapor began once more—and not just from the one cave but from several around the island. But the worst of all was the heart-stopping booms. Yes, they began again, each one proceeded by a great shower of ash, pebbles, and something new: rocks. The rocks, made out of hard black stone, were about the size of a man's fist. They slammed into facades of houses and apartments, crashed through roofs and were lethal missiles to anyone walking our streets. Between the ear-splitting booms and their barrages, our nights were sleepless.

Our fields—our precious fields—were covered in some places with as much as a foot of coarse, grayish-white ash. Even when the volcano was not exploding, there was no letup from the ash, which stripped the few remaining leaves and twigs off the trees and ravaged every vine.

Because the period when the wind sleeps had ended and the northerlies had started, the south coast was hardest hit by the ash. Metapontus was a city entombed, its great harbor clogged.

By the middle of the first month of the new year, all Kallisteans knew we would have to abandon our homes for the devastation showed no signs of slowing down, never mind ceasing.

We expected to hear from Catreus any day. All of our belongings—except what we needed for cooking—were already packed and piled in the wagons, ready to go. Our grazing animals were herded in tightly throughout the towns, sheltered wherever possible. I had worried that some of our older people would refuse to leave Phira, wishing to stand by the only homes they ever knew. But as the situation deteriorated, everyone, young and old alike, knew that there was no option.

The seven stars known as the Sailing Ones were overhead and the moon was full—though no one could see them—the night we knew we had spent our last on Kalliste. The deafening booms came so close together that you could not count to threescore between them. And they were so loud that their invisible force actually cracked our newly repainted and plastered walls. The downpour of ash and rock was like a hailstorm. We had to call in all our workers. The ash buildup on the roofs became critical. Late that night, the ceilings in some of the palace apartments began to sag. The floors trembled, even between the booms. With torch in hand, a daring young runner arrived at Phira to alert us to what we had already guessed: the next day, at dawn, one of the king's squadrons would be waiting for us at our wharf.

That last sleepless night, my weary people huddled together praying that the sun would somehow appear before its due time, while I, with a small lamp, made my way to the recently enlarged shrine. I found the lovely priestesses, the ones that had been so carefully painted on the walls, lacerated and dismembered by cracks. A net of fissures covered the fine stucco work on the ceiling, which bowed down dangerously.

Miletus appeared at the door, wanting me to leave the pitiful room, but before I departed, I bid a tearful farewell to my mother, my palace, my island. Would I ever come back? What would I find if I did? One thing was certain: Kalliste was no man's land and would remain so until the Goddess's reign of terror had ended.

THIRTEEN

THE SUN ROSE unusually slowly the morning we fled Kalliste—or so it seemed. As soon as the sun illuminated the monstrous cloud, we were on the move. I was never so proud of my people as on that awful day, because, even though they were piled with troubles, they walked with their heads held high. I wondered how I could ever have had such anger toward them over their feelings about Aphaea's and my proposed wedding.

I was at the head of the long caravan, and Miletus and the priestesses were at the rear. Except for the very young and the very old, and the ill and the injured, everybody went on foot. Harnessed to the carts and wagons, the beasts of burden strained, for the vehicles were laden with our valuable possessions and stores. The grazing animals were herded at the back of the caravan and were driven along by the shepherds and pig-herds and their yapping dogs.

During the first leg of the march, a shower of hot ash sprinkled our heads. The ash was accompanied by a few small rocks, but no explosions. For a while, I thought to myself, maybe these plagues are slackening off and will die out soon, maybe we are being too hasty, maybe we should stay on. Couldn't the Great Mother Goddess have been testing us, seeing how much suffering we could withstand before abandoning our beloved land? But when we crossed the bridge over the great chasm, the ash intensified, even though we were farther away from the volcano. I sighed with resignation, realizing that things were not going to get any better.

As we went along, every now and then, I would step to the side and allow the long column to pass me. Shouting a brave word or two at the Phirans as they went by, I tried to lift their spirits. I extolled their courage in the time of crisis. I sang of fair Crete, well-grown with trees, the fruitful Messara, and, of course, shining Phaistos, city of deep-based wealth. Since many of my people had never visited Crete—some had never even been off Kalliste—I tried to allay their doubts about their destination. The Kallisteans who traced their blood back before the Cretan colonists came were especially fearful.

Nearing the wharf, we caught sight of a tall forest springing up from the water. The unshrouded masts and yards of the ships in the squadron caused this illusion. Phira's tiny wharf had never seen such a sight. My people's spirits were lifted; never before had they had such a sense of importance. Just think, King Minos, Ruler of the Waves, had sent so many of his wide-decked merchantmen and fast-faring warships to aid the people of Phira!

The boost to our waning hearts came at a crucial time, because the full extent of the disaster was finally sinking in. As we squinted out through the ash shower, we saw a countryside covered by a thick white blanket of ash. The terraces looked like huge snowdrifts.

Upon reaching the wharf, I led my people to the first of our three merchantmen. When I went to step aboard, I had the strangest sensation, as if the vessel was not floating on water but was grounded on a brightly colored reef or sandbar that swayed gently beneath the beam!

In midair, I broke off my step, swinging my foot back onto the steady planks of the wharf. The thought streaked across my mind that we were trapped; the sea floor had risen, and all the ships were stranded. Almost as quickly, I realized what had really happened. The volcano-belched pebbles had reached the water and were so incredibly light—filled with air as they were—that they actually floated! And they were so plentiful that it looked as if the ship was surrounded by land. The unnatural movement made my stomach squirm. Bending down and scooping up a handful of pebbles, I saw that the water had stained the pebbles green and purple, which made them appear more solid than they really were. How bizarre.

Turning toward my gaping followers, I explained the phenomenon to them, letting the pebbles fall one by one as I did. "Step aboard as fast as you can and don't look at the pebbles," I told them. Then I demonstrated. Most of them followed my orders, but a few didn't, paying for their curiosity by bringing up their meager breakfast of bread and diluted wine. After that first ship was filled, mostly with women and children, I hopped onto the wharf and signaled for Miletus. We exchanged a few words, then he went aboard. He captained that first ship, bringing her out to the sea swells where he awaited other full-decked vessels to line up behind his.

When Phira's two other merchantmen and large-hulled fishing boats were loaded, I signaled for the first Cretan vessel to pull in. As my people began to board her, the deafening booms resumed. Our pace, which had been fast to begin with, picked up. There was no pushing and shoving, though. That swelled my pride in the Phirans; even the Cretans commented on my people's mettle in the face of such a calamity.

After each ship was loaded and had been rowed out to where Miletus waited, another hollowed-hull ship tied up at the wharf. We unloaded the wagons and carts, placing the goods and provisions aboard the Cretan ships. The commander of the squadron gave orders to his men while I gave orders to my people.

Every now and then during the back-breaking work, I looked up to see what kind of progress we were making. When twenty ships had lined up behind Miletus's, they all headed south for Crete. From the wharf, I could see their far-shining sails moving along the horizon.

All the Cretan merchantmen were full and we were loading jars onto a warship when the explosions reached a feverish pitch. The animals, the next to be boarded, were creating a tumult that was almost as earsplitting as the volcano. Farmers and herdsmen tried desperately to keep the beasts together, but it was impossible. Goats and sheep broke and ran, and donkeys kicked wildly. As we fought to get them aboard the last ships, the dumb animals were completely bewildered, having no idea, of course, that we were trying to take them to safety. All they knew was that we were pulling them onto some strange wooden surface that bobbed up and down and rocked from side to side. Many Phirans and Cretans had black-and-blue welts to show for that part of the rescue mission, and two of our farmers were badly gored by maddened oxen.

All of the large animals could be saved, but not all of the small. We boarded as many as we could; even the Dove was overloaded with a small flock of sheep. The creatures that could not fit stood milling around on the wharf and the adjoining shore. When it finally dawned on them that they were free they kicked up their heels and bolted, not realizing that their freedom meant almost certain death.

The Dove, with sheep encamped everywhere, was the last vessel to depart. Pitching and rolling, the boat slammed against the edge of the wharf as I helped the priestesses aboard. They had stayed with me to the end, blessing each passenger and sailor as the ships were rowed out. It was difficult finding room among the bleating passengers for those brave women, but we managed. Black rocks rained down around us, splashing water over the Dove and its live cargo. The air was thick and putrid.

I jumped onto the topside and shouted, "Row!" Just then, two distant voices caught my attention above the din. I turned around to see Taras and Deino streaking down the wharf, baying uproariously as they went. My heart told me to stop and go back for the mongrels, but, in their eagerness to get away, my rowers had propelled the Dove a good distance away from the wharf. Bang! A rock the size of a jug struck a ram next to me, caving in its dappled back. Swiftly, I gave the order to reverse oars. My crew was astonished. I lifted the limp body of the ram and threw it over the gunwale, saying to myself this spot is now for my canine companions.

Before stern touched wharf, Deino was aboard. But in his excitement, Taras misjudged his leap, and I had to pull the dog from the brine. His rump was stained purple, and he reeked of the strong-smelling water. Once again, I gave the order to row. Soon we were slapping over the breakers. Although it was not easy working on the crowded deck, soon we upped sails and headed for Crete. We all prayed to Diktynna, Protectress of Seafarers, for a safe passage.

The waters around Kalliste were filled with ships that day. The Dove found herself between the convoys from Enalus and Oia. When we passed by Metapontus, ships were still lined up there waiting to load. Sometime afterwards, I learned from Catreus that the last ship did not leave the port until late that night; there were many casualties due to deadly fumes, falling rocks, and collapsing buildings.

We were well into the Snow Month; the sailing was rough. There is no need to discuss how my people, landlubbers many of them, and their animals, landlubbers all of them, fared on that long day.

Far out at sea, far from death-dealing Kalliste, the Dove overtook Miletus and the others. The sun was hidden; indeed, we hadn't seen it since early in the morning. But it appeared suddenly at dusk, miraculously floating above the water and giving us an astonishing display. Usually when the sun sinks into the sea, its rays light up the clouds and the very ether itself, causing that grand fire that gladdens men's hearts. But on the day of our seaborne exodus, the sun selfishly withheld its rays, keeping them locked within. It looked like a glowing, blood-red ball hanging before a sheet of gray. Even when it was reduced to a shiny nick on the horizon, we could not take our eyes off it.

As we approached Crete, the wind was directly off our stern. Like the sun for most of the day, the moon and the stars were beclouded. The squadron commander took the lead from me, because he knew the Cretan shoreline so well. We smartly skirted Thwart-the-way.

Off the bow, the lights at Amnisos could barely be made out, but behind us, Kalliste, marked by its monstrous column of steam and white ash, lit the clouds as the sun, moon, and stars had not been able to.

How fickle the Goddess, Earth Mistress, Mother of Mountains. A year before the exodus, we people of Kalliste were like children, gay and carefree. Upon one of the most bountiful islands on earth, we lived the blest life. But we became wretched refugees the day we fled, pelted by rocks that came from the bowels of Kalliste. Standing on the decks of the ships, watching our motherland burn in the night, we could not help but wonder whether we would be homeless too. Early the next morning, we docked at Timbaki, the great port of Phaistos. When I leapt onto the pier, I shouted praise to Diktynna for allowing us safe passage. Rhadamanthys was standing there, and he and I embraced as if we hadn't seen each other in twenty years. Standing behind the prince was a legion of courtiers and citizens ready to help us unload and swiftly move us to our new homes. A few of the Phiran families had relatives in the city, so, of course, they were assigned to them. The remaining people from Phira-town were matched with other residents of Phaistos-town. And the Phiran farmers were matched with the Phaistosan farmers. The Phiran farmers and their families, possessions, and livestock were taken at once to farmsteads lying in the hinterland. I made sure each family from my town carried with it at least one month's worth of provisions. So enormous was the generosity of the Phaistosans, so great their readiness to open their homes, that not one Phiran child was separated from his parents.

After all the decks were cleared, the commander of the squadron bid us farewell. Those of my people who were still at the port, courtiers mostly, shouted their thanks to him and his men. I pledged my undying gratitude for the great service done the town of Phira. The commander graciously accepted our praise and complimented us for the way in which we handled ourselves during the hair-raising evacuation. "I have to set sail for the inland, now," said the commander.

"What? At this time of the year?" I asked in disbelief. "Surely this mission exposed you and your men to enough dangerous seas. Why must you go up there so soon? Thundering Goddess!"

"My lord, it is because the farsighted King Minos, our supreme commander, wants to make a show of force at this critical time. Good Prince Rhadamanthys could explain it much better than I, Sire."

Nodding, Rhadamanthys gave tongue to his thoughts. "Prince Idomeneus, the king wants to show our neighbors that things are well in the kingdom, that the evacuation of Kalliste has not weakened us in the slightest, that the Peace of Minos remains intact. You see, the news about your island has flown across The Deep Blue and no doubt the Achaeans have had wind of it. The way news, especially bad news about us, travels, I would be surprised if the Hittites or the Egyptians haven't received reports. But those peoples need not concern us. They have no navies, thus present no threat. But the Achaeans have navies, though not very good ones. They are close enough to warrant some concern. If the Achaeans felt that we were vulnerable—Minos believes, and I concur—they might attempt something bold. Well, you remember our discussion a while back."

"Yes, of course."

"Well, King Minos is sending about a third of the navy to cruise the coast along the inland. You know, to dampen the spirits of the barbarians if they were even dreaming of such a thing."

"Yes, I can see the wisdom in that. Until I heard your words, just now, my friend, I hadn't considered the impact of Kalliste's woes on the rest of the world."

"That's understandable, since you've been caught in that desperate situation at home," opined Rhadamanthys.

"At any rate," I said, shaking my head, "this show of navel force sends this captain and his courageous men over the windswept waves, again."

"Alas," said Rhadamanthys, shrugging his shoulders.

"So be it, my lords," the commander said. "When we return safely, we will all drink together and laugh about it at the Spring Festival!"

"Here is a stout-hearted man for you," I declared to all around us. "He and all the other captains and all their men and all the sailors who came before them are the reason why the Peace of Minos has lasted so long!" Everyone gave voice in agreement, crying "Yea!" I told the commander that I would be at the Spring Festival, too, and that I hoped I would be coming to it from Kalliste. I asked him and his men to be my guests at the festival, where I would put on a splendid feast, a small token of my gratitude for their help.

"My men and I would be most honored, Your Excellency," said the captain. "Now, I must depart. I bid a fond farewell to you, Prince Idomeneus, and to you, Prince Rhadamanthys. To all others, farewell! I pray your resettlement goes smoothly! Hail Minos!" Echoing the kingly acclamation, we saluted the commander and bade him Goddess-speed.

On our way up to Snow Crystal, Rhadamanthys and I had much to discuss, and so did Miletus and his counterpart, Rhadamanthys's chief yeoman. When we reached the base of the hill upon which the palace of Phaistos and Snow Crystal sat, that familiar palpitation began beneath my breast. I was surprised that feeling of excitement and high anticipation reappeared so quickly, considering the ordeal we had been through. But I welcomed it. Moving up the gentle slope, we stepped lightly on the perfectly shaped, limestone blocks composing the path leading up to the summer palace. On either side of the path stood gnarled cypresses. My eye jumped from tree to tree in the hopes of catching sight of my wood nymph. Presently the roofs of the shining palace came into view; upon them were people anxiously awaiting our arrival. When they saw us approaching, those retainers and servants scurried down and assembled in rows in the main court. On Rhadamanthys's command, his people stepped forward and began escorting mine to their suites. On the right, in a small portico, a lone figure stood motionless.

"Go ahead! We'll continue our talk over lunch," declared Rhadamanthys.

I said to Miletus, "Make sure everyone gets settled in. If you need me, I'll be —"

"Never you mind, Sire," said Miletus. "With all of this assistance, I'm sure there'll be no problems. I'll take care of everything." Good old Miletus.

I managed to keep my senses enough to actually walk instead of run to where she stood. I felt the eyes of my entire court on my back, but I don't think they saw me trembling all over. As I approached, Aphaea stepped from the shadows. I grabbed her hand, quickly leading her around to a small court, where no one could see us. Her lips were dewy. Lost to me now are the words we spoke. I remember only that at that sweet moment, the weight was lifted from me. It didn't matter that I was then a prince without a principality. It didn't matter that I was a sorry fugitive dependent upon the bread of a friend. All that mattered was that Aphaea and I were finally together. That was all.

By the time of lamplighting later that day, all my courtiers were settled into their rooms at Snow Crystal. Rhadamanthys and his people had left. With everything in order, I felt that I could disappear for awhile; I went to Aphaea's apartment at the main palace. We walked through the gardens, having each other's arms to keep us warm and the bright moon to light the way.

"What was it like those last days on Kalliste," Aphaea asked gently.

"It was horrible."

"Besides the great mountain spitting out steam and smoke, what else happened?" Like everyone else she was curious about the bizarre phenomena, but I didn't want to relive those terrible moments then. "Dearest, I'll tell you everything, in detail, later on. I'm just not in the mood right now to go into it all."

"Oh, I'm sorry, dear."

"That's all right. Let's talk about something else: our wedding."

"Our wedding, now?"

"Why not? Why should we wait anymore? There are no more obstacles in the way."

"True. But you and your people have just arrived; surely, we should wait until everyone's settled in."

"Yes, of course, you're right. Maybe we'll let a month or so go by, then hold a simple ceremony right here at Phaistos."

"That would be splendid! Do you think it would be all right with Princess Biadice and Prince Rhadamanthys?"

"Oh, I'm sure they'd be happy to have the wedding here. Biadice could conduct the "ceremony…it was supposed to have been my mother." Aphaea softly touched my hand. "Then after the wedding," I said, "we can go to Snow Crystal and stay until Kalliste can be reoccupied. It'll be our first home."

"Though it's not your palace at Phira," Aphaea said, "Snow Crystal is the next best thing."

Quite a few people in the palace saw me bring Aphaea back to her apartment that night. At that time of upheaval, we didn't worry about the ever-present gossips. If they had nothing else to occupy their thoughts, after all that had happened, then we truly felt sorry for them.

As I walked back to Snow Crystal that night, my mind was filled with images of my Aphaea. Night sounds drifted on the breeze and horse-fleet clouds sailed over the moon's heavenly face, blinking her radiant light on and off. How wonderful it was to be able to see that silver orb and not have her hidden by an unnatural veil. How pleasant it was to smell the fragrant air and not have fetid gas swirling through my nostrils. How delightful it was to feel the breeze on my face and not grind gritty ash between my teeth.

That day and the day before had seemed never-ending, so filled with sorrow were they. But that night, as I reached the stairs leading down to Snow Crystal, my spirits were flying high. I was amazed: in one short day I felt at home on famous Crete of the shadowy mountains.

FOURTEEN

A FEW DAYS LATER, Aphaea and I stood in the princess's brightly-frescoed throne room. "Of course, you two have my full blessing," said Biadice. "I hope your wedding lifts the spirits of everyone on Crete."

"Thank you, my lady," said Aphaea.

"Yes, thank you, Your Highness," I said. "Do you think we could have the wedding here at Phaistos?"

"By all means! It would be an honor for Rhadamanthys and me to host the celebration. If you'd like, I will conduct the ceremony, too."

"Yes, I was going to ask that next," I exclaimed. "When do you think the best time for this wedding would be?"

"Well, I shall have to consult the Great Goddess, Mistress of House, Hearth, and Love. It will take a little time for the answer, but I shall let you know as soon as I can."

"Excellent," I said.

Biadice turned to Aphaea and held her hands. "I'm going to miss you frightfully, my constant companion. But, at last, your countless prayers have been answered."

"Yes, when I first fell in love, it seemed my dream of marriage would never come true. Idomeneus was a prince—"

"And I still am," I asserted.

"Yes, of course, my love! You were a prince, and still are. I was a commoner and still am one. You lived on distant Kalliste, and I on Crete. And you were promised to a beautiful princess from your own island. All of those things were against us, and at times, I must admit, my faith in the Goddess's ability to remove those obstacles wavered. But, I never lost faith! I continued to honor Our Lady, under Princess Biadice's direction, above all else. And now look—before long we'll be man and wife. Surely, that bespeaks the workings of a passionate and attentive deity."

I was about to say that the man she was getting was a prince without a principality, and that, too, was the work of her deity, but with Biadice there I said nothing. Aphaea and I thanked the princess and left her throne room.

That morning, Miletus and I had planned to see how the resettlement of our people was progressing. We went first to the city of Phaistos to inspect the housing arrangements. We went without a loud-voiced herald to announce us, because we wanted to catch our citizens unaware, hoping to observe them in the most natural situations. When we entered a household, we insisted that the guests and hosts continue to do whatever they were doing and that they try to disregard our presence as much as possible.

In all the homes we visited, our hearts were warmed by the pictures of harmony we saw. In many instances, the Phiran family was holding court, so to speak, surrounded by the Cretan family. The principal speaker was usually the father of the Phiran family, who gravely told the tale of the awakening volcano on Kalliste. But his wife and children did not remain silent. Kallistean women and children silent? They were forever piping up with colorful details that the father had forgotten. The interruptions did not irritate the father, but instead gave him additional material to embellish upon. Hanging on each word, the members of the Cretan family were all agog.

As we went around, Miletus and I discovered that, in some dwellings, a Kallistean and his or her Cretan counterpart were discussing the plight of Kalliste. For example, two fathers might be found working in a storeroom having a somber discussion about the volcanic phenomena or the evacuation. In the kitchen, the two mothers might be observed reviewing certain parts of the story as they cooked. And out in the garden, the children might be seen interrupting their games to bring up a point that had been missed or one they wished to repeat. When we came upon those discussions, Miletus and I insisted that the participants not stop for our sake, and we made sure we stayed only for a few moments.

Our presence, mostly mine, altered the situation in one home, the home of Aphaea's parents. They were talking with their guest family: a baker, his wife, and their two small boys. Upon our arrival, the discussion stopped, and, of course, switched to my impending marriage to Aphaea. Her jovial father and her deep-waisted mother were overjoyed with the prospect of their daughter marrying a prince, even though that meant that their daughter and son-in-law would not live with them, as was the custom. They were elated by Aphaea's betrothal to me but not overawed. Ever since the sharp-eyed Biadice had selected Aphaea as one of her attendants, her parents had expected that something like that would happen; they were confident that Aphaea's unrivaled beauty would beguile a member of the royal family. Sharp-witted were my fiancée's parents, and Miletus and I enjoyed sipping wine with them and talking.

The following days, Miletus and I visited every abode in the hinterland where Phirans were housed. Using a wagon filled with supplies for our people, we drove to each village, hamlet, and farmstead. Sometimes big snow flakes fell on our heads and spread a thin blanket over our wagon, it being the start of the Snow Moon. Now and then a rabbit darted across the road, startling the horses and us.

One time, Miletus and I arrived at a farm when a Cretan was about to take his farmer-guest around his entire property. We accompanied the two, sharing the guest's wonderment upon seeing the wide fields and orchards. Most of Kalliste was taken up by Mount Kalliste, thus, our farmers were responsible for only small tracts of land.

Later, after a week or so of inspection, I was completely satisfied with the arrangements Rhadamanthys had made and with the condition of my people. The Cretan families received compensation from the palace, which helped defray the heavy burden of our presence.

Before we departed the island, I planned on paying Rhadamanthys back in precious metal for his outlay.

The citizens of Phira were happily established in their temporary homes and settled into their new routines. Soon we learned that the people from the other Kallistean towns had also been befriended by their Cretan hosts. From what we gathered, even things at Knossos were going well. That was the only place I had had my doubts about. Rhadamanthys had had his doubts, too. "You know, Idomeneus," he said to me one day, "I wouldn't have been surprised if Sarpedon had bitten the hand that fed him. In fact, I expected to hear that he had made all kinds of demands on Minos: better accommodations, more servants, more food."

"Well, I'm sure, just to avoid headaches, Minos and Catreus were exceedingly generous to Sarpedon."

"True. Nonetheless, I thought Sarpedon would be a thorn in their sides. Anyway, I'm glad I was wrong about all that."

"I, too. I just hope we remain wrong."

It was extremely important, we felt, that each Kallistean, commoner and noble alike, behave like a model guest. If our Cretan hosts could claim that we were the least troublesome visitors they ever had, it would be a great honor to us.

On the north coast of Crete, a diligent watch was kept by Kallistean refugees. On clear days, they could see our homeland easily, the huge cloud still hanging over it. They reported that, at night, the spectral light of the volcano competed with the heavenly bodies. And when the wind blew from the north, the sentinels could hear muffled explosions.

Soon after we evacuees arrived, Minos placed his navy—the two thirds of it not sent to the inland—strategically around Crete. So rough was the wintry sea that the warships did not venture far out. But small sturdy crafts manned by the coast guard did, cruising the waters between Crete and Kalliste.

It was there that they encountered the curious newborn isles. All white, perfectly flat, and only a few feet high, the isles wandered to and fro over the sea swells! The crew who spotted the first one tried to moor, wanting to examine the new land more closely. But when a sailor threw the anchor onto the isle, the anchor broke right through!

And the anchor rope sliced through the isle like a knife slicing goat cheese. The entire isle was made of compressed ash, similar to the pebbles that deceived me at our wharf the day we fled Kalliste; the ash created the illusion of solid land. The wind-driven sea had brought them, lighter-than-water as they were, all the way down to Crete.

Coming from our island as it did, we Kallisteans were relieved that the Cretans weren't bothered by the ash isles, which were harmless, for they broke up when they reached the beach. As offerings to the Earth Mistress, some of the material was gathered up and placed on altars; the priestesses claimed that She would be pleased to have some parts of Kalliste back. Personally, I wondered why the Goddess would want the volcano-vomited stones made of compressed ash and pebbles.

Laypeople found a more practical use for the odd clumps of ash, and, in my opinion, a better one. Somebody discovered that if good-size pieces were ground flat on one side they could be used as scrubbers. The ash scrubbers were finer-grained and longer-lasting than the sea sponges that divers risked their lives for. Famous for adopting the latest fashion in everything, the Cretans soon had a selection of the new items in their bath houses—large ones, small ones, and ones carved into different shapes.

Late one night, as the Snow Moon waned, I was strolling through Snow Crystal when I noticed that the lamps in the sages' study were lighted. Their cherished study and their suite had been left undisturbed by my courtiers' occupation of the tiny palace. I found the greybeards examining, under their magnifying lenses, some of the ash from the north shore. While they worked, they sampled some smooth wine, which I had brought them from Phira. I joined them. We decided to drop the talk about the Kallistean ash and simply enjoy ourselves.

"Here, here," bellowed Glaukus, raising his long-stemmed wine cup. "Dash down the winter. The best defense against its cruel cold is to mix plenty of wine with water and drink it down." And, so we did. I called for a harpist to come and play, and we accompanied his sweet music with some very sour singing. Nobody seemed to mind.

The potent wine loosened our tongues, and before long Glaukus began reciting a string of bawdy tales. Eventually the inevitable happened: the three cronies began teasing me about my forthcoming wedding. Well, that is, the wedding night. The more ribald they got, the more I had to laugh at those old goats; they still had plenty of fire left in them.

After I had been dragged over the coals, Ta-ch'ih tried to ask a serious question but was hooted down by the other two. Finally, they gave him the herald's staff, a lewdly shaped copper tube. "My most excellent Prince I-d-o-m-e-n-e-u-s," he said, slurring his speech more than usual.

"Y-e-e-e-e-s, revered seeker of wisdom?"

"Has the day been set for this most glorious event?" he asked, with a hiccup.

"Why, yes, good sage, it has. Princess Biadice of the beautiful cheeks has determined that the first day of spring would be most proper for our wedding."

"Ah, a perfect day indeed for a wedding, my lord! Most auspicious, most auspicious!"

"Please explain, O sage."

"It's the first of only two times in the whole year when day and night are equal."

"Well, yes, I know that." The others chuckled.

"Well, that equality of day and night, that equality of light and dark, makes a perfect time for the coming together of—"

"Excuse me?" needled Glaukus.

"Ahem, the coming together of man and woman," Ta-ch'ih continued, pretending he was above such humor. "You see, Your Grace, you stand for the masculine principle, its symbol being light. No one could better represent the feminine principle, which is symbolized by dark, than Aphaea of the dark tresses. The world is the way you see it because these principles are forever dancing together, trying to get into a harmonious state of balance. And for you two to get married on the day when this state of balance is achieved in the sky itself is truly propitious. Your marriage will be a perfect blend of the principles that rule the world."

"I'll drink to that," exclaimed Ananda.

"Here, here," shouted Glaukus.

All of us hoisted our cups and did not put them down again until they were drained. After a few moments, Glaukus said slyly, "But Ta-ch'ih, you have let our friend off much too easily. You must tell him how the feminine principle works its magic on the masculine principle."

"Oh no," I said, wincing in jest.

"Ah, yes! Thank you, old soothsayer, for reminding me," said Ta-ch'ih. "You see, Prince Idomeneus, the principle you represent is not only symbolized by light but also by strength and hardness, like un-yielding rock. The feminine principle is symbolized not only by dark-ness, but by softness, like yielding water. Little by little, Your Grace, the gentle water works its way over the hard rock, leaving signs of its watercourse way here and there. Eventually, the rock is carved with deep furrows, and the design of the water becomes clear to all!"

We laughed, refilled our cups, and drained them.

"Far be it from me," croaked Ananda, "to disagree with the wise Old Fool."

"Watch out," hooted Glaukus.

"But I must say," continued Ananda, "that a woman is not like water at all, but, rather, just the opposite! You see, her lap is like an altar, her pubis the soma press. And the lips of her vulva hold the fire within them."

"Well put," shouted Glaukus.

Ananda continued, "The man who knows this and offers liba-tions in the fire, obtains as great a world as the performer of the holi-est sacrifice, for he acquires the good deeds of the woman for himself. But the man who makes libations without knowing this has his good deeds acquired by the woman."

We rocked with laughter and filled our cups to overflowing. We talked and drank some more; it had been a long time since I had enjoyed myself so. Just before dawn, we stumbled back to our suites and collapsed.

FIFTEEN

MY PEOPLE'S easy acceptance of my forthcoming marriage surprised me, though I don't know why. After all, the notion that I had anything to do with the destruction on Kalliste had been dropped half a year earlier. Deep within my breast, I feared that my people still fanned an ember of the ill feeling that they had harbored against me and Aphaea. Happily, as the first day of spring approached, there was no sign that that feeling would be rekindled.

My surprise at the Phirans' reaction was coupled with my delight in seeing them and the Cretans work together, for they cooperated wonderfully on the arrangements for the wedding. It was then that I understood that the wedding was the very thing needed to cement the already flourishing friendship between the Phirans and Phaistosans. Even though the resettlement had gone well, there still seemed to be something missing or left undone that could unite the people further. The wedding of Aphaea, the Cretan, and I, the Kallistean, was to be that special something—a ceremony of unity.

The decision to hold the wedding at the main palace of Phaistos turned out to be a wise one. Not only were the courtiers from both

Snow Crystal and Phaistos going to be there, but, also, all of my people staying in Phaistos-town and the nearby farms and all of their
host families. Add to that the many folks, Kallistean, Cretan, and
foreign, who would be coming to the wedding from distant cities
and towns across the island, and the central court would be filled to
overflowing. Furthermore, at any wedding in our kingdom, there
were always those who showed up unexpectedly. They too were welcome. Accommodating the huge numbers was a big consideration,
especially for those preparing the food; they worked for one solid
week before the actual event.

As much as possible, I honored the age-old customs of Kalliste
concerning the groom's behavior before his wedding. One custom
required that the groom spend the night before the wedding day all
alone. He had to sleep in the house that was to become the couple's
new home. Well, Snow Crystal was completely full, what with my
court and the three sages. I could not tell them to go and find accommodations for one night while I acted like a hermit. Instead, as soon
as the sun set, I retired to my suite, taking my meal and spending my
evening in solitary meditation.

At last, the long-awaited day arrived. At dawn, Miletus came
tiptoeing to my door and knocked. I had just finished up in the
sunken bath that adjoined my bedroom. I told Miletus to enter. He
was decked out in his finest and wore a toothy smile. He carried the
magnificent headdress I was to wear, the same one my father, the
illustrious Cretheus, had worn when he took my mother, the lovely
Henithea, as his bride. Miletus carefully placed the headdress on a
low cedar table. "It's extraordinary, Your Grace," he declared, his
brown eyes sparkling.

"It truly is, old friend. My father wore it when he married my
mother. You know, there was a time when I wondered if I would
ever get to wear it."

A thin gold band, something like a diadem, formed the base of
the headdress. On top of the band sat a beehive-shaped dome, which
looked as if it were made of wicker, except that the twigs were cast in
pure gold. On the outside of the dome, colorful feathers were arranged in rows: the first composed of hawk feathers, the second of
partridge, the third of dove. As if growing out of the top of the dome,

three large peacock feathers swayed and shimmered, bowing backwards and down in an eloquent crescent.

Before donning the headdress, I put on the rest of my attire. Around my waist, I wrapped a white kilt with thin yellow bands around the bottom. Over the kilt, I pulled on a dark blue codpiece, and around my waist, I tied a narrow belt that matched the color of the codpiece. I wrapped white puttees around my legs, then put on some tan sandals.

Going through my jewelry box, with the advice of Miletus to guide me, I picked a pair of golden armlets I had inherited from my father. I'm not sure how or where my father came by them, but they were quite old, the workmanship impeccable. On each armlet, a large chrysanthemum was skillfully worked in the magic metal, which shone like the radiant sun itself. The flower had been cleverly placed over the seam formed by the two ends of the band.

Around my neck, I adjusted a necklace composed of alternating gold cockle shells and round beads of precious lapis lazuli. On the ring finger of my right hand, I placed the timeworn signet ring I used for only the most important documents. When he founded fair Phira, my great-great-grandfather, Cresus, had had that ring cast in the rarest and thus most precious of metals, iron. Since then, every Phiran prince had pressed the bezel of that ring into yielding clay or wax. The gold ring that I usually had suspended from a chain around my neck was a later copy of that antique.

Before Miletus placed the feathered headdress on me, I selected a dagger from my collection. I chose the grandest of them all: On either face of the bronze blade, a thin metal strip had been carefully inserted, and on each strip, a lively chase scene was wrought in gold and silver inlay. The scene showed exuberant lions chasing fleet-hooved stags, the beasts bounding over a landscape of many-shaded hills. The hilt and grip of the weapon were made of hardwood covered with gold plate. The grip was decorated with four-petaled flowers in filigree and within the fine wire outline of each petal was a layer of lapis lazuli. A pommel of warm-colored agate completed the handle.

After I slipped the dagger between my side and the belt, Miletus placed the sumptuous headdress upon my head. I adjusted it while gazing into a handheld mirror; I only had to squeeze the band a little to make it fit snugly. I thought of my father. The fit was so good that I did not have to recomb my hair, which reached all the way down to the middle of my back. I had not trimmed it in half a year and liked it that way.

Though I was never one to rival my courtiers in fancy attire, I enjoyed dressing luxuriously that morning. With that feathered crown upon my head I felt like a king. This is what Minos must feel like when he dons the bull-horned crown, I thought to myself. Miletus caught me daydreaming and smiled. "What do you think?" I asked.

"Sire, it is indeed fortunate that today is your wedding, for if you walked around Phaistos looking like that you would be ravaged by those Cretan beauties!"

"Go on, you old dog"

"No, no, Your Grace, really. You strike a figure in that outfit... like...well, like your honorable father on his wedding day."

"Thank you, my friend. There could be no better compliment than that."

When Miletus and I left the suite and walked out into the main court, we were greeted with "oohs" and "aahs." We returned the courtiers' praise, for they were all elegantly dressed and adorned. The combined gold and silver of everyone assembled brightened up an otherwise cloudy morning.

Miletus organized the processional line as soon as the sages ambled from their suite, noisily debating some point or other. They had taken special care to do some cleaning and preening; I felt greatly honored. Ananda had even washed his robe! He wore no jewelry, but he was clean and presentable. Ta-ch'ih wore a spotless white robe and hanging over the neckline was a green, disk-shaped pendant with a hole in the middle. Carved out of some hard stone that we men of Minos were not familiar with, the pendant was wonderfully cool and smooth to the touch. The stone resembled jasper but was much subtler and more beautiful; Ta-ch'ih said that in his homeland the stone was considered magical.

Though everybody shone that day, there was only one man who could truly compete with me in my wedding outfit, the old seeker of visions, Glaukus. His well-groomed silver beard and hair framed his royal features and ruddy complexion. He wore a wide headband, purple with sea dye. Behind the band, he had placed a row of freshly picked poppy bulbs. Covering his frail body and complementing the headband above, a robe of the deepest purple with delicate silver trim on the sleeves and hem flowed to the ground. When we spotted the old wizard, we all fell speechless.

By the time we started out from Snow Crystal for the palace at Phaistos, the sun was climbing the east sky. Leading the way, the musicians piped songs heralding our approach. Having refused my sedan chair, I walked behind the musicians. My soul was just too restless to allow me to sit and be carried; walking put me at ease. I had offered the oversized sedan to the sages, but they refused it, preferring to saunter along at the rear of the procession. The two bearers of the chair must have been elated. They had to carry it, empty as it was, however, because it would be needed later that day. Or so we thought.

As we walked along, a few raindrops fell on our heads. A little rain on one's wedding day was a good omen; it meant the Dove Goddess of Love and Fertility was shedding tears of joy for the couple. When we reached Rhadamanthys's palace, his people crowded the northwestern court and showered us with sweet-smelling blossoms, then fell into line behind us, joining in our happy song.

The procession advanced to the theater and the grand staircase. At the top of the stairs, handsome guards, their polished weapons slung at their sides, awaited us on either side of the large column separating the portals. Each guard hoisted a trumpet and sounded a blast to alert those within. From the columned gallery above the staircase, scores of palace residents showered us with more blossoms.

Colorful banners were waving from the western facade; on the roof, pennants fluttered in the breeze. The procession swelled as it wound its way through the northern sector of the palace, until finally halting at the door of Princess Biadice's suite.

With Miletus close on my heels shouting encouragement, I made my way to the head of the line. The throng pressed in around. I knocked twice, gently, then stood there shuffling my feet, anxiously awaiting the opening of the door. My heart was lodged in my throat, my body pounded all over. I waited and waited, but there was no sound from within, as if the room had been vacated.

Suddenly I knew what was happening.

"So, this is how it's going to be," I roared, turning toward the crowd with a broad smile. I proceeded to rattle the solid door with some heavy pounding. I heard giggles and squeals coming from inside, and thought I overheard some talking, too, but couldn't make out what was being said. I could only imagine.

The door creaked open, and Aphaea's sloe-eyed sister, Timandra, appeared, dressed in a saffron-colored robe. In front of her, she held a wonderfully wrought golden bowl and within, competing with the precious metal, was some glistening honey. My breast swelled at the sight of the bowl, and my people put up a cheer. On Kalliste, it was traditional to present the arriving groom with a bowl of honey. Aphaea must have learned of the custom from one of my people; even though I was on her native soil, she was trying to make me feel as if I were at home.

Aphaea's sister presented the honey, but just as I was about to scoop up a fingerful, she pulled the bowl away. A roar ran through the crowd, and I threw my head back in laughter. When she attempted the tease again, I gently grabbed her wrist so the bowl would stay put and calmly scooped up some honey. It tasted delicious. As tradition prescribed, I took a second fingerful, and with it made the sign of the double axe on the lintel of the door. At last it was time to see the bride and the other ladies. Timandra placed the honey bowl within the room and stepped outside. She was followed by Princess Biadice's two other dazzling handmaidens, who also wore the ceremonial orange robes. Large three-hooped earrings and shining necklaces and bracelets completed their striking costumes. The three ladies were admired by all, but, in truth, we could hardly wait for the next and last vision to appear.

Slowly, with imperceivable steps, Aphaea glided out into the light of day. She had never looked more ravishing. I was engulfed by a sea of people, but when I laid eyes on Aphaea, I saw no others. Though I was spellbound by her beauty, I was a little surprised by the way Aphaea was wearing her hair. She was well-known for her long dark luxuriant tresses, but on our wedding day they were curled up and piled high on her head. Though her hairstyle surprised me, I loved it. To accent her hair, Aphaea wore a gold foil diadem embossed with rose-like disks. Solid gold, flower-headed pins pierced the diadem, anchoring it into Aphaea's thick black curls. Pure white lilies, freshly cut and dewy, sprang up from behind the diadem.

Below Aphaea's delicate ears, large gilt earrings flashed brightly: hoops, cunningly decorated with four-petaled flowers, similar to those on the grip of my dagger. Suspended from her graceful neck was a token of my love, the bee pendant I had given her on the beach at Matala. The sparkle of the jewelry was matched by that in Aphaea's eyes, and the joy in them made me fall in love with her all over again.

Over her shoulders, Aphaea wore a jacket of material so sheer that it looked as if it had been spun by a spider. Underneath the jacket, an open bodice blouse with lace sleeves accented her heavenly form. Dyed slightly different shades of royal blue, the jacket and blouse looked lovely together. A broad white skirt with royal blue and crimson trim on the flounces, tied at her waspish waist by a golden tasseled cord, completed Aphaea's wedding outfit.

As we walked in the procession, it was hard for Aphaea and me to keep our eyes off each other. Before we knew it, we arrived at the second-story reception hall west of the central court. There, dressed in their regal best, Rhadamanthys and Biadice were waiting to greet us and begin the sacred rites. Naturally, not everyone could fit into the hall; many people remained outside in the corridor or below on the stairway. However, all of my courtiers, about half of Rhadamanthys's, all of Aphaea's relatives, and some others, including the three sages, managed to squeeze in, though a few had to crane their necks around columns to witness the event.

Biadice did a splendid job of presiding over the ceremony. At the end, big tears welled up in her doe eyes for, though she was truly happy for her loyal attendant, she was sad to lose Aphaea. I, for one, could not blame the princess for that. After we exchanged our vows and received the Goddess's blessing, the grand hall was rocked by shouts and cheers. Aphaea and I embraced and kissed amid a crush of well-wishers. Then it was down to the central court for wine, food, and dancing.

The entire court had been transformed into an enormous roofless banquet hall. On the four sides, large tables had been lined up end to end. The tables groaned under the weight of food: steaming meats, the first fresh fish of the season, crabs, lobsters, octopus, squid, snails, cuttlefish, stuffed birds, freshly baked bread, kettles of fava soup, artichokes, figs, nuts, candied fruits, honey cakes, and, of course, towering pitchers of rosy wine. Though I had supplied the food and drink with my riches, the Phirans and our Cretan hosts had worked long and hard preparing it all. Their labor was their wedding gift to Aphaea and me, and we were greatly honored by the effort and love they put into it.

In the northwestern corner of the court, the step-like structure that leapers made use of was converted into a platform by the addition of wooden struts and planks. Aphaea and I sat enthroned upon it, accompanied by Rhadamanthys and Biadice.

"Oh, what a blest day this is! The two fairest flowers in the kingdom joined together. Let's all drink to our good fortune at having this pair among us!" A lovely toast by a wobbly Rib-Addi, who, having been into the wine already had sidled up to the platform.

Over the din, I shouted, "Thank you, Rib-Addi, thank you! How are things, my friend?"

He thought hard for a moment, scratching his head and grimacing, then replied, "You know, Sire, I can't think of one bad thing at the capital to report! Prince Sarpedon and his people are as good as gold. There are no scandals. No juicy gossip. I tell you, my lord, it's very boring. Ah, well, enjoy yourselves, be merry…ah, but don't drink too much," he said with a crooked grin and a wink of the eye.

All day long, the combined musicians of Phira and Phaistos played lovely music. At this end or that of the court, male and female voices, thick with winey triumph, would break into song. The musicians got an accompaniment whether they wanted one or not. Prince Thoas and Oenopion and their wives led off the dancing, and before long, they had a throng of dancers circling around the tables. Though many people had journeyed from afar, that did not hinder their high-stepping movements. Soon Aphaea and I joined them, dancing until our legs shook from weariness.

With so many little details to worry about, it is said that one never enjoys one's own wedding. Ha! I can say in all honesty that I had the time of my life at mine. Aphaea did too. And why not, for there we were eating and drinking and dancing and singing with our closest family and friends.

At one point in the afternoon, while I was pouring some wine for Aphaea and me, Ta-ch'ih came up to the platform.

"You see, my lord and my lady," he said merrily, "The Web holds wonderful times and amazing goings-on. 'Tis best not to ponder things too much, but to savor them as they flow by."

"Right you are, Ta-ch'ih," I exclaimed, raising my cup. "I must admit, though, for a while, I thought that the thread we were on held nothing but sorrow. But just look at this," I said, extending a hand toward the tumultuous celebration going on in front of us. "Surely, my friend, your web is most complex and subtle!"

"Pardon, Your Grace, it is not 'my web,' but 'The Web,' and everything and everybody on it fits perfectly into place."

"Well, this day is a fine example of that, Ta-ch'ih. Just look over yonder at Ananda. He's actually being polite to those two priests"

Ta-ch'ih turned to see his old friend engaged in a loud but peaceful debate with a pair of priests who had been among those who had had Ananda expelled from Knossos.

"Ah, will wonders never cease?" mused Ta-ch'ih, shaking his head.

"You know better than to ask that question, my friend," I chortled, "for The Web is composed of an endless number of wonders. Just look to center court for another!"

There, surrounded by a half-dozen violet-wreathed maidens, danced the man of dreams, Glaukus. "Danced" may be an exaggeration, because the old sage was simply turning round and round, arms outstretched, head thrown back, in the middle of his admirers. He was in ecstasy.

When we stopped laughing, Ta-ch'ih said to me, "Watch, now, Sire, tomorrow we'll hear all about this dream he had.'" Ta-ch'ih mimicked Glaukus's crackly voice as best he could: "And there I was, floating on a cloud, surrounded by these worshiping fairies, their hair scented with wild flowers."

We both laughed until we almost split.

A little while later, some former wrestling opponents of mine—both Cretan and Kallistean—came over to the platform to offer their congratulations. After introducing them to Aphaea, I said, "I was sorry to miss the festivals last summer and fall. By-the-Goddess, I don't even know who won the wrestling wreaths."

"You had to ask, Prince Idomeneus," growled a burly Cretan smithy named Tectamus. The others hung their heads, pouting like scourged dogs.

"Why? What happened?

"Ugh, that Athenian! He defeated every man he faced," said Tectamus.

"Oh, I see—well, at any rate, he will be leaving the island after he and his teammates have competed in this year's Spring Festival."

"I'm not so sure, Sire," cautioned Tectamus.

"What? King Minos must let them go when they have leapt in four bull-leaping contests—that's by his own decree almost thirty years ago. The bull-leaping contest at the upcoming Spring Festival will be number four for these Athenians."

"Around the capital, word has it that the king will never release these barbarians," Tectamus said. "As you know, Sire, no one has ever performed in four bull-leaping contests and survived. These Athenians have a good chance. King Minos wants to keep them on, however, like some kind of sideshow, until they're all dead."

"How many have escaped death so far?"

"All, your grace. Well, all except the two who died at last year's Spring Festival. Prince Idomeneus, these barbarians have become virtual heroes on this island." The other wrestlers bobbed their heads in agreement. I sneaked a peek down the table at Rhadamanthys who had been listening in on our conversation; he raised his eyebrows and nodded, confirming the smithy's statement.

"Ah, Sire, we were wondering," continued Tectamus, "if you, yourself, would consider tackling Theseus." He threw a sideway glance at Aphaea who pretended she had not heard. "We realize that at last year's Spring Festival your bout with Theseus did not take place because of his injured leg. Clearly, he has recovered. Maybe too well. We know that you have had no time for wrestling with all that has gone on. But Sire, we would be more than willing to help you train for a bout with this Athenian."

I was astounded. Cretan wrestlers in their prime did not aid past or future opponents in any way. Wrestling—like boxing, running, and spear throwing—was not a team sport. Those athletes who stood before me in the central court, independent souls, every one, were banding together to topple Theseus, which indicated to me just how much they wanted him defeated by a man of Minos.

"We could start workouts right away—humph!" A sharp elbow to the ribs by a muscular muleteer named Oxylus stopped Tectamus in midsentence. The smithy appeared to be thankful for the blow. He turned to Aphaea with great big puppy dog eyes. Poor Tectamus, who had obviously been elected spokesman and was now hating it, tried to cover his indiscretion. "I mean, uh…I mean, your lordship, not right away, but…say, when the moon is dark? At least, it would give you a little practice before this year's Spring Festival… uh, not that Your Excellency needs much, I'm sure."

"What a generous offer! I thank you, Tectamus. I thank all of you. It's very tempting. You say that Prince Theseus has not lost a single bout?"

"Sire, he's not even been thrown more than once in any one bout," Oxylus blurted out.

"Hhhmm. Well…I'll do it! But not at the Spring Festival. Remember that the bull-leaping happens *before* the wrestling; Theseus could be injured again or even killed. Let's set up a bout for two or three weeks hence. And with sparring partners such as yourselves, I know we will be victorious. Come to Snow Crystal in seven days and there we'll begin training."

"Excellent, Prince Idomeneus, excellent," exclaimed Tectamus. Though the din of celebration was great, the wrestlers put up a shout that drew attention from all four corners of the court.

"Now, all of you, go eat and drink to your heart's content…let's not have any of you injured on the dance floor, though," I teased. "I'll need sound sparring partners for my training."

The merrymaking continued well into the evening, and only a handful of people left when the lamps were lit. Every now and then, Aphaea and I had to sit down and catch our breath, but we were soon up again dancing.

Before too long, it was time for the newlyweds to depart. It was I who decided this, in part because I was feeling the wine. But what really convinced me to leave was seeing Aphaea steal a few yawns: Thundering Goddess, she and I had more revelry in store for us that night!

It was difficult tearing ourselves away from the celebration in the central court, which showed no signs of ending. Every time we made for the grand staircase, we were pulled into "just one more dance." Finally, we resisted any more pleas to stay on and, bidding a warm thanks and goodbye to all, we scurried down the grand staircase, then up the smaller adjacent one, reaching the northwestern court in a flash. There we expected to find my sedan chair manned by the two bearers, ready to carry us home. The chair was there, all right, but it lay on the ground unattended, while the two bearers were admiring a much greater vehicle.

"Hail, Prince Idomeneus! Hail, Princess Aphaea! This chariot is a wedding gift from the Lord of the Seas, King Minos. And I am to be your driver as long as you stay in this fair land." Thus proclaimed Evanus, the good-natured fellow who had driven me last spring when I was on Crete.

"Idomeneus!" exclaimed Aphaea.

"What a noble gift this is, Evanus," I stammered. "Can it be true?"

"Indeed, your lordship. And these strong, prize-winning horses are part of the gift." It was the Hittite team that had pulled the vehicle on my previous visit—the steeds were decked out with jingling silver tassels and loud braying, bronze bells.

"Well, my old companion, let's be off!" I exclaimed to Evanus. After helping Aphaea into the chariot, I bade the sedan chair bearers to return to the festivities and drink their fill. As fast as one can lay feet to ground, they were gone; Aphaea's and my wedding day had been an easy one for them. Evanus squeezed to one side of the chariot and Aphaea and I snuggled on the other side. Along the way, the three of us laughed and exchanged small talk. By the king's order, Evanus had arrived at dusk and stayed out of view. I assumed that it was really Catreus who had given the order and had masterminded the whole thing. The ever-resourceful driver did manage to slip into the kitchen, filling his paunch with drink and vittles.

The moon was waning, bathing the glorious Messara in a milky, magical light. The night air was filled with metallic clicks and groans, mewing and wailing, the mating serenades of thousands of frogs in the ponds and pastures. When we reached Snow Crystal, I jumped down and helped Aphaea out of our magnificent wedding gift. We bade good night to Evanus, then shuffled through the moonlit corridors to my suite, where I led my bride to our first, albeit temporary, bedroom.

When we opened the door, we were greeted by the shouts of a dozen women. There was Aphaea's mother, her grandmother, her aunts, her cousins, and my priestesses from Phira; they had all been at the wedding feast but had slipped out early to be at Snow Crystal when we arrived.

After greeting us, they turned and tore apart the bed. Then they started to make it. The making of the wedding bed was a long-time Cretan custom. As the bed was being made, each layer of sheets and blankets was accompanied by a silly song about marital bliss or domestic life or childbearing. Each sheet and blanket was strewn with a particular kind of flower and sprinkled with holy water blessed by the priestesses. Before retiring that night, we had to shake our bed out thoroughly.

When the bed was made and consecrated, two babies, a boy and a girl—up well past their bedtimes—were tenderly passed from one woman to the next. As the babies were passed, the women leaned over the newly made bed, pretending that they were going to drop the babies. With each feint, a chorus of earsplitting screeches and squeals filled the room. Finally—and we didn't know who determined it—one infant was dropped on its bum, bouncing harmlessly on the bed.

Our first child was to be a girl! I was elated. Unlike the Achaeans, who wish for sons and more sons so that they can be made into fearless warriors, we people of Minos cherished both daughters and sons.

After the baby girl was picked up, the women resumed passing the fledglings around, and, soon, the boy was dropped. Then the girl again.

"Whoa," Aphaea and I exclaimed in one breath. Whether that caused the women to stop we didn't know, but they did. We thanked them as they filed from the room, bidding us good night.

After lying on our wedding bed for a while, talking and laughing and holding each other tightly, I slowly unfastened Aphaea's maiden's belt. Of the many times we had burned in one another's arms, that time filled us with the highest pleasure.

Asleep were the peaks and watercourses of the mountains, the headlands and ravines, before fair Aphaea and I put aside our lovemaking. Then sweet sleep took hold, falling heavily upon us, for our bodies and limbs were tired after such a day: our first as man and wife, prince and princess.

SIXTEEN

THE TIME AFTER our wedding was filled with wonderful golden moments. Aphaea's and my dream of being together—not in stolen moments, but all the time—had come true. Before we knew it, spirit-lifting spring was upon the land, and we took advantage of it by strolling through the rich-soiled Messara or going farther afield in our majestic chariot. When back at Snow Crystal, we found people very genial; the entire court had accepted my bride with open arms. It was a warming sight to see Aphaea chatting with a retainer or two or with old Miletus.

When not at my side, Aphaea was usually with the two Phiran priestesses. For the sake of all three of them, I was happy to see how fast they had become friends, a healthy friendship for the entire court and the town of Phira. Soon Aphaea would have to take over not only her royal duties but her sacred ones as well. By marrying me, she had become the Princess of Phira, and she was destined to become, after initiation into the Mysteries, its foremost priestess. It was very important that Aphaea and the young priestesses were close, for my wife had much to learn from them, and, if they really liked her for herself, they could ease her passage from laywoman to priestess, skipping the normal acolyte stage. Of course, having been a handmaiden to wise Biadice, my bright-eyed Aphaea had picked up much: She knew all the ceremonies thoroughly, she knew bits and pieces of the lengthy hymns, and she knew how omens were read. Aphaea needed that advantage, because the task that lay before her was formidable indeed. Going from baker's daughter to priestess-princess of a well-known town like Phira was a big leap; in fact, no one could recall it ever having been done before.

In those halcyon days at Phaistos, I thought less and less about windswept Kalliste. With my loving new wife, the relaxed atmosphere at Snow Crystal, the companionship of Rhadamanthys and the three sages, and the blessing of spring, I found thoughts about home drifting toward the back of my mind. Besides, I was deeply involved with my conditioning and sparring sessions as the wrestlers helped me prepare for my bout with Theseus.

The fleet-hooved horses from Syria sped me from Snow Crystal to Knossos on the first day of the Sailing Moon month. I searched out Rib-Addi, finding him at one of his favorite wine shops in the capital. He assured me that everything was ready for my wrestling match with Theseus the next day. Rib-Addi promised me that a good crowd was expected. He had seen to all the promotional aspects of the match, while Catreus had arranged for the event to be held in the palaestra. I was relieved to hear it. I would have been undone if I had had to deal with a snag in the match at such a late moment. After a light meal, I retired, wondering if I could fall asleep with all the thoughts I had. But as soon as my head touched the bed, I remembered nothing.

The next morning, a number of friends from the capital, including Rib-Addi, came to the royal apartments and escorted me to the palaestra. The colonnades that enclosed the large square practice field were glutted with anxious spectators, including a host of gamblers. It was clear from the turnout that the talkative Rib-Addi had spread the word as only he could, though I knew that Prince Theseus's sudden popularity had much to do with the showing.

The gamblers were divided: about three-quarters favored me, one-quarter the fleet-footed Theseus. Under usual circumstances, the split would not have been surprising, for I was undefeated in the capital and had a healthy following. In that particular match, though, one would have expected even more for me, since my opponent had only recently displayed his wrestling skills in our land. For keen-eyed gamblers to lay wagers on someone they had not seen wrestle in many bouts over the years, Theseus must truly have captured the Knossosans's imagination.

On the grassy field of the palaestra, I began to limber up with a few stretching exercises. There was no sign of the foreign hero nor his comrades. The wily Theseus kept me waiting longer than anyone I had ever wrestled, and some of my crew began muttering about how he was afraid to come out. I knew better. Finally, the referee sent a boy to discover what was keeping the barbarians, but before the boy could reach the exit, the Athenians appeared.

As he walked through the colonnade, I noticed that Theseus did not limp. But when he crossed the field, he started to favor his left leg. I said to myself that the first thing I'll do is test that leg.

As he approached, Theseus glowered at me, but I did not respond in kind, calmly continuing my exercises as if I were only too happy to have had the extra time to warm up. Two could play that game.

The referee called us both to the middle of the field. A former wrestler, the referee was one of the most respected in all of Crete. In his two careers, as a wrestler and as a sure-eyed referee, he had seen a thousand falls and ten thousand holds. Theseus and I coolly exchanged greetings.

A procession of ladies-in-waiting entered from the east. In the middle, walking in splendor, came the priestess who would sanctify our match, the lovely Ariadne. She was Princess of Knossos, the daughter of Pasiphae and Minos. The ladies formed a ring around the referee, Theseus, and me. Standing before us, the deep-waisted princess began the ceremony by reciting an ode to Britomartis, Lady of Strife. Then she assigned us our elements: Theseus stood for rock; I stood for water. I could tell that the Athenian was happy with the element Ariadne gave him; he did not understand it was Goddess-directed.

Throughout the ceremony, Theseus could not keep his eyes off the young priestess-princess. And who could blame him? Ariadne, decked out in her ceremonial finest, was a splendid vision. She had a long, flounced skirt, dyed in expensive purple and orange, and a tight-fitting blouse that tilted her ample breasts upward. Two magnificent golden bracelets in the shape of writhing serpents adorned her arms, and a high tiara topped with a carved leopard crowned her noble head. Being a woman, and in her prime, Ariadne read Theseus's mind; here and there blotches of red flushed her milky neck. Since bull-leapers were sworn to abstinence during training and the festival, I surmised that Theseus's blood boiled over. And even if the Athenian had foresworn the abstinence oath or had been with a woman after one of the festivals had ended, Ariadne was enough to distract him that day. All the better for me, I thought, that the brash foreigner had a distraction of his own, for since coming to Crete, I certainly had had my share.

The princess concluded the ceremony with a prayer to the Goddess, asking Her to choose the proper element for the particular place and time. Then, forming themselves in a line, the ladies escorted Ariadne to a special platform under the western colonnade.

At last the match was in the hands of the referee. He gathered us in so that we could hear his instructions. He stated the rules slowly and carefully for Theseus's ears, but the Athenian acted bored and kept glancing over at the western colonnade.

We were ready to begin our best-out-of-five-falls match. Theseus and I stepped back, anxiously awaiting the referee's word to begin. In turn, he awaited Ariadne's signal, which she swiftly gave by placing the back of her hand to her forehead.

"Wrestle," the referee shouted.

Theseus and I began to circle each other cautiously. My body was loose and strong, but I knew that my mind, sheathed in doubts about the recent past as it was, was not clear.

Soon we made contact, thrusting out our grasping hands and slapping away our opponent's. After several feints, Theseus came at me as if he were going to tackle me chest-high, but swiftly dropped his arms down around my waist and rammed his head into my ribs. With one arm around me, he searched with his free hand for my arms. If he had found one, I would have been the first to hit the earth. I reacted in the blink of an eye, jamming the palm of my hand under Theseus's chin and extending my arm fully. As if he were shot from a bow, Theseus flew away, reeling. After he stopped, his right leg—not his left—buckled, and his knee touched the grass. The crowd screamed and hooted! It was premature, though, because Theseus clearly had slipped, and the referee ruled correctly that no toss had taken place. Groans and shouts of disappointment echoed throughout the palaestra.

Theseus's face burned, for he was a man not to be embarrassed or treated lightly by spectators. I knew he would try to take his anger out on the person who caused him to lose face.

When he jumped up, I was there to meet him. We tangled at once. I went for a shoulderlock, which he skillfully slipped. We grappled for some time, each trying to gain leverage for a toss. Though wiry, Theseus was possessed of bronze-like strength, and I had real trouble moving him around.

With great effort, Theseus managed to twist my arm behind my back and push upward: It was a hold meant not for throwing but for punishing. And it worked. I knew I had to do something—and quickly. I took the risk of dropping my right knee until it almost touched the ground, which forced Theseus over my shoulder, though he held onto my arm for dear life. Like a big hook, my free arm shot between his legs, catching his right thigh. I squatted down, coiled like a serpent, then stood straight up, carrying Theseus aloft on my shoulder. But he still had the painful grip on my arm. With a loud grunt, I heaved Theseus headfirst down to the ground, and, as he went, he did a complete somersault, breaking his grip on my arm.

The uproar around the field was deafening! The referee declared what everybody already knew: the first fall of the match. From the corner of my eye, I caught Rib-Addi and members of my crew breaking into a spontaneous jig.

Slowly, Theseus pushed himself up onto his knees, then rose to his feet. He glanced over at the western colonnade sheepishly. Hmm...I thought, today this man is fighting for more than the sport of it. Theseus looked over to his teammates who were all joined hand-in-hand, shouting encouragement. When he turned to begin round two, his face was lobster red and filled with wrath. For a moment, I wondered if he had ever been thrown before. I remembered not liking the first time I was thrown in front of a crowd, but I know it had not put me into such a ferment. I had had to wipe the dirt from my mouth many times over the years, but never more than twice in any match. I was still undefeated.

The referee commanded us to go to again, and Theseus attacked like a savage lion with flaming eyes. Though surprised by the boldness of his lunge, I managed to dodge it. At the first opportunity, we locked arms and fought for position. By the way my opponent fought, I knew he wanted to make short work of the round.

All of a sudden, without warning, Theseus's right fist shot up and rapped me in the ear. The referee rushed in, broke us up, and warned Theseus against punching. My head rang like a bell. The din created by the spectators did not help, but they were upset by the flagrant violation.

We resumed wrestling. Before long I was in a vulnerable position. My stomach and chest were draped over Theseus's back, and my right arm hung over his shoulder. Grunting and straining, Theseus tugged on my arm with both hands in hopes of pulling me over. But the crook of my left arm was smack against his forehead, preventing him from exerting all of his force. We were frozen in that predicament, both of us refusing to give an inch.

By and by, the sure-footed Athenian managed to take two small steps forward, carrying me with him. Then, though it almost decapitated him, Theseus broke my headlock by tucking his chin violently into his chest and flipping me forward and down. The next thing I knew I was flying like a sparrow. My outstretched hands broke my fall, and, somehow, I had the presence of mind to do a few rolls.

A long moan, sprinkled with a few gasps, wove its way through the colonnades. But there was cheering from the Athenian maidens and youths and the gamblers who went with Theseus.

Looking up from the turf, I found the referee and my opponent looming over me; I expected to see the first, not the second. Our rules had evidently slipped Theseus's mind; maybe he was carried away by the action, for the referee was trying to prevent him from pouncing on me. Not about to linger on the ground prostrate before him, I swiftly scrambled to my feet.

Though it was a cool morning, dirt and grass began to cling to our sweating bodies. At the start of round three, Theseus came in with a menacing grin on his smug face. At one fell swoop I was on him, trying to return the favor by flipping him the same way he had flipped me. Unfortunately, he squirmed away.

Theseus and I stealthily circled the wrestling ground. All at once, we went for each other. In that split moment, Theseus ducked down and grabbed at one of my legs. Reacting just in time, I vaulted over his hunched back, landing with both feet firmly planted. Quickly, I reached around and put a shoulderlock on him. The hold was unblessed, for it was not as secure as it should have been; when I tried to adjust it, the sly Athenian wriggled free.

Next, I tried for a headlock, but my quick-witted opponent dipped under it, reversed himself, and came up with a beautiful armlock. His left hand held my right wrist aloft. His right arm entwined my right arm. As a snake reaches back to bite its own tail, Theseus's right hand clutched the back of his left wrist, creating tremendous leverage. The cunning barbarian placed his right leg behind mine. I was helpless. He had me. Every time I tried to grab him with my free hand, he tightened the hold and racking pain forced me to abandon my counterattack. In all my years wrestling, I had never seen such a hold.

For the first time in the match, Theseus spoke. Breathless and in haste, he said, "I should twist this damn arm off, Idomeneus, to repay you for that first fall! No man—especially a man of Minos—treats me that way!"

Though I was in no position to bandy words with him, I shot back, "May crows feast upon your carcass!"

Words during a match were forbidden; if they saw two athletes talking, the spectators might think the match was fixed. When the referee started in to caution us, Theseus's glowering stare stopped him in his tracks. Done using his mouth, the Athenian began to put all his strength into the hold in an attempt to break my arm. He wanted to end the match right then and there, avoiding more rounds, but I had a different idea. I allowed myself to fall backward over his extended right leg, taking the fall, but saving my arm.

Much to the dismay of my supporters, I took my sweet time getting up. They had rarely seen me in such an unfavorable position, down two to one. I spotted Rib-Addi wringing his hands like some old crone, and I would have laughed at the sight of him if I were not in such pain: My arm was throbbing from elbow to wrist. As I got up, I flexed the arm as much as I could, which was not very much. I tried not to wince, for Theseus stood opposite me gloating, a smirk on his face. He put on a show for Princess Ariadne, bowing to accept some imaginary accolade from her.

He would pay for this cocksure display I vowed to myself.

After assuring the referee that I could continue, I squared off with Theseus for a fourth time. With one more toss, the Athenian would defeat a well-respected prince of Minos. And he had already conquered the bull of Minos.

When Theseus came in, I assumed he would try to make short work of the round and the match by taking advantage of my sore arm. But as we closed, he landed a hammer-like punch to my head. Amid hoots and catcalls, the referee warned Theseus that he would forfeit a throw if he struck me one more time. The Athenian's face told me that the warning meant nothing to him, for he was trying to inflict as much punishment on me as he could, regardless of the rules. When he looked at me, I don't believe he saw the man who came to talk with him that night during the festival, but rather some wounded beast. Though he has the upper hand, I thought, if he allows his heart to rule him now, it will be his downfall.

Using his right fist like a boxer's, Theseus swung at me, splitting the air. I ducked it cleanly, and, as the force of his punch spun him around, I quickly grabbed his arm, stepped in, and pulled him up onto my shoulder. Holding him up there like a bundle of firewood, I did two full turns, then flung him - back first - down to the palaestra field.

Flowers, hats, and cushions sailed onto the field, accompanied with screams of delight. The throw had taken the edge off of the Athenian's confidence and enthusiasm. He got up very slowly, rubbing the small of his back. We were dead even.

Knowing that it was the last round we began very cautiously, feinting and probing in the same manner we had at the beginning of the match. After a while we began to grapple. Soon we both had each other in a bear hug, which neither of us could exploit. Nor did we dare break off for fear of being tossed as we retreated. Finally, the referee had to come in to separate us. We had had no clinches in the first four rounds because the action had been fast and furious. Only two clinches were allowed in any one round; if it happened a third time the round was declared a tie. If the fifth round were a tie, then the match would be declared a draw. Nobody—not I, nor Theseus, nor the referee, nor the spectators—wanted that.

Theseus and I went at it again. We seized each other in headlocks. Like two oxen fettered and locked horn-to-horn, we pulled and tugged each other around the field. It was more a matter of will and stamina than anything else. We were both exhausted, but would not give in.

Reluctantly, the referee began to approach us in order to break up the long deadlock. Loud shouts of protestations rained down from all corners of the palaestra. Regardless, he did his job, slapping both Theseus and me on the shoulder and ordering us to break. Then he reminded us of what neither one of us needed reminding.

Soon we were on each other for a third time in the round, both determined to quickly upend the other. Helped by the profuse sweat, we both slipped some very complicated holds.

Theseus started to work on my right arm again. He was so intent on it that I was able to catch him in a deadly necklock. The hold was not against our rules, but rarely was one able to slip it over an opponent. As I applied more and more pressure, Theseus kept on backing away. I, in turn, kept yanking him closer to me. The palaestra was in bedlam. I twisted Theseus's red face so that his eyes met mine. Gasping deeply, I shouted, "Well, my strutting woodcock, it's time to get your neck wrung! Do you think the princess will shed a tear for you?"

Not able to answer with words, Theseus's fiery eyes told me that I would have to carry out my boast if I wanted to win the match; he was not going down while there was still a breath of life in him. The foreigner placed his honor so high that he would rather die than lie defeated at my feet and endure the jeers of the Cretans.

Suddenly the referee was alongside us, shouting at me to stop my taunts. But I was done talking. The wild and screeching crowd drove me on, as I tried every possible way to land the prince without taking his life. Even in his desperate state, Theseus managed to ward off every trip, flip, and toss I tried. From the corner of my eye, I saw the referee signal to me indicating that if I did not settle it at once—one way or the other—he would be forced to step in. In a series of thunderflashes, visions raced through my dizzy mind: I saw Glaukus and

Ta-ch'ih prophesying about the Achaeans; I saw Rhadamanthys telling me to break the barbarian's neck; I saw the roles reversed and
Theseus not hesitating to break mine.

Cries of alarm from all directions shook me out of my stupor and
told me that the referee was approaching. I looked down into Theseus's
distorted face and said, "Your courage has saved you, Theseus. I will
not take your life for the sake of my glory. Go forth and live!"

My words were followed by the roar of the crowd, as a heavy
hand fell on my shoulder and another fell on Theseus's. The referee
proclaimed the draw, and I released my death grip, propping up my
slumping opponent. Soon we were mobbed. I gave Theseus over to
his comrades. A number of them looked at me in amazement, but one
of them, the golden-haired Eriboea, gazed at me in admiration.

With a youth bolstering him under each arm, Theseus made his
way out of the palaestra, his legs constantly buckling under him.
Surrounded by my crew and other well-wishers, I lost sight of him.
Nobody asked me the obvious question. They all knew me. And they
knew I was fortunate to have salvaged a draw, being down two to one
to the unyielding barbarian.

By-the-Goddess, they were right.

SEVENTEEN

RIGHT BEFORE the Spring Festival, we received the reports we had prayed so long to hear, reports from those patient, hawkeyed sentinels along the north shore. They claimed that the monstrous cloud hanging above Kalliste was shrinking, becoming less dense, and that the spiraling column, which engorged the cloud with poisonous vapor, had changed. From the crown of the volcano, only irregular puffs of steam rose skyward. Another result of the slowdown of activity on Kalliste was that the white ash isles drifting by Cretan shores were becoming rare, and when one was spotted and examined, it was found to be composed of small cindery pebbles.

To my mind, the best news of all was that the volcano had gone mute; on Crete's north shore, no one heard the muffled explosions anymore. Even the fishermen whose keels were then carving the fish-breeding sea heard not a whimper from Kalliste.

As they continued to flow in, the reports, each one better than the last, lifted the spirits of my people. Like I, they had settled into the easy life on Crete. When they heard the happy news about Kalliste, home-returning thoughts leapt to the forefront of their minds, as they did mine. We felt that if the good reports continued, we might be able to reoccupy our cherished island within a month or two. Spread across spacious Crete, we refugees talked of nothing else except the day when we could set foot on our blest soil again.

About five days before the Festival, Catreus invited me up to the north shore to go boar hunting. Besides allowing me some time with my friend, the hunting trip was a perfect opportunity to see for myself the present condition of Kalliste. Evanus and I set out for the forest north of the city of Palaikastro early in the morning when the Eagle still twinkled in the east. We arrived the next day, and by early afternoon, we were tracking our prey with Catreus and his people. Though there were plenty of tracks and droppings, we did not even get a glimpse of a boar, and so it went for the next two days. "Let's go back to the capital and sleep in warm beds," said Catreus on the third night. We all agreed.

As we approached Knossos, we saw more lights than usual flickering within and around the palace. Soon we heard a din, men fighting. We raced to the northern gate. There we encountered a palace guard covered with blood, staggering toward us. "What's going on?" demanded Catreus. The man reeled, pointed toward the royal apartments and cried, "Sire, Sarpedon is trying to capture the palace and slay the king." Then he collapsed.

"What!" exclaimed Catreus.

"I can't believe this," I shouted.

We sprinted through the Labyrinth heading for the king's suite, jumping over the bodies of men who lay dead or dying. As we neared the king's bedroom, we were joined by people from the four quarters of the palace; having learned what was going on, servants, clerks, and priests grabbed whatever was about—shovels, knives, even sacred axes—and came to the aid of their king.

Sarpedon's men were battering the door to the king's bedroom with a great oak table just as we arrived. Surprised by the attack from the rear, they turned and fought like wild dogs. A bloody battle ensued with many falling on both sides.

"Traitor!" I shouted at a high-ranking officer in the Royal Guard who came at me. He swung at my head with his sword, but I ran him through.

Next, I cut down one of Sarpedon's body guards, but I was after bigger prey.

Sarpedon was pinned up against the door, dueling one of the members of our hunting party, whom he dispatched with a deadly thrust to the neck.

"He's mine!" I screamed and started to hack my way through the rebels. And I would have gotten him, too, had not Catreus swooped down on Sarpedon like some high-soaring hawk. They dueled in close quarters, when suddenly Catreus surprised Sarpedon with a slashing upper cut. Sarpedon reeled backwards and fell against the door clutching his blood-covered private parts in his hands. So enraged was the king's son that he savagely un-strung Sarpedon's limbs with his sword and began to hack the body. "Enough," I shouted, grabbing Catreus's arm, "You'll offend the Goddess." Catreus turned and looked at me with wild eyes. "Look over there." I pointed to the captain of the Royal Guard hemmed in on all sides by warlike courtiers. "Let's spare the cap-tain till we get the whole story."

"Aye," growled Catreus.

All of the other rebels had fallen as the traitorous captain tried to ward off two axe-wielding priests. "Stop! Don't kill him! There's time enough for that," shouted Catreus. "I want to interrogate the dog." We subdued the badly wounded man and bound him. Then we turned to survey a hallway glutted with bloodied bodies. Wounded courtiers were treated where they lay.

Before long, a solitary figure appeared at the end of the hallway: Minos. He had escaped from his bedroom by secret passage. His eyes were dark with hate.

"How many of you were involved?" Catreus said, grabbing the captain by the hair. The man slumped to the ground and blood ran from his mouth.

"How many?" Catreus cried, yanking and twisting the hair.

"About three score," groaned the captain.

"Sarpedon put you up to this?"

"Aye."

"Did you really think you could do it...with three score?"

"I gave most of the guard off tonight. We only had to get through

Minos's body guard. And we did. We would have succeeded if you…
you…" He fell over face first, dead.

"How on earth did Sarpedon expect to get away with such a
thing," Catreus asked more of himself than anyone present.

"Why, he was mad, utterly mad, Catreus," I averred. "He probably believed in his twisted mind that all he had to do was capture
the palace, and all of us in the kingdom would follow him like
frightened sheep."

"Well, Crete would have run red with blood before he brought
his scepter to Knossos, that's for certain," Catreus declared.

"What claws at my heart is how close he came. I mean, my
Goddess, assaulting the king's very bedroom! If it weren't for the lion-
hearted people of the Labyrinth and you, Catreus, Sarpedon would
be sitting on the throne right now"

"Britomartis forbid," uttered more than one of those around us.

"I wonder how Sarpedon got to the captain of the guard and the
others," I said. "Must have been a huge bribe."

"Colossal," Catreus agreed. "The bastard probably promised
them each a colony or a city on Crete. That scum! We plucked
Sarpedon from danger on Kalliste. Housed him. Fed him. Treated
him with honor. And all the time, the traitor was plotting to over-
throw the palace." One couldn't blame Catreus for wanting to chop
up Sarpedon's body and throw it to the dogs. Catreus shook his head
in disgust. He mused to himself, then said, pensively, "I wonder if we
should destroy the remainder of Sarpedon's court."

"Surely, there must have been only a handful of courtiers roped
into this by Sarpedon," I declared. "I know the courtiers of
Metapontus. They're good people." I was thinking of Crito and
Himera. "Besides, how could a large number have been involved
and kept such a secret so well?"

"Nevertheless, Idomeneus, a thorough investigation must be carried out," demurred Catreus.

"But, of course, Catreus, I agree. All I'm saying is that I'll be
surprised if other conspirators are uncovered."

"Sire," one of Catreus's advisors piped-up, "shouldn't the investigation be extended to the other courts of Kalliste now being
housed on Crete?"

The hallway was hushed. I quickly ended the silence. "All of these precautions are necessary, I suppose, though I feel certain that none of the other princes from my island had anything to do with this mutiny."

Everyone quickly voiced his agreement: What else could they do with me there? Everyone except King Minos. Lost in thought, he stood there, staring at the design on the floor, though I'm sure his eyes did not see. It was unsettling.

Early the next morning, Minos canceled the Spring Festival. The year before, an earthquake on the island had not been enough of a reason to call off the festival, but an insurrection within the Labyrinth itself was. The king must have recalled the earlier rebellion in our history, believing that the volcano on Kalliste had affected Sarpedon and his henchmen the same way the earthquakes on Crete had affected the rebels two centuries ago.

Sarpedon must have thought that things were different, and that he could usurp the throne of the most powerful king on earth. Why? What had he seen that had led him to believe he could succeed? Did he really believe that we would follow him after he slew our king or that he would have enough power to force us to comply? Or, finding himself within easy striking distance of Minos, did Sarpedon simply hatch the plot, convince the guards it would work, then, without thinking of his follow-up actions, make his move? Those questions and others like them buzzed around Crete, and, I suppose, all around the empire. Besides questions, the failed coup effected actions to be taken. The members of the royal guard who were slain—both heroes and traitors—were swiftly replaced by experienced warriors; the number of guards increased threefold. A burly and courageous Kushite was placed in charge. The king's personal bodyguards were replaced; their number increased sixfold. The bold attack on his life had shaken Minos badly; he was determined it would never happen again.

Loaded with sailors expecting to celebrate their homecoming at the festival, the warships that returned from cruising the waters around the inland were sent back at once. Other ships were sent up the Cyclades, while still others were dispatched for the coasts of Syria and Anatolia. The overseas presence of Minos's navy would discourage any pirate raid or barbarian invasion. The lesson learned from the troubles two-hundred years before was that the Peace of Minos, though well founded, could be shaken. The best way to maintain peace was to discourage those who questioned its strength.

There were people on Crete who questioned the king's concern about attacks from abroad. Those people—many of them Knossosans—worried more about new Sarpedons rearing their ugly heads. A thorough inquisition took place. For more than a month, scores of people, Kallistean and Cretan alike, were questioned.

The inquisition turned up no additional conspirators. Even at the Little Palace, none of Sarpedon's courtiers seemed to have known that their ruler was plotting the hideous crime. I was especially happy to learn that the good name of Crito, the yeoman, remained untarnished. As I had guessed, the only guilty ones were the men at Minos's door that fateful night, Sarpedon and his henchmen. The mad prince had kept his strike force to an elite group, a brotherhood of scorpions. What audacious and desperate men were they.

The bitter news of the coup cast a pall of darkness over the light atmosphere that had prevailed ever since we Kallisteans had arrived. It was hard to believe that the grand celebration marking Aphaea's and my wedding had taken place less than one month before. At the wedding, Cretan host and Kallistean guest had danced hand in hand and had drunk from the same cup. But after the attempt on the king's life, we Kallisteans felt cold eyes upon us whenever we passed one of our hosts. The Cretans knew full well that the attempted coup was the twisted idea of only one of our people. Yet, our kindly hosts were wounded deeply by the fact that even one of us could be moved to such an outrage, especially after the incredible hospitality shown to us pitiful refugees. No wonder we Kallisteans were looked at with sideways glances.

If the promising reports from our sentinels on the north shore had not continued, the bonds between guests and hosts might have snapped. We Kallisteans prayed for the day when we would hear that the giant had gone back to sleep, and we could return home. The Cretans prayed too.

In the middle of the Sheep Shearing Moon, when the sun chases the Goat from the morning sky, that day came. The volcano belched steam and ash no more; the sky above Kalliste was clear for the first time in almost six months.

Though the celebration of the Goddess's and Her consort's return had been canceled at Knossos, the cessation of the volcano's activity moved the people on Crete—both native and refugee—to rejoice. Across the island, people laughed, and cares were lifted. In the Labyrinth though, celebrations marking the event were banned, but Minos did not try to stop the drinking and dancing that sprang up everywhere else. I felt relieved to see the Cretans and Kallisteans together in spirit once more; though, in fact, the reason for their togetherness was the hope that soon they would be parting company.

Within days of the news that all was calm on my homeland, I was summoned to the Labyrinth. When I arrived, I was taken to Catreus's study. As always, he was behind his huge desk, but I seemed to catch him daydreaming, not studying the thick scrolls lying before him. He jumped up, and we exchanged warm greetings.

"We called you here," Catreus confided, "because we believe now is the time to send an expedition to Kalliste. We need a full report on the damage to each town and the city of Metapontus. We need estimates as to how long it would take to clear the fields of ash so that plowing could begin.

"The volcano is silent now, but there may be great risks involved in setting foot on a land so smitten by the Goddess. We need an expedition leader with a stout heart and a quick mind. The king and his advisors believe—and I concur—that you, Idomeneus, should be the leader. Had Sarpedon not gone mad, the scales would have fallen in his favor; he was older than you, had a longer reign, and ruled Metapontus, a city prized by the Goddess. But now—"

"Yes, I see. When can I depart?"

""Wait, my friend, not so fast, not so fast," Catreus laughed at my eagerness. "We believe it's important to tell the four other princes of Kalliste of our selection and to do it with the utmost protocol. After all, we want no ill feelings between you and the others. Do you foresee any problems here?"

I thought for a moment about Oenopion, Thoas, and the others, then said with a shrug, "No. These men know me well. They have trust in my judgment and know that while my party surveys their towns, things will remain undisturbed."

"Fine, that's what we thought. Well, then, we'll send high-level deputies to the other princes informing them of our decision. I would think you could depart say…at the new moon? Or just as soon as you can organize your party. We can supply you with whatever you need in the way of ships, sailors, troops, provisions. Simply name it."

"I think it would be best to keep the party as small as possible," I said, "taking only the bare necessities. I wonder if some strong Cretan lumber wouldn't be useful? We might have to throw up a few temporary shelters."

"Sounds wise. We here in the capital feel that you should begin at Metapontus, survey the city completely, then go on to the towns in whatever order you like. We want the most thorough report possible."

"Yes, of course. I have no idea how long the work might take, though I guess a month's worth of provisions would do."

"Better take a month and a half's worth," Catreus cautioned. Over wine, he and I worked out the details of the expedition. I decided to take two dozen of my Phiran men, two squads of Cretan soldiers, and two master builders from Knossos. The Dove plus two of my trading vessels from Phira would carry the expeditionary party to Kalliste, stopping en route at Amnisos to take on provisions that the capital was supplying. Water was a big consideration. The Grain Harvest Moon was sometimes dry; if the ash had clogged the cisterns and blocked the streams, we would be in trouble. Catreus recommended filling the boats with as many water jars as they could carry.

When the planning was finished, Catreus and I discussed the terrifying night of the mutiny and its results. He told me that personally he had hated to see the Spring Festival canceled and had argued against it. His father, however, was so distraught that once the priests suggested canceling the festival, there was no changing the king's mind. That made for some disappointed people around the kingdom, admitted Catreus, especially the athletes and entertainers.

"What does that mean for Theseus and his teammates?" I asked.

"Why are you so interested in that barbarian?" Catreus said with a sideward glance.

"Just curious, that's all."

"Well, my father wants the Athenians to leap one more time, at the Summer Festival. Then, the survivors will be sent back to Attica."

"I'd like to see Theseus before I depart. Is that possible?"

"Only if you send someone for me if you and Theseus start wrestling again.

"Ha! I can just see us going at it in his quarters, overturning chairs and tables and the like."

"Oh, he's no longer in the athletes' quarters."

"Where is he?"

"He was separated from his friends and placed under guard at the guest house south of the palace."

"Why?"

"My father's orders. After the insurrection by Sarpedon and his fellow traitors, father thought this Athenian prince might get a wild idea about an insurrection of his own.

I thought to myself, what is happening to our world when the most powerful king is jumpy over an imprisoned barbarian?

Before leaving his study, I thanked Catreus again for my sumptuous wedding gift. I promised that when Kalliste was fully resettled, I would have the team and chariot shipped over, so, when Catreus came to visit me, we could go hunting in splendor. The idea warmed his heart. As he showed me out, he said that he would come to the port when my expedition stopped to pick up provisions. We said goodbye until then.

After leaving the study, I cut across the wide central court and proceeded toward the guest house. I walked through the southern corridor and descended the doglegged stairs on the south slope. My head was filled with the scent of pine, but I didn't pause to admire the stand of ancient trees, for my thoughts were on the expedition.

When I reached the aqueduct that crossed the broad-whirling Vlychias Stream, a quick movement among the trees caught my eye. I spied not a wood nymph but a being of flesh and blood. Though she appeared like a blur, I recognized light-footed Princess Ariadne. What was she doing on the south slope, weaving swiftly through the pines, unattended and unheralded? Handmaidens always surrounded that much-admired lady whenever she took so much as a step outside her royal suite. Strange. Oh well, I said to myself, maybe she's just sneaking a few moments of peace and quiet away from the commotion of the court. My mind returned to my forthcoming voyage to Kalliste.

I crossed the aqueduct and arrived at the guest house. Catreus had told me that the guest house was heavily guarded, but as I walked up the front steps and across the small porch, I was not challenged. I was all alone. As I raised my fist to knock on the door, a voice from behind called out, "Ah, your lordship, Prince Idomeneus, may I help you?"

Turning around, I discovered a guard who looked more surprised than I. It was as if he had seen a ghost.

"Why, yes. I'd like to see the Athenian who is housed here. I have Prince Catreus's permission. The Athenian is here, isn't he?"

"Yes, Sire, he is. In fact, the barbarian is the only one here. The real guests were moved up to the palace."

"Guard…uh, what's your name?"

"Pelius."

"Pelius, I understood that Theseus was being carefully watched. Where are the other guards? Who's in charge?"

Glistening sweat beaded the man's brow. He coughed once to clear his throat. "I am, Sire. I gave the men a short break in the woods. You know, my lord, for a little sip, to relax a bit. It's good for morale. Gets awfully quiet down here. I was just going to whistle for the men when you came up, Sire."

I didn't like the smell of it. "I suggest you do it right after you unbolt this door and let me in," I said brusquely.

Darting to my side, the guard slipped the bolt and kicked open the door as fast as he could; his shrill whistle echoed in the porch outside as I stepped into the room. A disheveled Theseus jumped from his bed. Looking into his dark eyes, I suddenly had the veil removed from mine. It was all perfectly clear. No words were needed to answer the riddle: Ariadne sneaking through the woods, the strange behavior of the guard, the barbarian's appearance in the middle of the day. Theseus's eyes told all. I recalled the day we had wrestled and how he had stared covetously at the princess. As I stood in the guest house, I knew—as well as I knew anything—that the barbarian prince and the Cretan princess were carrying on a secret and dangerous love affair only a stone's throw from the palace. Right under Minos's nose, thanks to the assistance of the officer in charge of the guard.

Theseus greeted me coolly; it was clear that he knew that I knew, "And to what do I owe this honor, Prince Idomeneus," he said dryly.

"I had business at the palace, so I thought I would drop in and see how you were faring."

"Well, you can see for yourself," he declared, theatrically extending his hand and directing it around the lavishly appointed room. "I'm being treated royally. I'm the royal prisoner!" I raised my eyebrows but held my tongue. I knew he had more to say.

"I mean, here I am, living in splendor, the guest of a king. Who could ask for more?"

I was not about to be goaded into a sharp exchange with him, for my mind was too busy reviewing the riddle I had just solved and considering its consequences. I kept an even keel. "Do you get to see your friends at all," I asked. "Are you allowed to visit them?"

"No, never."

"You must miss them—you all seemed so close."

"We are. Or we were, that is. But of course, we Achaeans are too dangerous when we're together. By the way, you and your people call us by this name, lumping all of the peoples from different cities into one group: Achaeans. But we don't use this name. We refer to ourselves by our cities and by our provinces. In our case, we are people of Athens, of the province of Attica. Anyway, Minos is afraid that I might incite those delicate maidens and youths to riot. We might jump those sword-carrying guards and take over the palace."

Just like in the palaestra during our wrestling match, there was no taming a wild boar like Theseus. I let him rail on. I was baiting him and would not be distracted. When his bristles laid down, I asked, "Well, does anyone come and visit you here. Or am I your first guest?"

Like two red hot coals, his eyes tried to burn through me. I withstood the heat and waited. He spoke at last. "I'm not allowed visitors."

"Then I'm the first."

"You're the first...given permission to see me, yes."

"Hhhmmm...must get lonely."

"Yes, it does." There was a pause. "How boorish of me," Theseus exclaimed, trying to sound like a Cretan courtier, but failing.

"What?"

"Why, I forgot to congratulate you on your marriage, Prince Idomeneus." He paused. "If things had been different, I might well have attended."

"And you would have been welcome, Prince Theseus."

"Thank you. I've heard there were some obstacles in the way of your marriage—like Prince Sarpedon for one. Anyway, the obstacles were overcome, and I'm happy for both you and your beloved." He paused, thinking for a moment. "When a man finds the woman he loves," he opined, "difficulties—no matter how great or in what form—should not be allowed to keep them apart. He who causes such difficulties between lovers incurs the wrath of the Goddess."

Like that day in the palaestra, once again Theseus and I were at a standoff. But in the guest house, I knew that I alone was my real opponent not Theseus. I battled with myself on whether to expose the politically volatile love affair I had uncovered. On the one hand, exposing the affair would surely mean taking the life of the Achaean, a life that I had spared in the palaestra, for I knew that if King Minos learned of the liaison between his eldest daughter and the hated foreigner, he would surely have Theseus's head. What would befall lovely Ariadne, I had no idea. On the other hand, if I said nothing, my silence could jeopardize the royal household. How might the forceful Achaean sway the princess? What might he persuade her to do for him? Already he had had her win over the guard, bribing him, no doubt. As I spoke, these questions whirled through my mind. "The Goddess, you say?"

"Why, yes…Immortal Aphrodite, the beguiling daughter of Zeus," Theseus exclaimed. "Hers is the realm of love, and whoever interferes with Her plans, whether he be god or man, is harshly punished."

A warmongering man, Theseus was not very skilled in the game of words; slick speech with countless veils of meaning is the courtier's stock in trade. Be that as it may, the Athenian's awkward allusion touched my heart, and the more he talked the less I felt like exposing his affair with Ariadne. "We believe," I said, "the Great Mother in Her manifestation as Dove Goddess of Love and Fertility is responsible for the love between man and woman."

"So I'm told. Don't you people also believe that this Goddess rules over the moon, mountains, earth, harvest, wildlife, the Underworld—everything?"

"Well, not everything, Theseus. The Great Goddess rules much of the earth, such as the mountains and the wild animals that roam it. You mentioned the Underworld; yes, She rules our Elysian Fields. Also, She steers the course of love, as I said. There are, however, other deities that we pray to for guidance and support. A huge part of our world, as you know, is the open sea, and our sailors and fishermen look to Diktynna, who controls the waves. During a hunt or in times of battle, we pray to Britomartis, Lady of Strife. Every morning, we salute the Young God, Consort of the Great Mother Goddess, He who pulls the sun across the sky."

"We know him as golden Apollo," Theseus demurred, "and He's certainly not an immature consort of a goddess. He is the son of Almighty Zeus and lovely Leto, and each day He drives his magnificent chariot across the sky."

"And Leto gave birth to Apollo on the sun-splashed island of Asterie," I said.

"So, you know quite a bit about our Gods, eh?"

"No, not really. It's just that Asterie is now one of my ports of call, and I've tried to learn something about it, even its legends. Isn't there a palm tree there sacred to your Goddess Leto?"

"Yes, it's the tree Leto leaned upon while giving birth to Apollo and his sister Artemis."

"With the help of Eileithyia.'"

"Why, yes, Idomeneus, of course! Didn't you know that we 'barbarians' pay homage to Eileithyia, Goddess of Childbirth, too? And we also sacrifice to Gaea, who seems very similar to your Mother Goddess in Her aspect as Earth Mistress. We Athenians see many Gods and Goddesses revealing Themselves all the time in many forms. Take Zeus, the cloudgatherer, for example. From high Olympus, the Holy Father comes down in any number of forms or guises: a snow-white bull, a wide-winged eagle, a downy swan, a flame of fire, a shower of gold—actually in any form He wishes. After all, He is Zeus!"

"And quite an amorous God He is, as I understand it."

"Undeniably. He can be whatever He chooses and can make love to whomever He chooses. A true king of the cosmos!"

"Let me ask you something, Prince Theseus, for I have wondered about it for some time."

"You'd be better off asking one of our priests; but go on, I'll answer if I can."

"Well, you people have many deities—as you yourself have just said—and most are either gods or goddesses, though some are half mortal and half immortal. What I would like to know is why your most powerful deities— the ones that you pray to most—are gods, not goddesses?"

"Why? Because they are! Just look around you, Prince Idomeneus. The most powerful forces, the most powerful elements in the cosmos all reveal their 'godlike' nature to man: the four winds, the thunderflash, the roaring sea, and the sun, which can wither the earth and dry up men's blood. And what about man-killing war? It's clear to anyone with eyes that the hand of a god, not a goddess, is behind each of these."

"Let's say it's clear to some."

"Well, what do you expect?" exclaimed Theseus. "Here of Crete, and on the other islands, priestesses rule. It doesn't hurt their position to interpret these forces and elements as goddess-directed."

"I could make the same charge against your priests. It doesn't hurt their position to interpret the thunderflash as the holy weapon of a god." That stopped Theseus in his tracks. For a few moments he considered my words in silence. I was silent, too, for it was the first time I had ever said such words, and I wanted to consider their meaning.

"I don't know if my people," Theseus said at last, "and your people will ever see eye-to-eye on this question of religion. Or any other question for that matter. You people are so different. You men of Minos are so isolated from all the other tribes under the Four Pillars."

"Isolated? How can you say that? Our warships and merchant-men have ventured farther and for longer than yours have. We have colonies all around The Deep Blue."

"Agreed," Theseus broke in. "Sure, it's true that, due to trade, you come into contact with different peoples. But you men of Minos don't live on the same soil with these peoples, as we Athenians do. The sea swells are convenient walls, protecting you from the many tribes and their armies that wander over our homeland, the inland—as you call it. And, also from those tribes and armies who maraud across Anatolia and Syria. There are savages out there, Prince Idomeneus, who wouldn't know the prow of a ship from its stern. To you they pose no threat, for they are far away and cannot burn your towns and steal and rape and enslave your wives and daughters.

"Where I come from, though, we must build great walls, walls of stone, to keep the marauders from our doors. We Athenians must always be on guard, always have our soldiers ready, and always sleep with our swords close at hand. Blood-streaked Ares, God of War, never gives us a moment's rest because if it is not hungry savages, it is an army from another inland city that comes to plague us.

"I would laugh if it weren't so pitiful," Theseus went on. "Here on Crete, a minor prince tries to usurp the throne—clumsily, I might add—and everybody is shocked. The people go around all moon-eyed, asking each other, 'How could this happen? Why? What could have poisoned Sarpedon's mind?' Unbelievable! That sort of thing goes on all the time where we live and, in the Near East, my friend. I bet if you took all the cities in all the lands beyond your Deep Blue, you'd find at least one coup a day. That's the way of the world, I tell you…except in your part of it, which has been mercifully spared.

"Your islanders and your Cretan cousins think that life is all honey and flowers, music and dance. Well, hear this: Where your fine ships bump the land and can go no farther, out there, life is not so sweet. Out there, Almighty Zeus, brandishing His rapid-fire thunderflash, keeps things from falling back into Chaos. Wisely, the Father keeps a rein on His arrow-loving son, Ares. Though it's a loose rein, indeed! Out there, Gaea, with buds of flowers in Her hair, is honored, to be sure. But She walks one step behind Zeus and Poseidon, and Apollo and Ares. Gods like these are not led by sweetness and soft ways."

"Prince Theseus, I've never been beyond the limits of our empire. But from what I've heard from those who have, I know that the picture you paint is true. And I'm sorry it is, because if the din of your spears beating on your shields was ever silenced, even for a brief time, you would learn that life on this bountiful earth can be warm, can be joyous, like a soft loving woman."

"You say this, Prince Idomeneus, even after what this 'bountiful earth' did to your home and loved ones on towering Kalliste," said Theseus wryly.

I was stumped for a moment. "Because one island turns against the people who live on it," I haltingly replied, "it does not follow that all the earth is the enemy of man. Our Lady was clearly angered with us, and She displayed that anger in the most horrible ways imaginable. To this day, I don't know why She was so angry, and I'll continue to ponder that. But, Praise-the-Goddess, the dark days have passed—as all things must—and, lo and behold, I will be returning to my island. Shortly, I'll be leading a small expeditionary party that will assess the damage on Kalliste. So, you see, Prince Theseus, at the threshold of the Mother Goddess's throne room are two jars to be distributed: one of evil, the other of good."

"Well, I'm pleased to hear that at least someone is returning home."

I caught Theseus's meaning. "I am sorry that Sarpedon's attempted coup and Mino's resultant cancellation of the Spring Festival," I declared, "have blocked your departure for home. I've heard that now you'll be kept here until this year's Summer Festival."

"Aye," Theseus said with a scowl.

"Well, since you're here, let us reach into the Goddess's jar of good. What I mean is, I would like to wrestle you again; this time in the central court during the Summer Festival. If all goes well on Kalliste, I'll come back to Crete this summer. What do you think?"

"A rematch! I wouldn't mind that, since our last match was declared a draw. You know, Prince Idomeneus, I haven't forgotten that I owe my life to your restraint. Thank Zeus, I was wrestling a man of Minos then." We both chuckled.

Then Theseus cocked his head and stared at me as only he could. He said in measured words, "Now, I hope to be indebted to your restraint once again."

I knew exactly what he meant. My mind raced over all the possible things that could happen if I kept Ariadne and Theseus's secret. Nagging questions about those things remained unanswered, but if I exposed the affair there was no question as to what would become of the bold prince whom I had come to respect.

"Your secret is safe with me," I said. As I spoke, I half-expected to see the spectre of my father once more. The only form before me, however, was Theseus's, breathing a sigh of relief, a thin smile creeping across his handsome face. "But allow me to suggest," I added, "that you two be more cautious from now on, or I won't be the only one who knows." His smile folded inward. He pursed his lips and nodded in grave agreement.

Once again, the warrior prince from the inland and I parted not as enemies, but as uneasy friends. Because of the dangerous secret I knew and the pledge I had made to keep it, the Athenian and I were closer than ever.

At the time, I believed that shielding the affair between Theseus and Ariadne was the honorable thing to do. Later on, I would twice curse their love.

EIGHTEEN

I RETURNED to Phaistos, and in ten days time, we were ready to sail for Kalliste. On the morning we were to depart, the sun was a brilliant crimson, looking like the fiery mouth of a kiln. Set against an azure sky, the sun looked redder yet. As the Young God hoisted it higher and higher, its color changed first to orange then to yellow. Even if you turned away and gazed at the limitless sky, you could still see the sun pulsating before your eyes.

The red sun was an auspicious sign. It could mean only one thing: the glorious resurrection of my island home. Just to make certain, I conferred with the two priestesses, who agreed with my augury, though I had no training in the art.

The sun, or rather the meaning we read into it, made me rejoice, for my mind had been divided. At first, I thought I could not wait another moment to set foot on soaring Kalliste. I wished to be transported there immediately, magically, thus having no need for seafaring. Just close my eyes and "poof," I'd be standing in Phira! That thought burned in my mind day and night, never dimming, not only because I longed for my home, but because I wanted to forget the things that had happened on Crete: Sarpedon's foul plot to usurp the throne and the reactions it caused toward all of us Kallisteans, and the affair between Theseus and Ariadne that I had accidentally uncovered and had sworn to keep secret. How good it would feel to be far away from all the charges, bad feelings, and intrigues.

But there was something that tugged my mind in the opposite direction. Something that countered the feeling of relief in leaving Crete: the separation from my wife. The mere thought of it so soon after the wedding filled my heart with sadness, dampening the excitement I felt for the adventure ahead. Thank-the-Goddess, Aphaea saw how my mind was being torn; she was very understanding. Throughout the long days of preparation, she tried to make things easier by constantly encouraging me, saying that the sooner my party explored Kalliste and made its report to the king, the sooner we Kallisteans, and she, could return to our homes. Aphaea already considered Phira her home, though she had yet to see it.

Not once did she mention the dangers involved in my mission, though during a few brief and unguarded moments, I spied some fear behind her bright eyes. The volcano had gone to sleep, I told her, and the expedition would be fully manned and lavishly provided for. All would be fine.

In order to turn her head to other things, I talked of the task that Aphaea had to accomplish during my absence. So that she would be the foremost priestess in Phira as soon as it was reoccupied, Aphaea had to be initiated into the Mysteries. We both wanted her initiation to take place as soon as I returned, so for the next month, as I reminded her, she would have to learn a great deal about her sacred duties. Both Aphaea and I had our work cut out for us: she studying hard on Crete, I surveying Kalliste.

The morning the Kalliste expedition began, the port of Timbaki was crowded with friends and family. Long goodbyes, well-watered with tears, serve no purpose. Everything my Aphaea and I had to say about our separation had been said. When all was ready on the three ships and the last man jumped over the gunwale, I turned to my wife standing on the dock and hugged and kissed her. Aphaea's delicate white arms did not release me easily, as if she feared they would never hold me again. Quickly banishing that thought, I jumped onto the

Dove and shouted, "Row!"' The clappers began their rhythmical song, and soon the Dove and the other vessels were away from the pier.

Waving to Ananda and Glaukus from the deck of the Dove, Ta-ch'ih had a big grin across his face. He had begged me to take him along, explaining that he just had to see the aftermath of the volcanic destruction that I had so vividly described. I had wanted to keep the party small, but I could not deny my long-time friend his fervent request.

From Timbaki, we sailed west along the south coast of Crete. It's a barren stretch of shore. The mountains reach down to the sea breakers, providing little room for man to plant his vines and olives. Here and there we saw a solitary hut or a lonely village, from which a few people waved as we passed. Though we couldn't make out what they were shouting, we felt that they knew who we were and what our mission was. Could word have spread so fast over the island, reaching down to such isolated cliff-dwelling people?

Because we were beating against a stiff westerly, a good part of the morning passed before we reached the west coast of Crete and began moving up it. Along the north coast, we passed the famous temple of Diktynna near Cape Spatha and entered the wide Gulf of Kydonia. Though we were far away, the flashing of bronze mirrors at the port caught our eyes. In order to learn why we were being signaled, I ordered the helmsmen to swing by.

As our ships approached, an army of people began waving and shouting. Some folks were crashing cymbals; others were beating drums. The Kydonians and their guests, the Kallistean Therasians, sent scores of small fishing boats out to greet us. Festooned with flowers, the boats were filled to overflowing with royalty and commoners of both Kydonia and Therasia. Aboard the lead craft, Prince Lacinius was cheering as loudly as anyone, wishing us a safe and successful voyage. In their enthusiasm to wish us well, a few boys fell into the brine and were fished out amid much joking and laughter.

A garishly painted skiff weighed down with a merchant and his family pulled alongside the Dove. The merchant held his daughter up in his arms and pointed her toward us, as if he was making an offering of her. She screeched like an owl on a roofbeam. But the din was so great, I could not make out a word she was saying. I had the Dove's sail slackened and leaned over the gunwale to try to discover her urgent message.

"Yes, what is it, little one?" I shouted.

"Alecto! My dog," she yelled, her eyes begging. "We left him behind on Kalliste, and I've been crying ever since! Could you please look for him, your lordship? Please!" She was so fetching, I wanted to reach over and give her a hug. At the same time, my heart felt for her. What could I say? The odds against anything surviving on Kalliste were incredibly low.

In all earnestness I said, "Yes, my dear! While we're in Therasia, I promise to scout around for Alecto, but it's been a long time, you know."

"Yes, I know," she said sadly.

"What does he look like?"

"Oh, he's beautiful, Your Grace! Big and black, with a white face, white paws, and fluffy ears. Thank you, Your Grace! Thank you! May Our Lady Diktynna bless you a thousand times!"

Seeing the great display of support that the expedition received at Kydonia, we all felt proud being a part of it. Shouting our thanks to the throng, we waved farewell and headed around the mushroom-shaped peninsula to the east.

As night fell, we arrived at Amnisos where we found another joyous throng, made up of Knossosans and Metapontusans. We overnighted at the port, and the next morning we loaded aboard the stores, lumber, and other materials the capital was providing. As promised, Catreus came to see us off.

We skirted Thwart-the-Way, the tiny island just north of Amnisos, as a Zephyrus swept across our decks. With ease, our prows carved the indigo sea. If the wind stayed strong, we figured we would arrive at Metapontus as the last rays of the sun were dying.

What a delight to see my crew on the open sea once again. They flung themselves into their work with a passion unlike any that I could recall. And having Ta-ch'ih aboard doubled my joy. He was intrigued by everything going on around him, as if he had been born that very day and was seeing the world for the first time. In truth, he had not been away from Snow Crystal—let alone across the sea swells—in over six years. The working of the ship amazed Ta-ch'ih. The sea breeze amazed him. The motion of the water, like streaming hair, and the sea creatures that gamboled alongside the Dove amazed him. Like a noble who savors a fine meal that is set before him, the old sage relished each moment of the voyage.

Every now and then, I peered over the side, looking for the sea-people. I didn't know if I really wanted to see them, since last time, their appearance proved to be an omen of bitter suffering to come. If they surfaced as we were returning to our motherland, I hoped they would appear playful, taking rides on the waves off our bow and stern. Instead of the lamentable whines, I longed to hear chirping and squeaking, clicking and whistling as they escorted us to Kalliste.

The brilliant sun on the morning of our departure from Crete had been a clear sign. Nevertheless, I desperately wanted the dolphins to confirm it by showing their shining snouts. None did. At least, I didn't see any. And neither did clear-eyed Ta-ch'ih, who, at my request, kept a watch for the creatures. Though disappointed, I tried to find something good in it, a folly man commits to ease his doubts. It's better that the sea-people don't appear, I whispered out loud to Diktynna, than to have them present me with another riddle.

As the westering sun dipped below the horizon and the evening sky turned green, then vivid purple, the port of Metapontus came into view. We could not have prepared ourselves for the way our island looked that evening, for it seemed as if the thick mantle of ash covering the island had made Kalliste look like a corpse that had been refused a proper burial. The tall cypress and pine trees covering the slopes of the Metapontusan valley were half buried in volcanic debris. No needles survived, only spiny branches and trunks, which stuck out of the ash like an army of skeletons.

My idea had been to spend the first night along the wharf, then, the next day, to search the city for a suitable campsite. As we came close to land, I began barking orders, but none of the Dove's crew seemed to hear me. Nobody moved. Soon I realized why: A look of terror was etched into their eyes, terror caused by what they saw before them. The pebbles and ash had completely buried the port.

The worst part of all was the silence. When you pull into a port anywhere in the world, the sounds of the place surround you well before you tie up: the sailors laughing and swearing, cups clinking together or being pounded on tables, itinerant traders announcing their presence and hawking their wares, footsteps echoing on the wooden planks, boats creaking as they bob over the swells, ropes straining to keep the boats from escaping. But the evening we returned to Kalliste, we heard none of those familiar and reassuring sounds, only the slapping and gurgling of the sea.

All the members of the expedition had been prepared to see Kalliste laden with white volcanic ash, like some freak snowfall in springtime. But when we actually saw the island, we were stung to the marrow. I quickly decided it would be better to spend that first night aboard ship and informed the expedition members of the change in plan. The first steps upon our battered homeland should be taken in the full light of day, I thought to myself, not by the dancing light of torches. We dropped anchors in the shallow water just fifty feet away from the land many of us had loved all our lives but were afraid to set foot on that evening.

When we awoke the following morning, we were better able to get an idea of the damage wrought by the volcano. It was dreadful. Judging from the shops and storehouses fronting the port, the volcanic debris reached as high as five feet or more. Without even setting foot on land, we realized that the reoccupation of our island would be a colossal task, taking many months, maybe years to accomplish. Yet at the same time, we all pledged to accomplish that task for, after all, Kalliste was our home — it was all we had.

We devoured our breakfast of hardtack and diluted wine. Then the rowers brought the ships alongside the wharf. We dropped anchors because there were no mooring posts to tie up to; all of them were buried under the ash deposit.

I was the first to set foot onto Kalliste. What a weird feeling to have to jump up onto the wharf, when in the past I always stepped down to it from the gunwale. The parched top layer of ash crunched and crackled beneath my feet. But it held, I surmised, because the layers had been compacted due to the pressure of their weight. Every step I took left a deep footprint. Soon the others joined me, at first walking like toddlers, then stomping like dancers. Ta-ch'ih's eyes practically popped out of his head when he tested the strange new earth. I allowed the men to get their footing before I ordered them back to their ships to begin unloading.

The men worked quickly, and soon all the stores and supplies sat piled high on the wharf, or rather on the thick blanket of ash that covered the wharf. Hoisting a bundle on a shoulder, each man fell into line, and I led them up the valley. Since there was not the slightest trace of the road, we marched where the road should have been. More alarming than the absence of the road was the absence of the richly flowing stream that used to murmur alongside it before emptying into the sea. Only a long ghostly three-foot deep depression in the ash layer marked the stream's position. We were wise to have brought as much water as we did.

There were some promising signs, though. Spring runoffs had carved thin, snake-like ruts into the ash deposit. Slowly, nature was creating another stream to replace the old one. But if we Kallisteans wished to reoccupy our island in the near future, we would have to aid nature by removing the volcanic filth glutting all the streams. A monumental job, indeed.

On the outskirts of the city, the upper walls of houses stuck up through the ash layer, though all the roofs had collapsed under the cruel weight of the ash. We peered down into the houses as if they were mineshafts, and we were miners looking for copper or tin.

Within the city proper, every ground floor of every building had disappeared, as if swallowed up by the earth. Supported by the compacted ash layer, we stood level with the second stories, gazing dumbfoundedly into gaping windows. I surmised that the compact street plan of the city somehow funneled more ash into the city; thus, the ash was deeper here than on the wharf. As with the buildings on the outskirts, all the roofs had collapsed, causing the floors of the second and third stories to be driven down to and stacked upon the ground level floors. Members of the expedition kept squatting down to look through this window or that window. When a few men leaned precariously on the damaged sills, I quickly ordered all the men back in line; I was afraid that someone might slip and fall or that the poorly-supported walls might crumble. I remembered how it was in the shrine at Phira after the earthquake.

We moved cautiously along the cinder-covered streets. Here and there, walls of buildings bulged as if giants were pushing against them from inside. Occasionally, we came across a wall that had toppled over, shooting its splintered crossbeams and shattered bricks in all directions.

The south square had been my first choice for the camp. Arriving there, I sent the two master builders from Knossos around to check the bordering structures. Almost immediately, the builders returned with the sad report that the upper stories of the apartments facing the square might topple at any moment, so badly were they damaged.

Swiftly, I moved the party farther north, deeper into the deserted city. We came to a massive gateway spanning a road and its ash deposits. We stepped over the huge stone lintel of the gateway. After taking that step, we were within one of the biggest open places of Metapontus. Once again, I dispatched the builders to examine the structures surrounding the square, unusual because it was three-sided. They came back with a good report: the walls were secure, being extremely well-built and massive in that part of Metapontus.

For the remainder of the day, I supervised the construction of the shelter that would house us while we stayed in the city. Because they all wanted a roof over their heads that first night, the men worked straight through the noon meal. By late afternoon, the large single-room shelter was almost complete. The lumber, which had been cut to shape back on Crete, filled the square with its sharp piney scent. After the absence of noise, which, of course, we had expected, the absence of odors of any kind unsettled us the most. Try to imagine, if you can, a city devoid of the smell of bread baking, food cooking, fish drying, freshly cut flowers, people, animals, sewage, and countless other common odors. That was the way Metapontus was when we first arrived.

Darkness followed hard on the heels of the setting sun. Thank Goddess we had finished most of the wooden shelter by then and had stacked all of our provisions within it, because, as the sunlight was replaced by our torchlight, the entire feeling of the city changed. The sky turned pitch-black, and the city closed in on us. The fire from our cooking pit and our torches produced flickering beams of light, which danced on the walls of the nearby buildings. To add to the unearthly display, our voices seemed to echo more during the night than during the day. When we stopped talking, the silence was even more ominous. One of the crew of the Dove was a pretty fair hand with the lyre and, to keep our spirits from flagging, I asked him to strum it. A lanky soldier began to sing the words to a bawdy song, and soon he had everybody singing and laughing around the sputtering fire.

That night, after the two exhausting days—one at sea and the other on our stricken island—we ate ravenously. I made sure that the cook and his helpers served up plenty of everything, including strong wine. We dined almost as if we had been back on Crete. Tasty lamb, dried fruit, a selection of mellow cheeses, crispy radishes, fruit, bread, and other good things made our bellies happy. After the hearty meal, the lyre music did the same for our souls.

The stars turned slowly overhead, the Bear smiling down on our camp, a lonely but brave outpost on a desert island. I allowed my men to consume more wine than their normal daily ration, for it was important that they be at ease that first night. After a while, sweet sleep beckoned. Beneath the hastily built but sturdy roof of our shelter, we curled up in our sheep skins. The two days of back-breaking work caused the men to slip off at once. A chorus of snorers produced a jarring cacophony.

Before dozing off, I uttered a prayer for the once great city. "O shining city of song, great outpost of Minos's realm, glorious Metapontus, place full of divinity, you were once wreathed in violets, now a winding sheet covers your great palace and homes. I humbly ask your Divine Protectress, the Great Mother, to roll back the heavy shroud, thus exposing to all the world your sublime radiance. And I pray you, Mistress of Nature and Mountains, will allow the rest of Kalliste to rise from the ashes like a lovely spring rose pushing through the frost. This, I, Idomeneus of Phira, do beg on bended knee, presenting myself to you, Great Goddess, to be used as You see fit." Peace came over me, and, despite the trumpeting of those around me, I fell heavily into blissful sleep.

I don't know what I was dreaming, or if I was even dreaming at all, when suddenly I was awakened by a bloodcurdling cry from outside. I shot up, as did my comrades. Confusion reigned as we tried to light some torches in the darkness. We worked feverishly, because the cry was quickly followed by more, each as terrifying as the first. Soon five or six torches lit up the sleeping area, and we quickly discovered that one of my sailors, a lad named Dymas, was missing. Throwing off their covers, the men made for the door, but I yelled for them to stay where they were. I ordered the Cretan officer and two of his soldiers to go with me, and, in a flash, the four of us were outside, each with a spear in one hand and a torch in the other. There we froze, waiting for the next cry to rend the air and tell us which way to go. We didn't have long to wait. From the south a desperate cry rang out.

We flew over the lintel of the half-buried gateway, heading for the unsuitable first square we had come to that day. When we reached the square, our torchlight revealed nothing. We knew we were close though; the screams were clearer and louder.

Suddenly an anguished groan, accompanied by a frightful growl told us exactly where to go. We approached, spears raised, a dilapidated structure on our right. Peering over the partially collapsed northern wall into the shell of the building, a ghastly sight met our eyes. A blood-streaked Dymas was pinned against the south wall by a hideous dog. The cur had buried its fangs deep into Dymas's shoulder and neck and was shaking the youth's body like it was a sack of grain. We held our spears, afraid of hitting the youth.

Because of the terrible noise it was making, the beast did not hear us. But somehow it knew we were there. It looked up with savage eyes. Releasing its grip from the youth's limp body, the dog swung its head toward us. It snarled so ferociously its entire body shook. It meant to attack us — all four of us — straightaway!

Clutched in my right hand, the spear felt as if it were made of stone; I stood there as motionless as a statue. Thank Britomartis, Goddess of Hunters, the others were with me. Before the grisly dog took two steps toward us, the soldiers let fly. With great impact, all three spears struck home, skewering the wild dog and pinning it to the cindery floor. At once, the fire in those monstrous eyes was extinguished. The beast never made a whimper: such a thing— monstrous as it was — must have been thankful to die.

Swiftly we were at Dymas's side, surprised and relieved to find the breath of life still within him. His eyes were open, but they were glazed over, they saw nothing. A good thing, for it was best that he couldn't see his mangled body. The officer sent his soldiers to get rags, blankets, and a pot of boiling water. I instructed the men to bring Ta-ch'ih back. Having learned much from Glaukus over the years, the old sage knew more about healing than most men.

After making Dymas as comfortable as we could, we turned toward the impaled creature beside us. Oh, what desperate and unspeakable days that half-crazed beast must have seen on Kalliste. Its body was a battlefield of scars. Huge swaths of fur were missing from its sides and along its back. One ear was chewed off, possibly in a life-and-death struggle. As if the dog had turned to hardwood trees and rocks for sustenance, many of its teeth were broken or cracked. We shook our heads in horror, then quickly heaved the boney brown carcass over a nearby wall. Why should the others see such a sight? For the rest of the night and into the morning, we tended Dymas's wounds right where he lay. I had guards posted around the shelter, and for the remainder of our stay, it was patrolled day and night. It didn't seem possible that any creature could have survived the volcano's wrath, yet, that tenacious dog had. Maybe there were more.

NINETEEN

IN THE MIDDLE OF THE NIGHT, when we thought he could take it, we moved Dymas on a litter from the dilapidated building to the shelter. As morning broke on Kalliste that second day, it was Ta-ch'ih who stirred me to action. Leaving the side of the wounded youth for the first time, the weary sage shambled over to where I sat.

"How's Dymas faring?" I asked in a hushed voice.

"He's sleeping soundly, Your Grace. For now, that is the best thing. It will be a while before he is up and around again. The shock to his tender body was great indeed."

I hung my head. I could feel the sage's kind eyes upon me; he knew what was running through my mind. I waited for his words, knowing that they would be a salve to my troubled soul. I could barely hear it, but he sighed before he began to speak. "Neither Glaukus, the dreamer, nor old Ananda asked if they could come on this expedition, did they, Your Grace?"

"No.

"Aaah, both those sages are blessed, indeed. Both are true soothsayers. They can see from a distance the good or evil coming to a man whom the ancestors attend. Neither of them needs to trouble himself anymore venturing forth over the sea-forest nor the shadowy mountains, where savage beasts dwell. I swear, that strange Ananda would never move off his spot if I weren't at him all the time. And Glaukus. Well, if I let him, he would just dream his life away. Alas, I am different from my dear friends. I must go forth and examine this or that. Turn over the rock to see if the lizard really lives there. I know that everything is properly attached to The Web. Yet, with these," he said pointing to his eyes, "I must actually see if it is so, even though my eyes are poor specimens now and soon will close for good. Sire, I have traveled to the ends of the earth, using my eyes to confirm what I had already seen in my heart. And I will continue to do so——"

"Yes, but why, Ta-ch'ih, why," I broke in, looking up and holding his eyes. "Why not simply divine with your tortoise shells and bones and leave it at that? In your own way, you're as skilled at looking into the future as Glaukus and Ananda. I've seen you do it many times. Why go about endangering your frail body, putting yourself in jeopardy, when you know your observations will only confirm your prophesies? Besides, you cannot... I cannot...alter destined things." Pausing, I thought about our present predicament. "It seems all I ever do is drag others along on my perilous missions," I said, "rushing them headlong toward what is inevitable and what they can't possibly change."

"But, good Prince, that is what you must do! And all who follow you, that is what they must do, including me. Our natures, plus where we stand on The Web, compel us to be the kind of men who must look and touch, explore and discover, even though all of our labors may come to naught. 'Tis true, as you say, sometimes I can predict events before their time. As you know, I did not ask the bones about our adventure on Kalliste, feeling that I should enter into this adventure without any foreknowledge. And I believe I was correct in making this decision."— Ta-ch'ih stopped. Then he did something unusual for him: He came right to the point. "I know this expedition has soured in your mouth, Your Grace. And it is possible that we may all come to an evil end here, our flesh and bones forming a new layer of earth. Nevertheless, to return to Crete now, before we see what we must see, would be to go against our very natures, and we would truly accomplish nothing. Prince Idomeneus, I stand behind you. So do your men. Put us to work and we will carry out the missions we have been assigned by King Minos and by the Cosmos."

We stared into each other's eyes for a long time. I knew that he was right, and he knew that I had made up my mind to stay and complete our work. We both smiled, grasping each other's hands.

Disregarding the pall hanging over the compound, I went about explaining to the men what I expected to be accomplished that day. At first, I could feel their cold, unflinching eyes all over me. The men were thinking, how could he be so callous, so bullheaded? After all, the message from the Goddess, in the form of Dymas's attack, was crystal clear: She did not want us on Kalliste. Before long, though, the icy stares began to melt away. The men looked at me the way they had the morning after I wrestled Theseus. My confident words and my manner, the warm food, and the bright sun began to stoke the coals that lay deep within each of them.

After breakfast, I organized a survey team. The two master builders and I would direct the survey, and the two Phiran scribes would record it. Needing broad-backed men to do the pick and shovel work, I had the officer select ten of his soldiers while I chose ten of my sailors.

Those who stayed back at the compound had their work cut out for them, too. Under the supervision of the officer, they were charged with finishing the work on the shelter, then searching for serviceable bricks and stones. The idea was to reinforce the wooden structure with stronger materials. Thus, when the Metapontusans returned to their city they would have a solid building for their headquarters. Also, using the debris spread around the square, I wanted the men to construct temporary barracks for the returning citizens.

After some last instructions to the officer, I led the survey team out of the square into the narrow streets of the city. Knowing Metapontus as well as anyone, I decided to begin at the southernmost limits with a stately building that had been donated to the priesshood by a wealthy merchant. Though the preeminent priestesses of Metapontus had held their secret rites in the building, on special days when public ceremonies were called for, the doors were thrown open to the people.

Once, happening to be in the city on one of those occasions, Miletus and I attended a ceremony. We were astounded by the beauty of the place. In the lower level, the most superb fresco I had ever seen in my life was painted along the walls of the lustral basin. Metapontus was famous not only in the Cyclades but throughout the entire kingdom for its wall paintings. There were two well-established families in the city, and between them they had turned out scores of talented painters. For several generations, the Mimas and the Lynceus families had had a competition going to see which could produce the best artists. The true beneficiary of that friendly rivalry was the city: the palace, the shrines, most of the public buildings, and many of the private ones were adorned with works by artists from both families.

On these lower level walls, two artists of the Lynceus family had depicted elegant priestesses gathering up crocuses. As the priestesses moved through the colorful field, they conversed amongst themselves, smiling and chatting the way they would in real life. Each was gayly dressed and bejeweled. There were young initiates, their breasts not having swollen; others were clearly in their prime, reminding me of our lovely priestesses from Phira. But one full-breasted figure, gliding effortlessly among the painted flowers, clearly outshone the rest. Thick folds of blue-black hair fell from her lovely head, cascading over the nape of her neck and concealing the collar of her sheer, loosely fitting jacket. In her left hand, she proffered a necklace of amber beads. The priestess resembled my Aphaea.

The two figures completing the scene were matronly priestesses, in a slightly larger scale and as wonderfully lifelike as the younger ones. With their regal heads and wise eyes, they resembled my mother, and I remember commenting so to Miletus that day as we entered the sacred building.

As the survey team picked its way over the remains of that once great building, I had trouble locating the room which was graced by that much-admired fresco. By and by, I determined approximately where the room should have been. I stood over the spot in sadness. Only about three feet of the walls were standing; the upper part of the walls had plummeted down to the lustral basin, along with the ceiling and slate-paved floor. Somewhere in that confused heap, covered with pebbles and ash, the fresco lay smashed in hundreds of pieces.

Directing the soldiers and the members of my crew, the master builders had trenches dug around the outside of the building in order to get a better idea of the structural damage. If the huge stones that formed the foundation were smashed, the reconstruction would be lengthy and expensive or unrealizable and the mansion would have to be torn down. If the stones were merely cracked, though, and could be patched, or if they were knocked slightly out of alignment and could be readjusted, then to raise the upper stories upon them would not be difficult.

The builders measured every foot of the sacred edifice. As they moved along, they jabbered back and forth about support, weight, stress, and other things of which I knew nothing. As the soldiers and sailors dug the trenches, it became clear that the excavation of the building, and also the city and all the towns on the island, would not be as difficult as we had first thought. The men did not even need their picks because the layer of ash and pebbles broke so easily under the blades of their shovels. Working quickly and with little strain, the men were able to expose considerable sections of the building.

The morning was spent examining and discussing the sacred building. If we were to accomplish our mission in the time dictated by our provisions, I knew full well that we would have to work faster. But, since it was the first one, I allowed the men to spend more time on the building than was necessary.

By midday, we had moved over to Sarpedon's palace, and the workmen were busy dropping trenches as the builders instructed. Without purpose, I wandered over the copious debris of the stupendous ruin. At every turn, ghosts of people — friend and foe — jumped out at me, and visions of events that happened long ago danced before my eyes.

I reconstructed in my mind the rooms of the palace exactly the way they looked before the Goddess laid Her heavy hand on them. At one point, I found myself standing over the spot where the doorway of the throne room should have been. With a small piece of broken crossbeam, I began scraping through the overlaying silt. Soon I struck the massive lintel. A few more passes with my makeshift shovel revealed the top of the door. As if it had happened the day before, I recalled the guards bursting through that same door and interrupting my heated exchange with Sarpedon. Both of us burned with such a hateful passion then that we almost leapt upon one another like savage lions.

How stupid we were. As I stood in the shattered palace, I cursed human beings, we wretched creatures, and the feeble notions we have about ourselves. I threw my shovel down in disgust; it made a dull thud on the white surface, and a small dust-cloud rose up to engulf me, sprinkling my head with ash. I addressed my mournful heart, saying The Goddess Steerer cares as much about the affairs and thoughts of humans as She does about the chaff that is winnowed by the wind. What really matters on earth are the wishes and deeds of the Death-Dealing Goddess, not those of men.

If it weren't for the high spirits of my companions, mine would have remained down for the rest of that day; the builders and the workers seemed almost to enjoy exploring the battered palace. At first it was thought that a completely new palace would have to be built over the flattened and mutilated body of the old one. But after examining and testing all of the intact walls, the builders concluded that wouldn't be necessary. Much of the massive northern, eastern, and southern walls had survived the earthquakes and heavy ashfall. After being cleared, the outer shell of the palace would be in much the same condition it was when new, the builders promised. The job of rebuilding the upper stories would not be a small one, but they insisted that it was possible.

At dusk, we returned to the camp, having surveyed only two structures that day. Those structures, however, were the two most important in the city, and we felt our time had been well spent. As the evening gloom seeped in around us, it was good to be by the bright bonfire dancing in the three-sided square.

After throwing down a cup, I went directly to the shelter to see how Dymas was doing. He was asleep, the old sage kneeling by him. Ta-ch'ih told me that the youth had taken some soup and said a few words; those were encouraging signs. Dymas told Ta-ch'ih that he had left the shelter to relieve himself, wandered a bit too far, got lost, and then was cornered by the wild dog.

The night before, I had raised the possibility of sending Dymas back to Crete if his wounds did not heal quickly. That was not necessary, though, for the constant change of bandages, the nourishment, and the sage's chanting were doing the trick.

Before dinner, I had the captain take me around the compound to see how the work was progressing. I was elated to see how much had been done, for those who had remained in the square had managed to collect enough bricks to line the outside of the shelter almost up to the windows. I was sure in a day or two that the entire wooden structure would be encased in durable mud brick. Also, the officer had had his men collect loose stones, which were stored behind the shelter where they would be used for the foundations of the barracks.

All in all, that day on Kalliste had been a most productive one; a sense of accomplishment pervaded the air as we sat around the fire and ate heartily. No one felt like singing, but our discussion was salted with a chuckle or two. We believed our feet were at last firmly planted on Kalliste, and we pledged once more to complete our mission—no matter what.

The men retired early that night. I stayed up a bit longer with the master builders from Crete discussing the following day's plan. After we finished, we entered the shelter, leaving the guards to stand their lonely posts.

As I wrapped myself in my cover, there were only a few snores to endure. Mostly I heard restless bodies tossing and turning. Before long, I noticed some dust drifting across the large room, moving from south to north. It could only mean one thing: the Notus was blowing up from Africa. We had much work to do during the remainder of our stay, and the last thing we needed was the sultry south wind making our knees weak and our heads soft. After a while, the dust was suspended in midair, then gently glided down to the earthen floor. The wind had stopped. Only then did sleep take hold of me, easing the cares of my heart.

During the following week, the survey team covered almost every apartment complex and public building in Metapontus. Some were examined more closely than others, though none more carefully than were the first building and the palace.

One edifice at which we spent a good deal of time was the huge storehouse in the northern sector of the city. Being extremely well-made, the storehouse had survived better than most of the structures. When we excavated the area in front of the door, we found the carcasses of small animals—rabbits, foxes, bats—that were no doubt trying to scratch their way into the storehouse. Their pungent odor filled the air. When we got inside, we dug down to the basement and were surprised to find many of the pithoi, some the size of men, still standing. Debris from the building and gritty pebbles from the volcano had fallen all around and within the large storage jars. The valuable foodstuff contained within the jars was ruined. All that remained of the olives were their pits. The barley, wheat, and spices had become inextricably mixed with the debris from the building and the volcano. Sandy cinders had mixed with the wine and olive oil, forming unsightly plugs of mud at the bottom of the pithoi. Some of the precious liquids had drained out through cracks, forming thick dark curds on the floor. One of the builders surmised that the cracks occurred because of the great force of the earthquakes. The other builder disagreed, proposing that the heat of the volcanic ash and pebbles had caused the cracking.

Millhouses, lodging-houses, wineshops, artisans' workshops, and merchants' homes were surveyed during our stay in the city. The Cretan builders had my scribes fill rolls of papyrus with pertinent information needed to rebuild Metapontus. A large plan of the city, requiring several papyri pasted together, was drawn with color and brush. The plan indicated where the major damage was and noted what remedies might be taken when the Metapontusans returned.

During our work, we pocked the city with our deep pits. Each time we dug one, we were afraid of finding the body of an unfortunate man or woman; we had all heard the grim reports about those who had perished the day the city was abandoned. When the last spade went down into a pit, we held our breath until it rose again. Thank Goddess, that in all the ditches we dug, not one decomposing body was unearthed.

The building we saved for last was the one closest to our shelter. Forming the northwestern side of the square, the large mansion was owned by a wealthy trader who had made his fortune cruising the Libyan coast. I had been inside the building on a number of occasions, and during one visit, I remember the trader proudly taking me around to see his paintings; the man favored the Mimas, and all of the works in his home were executed by one or another of that family. Some works were frescoes, others panel paintings, still others, frescoes painted on small slabs of plaster, then displayed like panel paintings. Works of this last class were well represented by panels depicting fisher boys. Poised in opposite corners of a large room at the back of the mansion, each boy proudly displayed his catch of the day: One held a string of mackerel in either hand, while the other—not as successful—held but one string. Colored a vivid red, both lads were as naked as the day they were born.

Even more skillfully rendered than the fisher boys was the long, continuous fresco that wrapped around the tops of the four walls. Since it depicted a large naval operation, the painting was the trader's pride and joy. Three cities were colorfully portrayed: Metapontus, a city on Crete, and one on the Libyan coast. Tricolored dolphins led the way, as handsome ships with fantastic prow ornaments plied the waters between the well-built cities. On the eastern wall, an undulating stream snaked through a Libyan landscape as a griffin and a lion pursued birds and fawns. Every rock, tree, animal, and human was done in incredible detail; yet, there wasn't a figure in either the Libyan landscape or the naval scene larger than your small finger.

As I stood on the rubble of the roof and second story that filled the first floor, I tried to place in my mind where each element in the painting had been, for, as with the painting of the priestesses in the very first building we surveyed, not one scrap of the fabulous miniature fresco was to be found. I despaired in my task, saying to myself: well, maybe when the master of the Mimas family returns, he will recreate his vision on the fresh plaster of the new walls. Suddenly, I realized that would be impossible. Maybe the son or the grandson of the master would take up the brush and try to duplicate the brilliant work, but not the master himself. The old man was one of those who had failed to escape from the crumbling city; somewhere below us, he lay entombed in stone and ash.

TWENTY

BY THE END of our tenth day on Kalliste, we had covered the city of Metapontus to my satisfaction and the satisfaction of the Cretan builders. There were many other structures we could have examined, of course, but we felt we had an accurate picture of the damage and how much work would be required to resurrect the city. Besides, everybody in the expeditionary party was eager to move on to the five towns of Kalliste in order to assess the damage to each of them. Naturally, I was dying to head for Phira; I had been ever since setting foot on the ash-embalmed island. So had my sailors. Unfortunately, since we had begun at Metapontus and would have to finish up there, it was just not practical to visit our hometown next. We all agreed that beginning on the west side and circling the great volcano would be the easiest route to take.

Before the sun awoke on the next day, we prepared to depart for Therasia. Although the constellations were faint, we saw the Serpent and Scorpion glide overhead, watching our every move. Without warning, a stiff northwesterly began to howl, picking up ash and swirling it around in dense plumes that looked like waterspouts. The officer, the two builders, my advisors, and I debated about staying back until the dust-laden wind died down. How long would that take, we asked each other. After I heard each man's thoughts on the matter, I reached my decision. Since we had planned to leave that morning, I felt it would dampen our spirits to be turned back by the wind—bad enough it had us hesitating before our first steps.

Each man who was to go to Therasia was instructed to fix a moist linen strip over his nose and mouth; the cloth would provide some protection from the abrasive grit.

As the shining beams of dawn lit the sky, we who were to circle Kalliste said goodbye to our comrades who were to stay behind: Ta-ch'ih, Dymas, five other sailors, and five soldiers. The men had their orders to improve the compound. By digging through the volcanic deposit, they could reach dirt, which, with the addition of sea water, could be turned into mud bricks needed to enlarge the shelter and work areas and build the barracks.

As we who were to explore the five Kallistean towns left Metapontus, the wind was funneled down the streets and flew shrilly into our faces. Reaching the outskirts of the city, we climbed the west ridge, and, once on top, we looked back. The city had disappeared beneath an ominous cloud of dust, or rather many small clouds of dust, each twisting and churning to its own beat.

As we headed north along the ridge, the wind died down noticeably. When our eyes adjusted to the near-blinding white of the ash-covered landscape, we saw a good deal of the island and quickly discovered something that gladdened our hearts. The deposit of pebbles and ash was not of equal thickness around Kalliste. In the direction we were heading, northwest, the deposit appeared to taper off. At Metapontus, we had found drifts over ten-feet high, but as we moved along, we found the mantle to be five feet or less in some places. We were able to judge the depth by the skeletons of farmhouses piercing the surface. Approaching the base of the volcano, we discovered furrows, five feet deep, cut into the ash by the spring runoffs. At the bottom of the furrows lay the once thriving soil of Kalliste.

"This wind that plagues us now," I said to the men, "must have been blowing when the volcano roared, sweeping ash from the summit and driving it in a southeasterly direction. That means that the five towns, except for maybe Enalus, may have received only a fraction of the ash that Metapontus did." Cheered by my words, the men stepped lively as we continued our trek.

A little ways on, we had to take a detour around a huge mound composed of great blocks of compressed ash and pebbles. From the wide gash in the volcano's southwestern slope, it was clear that the mound had been created by an avalanche.

As we walked along, we soon realized that the major problem wouldn't be the removal of ash from the city or towns, but from the farmland. Even if the deposit averaged only four or five feet around the island, digging it up and dumping it into the sea would still be an enormous task; I estimated that it would take at least two years, maybe more. But it was truly a guess. During that period, rich Crete would have to supply us with virtually everything. How could our pride ever accept that? We Kallisteans thought of ourselves as rugged, independent people. We would just have to swallow our pride, I mused to myself, get our homeland in order, then, somehow, repay the generous Cretans.

The evening light was fading as we reached the outskirts of Therasia. The sky was a royal purple and small red clouds edged in silver sailed overhead. I led the survey team to an open square in the center of town, and we set up camp.

Before night fell, I walked cautiously through the streets surrounding the square. In the back of my mind, I saw the big black dog, the one which the little girl had told me about, and I had promised to search for. As I wandered the deserted streets, my feet crunching the ever-crumbling ash, I was prepared to kill the mongrel on sight, if necessary. Thank Goddess for the both of us that we never met.

From what I could determine on my brief walk in the failing light, Therasia was covered by only a few feet of ash; the job of digging it out would not be that great. The earthquakes, however, had been quite severe, buckling some walls and pulling others down. A thorough survey would tell us how much work would be needed to breathe life back into the town. The next morning, we awoke eager to explore Therasia and to take stock of the damage. Having risen first, the cook had our breakfast waiting for us. Wherever we could find room, we squatted or sat cross-legged amidst the debris and, between mouthfuls, discussed the plans for the day.

The rays of the newborn sun began to heat up the atmosphere; beads of sweat appeared on everyone's brow. Though we had just awakened, drowsiness made our knees weak. The air was heavy and dry and felt as if it were closing in on us. Even the brisk breeze didn't help. I had hoped to accomplish much that day; the strange beginning, however, was a bad omen.

Not wanting them to dwell on the oppressive atmosphere, the Cretan builders and I hurried the men along. The sailors and soldiers did not seem to mind being rushed, for they too wanted to put the ominous start behind them. They lost no time downing the last of their bread and salted meat and springing to their feet.

Presently, our survey team was away from the campsite, making for the palace of Prince Lacinius. Though I marched the men slowly, we all sweated like hard-working oxen. It hurt to take deep breaths. The searing air also affected the deposit of ash, which became hotter and hotter. I thought my sandals would burn right off my feet.

I took more than one glance at the glittering massif looming over my shoulder. The volcano was silhouetted against a mackerel sky. There was not a trace of steam feeding the clouds above.

An occasional cough of a sailor or soldier and the crunching of pebbles underfoot punctured the silence. There was no other sound except the pounding of the surf, which seemed unusually loud.

When we reached the palace, all of us looked as if we had put in a full day's work. We were coated with a sticky white paste produced by the mixture of our sweat and the bothersome ash. I said nothing, but it struck me that we looked like a phantom patrol trooping through a ghost town.

Under ordinary circumstances, the work would have begun at once, the master builders surveying and measuring and the men digging. I felt it best, though, to allow the men to sit and rest, to catch their breath and to try to wipe off the unsightly paste. I was kneeling, talking to one of the soldiers, when I heard the shouting.

"By-the-Goddess!"

"What on earth!"

"We're trapped! We're trapped!"

"Prince Idomeneus! Sire! Come quickly," cried Hyllus, the older of the Cretan builders. Out of all of the men on the expedition, Hyllus had been moved the least by the sights and sounds we had experienced. He was always calm, never shaken—until that moment. I knew that whatever it was he had discovered, it was dreadful. The men knew it too; they were right on my heels as I dashed off.

I quickly reached the second floor of the dilapidated palace, where Hyllus and the other builder stood motionless. I looked out to the west where they were both pointing. From the vantage point of the palace, we could see Therasia's small port and the limitless water beyond. What a sight. As if the sea were a great cauldron, fired up to boiling, agitated beyond belief, the water was seething and roiling. Huge sheets of billowy foam leapt into the air, stayed suspended there briefly, and then came cascading down onto the turbulent surface. The wind scooped up and scattered small patches of foam, and some came close to where we stood.

In all my days at sea, in all the raging storms, I had never seen such a display. Neither had anyone else amongst us. Crowding the shell of the once well-appointed room, we stared in awe at the amazing sight.

We hadn't been standing there long when the level of the water appeared to drop several feet right before my eyes. I gasped. It was as if the liquid in a great basin was being sucked through a large crack or hole in its bottom.

The sea stopped its shocking plunge, and, for a moment, stayed level. Then, gradually, the water began to rise until it reached its original height.

To our amazement, the water did not stop there, but rose higher and higher, and, for a while, I thought it would never stop, that sad Kalliste, so hated by Diktynna, would be flooded, and all of us drowned like miserable rats. The water overflowed the dock. Adjacent wine shops and warehouses were inundated.

We were just about to take flight when the sea began to recede, again, leaving the buildings and the dock and draining away as it had done before. For as long as we watched the sea from the palace, the pattern of falling and rising continued. The whole time, the surface was a confused battleground, with foam and spray being spit into the air and oddly shaped, loud-crashing waves appearing and disappearing at random.

Diktynna's sacred name was spoken aloud by everyone: in prayer, in supplication, and in blasphemy.

"We're doomed! We'll never leave this damned island," someone cried.

"Hold your tongue," I shouted, half-heartedly searching out the man; I didn't discover who it was, which was just as well.

We stared silently, but if thoughts made sounds ours would have created a din. My mind reeled over the prospects of our ships back at Metapontus. Surely, I thought, they had not survived these feverish, frenzied waves. I remembered the watery wreath around Kalliste, first multicolored, then milky white, then virulent green and purple. I remembered what it presaged. As we watched from the Therasia palace, the sea was not discolored, but I wondered if the maddened water meant the same thing.

The question was answered by one of my crewmen standing beside me. He must have been thinking the same thought, for he turned away from the tumultuous scene and cast his eyes on the great mountain behind us. The expression on his frightened face told me the dreadful answer. Slowly, haltingly, I sent my glance after his, turning toward Mount Kalliste, the colossus that had once been our proud emblem. I beheld a yellowish wisp of steam issuing from the summit and curling skyward. The wisp was thin and transparent in places, nevertheless, it was enough to proclaim that the giant had awakened.

All of the others turned toward the east and stared. We knew it would not be long before we would be showered by sizzling ash. Pebbles and rocks would follow.

"What about all the trenches we dug at Metapontus," someone moaned. "They'll be filled with new debris from the volcano."

"That's the least of our worries," Hyllus replied.

We had been the target of a cruel and sinister hoax. Having lulled us into believing that the volcanic activity had ceased, the Goddess permitted our passage over the sea swells and our return to Kalliste. She let us work long and hard at Metapontus, surveying much of that once fair city, and allowed us to leave with high hopes for the rest of the island. The All-Powerful Mother had only wanted to ensnare us, to smash our ships to splinters, then to bury us in a cindery tomb.

A vision appeared before my eyes; Aphaea, my lodestar. Had I made her wait so long to become a bride only to make her a widow so soon?

A firm hand grasped my arm, breaking the dark spell I had slipped into. The hand belonged to Hyllus, who was overcome by what he saw and wasn't aware of his impropriety. He asked simply, "What do we do?"

I gazed at the desperate eyes around me, especially those of the Cretans who had not experienced the volcano's wrath before, and without a moment's delay I declared, "We make for Metapontus at once! By some good fortune, our ships may have survived this wild sea. They were well-built; they would have put up a good fight. If they're sea-worthy, we must beat a hasty retreat for Crete. As you can see, the Great Mother plans more destruction here. Whether we're woven into the fabric of ruin or not, only She knows. But I, for one, will not sit still and watch Her plan unfold! She must catch me first before She dashes out my life!" I pronounced the last part with a defiant fist raised to the mountain. It seemed my words lifted the downtrodden hearts of those around me and a burst of spirit ran through the survey team.

With all haste, we fled the palace and began scurrying through the narrow streets. The vile ash began to fall. Though it was a light shower, it portended worse to come.

When we arrived at the campsite, the cook and his helper were already packed and anxious to leave. The men of the survey team quickly gathered their supplies, threw them into their haversacks, and fell in behind me.

As we headed out, the first quake struck. It was a slow, sly one. Indeed, it may have been going on for some time before we became aware of it. At first, we noticed an increase in ashfall. Then I realized that the ash was coming not from the sky, but from the battered walls, which were vibrating, sloughing off their cindery coating onto our accursed heads.

Ordering the others to follow closely on my heels, I began dashing through the streets, hoping to make it beyond the confines of the town before the shaking reached its climax. Soon I knew that would be impossible. I decided on the closest square and headed for it, as bricks shook loose and tumbled into our path.

As the full force of the earthquake struck, we entered the desolate square and dove to the ground. Like lizards, we crawled on our bellies to the center of the square, far away as possible from the feeble walls. Several collapsed, spraying us with broken bricks, splintered timber, chunks of plaster, and choking dust. Even more frightening was the awful rumbling of the earth, which seemed to drown out everything. It was much worse than I had remembered it being at Monolithos.

When the shaking finally stopped, I rose to my knees, spitting out the grit and calling to my men. I couldn't see the person on either side of me, so thick was the cloud that hung in the square. When it lifted, I checked to see if anyone was injured. By some miracle, no one was. The walls around us, which had seen so much misery, did not fare as well. All were completely flattened, making the square as safe a place as any to wait and see if there would be any more quakes.

Again, the ground heaved and lurched, and rumbling filled the air. After five or six jolts, stillness fell over the square. A dust cloud rose from the ground, and, as it did, we tried to glimpse what was happening on the summit of the mountain. What had been a wisp of steam had become a tremendously engorged shaft that climbed higher and higher. It had taken on the shape of a building's column with a bizarrely bloated capital. The ash that rained from above was coarser and warmer. At first it prickled our skin. Then it stung. Our dark hair turned gray, then snow white. Everything turned white, except our terror-stricken eyes.

Suddenly, the heart-stopping sound—the sound that I had hoped never to hear again—echoed across the island. BOOM! Each explosion was louder than the previous one, the ashfall worse with each. Soon pea-size pebbles fell from the sky.

Though there was no shelter to be had, some of the men searched frantically in the ruins. Even if there had been shelter, I would not have allowed men in my charge to be buried alive under some dilapidated building. Therasia was doomed. I ordered the men to lighten their loads, instructing them to place their haversacks upon their heads as protection against the blistering fallout. I led the survey party out of the Goddess-forsaken town, heading south for our only hope—the ships.

Hard on our left throughout the retreat, the great mountain bellowed like an enraged bull. Standing on the mountain's head, the gigantic shaft of steam and ash had changed again: instead of an ever-growing limestone column, it looked more like a colossal black pine tree. Bright thunderflashes ran up the trunk and spread throughout the branches.

For all their spectacular displays, the flashes did not improve the visibility down below. Though it must have been midday by then, the light, instead of increasing, was rapidly dying, as during early evening; the pine tree cloud grew so fast and was so dense that the sun's rays had trouble breaking through. The air was acrid, sluggish. Our pace slackened. We barely crept along.

The reports from the volcano became more and more violent. Before each explosion there was a strange noise. I can only describe the noise as *"whomph!"* It sounded as if water was being forced through a tapered pipe and then ejected.

After a while, the individual booms merged into one continuous roar, which drowned out every other sound; we could not even hear our own feet falling and crushing the pebbly surface. If we hadn't been together or hadn't had a glimmer of hope of reaching our ships, I believe the unrelenting din would have driven us mad.

What a pitiful sight our scraggy line must have been, trudging its way over the lifeless land. It did not seem possible, but once again Kallisteans were to suffer greatly. The length of time before another person set foot on this ravaged earth would be reckoned in years, not months, I thought. The real question in my mind was whether the Great Goddess would allow men to live on the island ever again?

On that sinister day, as we stumbled along, I thought I knew the answer.

We managed to get lost several times. The day before, we had had no trouble going in the opposite direction, though we had neither road nor path to guide us. We could see. When the volcano turned day into night, though, we became blindmen. Confused and choking, we staggered through the blizzard of dust and pebbles; blazing torches shed but little light on our feet. Familiar landmarks were impossible to make out—Mount Kalliste itself was shielded. Jabs of thunderflashes, like the flickering of a serpent's tongue, were the only things visible overhead. The bloodcurdling stories told by the Achaeans came to my troubled mind, though I doubted if Hades could be worse than what we were walking through.

Exhausted and famished, ash-singed and grief-stricken, we arrived at Metapontus sometime the following day: I think it was early morning, but there was no way of knowing for sure since the sky was hidden. What a relief to see a modest bonfire going in the middle of the wedge-shaped square. Piling on scraps of wood as quickly as they could, the sailors and soldiers worked feverishly to keep the fire going. I could see that they put up a great hurrah when they spotted us, but I could not hear it over the berserk din of the volcano.

Upon entering the square, we were surrounded by the men who had stayed back. They offered us jugs of soothing water, which we downed straightaway. I drank like a beast, my eyes darting around the square for old Ta-ch'ih. He was nowhere in sight. Competing with the noise of the volcano, shouting filled my ears.

"What are we to do, Sire?"

"We shall all perish!"

"The accursed Goddess has deceived us!"

"Silence! Silence, I say," I yelled above everyone. "You brave men of Minos get hold of yourselves! Here, now, answer my questions, quickly! Where is the old foreigner and how does he fare?"

"He's alive and within the shelter, Your Grace," answered a trusted pilot of one of the merchantmen. "Dymas has taken a turn for the worse, though. The old foreigner is trying to pull him through."

"Have there been any injuries?" I asked, wiping the grit from my eyes.

"Nothing serious, Sire," replied the pilot.

I looked the man deep in the eyes. "And the ships?" I quavered.

"Sire, we just finished checking them. The Dove and my ship are all right, but the other merchantman has been scuttled! Smashed to bits! Planks and shreds of canvas lie strewn everywhere, Your Grace."

My mind burned like the volcano. "The water! What is the water like?" I exclaimed.

"Crazy," replied a young soldier, his face pale as death. "It's boiling and churning, rising and falling. We can't board those ships. We'll never get off this cursed island!"

"Easy lad," I said firmly. Turning to the pilot who had spoken, I said, "Here's what I want you to do: Take some men down to the wharf; shelter yourselves as best you can. Keep a close watch on the wicked sea, and, at the first sign of it letting up—and By-the-Goddess, it will let up—send two runners back here at once. We'll get off Kalliste at the first chance. Go now—quickly!"

The pilot tapped the shoulder of each man he wanted with him, four in all. As the sentinels raced from the square, they grabbed torches from some of those who had come with me from Therasia. In a moment, their torches were lost in the inky darkness of the city.

"All of you others—soldiers and sailors alike—take food now," I ordered. "Fill your stomachs. Goddess only knows when we'll eat again."

"Or if we'll eat again," said one of the soldiers as he turned away. I let the comment pass and walked smartly to the shelter. Lifting my torch up high, I examined the roof of the structure. I winced inwardly when I saw the dangerous overlay of ash and pebbles, nearly a foot high; the sturdy shelter was holding, just barely. I prayed to see the runners' torches as soon as possible.

The heavy oak door was out of line; I had to practically knock it down to get in. In the middle of the room, a disheveled and weary Ta-ch'ih was kneeling over Dymas. Death pervaded the dimly lit space. The sage slowly rose and staggered over to where I stood. My heart was pierced by severe pain, for, somehow, I saw that the hand of death, when it had come to claim Dymas, had brushed my old friend.

Though apart for only a couple of days, we embraced and kissed each other's cheeks. My throat was drier than when I had walked from Therasia. I could not speak. The wise sage knew all. He broke our silence with his inimitable words. "My dear Prince, for a long time to come your cherished land will be barren. I am sorry." He thought for a moment, then said, "As sure as the stars are above, one day people will return to this place and sounds of laughter will be heard once more." He added, "But this won't happen until many aeons have come and gone."

We searched each other's eyes. He looked tired and drawn, yet calm and serene. From my grief-stricken eyes, Ta-ch'ih saw that I knew of his fate. Slowly he turned away, motioning toward the frail body lying perfectly still. "At last the youth's spirit is free to fly with the Wanderers. The graceful butterfly has left the awkward caterpillar behind. Who is to say it is not for the best?"

My head pounded. I was too unsettled to think high ideas. In order not to break, I had to concentrate on what was before my eyes.

"His fate seemed tied to the great mountain," explained the sage. "When it began to spew forth its wrath and trumpet in anger, Dymas's recovery stopped. Each tremor of the earth he matched with fits, shivering, and shaking. Each boom he echoed with anguished cries. The warmer it became outside, the more he burned from within. Finally— just before you arrived, Sire—his soul decided it had had enough…it was time."

We bowed our heads. The creaking of the roof startled me. "I will have poor Dymas buried now," I said. "He will remain on the island of his birth. As soon as we can board our ships, Ta-ch'ih, we'll push off for Crete. I have posted men down at the port to alert us when the sea is calm. We'll be safe as soon as we leave this hellish place."

"Prince Idomeneus, you cannot outrun death."

I swallowed hard. "Maybe so, dear friend, but you can give death a run for the gold. Dymas is the last one we'll bury on Kalliste. I swear it!" With that, I led the old man to the door. In the square, the men had constructed lean-tos out of ox hides. Their heads shielded from the hailstorm, they crouched and hungrily gobbled their food like so many monkeys.

"You should eat something before the long sail," I advised Ta-ch'ih.

"No, your lordship, thank you. I wish to keep my stomach light, my wits sharp. Man is permitted to witness this kind of phenomenon only rarely. I want to take in everything while I still can."

I said nothing as I led the old sage to one of the lean-tos and sat him down.

Those who had finished their meager bread and cheese were busily scurrying to and fro, collecting wood for the fire. I grabbed two sailors and instructed them to dig a grave behind the shelter with as little fuss as possible and to tell me when they were done.

The continuous clamor had stopped. Instead, each explosion was spaced about eighty or ninety counts apart. In an eerie way, the quiet, the stillness between booms, was worse than the booms them-selves. Each interlude seemed like death. Even though we expected them, when the reports shattered the unholy silence, we jumped like surprised fawns stepping into a lair. The earth was ashake after every boom, and a wave of hot air—hotter than the air that engulfed us—rolled over our heads. The air had the strong smell of the lethal vapor that had plagued Kalliste earlier. It made us cough, sneeze, and spit all at the same time.

When we glanced skyward, we saw amid the thunderflashes great white balls of fire spinning across the dark shroud. At first, I was dumbfounded by the new phenomenon, then, as with all the others, I got used to it.

When several writhing flashes and blazing balls of fire occurred at the same time, the entire city was illuminated. Everything stood out in sharp contrast then: the buildings, the debris, and we humans. We appeared to be ghostly specters and could hardly bear looking at one another.

When neither the flashes nor the fireballs were igniting the air, an incredible darkness, a darkness you could feel, covered the city. Metapontus closed in on us. I felt as though we were in a tiny door-less, windowless room. We huddled around the fire like terrified sheep before the slaughter.

The two gravediggers motioned to me from the south side of the shelter. With Ta-ch'ih on my arm, I walked over to where they stood and told them to fetch the body and join us around back.

With the light and darkness alternating, it was slow going leading the sage around to the grave. The men brought the limp body and placed it gingerly in the trench. Even though he was not a priest, I asked Ta-ch'ih to say a few words. He asked me if he could speak in his native tongue. I said yes.

What a bizarre sight it was, the four of us standing there in the blinking light, one of us chanting in a barbaric tongue, and the volcano tattooing a deafening drum roll. When Ta-ch'ih finished, we filled the grave with ash and returned to the campfire, where we waited with the others. It was the longest wait of our lives.

TWENTY-ONE

OUR BODIES were wracked by weariness as never before. Yet, not one of us put his head down to rest; nobody could take his eyes off the volcano's display. Cowering beneath the sagging lean-tos, we mumbled prayers and begged to be spared as the doomsday cloud mushroomed overhead. If we hadn't known that the angry Goddess was destroying only Kalliste, we would have sworn that that day was the world's last.

In the gray swirling maelstrom, we were pelted with airborne pebbles and stones — sizzling hot. We picked off the scorched clothing that stuck to our burned skin.

Now and then, the sky overhead would burst into unimaginably brilliant light, caused not by the thunderflashes nor the fireballs but by the explosions on the summit of the volcano. When the explosions occurred, every detail of Metapontus stood out starkly, as did the surrounding landscape, including Mount Kalliste. Someone noticed that in two ravines midway up the mountain there were clearly rivers of some sort of material flowing downhill. The material was viscous and red. And it glowed as though it were extremely hot. What was it? By this point, any new phenomenon—no matter how bizarre—would not surprise us. It did frighten us, however, because if these rivers remained funneled within the ravines and continued their rapid descent, they soon would be upon us. When the brilliant light stopped and we were cast into utter darkness, we waited impatiently for the next explosion and its accompanying light so that we could track the progress of the flows. How long we experienced the weird alternation of day and night and witnessed the strange bleeding of Mount Kalliste was anybody's guess. Time had no meaning then. It was as if we were trapped not on an island, nor even on the earth itself, but rather on some pulsating star.

Eventually, the startling bursts of light became less frequent and then stopped. A pall of darkness reigned. The downpour of ash and pebbles abated. The air was cool, the putrid smell diluted. Each one of us was afraid to say so for fear of endangering our chances, but I know the others held the same thought: the turbulent sea will soon be stilled.

Before long, two flickering torches lit up the road that entered the square from the south. The men stirred, bolting out of their lean-tos, knocking several over in the rush. Expectant voices filled the square.

Soon we heard racing footsteps. The runners appeared, heading toward us at breakneck speed. "Prince Idomeneus, the waves are subsiding," yelled one of the sentinels, gasping for breath.

"Does the pilot believe we can board now?" I demanded.

"He says we should try, your lordship," replied the other sentinel. "You must understand, Sire," he added in a guarded manner, "that the sea is far from calm—but it's improved considerably"

"Strike while the iron is hot, Idomeneus," I said under my breath.

Ordering the men to fall in two abreast, I led Ta-ch'ih to the front of the line and tightly entwined my arm with his. I vowed to myself that he would not leave my side until our feet felt the planks of the Dove.

As swiftly as the sage could go, we made our way through the once busy warren that had been Metapontus. An uneasy quiet pervaded the deeply shrouded city. The volcano was mute. The ground still. The thunderflashes and fireballs were extinguished. Only a light shower of ash and cinders and an indescribable blackness made that night different from any other, if, in fact, it was truly night.

When we reached the wharf, the three other sentinels were attempting to lay planks across to the gunwale of the merchantman. They were failing miserably, for, as the craft rose and fell, each plank in succession slipped into the brine. The runners had not lied, the waves had gone down all right, but our boarding would nevertheless be dangerous. "Forget the planks," I shouted to the frustrated men. "We'll jump for it!"

I sent the officer and about three quarters of the men over to the large ship and the rest scurried alongside the Dove. Five or six men at a time toed the edge of the wharf, waiting for the merchantman to rise to its highest point. When it did, the men leapt for all they were worth, landing with thuds onto the well-made deck. Once aboard, the men scrambled to their feet and tried to aid their comrades who were about to leap for their lives.

At the same time, the Dove was being filled to overflowing as valiant soldiers and sailors leapt onto her deck. It didn't take long before all of the men except Ta-ch'ih and me were safely aboard either the merchantman or the Dove.

"Ready to fly, my friend?" I asked the wizened sage. I didn't wait for his reply but instead picked him up and cradled him in my arms like a babe. I leaned over the rolling Dove and threatening water, the live cargo held tight to my body, and, timing the ascent of the craft perfectly, I released Ta-ch'ih. Like a sparrow tumbling out of a nest, the old man dropped straight down, into the waiting arms of two of my crewmen.

The Dove was crammed with men, but they squeezed together and made an opening for me. I took off. My feet struck the mantle of loose ash and pebbles on the deck, slipping right out from under me. Fortunately, the circle of men was so tight that I was buttressed before I crashed to the boards.

We weighed anchor. The metal was warm to the touch and its usual coating of barnacles had been stripped away, as if cleaned and polished. Down went the oars. They plummeted through the layer of lighter-than-water pebbles clogging the port. Most of the pebbles were small, the size of olives, but some could rightly be called rocks for they were the size of a newborn's head. The Dove left a narrow wake through the bizarre layer of pebbles, so narrow, in fact, that I had to lean over the stern and look under to see it. I had to look quickly because the dark swath in the pebbles healed at once, as if the ship was a plough tilling the land, making a furrow that wouldn't remain open. Our passage through the pebble layer created a soft crunching noise, a noise like no other.

The weight of ash on the rigging and yardarms made the ships list; I put some men to work busily brushing and knocking the ash overboard. As soon as we were a good distance from the port, up went the sails. It's a good thing they had been stowed away so carefully, because the smoldering rain would have burned them into useless rags.

The sea was nothing but white caps, though it wasn't nearly as rough as it had been in the bay. We headed due south, for Crete.

While the bone-weary, defeated men tried to doze off where they could, Ta-ch'ih sat quietly, safely tucked away in my overcrowded cabin. I took some pleasure—the first in several days—thinking how I had cheated the Goddess by stealing the foreigner away from Her death grip. The feeling that he was doomed had been so strong back in the shelter; yet, there he was sailing for Crete. I began to believe that maybe Diktynna's grand design could be circumvented, just a little, thus keeping intact a thread in The Web that might otherwise have been torn asunder.

Visibility was poor—only a few feet at most. The Dove pitched and rolled unpredictably. As I moved along the deck checking the men, my hands clung to the rigging, the gunwale, the shoulder of a man. Peering out from underneath an oxhide, two dull eyes caught my attention: they belonged to the master builder, Hyllus. "We made it, Hyllus." No reply. "We made it Hyllus," I say." No reply. The Cretan stared at me as if he were lost in another world; he would not or could not acknowledge my presence.

Sometimes in war, a man will freeze, become lifeless. No one can reach him. The savagery of battle, the gore, the maimed bodies can draw a shade over a man's eyes, and he comprehends nothing. That is what happened to Hyllus. For the sake of the others aboard, I did not make a stir, instead leaving the poor Cretan to his thoughts, if, indeed, he had any.

We had been out for some time, when the watch bellowed, "Ship dead ahead!" Muscling through the throng, I made my way onto the bow and caught sight of a rapidly approaching vessel, its mast and sail underlit by flickering torches. It must be a rescue ship from the capital, I thought. Why only one, though? Maybe they're pirates or raiders from the inland, taking advantage of the chaos caused by Kalliste? Why else would a ship be headed north, now, daring to skirt the fiery island? It was two against one, but we were in no condition to fight.

On my command, the rowers took their benches. I instructed the helmsmen to be ready to run to the east. Soon the mysterious vessel was within hailing distance.

"Ahoy, there!" I sang out as loud as I could. "Under whose banner do you sail?" There was no reply. My body tensed as did, I'm sure, those of my comrades. I hailed the ship again. Still no reply, though we could hear voices and movement on the deck. I was about to give the order to fly when, belatedly, someone on the advancing vessel yelled out. He spoke in our tongue, but the words were butchered so badly that I had to ask the man to repeat himself.

"Your language is difficult," explained the gruff voice, "but I'll try. My name is Jason, son of Aeson. I was taught by the wise Chiron. I captain this vessel. It flies the banner of Iolcus, far to the north."

A barbarian. Do we run for it or stay and talk? Before I could reach a decision, the captain spoke again. "You must be Prince Idomeneus of Kalliste. May we pull alongside? We have some fresh water and provisions we can spare." Though his manner was crude, his words rang true.

"You're right, Captain Jason, I am Prince Idomeneus. Yes, please, pull between us. Our throats are as parched as summer grass."

As the Achaean ship emerged from the haze and came up to us, we were startled by its dimensions, for it was the largest craft we had ever encountered: at least fifty oars. Cruel waves and sharp reefs had clawed its hull unmercifully. The ship must have been at sea a long time; it badly needed repairs. The pilot eased her between the merchantman and the Dove. Lines were tossed out, and all three vessels were drawn together. On the unadorned prow, an Achaean word—the craft's name I assumed—was crudely carved and considerably worn. I read it as "Argo." I did not know if it was someone's name or a thing.

The crew of the Argo swiftly passed jugs of water over to my men, who just as swiftly drained them. Captain Jason walked along the spacious deck until he came opposite me. We exchanged salutes. He held out a crudely made gray pitcher and offered it to me. My dry lips tingled as the cool water ran over them.

"By-the-Gods, how did you escape?" the Achaean asked, staring into the blackness to the north. He didn't wait for an answer, declaring, "It was either a miracle, or fiery Vulcan took pity on your mortal being and spared you." I shrugged my shoulders and drank. He continued. "The Kallisteans and Cretans think you and your men have perished. There was some talk at Amnisos of sending out rescue ships. But they decided that it was too late. They're back there mourning you now...when they're not praying to save themselves," he said.

"Does this pall of darkness cover Crete?" I asked fearfully.

"It's getting darker there well before its time, but the darkness is not as bad as this."

"Back at Kalliste, it's like the blackest night you've ever seen. What time of day is it, anyway?"

Turning his head to the south, Captain Jason peered through the dense murk and said, "It should be close to midday, but without the sun —"

"You know, this course you're on will take you straight to Kalliste," I warned. "It would be best to give her the widest possible berth. I'd say swing east of Analfi, and possibly all the way around Astipalaea and use those islands as shields...shields from the bombardment of stinging ash and scorching rocks, from insufferable heat and poisonous gases, from earsplitting explosions and wild thunderflashes —"

"Almighty Zeus!"

"No words can describe the horror we've seen. None of your bards — no matter how great — have ever sung of such sights."

"I assure you, Prince Idomeneus, I will heed your advice and head for Astipalaea."

"But what puts you on the water at this dangerous time, anyway, Captain Jason. Surely you could have remained on Crete until things died down?"

"I'm not so sure of that, Prince. The Cretans are filled with uneasiness. Ash sprinkles their well-combed and oiled hair, and they're afraid it's going to get worse."

"Ash falling on Crete? Oh, Earth Goddess, why do you do this thing?" I asked the blackness around me.

"Reports say that the east part of the island is covered with the stuff. Crops are suffering terribly. West Crete has been spared, though."

"So far," I said glumly.

"Also, it has gotten unseasonably cold. Like the dead of winter. The uneasy atmosphere, coupled with yesterday's escape by the Athenians, convinced me that foreigners, inland foreigners, had better leave at once."

"Escape of what Athenians?"

"Oh, the son of King Aegeus and his people...what's his name—"

"Theseus?"

"Aye, that's him. King Minos's men were holding him prisoner, but in the confusion that swept over Knossos the last few days, the daring Theseus broke out. Don't know how he could have made it through the Labyrinth without inside help," Jason said out of the corner of his mouth. "The Cretans know the full story, but, whenever we were around, they clammed up. All we know is that this Theseus sprang his friends loose, stole a boat, and shoved off. They could have been over-taken, I'm sure, but the king's navy did not pursue. Old King Minos probably figured that the enraged sea would do his work for him."

Half to myself, half out loud, I said, "Maybe, maybe not."

"You know, the Cretans lump all of us Northerners together: Mycenaeans, Tirynsians, Thebans, Corinthians, Athenians, and Iolcusans like me are considered all one tribe. Thus, when Theseus escaped, we felt the Cretan ire, as if we had conspired with a man we didn't even know. Best to take our chances on the open sea, I thought. After all, we sailed all the way to Colchis in the far north, then on the return voyage faced many dangers and monsters, including having an evil wind blow us all the way to Libya. But when we finally return home with the Golden Fleece in hand, the bards you referred to will sing our tales for centuries to come."

I had no idea what Jason was referring to and didn't bother to ask. "But don't underestimate what's directly ahead of you, Captain Jason. It could be fatal."

The Achaean nodded. "We were told you had three ships. Where's the other?"

"Smashed to splinters by frenzied waves."

"And lives lost?"

"No one perished at sea, but we buried one youth who was brutally attacked by a wild dog. The volcano sealed his fate."

"Wild dog? Sounds more and more like Hades itself." Jason cast his eyes up and down my body, then said, "Indeed, you and your men—if you don't mind my saying so, Prince—look as though you have traveled through the nether world."

"We owe our condition to days without seeing the life-giving sun, lack of water and food, no sleep, and squatting at the foot of an unpitying giant."

Jason took my words as a bold request. "My provisions are meager, Prince Idomeneus," he said, "but you and your men are welcome to some gruel and hardtack."

"No, thank you kindly, Captain. I reckon we're about half way to Crete." Jason nodded in agreement. "We're eager to touch land, to see our loved ones. Nourishment can wait till then."

Looking across to the merchantmen and around the deck of the Dove, I saw that the men had slaked their thirst. Picking up the pitcher again, I gulped down the last of its water. "We must be gone," I said. "And I recommend you depart, too, good Captain. There's no way of knowing when things might get worse. For my men and me, I thank you for your kind aid. May you bestow glory upon your motherland."

"Prince Idomeneus, man of much sorrow, I bid you farewell. May Poseidon see you safely to Crete, and may you somehow prosper when this sad tale is over. Farewell."

"Farewell, Captain Jason."

The crews shouted their goodbyes. The Kallistean vessels headed south toward the light and the Argo headed north toward the abyss. Before the torches on the Argo faded, we saw her veer to the east, and, I presumed, for Astipalaea.

The decks of the merchantman and the Dove buzzed about the fact that Crete was being plagued by the ash. If and when the volcano resumed its violence, would Knossos and the other north coast cities be silted over, we wondered? And would pebbles, rocks, and boulders come flying across the sea, raining down death and destruction on the most cherished island on earth? Kalliste and its people would be blamed, of course, for the ravaging of Crete. Phanus, the Dove's pilot and of island stock, recalled a Kallistean legend that predicted that one day the islanders would get revenge for the Cretan conquest of the Cyclades. Those of Cretan stock aboard mumbled or cursed out loud. One soldier said that Minos would send us Kallisteans packing and we would be lowly refugees once more. Beyond the lap of the waters, in some savage land, we would have to set up our lonely colony. Once talk like that started, there was no way to squelch it.

Soon the talk was fueled by the volcano's wrath; once more, Kalliste began banging out its message of doom. We looked to the north in search of other signs of renewed activity and caught glimpses of thunderflashes flecking the dark sky.

Before long, we felt a storm brewing. We ran ahead of the storm as fast as we could. But a blinding squall, composed of rain and ash, overtook us and soaked us to the bone. Each raindrop was as big as an eye and filled with sharp particles. I ordered the sails brought down and the oars dropped.

Whipped by the wind, the sea rose in frenzied wrath. Both the water and the air howled like tortured demons. The turbulent air was aswim with ash, sand, and pebbles. Gigantic rollers lifted the ships like childrens' toys, spraying the decks with gray salt water laden with grit that stung like needles.

Crete was not far off, but the Goddess was determined to stop us and cast us into a watery grave. Phanus and the helmsman tried to control the Dove as best they could, until they were forced to up oars and just ride the waves. I don't know what happened to the merchantman for we lost sight of her. We never saw her again. Ropes snapped across the Dove's beam, whipping the deck and human beings alike. We lashed ourselves down and held on.

The din reached a feverish pitch. Thunderflashes as bright as silver shot overhead on both sides of the Dove. Soon the flashes began to strike the mast and rigging, causing them to crackle and glow. Then the men began to shriek, shouting out that they had been hit and frantically shaking injured arms and legs, as if to bring them back to life. I was struck twice myself.

To add to the chaos, fireballs fell from the sky, glancing off the mast and yardarm and causing huge hungry pink flames to dance across them. Several fireballs crashed onto the deck, and though no one was hit directly, we were all sprayed with singeing sparks. After a while, the shocking flashes and fireballs abated. We counted ourselves lucky to be alive.

Though it no longer carried the cursed ash, the rain beat down harder and harder, bringing instead a new tormentor: mud. The red sticky mud clung to the rigging and produced a soft white light, like the kind sailors see when an entire ship will glow for no reason. As with those times, when we ran our wary hands over the ropes, the glow went out. As far as their flailing arms could reach, the men blotted out the spectral light by wiping away the mud. Working like mad, some even untied their safety lines in order to reach farther. It was as if obliterating the glow would remedy everything, and all of the bizarre phenomena would suddenly disappear.

Day blinked on and off just as on Kalliste. The muffled reports of the volcano could be heard above the howling storm. At times, the Dove rolled ahead of the waves broadside on her beam. She pitched and rolled but wouldn't heel over. Throughout the ordeal, I never lost heart. I knew the storm, coming from Kalliste as it did, was driving the Dove south, closer to Crete.

Little by little, the downpour slackened and the gloom lifted, the wind died down and the waves subsided. By late afternoon, we saw the spiny backbone of Crete. Correcting our course, we sped for the west side of Thwart-the-Way. When we entered the broad harbor, the ash-coated water was choppy, but nothing compared to that over which we had made our escape. An armada of vessels lurched to and fro, circling their anchors. It looked as though the entire navy and most of the trading fleet were in; they were lucky not to be on the high seas at such a time.

A shower of fine ash sifted through the atmosphere. Having watched our approach, the people milling on the broad dock eagerly awaited us. Before we could even toss out our ropes, questions were shot at us from excited townsfolk, merchants, and sailors. From the gunwale of the Dove, the sailors and the soldiers shouted back their answers. The whole scene was deafening and chaotic.

Disembarking, we were embraced — almost crushed — by the Kallisteans present. The Cretans did not seem overjoyed at our safe return. Water and food were produced, and we swilled and gobbled in between answers.

The sound of a familiar voice caught my attention. "Let an old man through, will you," growled Rib-Addi. "I must see the prince. Out of my way! Damn, let me through!" I shoved by some bodies, meeting the old foreigner in the middle of the throng.

"I never gave up on you, my lord. Never," cried Rib-Addi, hugging me to his boney chest. He gazed heavenward, saying, "Oh, Merciful Mother, thank you for sparing the bravest of the brave." For his thanks, Rib-Addi got a mouthful of ash. He spat it out in disgust.

"It's good to see you, my friend. You don't know how good," I said. "Listen, how fares Crete? What about Phaistos?"

"It's been the way you see it now, Sire, for about two days. During the day, the vault gets brighter, but we don't see much of the sun. This confounded ash is silting up most of the island. Vines are being crushed, leaves are being sheared off trees, streams are being choked to death."

"And Phaistos, what about Phaistos?"

"The palace at Phaistos reports only dark skies, no ash...yet. Palaikastro, Kato Zakro, Gournia, and other places to the east are suffering the most because the Boreas and the Zephyrus have joined forces."

"Has the earth remained still?"

"Aye, my lord. We are plagued only by the ash and oppressive cold sent by Kalliste," Rib-Addi declared, shaking his disbelieving head.

"How do the Kallisteans and Cretans behave?"

"Everyone is deathly afraid, Prince Idomeneus. Some say the end of the world is at hand. Everytime the volcano makes a noise the people go crazy. Cries ring out across the countryside. Beasts of burden go berserk, forcing their way into households, braying and screeching until the noise subsides.

"The priestesses are performing secret rites day and night at the palace and on top of Mount Juktas near Arkhanes. King Minos and his advisors have been assuring the Cretans that the sky will clear soon. The people—at least the ones down here at Amnisos—don't believe it. They say the Earth Mistress won't be happy until She's pulled down the whole kingdom!"

Casting my eyes toward the crowd, I said to Rib-Addi, "In this time of crisis, I hope that the Cretans and Kallisteans are working together, aiding one another."

Rib-Addi cleared his throat, then put his mouth to my ear.

"There are some troublemakers who are grumbling, Your Grace. They're trying to start something against your people, but nothing's come of it. I hasten to add that most of the Cretans are levelheaded; they know you Kallisteans are innocent in all of this. I mean, you folks have suffered the most! Sire, the Cretans are just concerned about their homes, their possessions. They're confused and frightened. The thing with Prince Theseus didn't help matters."

"Aye, I heard about it."

"What! How could you?"

"One Jason, a captain of a many-oared Achaean ship, came upon us halfway down. He gave us water. It was he who told me the shocking news. But this Jason—poor man, must have been swamped out there—didn't have the full story. Rib-Addi, how on earth did Theseus pull it off?"

"With the help of Princess Ariadne, that's how!"

My throat constricted as if I had gulped poison. I managed to get out, "Wha...what happened?"

"It appears that the princess and the barbarian were carrying on an affair! No one knew about it! A few guards conspired with them—paid off handsomely by the princess, no doubt. Much good their ill-gotten gold got them."

"Why?"

"The guards were exposed and swiftly beheaded early this morning. But the real culprits, the lovers, got away. Before they fled, though, they did a strange thing that I can't figure out, Your Grace.

"What?"

"Instead of fleeing straightaway, Ariadne led Theseus through the Labyrinth, past the busy guards, and right...right into the king's suite!"

"No! What on earth was she thinking of? Was she out of her mind?"

"As I said, Sire, I can't figure it out. I don't know, but maybe she knew she would never be allowed to set foot on Crete again and wanted to see her father one last time. That's only a guess."

"My Goddess, what did Theseus do?"

"As soon as he saw the king, he reached for a double axe, that's what! Raising it high in the air, he roared that he would have his revenge for all of the indignities he suffered at Minos's hands. That would have been it for Minos."

"What happened?"

"As Theseus went for the king, Princess Ariadne darted between them, wailing that Theseus would have to take her life, too, if he took her father's. Tears gushed forward, she tore her hair out in clumps and pleaded as no one had pleaded before. We have all this from King Minos himself.

"For a moment, it seemed as if the ruinous Theseus would split both father and daughter in half with a single stroke. That heart of stone which beats under the barbarian's breast miraculously softened, for he swung the double axe off to the side, bringing it down right on the king's ancient headdress, the one worn at the festivals. That proud headdress was cleaved in two, one bull horn on either side. 'There, you damnable tyrant,' Theseus ranted, motioning toward his handiwork. 'That's what I'll do to your ocean empire! I've spared you this time, thanks to your daughter. But your days are numbered, King!'

"Grabbing Ariadne by the arm and practically pulling her through the air, Theseus fled the innermost confines of the Labyrinth. The lovers made their way to the guests' apartments where, with the help of more traitorous guards, they sprang the other Athenians. Carts took them down to the shore where a ship—the very one they arrived on—was waiting for them. No one spotted the getaway, because the ash cloud dropped a curtain for them." Turning toward the north, Rib-Addi said, "Somewhere out there, they are making their escape, no doubt, to the inland and Athens."

Through my mind swirled back-eddying thoughts. I put words to them. "Goddess, when I had the chance…nay, the chances…I should have sent that barbarian's soul down to Hades, wailing for its fate."

TWENTY-TWO

KALLISTE RUMBLED in the distance as we threw our haversacks over our shoulders and headed out of the port. I felt that if we could only make it to the palace—a short walk to the south—we would be out of earshot, thus, somehow safe. My men from Phira and the Cretan soldiers must have felt the same way. When I gave the order, they fell in before the blinking of an eye.

For the time-worn Ta-ch'ih and Rib-Addi, I secured sedan chairs from an Amnisosan merchant with whom I had had dealings. Some of my men grumbled as they hoisted the carrying poles onto their shoulders. "Stow it," I said sternly. We were all a bit jumpy.

As we hurried through the streets, it felt good, strange to say, having only a thin layer of ash under foot. When we reached the outskirts of Amnisos, we were stopped in our tracks by five tremendous explosions. Our hands shot to our ears, pressing tightly in an attempt to seal them off. The sedan bearers dropped their loads; Ta-ch'ih and Rib-Addi went sprawling but managed to save their hearing by covering their ears.

After the fifth report, we waited a long time before bringing our hands to our sides. Suddenly, five powerful blasts of debris-laden air hit the north coast, almost knocking us off our feet. What had happened on our island home, no one could begin to imagine.

"Pick up the chairs," I shouted. "Let's keep moving! The farther south we go—the farther away from Kalliste—the better off we'll be!"

We went over the bridge spanning the Amnisos River at full gallop, then skirted the ridge that lies to the west. Daylight began to fail. The atmosphere was frigid and smoky. We pressed on.

We were surprised to hear a commotion behind us coming from Amnisos even though we were downwind and the wind was strong—the shouting at the port must have been uproarious. Animals added to the din, braying and barking dementedly. If a reaction to the explosions, why, we wondered, was it so delayed? I sent one of my crewmen scrambling up the side of the rocky ridge to see if he could learn what was happening. Though a fair climb, the man went as if he were a mountain goat so anxious was he to discover the reason for the commotion. We lost sight of him for a moment. He reappeared on top of the ridge waving his arms vigorously for me to join him. Though my legs ached, I made my way up the ridge. When I approached him, the man screamed, "My lord, the sea has vanished! Come!"

I didn't doubt him—at that point, anything was possible. Panting, I came directly alongside the sailor. We stood on a spot that gave us a full view of the north shore. By-the-Goddess, the man was right. The port of Amnisos was dry. The rugged sea floor was completely exposed for a couple hundred feet out. Beyond that, I could see the water streaming away from us, away from the coast, out toward Thwart-the-Way. The sea was running the wrong way! There were no waterspouts or whitecaps. The surface wasn't tortured as it had been around Kalliste. The water was simply being sucked toward the north by some unknown force.

Minos's mighty navy, one of the great wonders of the world, sat beached on the muddy bottom, its famous ships looking like so many toy boats keeled over in an empty tub. Still securing ships to their anchors, the once taut ropes lay limp, crisscrossing one another in a confused jumble. I spotted the faithful Dove. What a sight. Her stern was buried in the mud, but her bow, still roped to a mooring post on the pier, was ten feet higher; the Dove just hung there like some fowl strung to a rafter. Her mast was split in half; her rudder crushed beneath the stern.

The buildings of Amnisos were emptying as townsfolk raced down to the wide dock to view more closely the incredible scene. Stampeding in the opposite direction, up the ridge or down the adjacent valley, mules, dogs, and other creatures were evacuating the town, outstripping the wind as they went. No wonder the frenzied din had reached us.

From our high vantage point, my crewman and I saw all. In the shallow pools in front of the dock, we saw wild splashing, and we guessed that sea creatures had been trapped when the water receded. Soon a handful of men climbed down from the dock with baskets in hand and reaped the unexpected harvest. Amazed, I stood on the ridge watching the men — probably greedy fishmongers blind to the ominous signs all around them — elbow each other for the biggest fish.

Not only at Amnisos, but all along the coast, as far as the eye could see, a wide swath of land was exposed. Where the waves had lapped the shore a short time before, large sections of sea bottom and bizarrely shaped rocks could be seen.

I hollered down to the expeditionary party, "Bring the two foreigners up here at once!" The sweating sedan bearers lumbered to the top of the ridge, and Ta-ch'ih and Rib-Addi were helped to their feet. I ushered them over to where they could see the bewildering sight. "Have either of you ever encountered or heard of anything like this before?"

"I don't believe it," Ta-ch'ih uttered

Rib-Addi stood silently, gazing transfixed at the port. Suddenly, he began to shake all over.

"Rib-Addi, what is it," I cried. "My friend, do you know what this means? Tell me at once!"

Wheeling around, the Easterner stared at me with eyes filled with terror. He stammered, "Sire...I...I remember stories...old stories...from back...back home about waters like this along the coast of Canaan before...before—"

"Before what! Before what!"

"Before waves, Your Grace, waves!" Rib-Addi broke into rapid speech, almost swallowing his words. "Huge killer waves. They come from nowhere and can sink ships, flatten buildings, wipe out whole cities. I thought the stories were just the nightmares of old sailors, but—"

My chest was tight with fear. I cried out, "By all that's sacred, we must warn the people!"

"Too late, my prince," interrupted a distant and dispassionate voice. It was Ta-ch'ih. He was standing a few steps ahead of us, staring not at the port, but beyond. I looked out and beheld what the old man beheld. All that the greatest magician could conjure up would be far, far less than that awesome sight. Behind Thwart-the-Way, there arose a monstrous wall of water. Its height was incalculable. Imagine how it would be if the horizon suddenly sprang up hundreds of feet higher. That is what it looked like; from east to west the wall of water rose to the sky.

In no time, a howling wind was upon us, carrying with it the desperate cries from the port. As if they had been staked down, our feet were fixed to the ridge. We watched dumbfounded as the massive wave rolled in, growing bigger and bigger.

Suddenly something snapped in my head: the others. Warn the others in the expeditionary party below! I dashed to the edge of the ridge and shouted as loudly as I could. Though the wicked wind muffled my voice, my frantic arms told the men down below to flee at once, and straight up the valley they went. When I turned back toward the shore, I saw the wave—like some mountain rushing onward—almost upon the port. At that sickening moment, I, along with the others on the ridge, realized that the wave would reach well beyond the port.

Those around me broke like terrified deer; Rib-Addi was as swift as an arrow. But, like the stone that stands unmoved before the tomb of a dead man, Ta-ch'ih stood motionless. I picked him up, flung him over my shoulder like a sack and bolted.

I had no fears nor thoughts then. My body knew only to run, run, run.

I don't know how far I got—a couple of court lengths, maybe—when suddenly I became aware of a rumbling that was overtaking me. It was then I knew fear. One moment I was running, my arm firmly clasped around Ta-ch'ih, the next I was treading water, having been picked up by a frothing, twisting maelstrom. I didn't let go my precious cargo, nor did I sink. Instead, like a feather, I rode high above the chaos. It was as if time had stopped. My legs were thrashing, but it seemed as if they were moving at slow speed. Buoyed, Ta-ch'ih and I were carried along.

The ride ended abruptly. All at once we dropped like an anchor. I knew we would die. Down, down Ta-ch'ih and I went into a tumultuous, black abyss. We were dragged and hurled, shoved and jerked, lashed and battered. Then, Ta-ch'ih was gone.

I don't know how, but I remember seeing shadowy images of people I knew. Were they before my eyes, within my head, within my heart? Never mind, they were there. My father and mother. Good old Miletus. Rhadamanthys, Catreus, and the three sages. My Aphaea. Even hideous Sarpedon. Their presence seemed right and proper. I was, somehow, at ease.

The breath of life I had taken down to the murky depths was just about extinguished. So at peace was I, though, that I began to open my mouth, heedless of the result.

Suddenly, I felt pain, excruciating pain. It shot from my right arm down my side. I had struck something hard and immovable, and it nearly broke me in two. I clutched for it. My arms and legs were darting snakes, wrapping around the thing and pulling my entire body up against it. It was a tree.

My peaceful state was shattered. My mind reeled. This is it, one chance to live. Climb! Climb I did, using every bit of strength, every part of my body. Now that I think about it, I didn't even know if I was climbing up or down, toward air or earth, so pitch black and chaotic was it down there. My body simply moved in the direction my head was pointing.

The tree trunk was without end. Or so it seemed. My chest felt as if it were being crushed in a vice. My arms and legs began to fail me. My back bent in sympathy with the swiftly moving current, which tugged relentlessly at me. I started to melt into the surrounding darkness.

All of a sudden, my head popped through the surface. Air! My jaw snapped open. I gasped loudly. My nostrils flared. My chest hurt as much as when it was crushed by lack of air, for I hungrily swallowed the life-sustaining air.

Good thing, for without warning I was submerged again; it was as if a smaller wave had run up the back of the giant one. Scaling the trunk as quickly as I could go, once more I broke into the sweet air. Overhead my groping hands discovered the crotch formed by the branching of the tree. Summoning all the strength I had left, I hoisted myself up and into the crotch, slumping there exhausted. Like bronze clamps, my arms and legs clung to the tree. It was an oak, shorn of its leaves and most of its upper branches.

Not even the substantial tree could convince me that land was below and that I was not lost at sea. The wind raged on. The water ran by at an incredible speed, straight for Knossos. It was useless to look for Ta-ch'ih or Rib-Addi, or any of the others.

I reckoned that all of Crete had been inundated by the gigantic wave. It was the end of everything and everybody I knew and loved. For a moment—a brief moment—I thought of releasing my life grip and just sliding off the tree, falling back into the water and joining my beloved friends.

My head unclouded. I saw then how impossible it was for a wave, no matter how great, to climb over Mount Juktas, Mount Dikte, Mount Ida. The north shore of Crete may have been obliterated, but certainly not the south, certainly not the Messara, certainly not Phaistos.

After a while, distant thunderflashes streaked the realm of total black, illuminating the surface of the restless water. Floating upon it were huge blocks, some the size of houses, composed of compressed ash and pebbles. Pushed in front of those snow-white islands, trees, branches, and confused heaps of I know not what streamed by at a frightening speed. A few of the pebble islands carried the remains of buildings and their holdings from Amnisos. In the eerie light, I could make out buckled doors, sections of plastered walls, broken furniture, and carpets, curtains, and clothes. The remains of the buildings were inextricably intertwined with uprooted trees, shrubs, and with twisted forms I knew were human corpses.

While I clung to the tree, I did not see another living thing. Now and then above the roar of the wind and water, I heard a faraway moan or a cry. There was no possible way of helping anybody, though I did call out. No one answered. No one except a goat that bleated after one of my calls.

It wasn't long before the water slowed its surge to the south. The current turned sluggish, then stopped altogether. The pebble islands, laden with debris, bobbed gently on the surface. Then, the sea began moving in the opposite direction, toward the shore. As the water reversed itself, my tree, having withstood the onslaught of the killer wave, groaned and shuddered. A whirlpool spun around the trunk, which began to bend alarmingly. Soon only my head was above water.

When the ghostly islands of ash and pebble had sailed by earlier, they had kept their distance, but on their return, they came dangerously close to my tree. None hit it or that would have been the end of me. But I had to duck under when branches and planks from ships sped by on their own.

My tree weathered the reverse floodtide. The water level dropped rapidly and in a short time was only a few feet deep. Even so, if I had jumped down, I would have been swept away in a moment; the current was still formidable, clawing unmercifully at the earth, tearing up low-lying bushes and grass, and churning up the soil. Soil and plants were mixed into an ugly gray gruel. The precious land of the Cretans was being destroyed by the sea water.

Eventually the water retreated from the ridge, leaving a ruinous battlefield behind. I was afraid that another wave or several might strike Crete; thus, I remained high in my sanctuary. Except for the thunderflashes, there was not a glimmer of light to see by, anyway. I figured I'd stay put until morning. I grabbed a tattered bed sheet as it went by, tore it in half, and used it to tie my bone-weary body to the oak. Soon I was overtaken by a numbing sleep. If the sea returned to the ridge that night, it did so quietly, for I slept straight through till the following morning; I guessed it was morning because the sky was not as black as it had been. There was no sun, just an orange haze and a steady rain of fine ash. What caused me to stir was not the feeble half-light of dawn nor the ashen shower. It was the temperature. It was freezing.

I tried to bring heat to my body by running my left hand over it vigorously; my right hand was useless, for my shoulder and arm were terribly bruised. While trying to warm myself, I peered through the haze and became eyewitness to the unimaginable. Fair Crete was no more; it had melted. It appeared so because of the all-engulfing mud.

Twisted and tumbled, dismembered trees lay strewn over the ravaged ridge. A few—like my oak—stood defiantly, stripped of their branches, bent but not broken. The earth was brutally torn, as if thousands of ploughs had been pulled helter-skelter over it. In the furrows, still pools of ash-laden water reflected periodic thunderflashes.

Half-climbing, half-slipping, I made my descent. When my feet touched the earth, I sank up to my calves in sticky, smelly, red mud.

I felt compelled to see what had happened to Amnisos. I moved slowly along the ridge, a loathsome place. Planks from ships and houses and people's bedding and clothing made me pick my way carefully, afraid of what I might step on. Next to a large pool, I came across a ghastly sight: a hank of black hair and a gnarled hand sticking up through the glistening mud.

Eventually, I reached a spot where I could look down on the entire coast. Where once stood world-famous Amnisos, the harbor town of Knossos, there was only a waste of water. The water was a couple feet deep, I guessed, and it moved sluggishly. I could see from the destruction that the Goddess had taken no pity on Amnisos. Not a house nor a shop was left standing. Minos's navy and trading fleet were wiped off the face of the earth; not one intact hull did I see. The Dove was gone.

Tangled heaps of debris rose up through the soupy water. Jammed amidst the debris were twisted bodies, both animal and human. Those poor beings never had a chance.

As my stomach sickened at the sight of Amnisos, my arm throbbed with pain. I scooped up a handful of mud and applied the cool slop. I looked north, straining my eyes. Kalliste was hidden by the darkness. Nevertheless, I addressed my island: "I hope you sank into the sea, destroyed by your wickedness!" I turned away and headed for Knossos, plodding through the morass.

Descending the barren ridge to the valley floor, my movement was slow and labored. I waded through foul-smelling pools, tripped over slashing coral heads, and stepped on half-buried bizarre sea creatures. I worried that the killer wave had reached all the way to the capital.

As I went, I kept my eyes peeled for members of the expeditionary party. The farther I went, the more firmly rooted trees I saw. Maybe one of my sailors or a Cretan soldier had latched onto a sturdy tree, as I had done, and saved himself. Alas, every tree I came upon was empty.

Eventually I reached the outskirts of Knossos. Soon my feet were sinking not into yielding mud, but, instead, into soft ash. Scraping through it, I discovered that it was about four inches deep, about the same depth it was at Amnisos before the wave. There were no pools nor sea debris in sight. The wave had fallen short of the capital. Knossos stood! And as long as it did, we men of Minos still had a chance.

Though my legs were wobbly, I began to jog toward the palace. Soon my feet felt a firmer base beneath the ever-crumbling ash. I was on the Sacred Road. Ahead: dancing lights. I tried to call out, but nothing came forth; my throat was too swollen. All I remember is my foot knifing through the ash and catching the edge of one of the great stones. I flew forward, headfirst. Everything went black.

TWENTY-THREE

WHEN MY EYES OPENED, they were looking up at a sumptuously decorated ceiling. The intricate spiral and papyrus relief and the beautiful painting told me that I was in one of the palace rooms. Softened by luxurious pillows, the small cot that I lay on did not seem worthy of such splendor. In order that I might learn exactly which room it was, I rolled on my side. Like a shot, a wicked pain ran through my arm. I groaned, then heard someone rustle behind me. Craning my neck, I caught a glimpse of the fellow's back as he dashed from the room, pulling the door closed and locking it. Shouting did no good, the door remained closed. Strange, I thought.

Glancing around the room, my eye stopped at the grand table, piled high with documents and the like. It was then I knew where I was.

Before long, the thick door flew open and in strode a drawn and weary Catreus. He pulled a chair up alongside the cot and looked at me with worried eyes. "How are you, Idomeneus?"

"Better. Better since I've rested…and seen your face, good friend." A smile crept over his thin lips. "How long have I been out, Catreus?"

"Two full days. You woke briefly, once, and were given some broth. Don't you remember?"

"No. The last thing I remember was reaching the Sacred Way, seeing some lights, tripping, then— What happened next?"

"One of the search parties found you collapsed there and brought you in."

"Have they found any of my men? Ta-ch'ih or Rib-Addi, by some miracle?"

His brow wrinkled. He grasped my hand. "I'm afraid only two of your men have been found. They were making their way to the palace, like you."

"Who are they?" I asked weakly.

"I don't know. You'll see them soon. I believe only three or four of the soldiers who accompanied you have been found."

"And the poor people of Amnisos?" I muttered.

The son of Minos cast his grief-darkened eyes to the floor and said, almost in a whisper, "Only a dozen or so survived. A dozen or so from a town of hundreds," he moaned in disbelief, "The survivors flung themselves on floating debris, or—as they were pushed along by the wave—latched onto trees."

"That's why I speak to you now, Catreus, and why this arm and shoulder are damaged. I was driven into a proud oak."

"I thank the Goddess for placing that tree in your path, Idomeneus, but I curse Her to the stars for all the calamities She has wrought!" He dropped his head in his hands and was on the verge of tears.

"Tell me, dear Catreus: Are we doomed? Is the empire shattered?"

The prince turned his head to one side, trying to pull himself together. He said, "Every city, every town, every village on the north shore has been destroyed by the monster wave. At Palaikastro, Gournia, Mallia, and Kydonia, there is nothing left. Nothing!

"Nor at Amnisos," I added bleakly.

"Aye. We've dispatched orders to our remaining ships to return to Crete at once, regardless of the condition of the sea.

"Idomeneus, we are vulnerable and can only pray that Kalliste had thrown our adversaries into confusion, too. It will take us months to clean up the coast. Months! And to rebuild, well," he shook his head. "Right now, we're mustering rescue teams to help those poor souls who were left homeless and without families. As you saw, the great wave rolled inland a long way, a league or two in some places. The biggest problem we face now is pestilence."

"Pestilence?"

"Yes, all of those corpses lying unburied. Everywhere, stagnant pools breeding insects and vermin. We've called for aid, supplies, and men, from the central, south, and west parts of the island. Already, help is streaming in. We must try to ward off an epidemic." Catreus looked at me with a troubled expression. "We may be able to pull ourselves back together the way our forefathers did two centuries ago," he continued, "but not if your homeland doesn't stop tormenting us."

Shocked, I sat straight up. "Surely, Kalliste has exhausted itself by now. It can't still be ablaze."

"We're not sure of that; it's been black outside these last few days. But the field-burying ash keeps falling, and violent explosions can be heard now and then."

"After the killer wave, I cursed my island," I admitted, "hoping it had destroyed itself."

"You weren't alone in that wish."

Catreus went on to tell me some of the reports he had received. Up and down the north coast, children had seen their parents drown before their eyes, and husbands their wives. Entire families, entire clans, entire hamlets were wiped out. Fleeing the wave's lethal reach, fugitives ran down ravines and up hillsides, only to be killed or maimed by water-born oaks, elms, and pines, hundreds of years old, which were uprooted and carried along by the wave. As they tried to scramble to high ground, some people died of pure exhaustion.

At Kydonia, the popular market had remained open well past its usual closing time to accommodate the hard-pressed citizens, goods being difficult to procure since the volcano had reawakened. When they finally were able to reach the city, rescuers found the market glutted with bodies, many belonging to the merchants who kept the shops and stalls.

The sea completely inundated Mallia, where terror-stricken survivors reported that the water itself was on fire. What they meant was that in the towering torrent there were floating pebble islands upon which piles of debris burned brightly, the result of overturned lamps and braziers.

At Amnisos, the wave snatched up a warship and carried it eastwards and halfway up a hill. As if Dyktynna were making a bizarre offering to Eileithyia, the ship—its mast snapped off and its hull smashed in—was deposited at the mouth of the Eileithyian cave. An offering not to birth, but to death. A half day's walk inland from Amnisos, shepherds found coral blocks the size of oxen perched precariously on hillsides.

Though not even on the north coast, Kato Zakro, its gentle bay opening to the east, was pounded by heavy surf and suffered considerable damage. After the water receded, that once shining city was buried in a downpour of mud, ash, and gravel.

And, finally, Catreus told me that when the water departed the city of Palaikastro, the rescuers reported finding total destruction. Everything had been dragged off by the retreating sea, except—as if by some sinister hoax—all the bodies. Diktynna wanted to make sure an accurate count was made of Her foul deed.

When Catreus finished his lamentable account of the catastrophe, I lay back on the cot stunned. The respected son of Minos spoke to me softly. "I know as soon as you are well enough to travel, you'll want to return to your people. There'll be a chariot waiting for you and your two men."

Surprised, I stared at my friend and asked, "Don't you need me here at Knossos to direct rescue teams or to help organize the incoming men and supplies?"

Catreus stared back at me without expression. I waited for him to reply. "Idomeneus, I cannot promise you protection if you stay here much longer," he said.

"Protection," I stammered, taken aback.

"Oh, it's those confounded priests. They're looking for scapegoats for all this, and they've got my father's ear. They keep reminding him that some of your princes from Kalliste disobeyed him by refusing to carry out the human sacrifices."

"That was nonsense!"

"Yes, maybe. But the priests insist that had all those sacrifices been performed, none of these tragedies would have happened."

"Surely King Minos—"

"My friend," Catreus broke in, "nothing is sure these days. My father's mind is beclouded by all that has happened. One moment he takes my council, the next a priest's, tomorrow, who knows, a servant's! No, dear Prince of Phira, it's best you depart as soon as you're able. I only hope" — He looked down on me gravely, placing his hand on my good arm —"I only hope that the people of Phaistos do not feel the same way about you Kallisteans as my people here at Knossos do."

"Catreus, I thank you from my heart for your loyalty and love. If one of my men can drive, I think I can leave for Phaistos right now."

"Oh, you can rest here a little bit longer. I've got guards —"

"No, no, it's all right, friend."

"Sorry it has to be this way. Will I ever see you again, I wonder."

"I doubt it not."

Catreus stood up and walked to the door. "I'll have the chariot and your men brought around at once. May the Goddess Steerer leave Her wrathful ways, sparing those of us who remain."

"If there is a Goddess."

The prince did not rebuke me for my impiety, but simply turned his back and said in a quiet voice, "Farewell."

I never saw him again.

The guard entered and helped me from the cot; with bandages covering my upper body, I had difficulty moving. The guard wrapped my head in linen. I must have looked like one of those Egyptian mummies. The head bandage was not to protect a wound, but, alas, to conceal my identity.

I was led out of the study and down a broad corridor. After a few twists and turns, we were standing before a team of roans and a large chariot, upon which stood two heavily bandaged men. For a moment, I didn't recognize them as the helmsman, Otus, and a rower, Pteleon, both from the Dove. I was helped up into the chariot, and after a few words, determined that Pteleon's injuries were less severe and told him to drive. Though he had never driven before, Pteleon soon had us rattling over the cobblestones. Having been caught up in the turmoil of the last few days as well, the horses were tired and unruly. Pteleon showed them who was boss very quickly; after what we had been through, none of us was in a kind mood. Besides, being forced to sneak out of Knossos like thieves made our blood boil. So busy were they, sweeping, shoveling, and carting away the troublesome ash, the people of the palace paid us little attention.

When we passed through the city gate and headed up the valley, the three of us sighed as in one breath. Instead of its usual vibrant green, the winding valley looked as if it were wearing a rarely-seen blanket of snow. Frantic farmers knocked the white ash off the fruit trees and vines. But it was a losing battle; the smothering ash continued to fall.

During our drive, each of us told his story about the great wave. When I had signaled down to them from the ridge, Otus, Pteleon, and the others had broken and run as fast as their weary legs could carry them. Before they knew it, the wave overtook them. Otus lighted upon a tree and was saved.

Pteleon's story was incredible. When plunged into the turbulent water, he was turned topsy-turvy. He groped for any kind of help. Striking something large and solid, he grabbed it and held on for dear life. The object and he were slowly spun upward, like a lotus rising out of a murky pond. When his head broke the surface of the water, Pteleon discovered what had saved his life. A dead hog. The animal must have been a prizewinner, the rower said, for it had huge rolls of fat and was as big as a rowboat. The hog buoyed him throughout that unspeakable night. After the land seemingly rose from the sea, the two men stumbled toward Knossos, each believing that he was the expedition's sole survivor.

Even if Catreus had not had a basket of food placed in the chariot, we were determined not to stop to eat, hoping to make Phaistos in one day. As we went farther south, our minds reeled at all of the ash—a half-foot deep in some places—that had been spewed out of the Kallistean volcano. We wondered when on earth it would be exhausted. The first time the volcano erupted, Kalliste had received a heavy dose of ash. Heaven only knew how much it received that second time. What about all the ash falling on the nearby islands? And what about all of it falling into the broad sea.

Upon entering the Messara and heading for Phaistos, we noticed that the ash deposit was not as thick. The farther west we went, the thinner it got and the more vegetation we saw struggling through the ashen shroud. What we had heard in the capital was true: the southern and central parts of Crete had not been badly hit.

The sunset that evening was like none I had ever seen before nor ever could have imagined in my wildest dreams. As it started to go down, the sun turned a ghostly greenish-blue. Then it became a metallic green, the color of bronze when it has been buried under the earth for centuries. Even when the sun disappeared, the sky lit up in brilliant succession yellow, gold, orange, then, finally, blood red. The evening sky stayed aglow long after its usual time.

Late that night, we arrived at a place we thought we'd never see again: the palace of Phaistos. From the startled expression of the guards, we knew they hadn't expected us to return either. Their reaction was due in part to our ghostly appearance, for we emerged out of the blackness wrapped in white bandages. The guards practically carried us to Rhadamanthys's suite, where we awoke the prince from a sound sleep. Even amid the terrible crisis, my reunion with Rhadamanthys was sweet. "Oh, My Goddess, you're alive," he cried as we embraced. "I thought either the volcano on Kalliste or the great wave it generated had destroyed you."

"They both tried their damnedest."

"Everyone at Phaistos is grieving for you and your expeditionary party—where are the rest?"

"We're all that's left, Rhadamanthys."

"And, and Ta-ch'ih?"

"Gone. The wave took him."

Tears welled up in my friend's dark eyes.

I told Rhadamanthys of some of the calamities that had taken place over the last few days and how and why we had to flee Knossos in such haste. He was appalled. His tears of sorrow turned to tears of rage. "Not one Phiran will be troubled. Not one hair on one Phiran's head will be plucked, as long as I rule Phaistos," he roared. "None of you will be cast out; I swear it."

It did Pteleon and Otus good to hear the prince's resounding words, but for my part they were not necessary: Rhadamanthys and I were like brothers. I told him a few things Catreus had told me, then promised to return the following day to report further. Without me saying so, he understood how I yearned to go to Snow Crystal.

As he walked us to the door, Rhadamanthys grabbed my arm and said, "My Biadice is ill, very ill."

"Why?"

"We're not sure—she's had trouble breathing—it might be this smoky air."

"Kalliste's evil has finally reached Phaistos," I declared.

"Rest seems to be the best thing. Biadice has been in bed for three days."

"If Aphaea and I can be of help, let us know."

"Yes, I will." As we left, Rhadamanthys tried to buoy our spirits. "Though you bring tales of unbelievable woe, Prince Idomeneus, you and these men are the first good signs we have had. Now maybe things will change—maybe the worst is over."

Pteleon and Otus were anxious to be reunited with their families down in the city, but, by the time we reached the chariot, I had decided against it. Though I knew exactly how they felt, I saw no reason in rousing the people of Phaistos from their beds with the tragic news that three out of some fifty men had survived. I promised to go with them the next day to speak to the people. All things considered, they took my order well and climbed into the chariot behind me.

Along the familiar road to Snow Crystal, my heart fluttered back and forth between sorrow and gladness. For what had seemed forever, my comrades and I had been subjected to the worst barrage imaginable: earthquakes, sizzling ash and rocks, blinding thunderflashes and fireballs, and then, the wave. Countless times, our lives hung from threads. Finally, at Amnisos, the wall of water chose us to be the sole survivors, battered and bruised. And yet, there I was—my heart swelled with eagerness—approaching the tiny palace, housing the people whom I loved. Though as weary as their passengers, the solid-hooved horses were urged on by Pteleon at my command.

When we rolled up to the main entrance, a guard challenged us. He hooped and hurrahed like a madman upon hearing my voice. I ordered him to keep it down; as I had not wanted to disturb the citizens of Phaistos, neither did I want to wrest blest sleep from my courtiers. In a hushed voice, I explained that to the guard. I instructed him to find a room for the two sailors and to bring them whatever they desired.

"At once, my lord," whispered the man.

I answered his question before he could put words to it. "Aye, we're the only ones left." Even though it was as dark as a raven's back outside, I could see the guard shudder, for he realized our homecoming was truly lamentable.

"Tomorrow, first thing we'll go straight to the city," I promised Otus and Pteleon. With that, the guard led the two away and I headed for my suite. I thought of ways of waking my wife without startling her to death. When I reached the bedroom, I was spared the task as a light shone from underneath the door. I tapped gently on the bolt.

"Yes, Baucis, what is it," said Aphaea. Though she tried to hide it, I could tell by her voice that Aphaea had been crying. Nudging the door open, I stepped into the lamplit room.

In my dear wife's face, I saw surprise, joy, and worry all together. Before I uttered a single word, she held me tightly, her face buried in my chest. Tears streamed forth. Without the slightest desire to staunch them, my tears mixed with hers. I cried because I was holding my love and had never thought I would again. I cried because my ordeal was over. I cried because Ta-ch'ih, Rib-Addi, and all the others were no more.

We collapsed on the edge of the bed, enfolded in each other's arms. Whenever we tried to speak, we choked with tears. We sensed that the best thing was to simply hold one another. Words would come later.

Aphaea began caressing my damaged shoulder and, at last, was able to speak, asking how my body became covered with burns, bruises, and welts. I left out much, giving her only an outline of what had transpired on Kalliste and out at sea. She sat up openmouthed, horrified by my account of the baleful events; they sounded unbelievable in the telling, even to me. More tears flowed when I told of our losses to the wave on the north shore.

Much of that night passed in that way: talking, embracing, weeping. Finally, with each of us totally exhausted and me cradled in Aphaea's arms like a child, we fell asleep.

The next morning with its sad duties came much too quickly. Aphaea and I awoke not to a warbling lark nor a tap on the bolt, but to the buzzing of voices and the shuffling of feet. Word had gotten out. I was foolish to think our return could be kept secret, even for one night. After all, Snow Crystal was a palace and the people who occupied it were courtiers. When I opened the bedroom door, I was confronted by a throng headed by Otus, Pteleon, and good old Miletus. I was warmed by the sight of the staunch yeoman, a half-smile upon his wrinkled face.

Like poppies rippling in a crosswind, heads bobbed back and forth as my courtiers tried to catch a glimpse of me. In a twinkling, I was encircled by a boisterous, gesturing group of friends, showing me love and relief at my return, though it was hardly a happy time.

Ananda and Glaukus were not in the crowd. They sent word that they were spending the morning in silent prayer and fasting. I understood. I would have joined them if not for my responsibilities.

For the sole reason of having support, I asked Miletus and several of my courtiers to accompany Otus, Pteleon, and me to the city; one does not relish the job of telling mothers, wives, and children that the men in their lives are never coming home. Chariots supplied the transportation, and before I wanted to be, I was standing in the agora of Phaistos, telling my woeful tale once more. Wailing drowned out every sound of the city.

Though my heart was torn asunder, I couldn't join in the lamentation; I was dry from the night before. My tears had already run for my men, for the thousands of Cretans killed, and for ravaged Kalliste. I addressed my despondent soul, vowing that somehow, someway, we would have to piece our lives back together and I, as prince, would have to lead the way. The rest of the morning, I spent in Phaistos-town consoling my grieving subjects as best I could.

Later, I held a brief meeting with the Phiran town elders, telling them I had no solutions, no predictions. All we could do, I told them, was wait until calm returned to the empire, then decide whether to remain on Crete or sail off in search of a new home. Neither choice was acceptable to the old ones, though not one among them suggested we resettle Kalliste at some future time. They had no answers themselves.

In the afternoon, my small party drove up the hill and entered the palace, where I conferred with Rhadamanthys and his advisors. I was told that I had just missed the departure of a rescue caravan, which carried everything Minos had asked for: food, bedding, blankets, fifty mules, and a hundred men. Since the cleanup might take months, Rhadamanthys had no idea when he would see his men again. Sitting in a circle, we discussed the future and our fate. Two questions troubled everyone. The first was when would the wind shift, carrying with it the volcano-belched ash. So far, the orchards and the fields around Phaistos had been spared, receiving only a dusting. But, from the east tip of the Messara to the Lasithi Plateau and all the way to Palaikastro, the pasturelands and ploughlands were ashed over. Crete couldn't afford to have any more barren land. We needed to know as soon as possible when the dusty wind changed; thus, we devised an elaborate signaling network utilizing bonfires. Certain magistrates were chosen as overseers and charged with the responsibility of putting the network into operation at once.

The second question—one we had mulled over in the past—concerned dangers from beyond Crete's shores. Would a barbarian hurl his spear into our wound and twist it? Certainly no one would enter The Deep Blue, one of Rhadamanthys's top advisors declared, until the sea was calm again. Thinking of far-sailing Jason, I said not to count on that; there was no telling what the Achaeans might do. Rhadamanthys agreed and said there was no way to deter an invasion with our navy swamped. We could only pray that the fiery Kalliste would ward off all corners until we had time to regroup.

We decided on two precautionary measures: to post sentinels from Timbaki down the coast and to muster a small fighting force. I offered Phira's share of men for both duties, and the offer was well received. Detailed plans were to be drawn up by Rhadamanthys's people, and I was to return the following day with my roster for each duty. The meeting ended with our feeling that, at that perilous time, we were doing something useful.

Before I left, Rhadamanthys took me aside and asked if I would bring Glaukus with me the following day; Biadice had had a terrible night and seemed to be getting worse. I said I would, of course.

When I returned to Snow Crystal, Aphaea and I took the evening meal together in my suite. We kept our eyes glued on one another, afraid that the other might vanish in a puff. Although we could not stop ourselves from bringing up the dire straits we were in, we were thankful for being able to hear each other's voice and see each other's face across the table.

Later that evening, I found it difficult to leave Aphaea's side, but I had to, for awaiting me across Snow Crystal were the two sages. They wanted to hear, step by step, what happened to the expeditionary party after it left Timbaki. As I reconstructed the bizarre events on land and at sea, their astonishment turned almost... worshipful. When I got to the part about the wave, and Ta-ch'ih's death, they leaned forward.

"Considering the importance of the sea in his life," Glaukus said, "no wonder he stood there motionless as the wave approached. It was such a fitting way for him to die."

Since the wise men had an opinion on everything, I was surprised that silence filled the study when I told them what was being done to aid the refugees, and our plans for early warning and protection. Ananda sat there blank-faced, idly thumbing a crinkled papyrus. Glaukus peered out the window into the darkness. My skin started to crawl. I had to say something. "All right, you two, what is it about these precautionary measures that ties your tongues? Don't you think these steps are needed?"

The old Cretan turned his head toward me and looked deep into my eyes. "Prince Idomeneus, if the barbarians do come, I wonder if there will be anything left here worth defending."

"You've had a vision," I quavered.

"No, Your Grace...just a feeling. A feeling that Kalliste and the Goddess are not done with us yet."

"By all that's holy," I muttered. "How much more can either of them do to us?"

"They can entomb us in ash or cause some new catastrophe," Glaukus said. "My whole being tells me that before foreign troops appear, nature will plague us one more time."

"And escape is impossible," I broke in numbly. "Even if we could herd the people to the shore, we haven't enough ships to evacuate them. Besides, the sea is still stirred. Our skiffs would be swamped!" My mind raced on. "Maybe if we fled up the great mountains of Crete, we could outdistance this new catastrophe, eh?"

Glaukus shrugged.

The deep-thinking Ananda had been holding back. Finally, he spoke. "My friends, no matter what is done in the way of protection or prevention, no matter where or how we hide, the pattern of things to come will not be altered. You see, we have come to a most remarkable time and only one whose eyes and heart are blind could fail to see it. Ta-ch'ih saw it clearly. We are in a time when all will be torn down so that something new may be born into the world. Like a dazzling flower, or a human being, a great empire is born, prospers, grows old, and dies."

"No," I protested sharply. "We won't be wiped off the earth! You speak so coldly, Ananda, because these are not your people, this land is not your land!"

"Prince Idomeneus, my dear friend, if I have any people on earth, they are the people of Phaistos. I consider this my home. What I say, I say without malice, without wanting to harm. From deep within me do these words rise, and it would not be right to swallow them."

Ananda always spoke from the heart. I knew that. Gesturing for him to continue, I resigned myself to hear his prophecy.

"There is but one certainty, Your Grace, one constant factor in the cosmos: change. Right at this very moment, we are in the middle of a stupendous change, a change so enormous, so unimaginable, a change powered by such mighty forces that we should bow our heads to it, not cower before it. We should stand in awe. Respect it. Worship it. Ta-ch'ih understood."

"Respect and worship a change that devastates our islands, leaves us homeless, slaughters thousands?" I said.

"Try to understand, we are being given a brief and rare glimpse of Divine Work. The fabric of the cosmos is unfolding before our eyes. We're seeing through the form and the design; we're seeing the weft and the warp. We're seeing The Web."

I didn't dare to hear any more yet didn't dare not to.

"Remember," Ananda continued, "something like this occurred in the place I came from. As here, Nature Herself played a part in the change, for She dried up our land. But it was Her offspring, men, who ended our way of life. These men came in hordes from the cold north. They were forest-dwelling people, and they swept down and razed our shining cities. There was great suffering, great upheaval, great change. Yet, from what I understand, when the blood was washed away and the dust cleared, a new kind of civilization arose. Different from ours but laced with our thoughts and discoveries."

"Surely your people were not conquered without a struggle," I demurred. "They must've resisted?"

"Oh, yes. Yes, indeed. They fought and they died, and they shed oceans of tears. But these actions accomplished nothing. You see, the design was clear at the very beginning: our time had come. Those who refused to accept it agonized and tortured themselves needlessly."

"Ananda, listen, I know my people," I declared, "and I assure you they will not prostrate themselves. They will fight or flee, but they will not stand by and just accept, as you would have it."

"Whatever they do, Sire, it will matter little," the aged-one said. "The forces have been set in motion. Everything will be overturned. For a time, there will exist a void, but, before long, it will be filled by other people, new people. They will have their day of glory. What is true for us, however, will be true for them: their days are numbered by the gods. Shiva-Rudra, especially, will keep a careful watch and when their allotted time is through, He will plow them under. Thus, He will make room for others, and so the cycle goes on, spinning through the aeons. This is the way of the cosmos."

As the three of us sat silently in the study, the words of Ananda rolled across my mind. When I looked at Glaukus, I thought of his dream, over a year before, and about the cave that he and I had entered. The creature that spoke to us, half-deer and half-man, said that soon we would pass on to a place where the light was brighter. As I sat there with Glaukus and Ananda, I knew that "we" meant all the people around The Deep Blue ruled by Minos.

Numb, I got up and left the study, groping my way through the corridors of Snow Crystal. I arrived at my bedroom. Aphaea tried to comfort me, stroking my brow and asking if I wanted to talk about it. How could I speak the dreadful words of Ananda, speak of the truth of Glaukus's prophetic dream, speak of our utter hopelessness? As it was, I did not have to say a thing, for, when I gazed into Aphaea's purple eyes, so wise, I saw that she somehow knew.

TWENTY-FOUR

THE NEXT MORNING was cruelly cold, seeming more like midwinter than early summer. From the moment the great wave smacked Crete, the weather had been unseasonably harsh. Overhead, smoky yellows and oranges issued from a scarlet sun. Fine ash sifted down through the atmosphere, dusting the Messara. Rhadamanthys's bonfires warned the farmers early of the wind change, and they were out in force trying to keep their crops from being crushed.

Concerned over Biadice's health, Aphaea asked if she could accompany Glaukus and me to the palace. As the three of us bumped along the road in the chariot, my mind stumbled across Ananda's prophetic words of the night before.

Arriving at Phaistos, we found the palace buzzing with activity as courtiers tried to deal with the rain of ash. Wasting no time, we made for the royal suite in the northern part of the palace, where we were told that Biadice had been moved to a bedroom in the southeastern corner of the palace because the north wind was too cold and ash laden. A page led Glaukus and Aphaea off to Biadice's quarters, while I entered Rhadamanthys's study. I found him all alone, staring out a window.

"She had a dreadful night," sighed Rhadamanthys, not hiding his fear, "This evil wind makes her breathing terribly labored." He turned away from the window and the bleak scene outside. Grasping my hands, he said, "I'm thankful you came early, friend. I know that Biadice will be buoyed by the presence of Glaukus and Aphaea."

Rhadamanthys's advisors began filing into the room, and after the prince took a chair at the head of a broad table, the advisors and I selected chairs along the sides of the table. Before he spoke, I could see that Rhadamanthys was pulling himself together. "My good men and brave Prince Idomeneus," he said, "I must tell you that late last night a runner sent by King Minos arrived here with some heartening news." Like hounds that hear a twig snap in the forest, our ears perked up at the sound of those words. Rhadamanthys explained. "I was informed that the rescuers on the north coast were making good progress in locating the survivors, feeding them, treating their injuries, and carting them off to cities and towns farther inland. Also, the clearing and salvage operation is moving along swiftly."

It appeared that the Cretans had responded rapidly and generously to Minos's call for aid and so soon after the influx of Kallistean refugees had taxed their kind nature and their stores. What other people would be so generous to their neighbors in time of need? Egyptians? Achaeans? Never.

"Also, the runner informed me," Rhadamanthys said, "that the ash is beginning to slacken off around the island." We all glanced out the window and beheld the white flakes. "Maybe, this is just the last gasp before the volcano dies out completely," Rhadamanthys said. Everyone around the table nodded in agreement.

Rhadamanthys's spirits seemed raised. He spoke with fervor. "All these signs point to a recovery of our north shore, my friends. And a speedy one at that! We can now, I believe, put all our energies into mustering and organizing the sentinels and troops we spoke of yesterday."

During the discussion that ensued, we worked out all the details for establishing both the signal and the fighting corps. As we spoke, it struck me that we men of Minos had never called out an army before, so protected were we by our navy. I remembered how the rest of the world was and that Theseus had spoken about our special place in it. As we planned to defend our homes and our loved ones, however, we were no different from any other people. When the lists of available men were produced, the leaders of the broad Messara did not find Phira wanting; my papyrus was as long as anyone's except Rhadamanthys's.

Our meeting lasted throughout the morning. When it concluded, we rose from the sturdy table, and I approached Rhadamanthys. Others reached him before I did and caught his ear. I stepped outside and waited.

Within the corridor, the hubbub made it seem like everything was normal; priestesses, merchants, servants, and others walked by me briskly, headed for the four corners of the large palace. Now and then, a small child's voice rang out, making me think of brighter days on Kalliste when all of us were children.

As in a dream, the busy but peaceful palace scene disappeared in one stroke. My fingertips felt it first. I had my hand on one of the well-built walls; it started to tremble ever so slightly, then rock back and forth. So did its partner across the corridor. The talk in the room that I had just stepped out of stopped. So did the chatter in the corridor, as the sound of human voices was swiftly replaced by the creaking of timber and the cracking of plaster; palm-size chunks of the molded ceiling plummeted to the floor, shattering into white dust.

I screamed into the room for Rhadamanthys to get out, then took off for the stairway. As I scrambled down the stairs, the entire palace shuddered like some giant fish cast upon the deck, gasping its last breath. I was thrown headfirst down the last few unyielding stairs, my abdomen bouncing off their hard edges. With a thud, I struck the tiles below. Though I had the wind knocked out of me, I struggled to my feet, determined to keep going. My only goal was to reach Aphaea on the other side of the palace. As I battled through the throng in the ground floor hallway, no pleas—no matter how urgent nor from whom—slowed me. I heard people choking and coughing. Soon my nostrils were filled with vile smoke, too.

Just before the entrance into the central court, a terrible jolt sent me and everybody around me sprawling. Never before did I wrestle more ferociously—more like a beast than a man—as bodies crushing me went flying this way and that. I struggled to my feet, bounding into the court. As I looked over the wide-open space, north to south,

I saw nothing but blurs of people running pell-mell, bouncing off one another and tumbling to the flagstones. Some walls on the second and third stories teetered threateningly over the chaotic scene. Other stories had already succumbed, their debris creating hazards at every turn. Flecked with sparks and tongues of flame, black smoke billowed out of windows and doorways.

With my eyes riveted on the southeastern corner, I ran through the chaos of crashing, twisting bodies and falling debris. Though I was shoved and pulled, punched and gouged, I did not lose sight of that corner. And when I was halfway across the court, Aphaea came into view. I'm sure of it. One arm wrapped around Biadice's waist, Aphaea was trying to drag her friend out of a doorway and into the court.

I yelled out with everything I had, but my cry was swallowed by the din. Aphaea never saw me. I clawed and kicked to reach her. My eyes burned as they drank in the sight of her.

Then, as if we were in the clutches of some berserk giant, the palace shook violently. Flagstones slid from underfoot. No one remained standing. The air was filled with the chilling sound of earth and stone cracking, crunching, grating.

While everyone else around me hugged the ground, I pushed myself up onto my bloodied hands and knees. When I recall that moment, bitter suffering comes to me once again. For the thousand treasures I conveyed to the Goddess over the years, I did not deserve to witness such a sight. Before my very eyes, the southeastern corner of the palace of Phaistos—all three stories—pitched backwards and fell away into the valley below. My love went with it. So did Biadice and many others.

Shattered, my knees and arms went totally weak and gave out on me. I fell forward, face first onto the limestone.

How long I lay there in shock, groveling and sobbing, I don't know. All I know is that at some point I realized there was no longer any reason for my existence. The earth had snatched my Aphaea from me. Had snatched my dear mother a year ago. Had washed away Ta-ch'ih and Rib-Addi. Like a sleepwalker I rose, stepped over the human forms scattered over the court and walked to the edge of the precipice. The southeastern corner was severed from the rest of the hill, hacked away as if by some huge axe. Peering over the edge, I

discovered a cloud of dust rising from the city below, obscuring everything. I knew that no one who fell over the side from that height
could have survived. Nor for that matter, anyone living in that sector
of the city buried by the debris from the palace above.

Though my vision was clouded, my mind was clear: I must jump
and join my loved ones — or go mad. The swirling dust which veiled
the broad Messara below made me believe that the one step required
to enter the Elysian Fields would be easy, painless. Without fear, toe-
ing the jagged edge, I prepared to free my soul.

A voice stopped me. "My son, for you this is not the way." Like
a smooth pool disturbed by a pebble, my stupor was broken by those
words. Struggling against myself, I scraped the ground with my foot
like a bull before he charges. I guess I shall never know what would
have happened if that firm hand had not clasped my shoulder and
turned me around. I stood face to face with Glaukus, his time-ravaged mien, calm and controlled. "While those who go before us are
legion," he said, "I'm afraid we're destined to remain behind and
taste more suffering."

The next thing I remember was being held in the arms of the
sage. Completely covered by dust and soot, old Glaukus looked like
some spectral vision. Only a bright red trickle below a gash on his
cheek told me otherwise; ghosts do not bleed.

Although we were unaware of what was going on around us,
we were, no doubt, surrounded by life and death spectacles. In
truth, I couldn't have cared less — nothing mattered to me after
Aphaea's death.

My wailing was matched by that of others in the fractured court.
Men and women cursed, gazing around themselves in horror at the
once magnificent palace. Children wept uncontrollably. Not one upper story around the central court remained. Water was everywhere,
the result of broken pipes. Fires crackled around us, though, for floating piles of rubble were ablaze. As if I were a blind man, Glaukus led
me away from the abyss. Later I learned that Glaukus had left
Biadice's side a little before the earthquakes hit and had gone to talk
with an official in the northern part of the palace.

Out of the same corridor I had fought my way through, two men
carried a limp body: Rhadamanthys. Though I thought I had no feel-

ings left, that sight touched me deeply. Brushing away my tears, I broke from Glaukus, running to the bull-leaper's step in the northwestern corner just as the men laid Rhadamanthys on it. He was alive, but horribly battered.

Soon Glaukus was stooping over me. "We must depart at once this house of death," he said anxiously. "See how the flames spread." The isolated fires had joined forces, devouring splintered beams and furniture, licking shattered stone foundations and plastered walls. The heat was unbearable.

The tragedy of Kalliste had turned me into a survivor: I searched wildly for a passageway to flee through. There was no need to look for one through the eastern or southern sectors. The north was like the mouth of a raging kiln. The only way out was up some stairs in the western sector, then down the grand staircase. That meant that we would have to skirt the magazines filled with the oil pithoi, which were sending up towering columns of smoke.

"Pick him up and follow me at once," I shouted to the men who had carried Rhadamanthys. Frozen by fear, they looked at me with crazed eyes. "Curse you! Do as I say!" They picked up Rhadamanthys and quickly followed behind Glaukus.

Our actions had not been lost on the others huddled around the court, for, like lost sheep, they bolted to the northwestern corner and followed us. We stayed clear of flames and everyone lived to tell of their sprint through the deadly maze.

Gathering a little ways beyond the western court, we began to treat the injured as best we could. Behind us one of the most magnificent buildings in the world, maybe second only to the palace at Knossos, burnt to the ground. It was a blessing that Rhadamanthys did not regain his senses until after the flames died.

By midafternoon the injured prince came to, raising his head and staring at me in confusion. "ldomeneus, is that you?"

"Yes, Rhadamanthys, dear friend, I'm here. Easy now, the earthquake has treated you roughly."

"My wife…Biadice…where is she?" he implored.

I could not find the heart to lie to him at that point. Why put off the anguish he had to face? Taking a deep breath, I said, "Gone, Rhadamanthys. Gone to a better world than this…this hellish place."

Rhadamanthys's eyes went murky; though they remained open, they saw not.

"My dear friend," I whispered gently, "our wives went over to the other side arm in arm. There, dancing in meadows, they await us."

Pungent smoke drifted overhead. Smoke not only from the flame-ravaged palace, but from the city as well. A continuous stream of citizens and Phirans, bloodied and burnt, flowed into our make-shift camp, mumbling horror stories they had seen below. The earth-quake and the part of the palace that pitched off the hill, had laid Phaistos low; raging fires finished the job.

Although most of my being cared not a straw for anything on earth, there was a small part that hoped for Rhadamanthys's recovery. Somehow, even though his heart was full of anguish, Rhadamanthys sensed my surrender and, gazing up at me, muttered, "Idomeneus, you must lead the people."

A swelled riptide rose up within me and I roared, "No!" There was great rustling around us; the people were startled. I felt their questioning eyes upon my back. I clenched my fists and fought for control. Soon I was master again and lowered my voice. "No, Rhadamanthys, no. I'll never lead another person as long as I live. All my leading took us in one great circle."

The voice that had stopped me at the brink spoke once more. "Sire, Prince Rhadamanthys is right. You must take us away from here—at least to Snow Crystal. Maybe there the well-placed palace fared better. These people—many of them your own from Phira—need water and soon will need food and shelter. Maybe we shall find these things at Snow Crystal. Besides, what about Ananda? What about Miletus and the others?"

"Glaukus, I'm through. No more will I shoulder responsibility for others. No more will I direct or advise others. I'm prince no more."

"But my lord," the graybeard implored, "at least let us take Rhadamanthys to his beloved Snow Crystal. He'll die from exposure if we don't."

Looking up into the wizened face of the dreamer, I knew he was right. And I knew as long as I drew air there would be more things for me to do, more decisions to make. I nodded in agreement, saying "Let's prepare a litter."

With the help of another survivor, we hastily made a litter from a blanket and some branches. The other man, a palace smithy, and I lifted our burden. There were no other volunteers that day. Glaukus led the way.

Those scattered around the field alongside the western court, Cretans and Phirans, stared at us in anticipation of a signal or an order. When none was forthcoming, a few of them raised their hoarse voices.

"Where are you going with Prince Rhadamanthys?"

"Are you coming back?"

"Don't...don't leave us!"

When one frog begins to croak, all the others chime in. So, it was with the people that day; some were desperate, others angry. Before things got too heated, I had to quell the throng. "People of Phaistos and Phira, hear me," I shouted. "We're taking poor Prince Rhadamanthys to Snow Crystal in hopes of saving his life. We don't know what we'll find there, though. That building may be standing or may have been razed."

"But here we know for sure there's nothing," someone exclaimed. Others grumbled in agreement.

"Indeed," I said, "but, I can't promise you anything better on the other side of the hill."

"We'll go anyway! We can't just stay here," a man shouted. The crowd echoed similar thoughts, everyone yelling at once.

By putting the litter down and holding up my arms, I stemmed the hue and cry. I barked as loudly as I could, "All right, come along if you want! But know, each and every one of you, that I promise nothing. No food. No water. Nothing!"

By that time, those who could stand had scrambled to their feet, while others had been picked up and propped on shoulders. No one knows how many of us there were, for it was not the time for a head count. But our numbers stretched a great distance along the cobble-stone road. We moved at a snail's pace, with wails and groans haunting our every step. I could see animals, domestic and wild, scampering hither and yon down in the valley. Ribbons of dark smoke marked the spots where once gracious mansions and proud farmhouses stood.

When we were about two thirds of the way to Snow Crystal, the smell of smoke filled the air. Soon our worst fears were confirmed by a black spectre climbing towards the clouds. We rounded the slope above Snow Crystal and came upon the smoldering summer palace. In total disarray, a handful of courtiers lay upon the clearing above the main stairs. Though no doubt they had already spilled many, tears welled in their eyes. They rose and approached me. They filled my ears with mournful and, by then, all-too-familiar stories: loved ones crushed, burned, and trampled; the earth torn asunder; walls toppled over; suites, workshops, and magazines ravaged by hateful fire.

I said nothing. Instead, when the voices died down, I walked slowly over to the stairs and had a half-hearted look for myself. All I had experienced had deadened my senses, but the sight of that once-perfect building pierced my heart like a dagger. The name Rhadamanthys had bestowed on his lovely summer residence was no longer apt. Raven's Back or Charcoal would have been more accurate; the once glistening alabaster walls of the ground floors were charred. On the tops of the walls stood a few timbers, reminders of the upper stories that were no more. Transformed into charcoal by the fire's intense heat, the timbers resembled bony fingers pointing toward the sky.

As I stared at the macabre scene, someone sidled up to me. Feeling his presence, I turned around. I didn't recognize him so badly was his face blistered and discolored from the fire. When he saw I was at a loss, he quickly identified himself. "I'm Althaemenes, your scribe, Sire."

"Althaemenes," I said numbly.

"Sire, we have lost over half of our people. Over half!"

"Miletus?"

"Dead, my lord. He was crushed under a wall while trying to lead others to safety. It happened swiftly…he didn't suffer."

"The foreigner, Ananda?"

Althaemenes shook his head incredulously. "That old man would not leave his room, Your Grace. We yelled for him to run. We pounded on his door, but he had it bolted. As the flames consumed his room, we heard not a sound from within."

Though I felt a chill and dreadful emptiness, no tears came. The final blow had been delivered. Not I nor anyone else would ever be the same. There were no more plans, no more schemes to ward off disaster. Disaster was before us, and it was total. Our entire struggle had been in vain. Our offerings and prayers and curses had gone unnoticed. The sages had been right.

When I think about how little time I had shared with lovely Aphaea, my heart brims with regret. I would rather have seen her graceful way of walking and the bright radiance of her face than the sun itself. In the brief moments allotted to us, I should have stayed by Aphaea's side, instead of being drawn away to cruel Kalliste for no reason. There is no sense in the world. No beauty. Only dreams of what once was.

For the remainder of that long day, the day the earthquakes destroyed Crete, we survivors remained on the clearing above the main stairs of Snow Crystal. No one issued orders. Everyone went about his own business, trying to feed and care for kith and kin. Whether one was a Kallistean or Cretan no longer mattered, for each person was concerned only for his nearest relatives. Blood was the only bond that mattered.

Glaukus and I were the only exceptions; but then we had no family left. Caring for Rhadamanthys was the only thing that kept us going; none of the Phaistosans cared about their injured prince. Rank, position, and loyalty meant nothing for everyone knew that the world had changed forever.

TWENTY-FIVE

ALL COMMUNICATION was shattered by the earth-quakes and thus it took some time for the tragic story of Crete to be disseminated. Within a month, it was clear that the power and peace of Minos were gone forever. Prior to the eruption of Kalliste's volcano, earthquakes had struck only one or two places on Crete at a time: for example, Mallia and Gournia might have been hit one year, and later, maybe years later, Kydonia might have been damaged or, later yet, Knossos or someplace else. Only once before, two hundred years ago, had the entire island been jolted, each city being severely, but not fatally, wounded.

When the hill of Phaistos was torn asunder and Rhadamanthys's palace went up in flames, every other seat of power on Crete suffered a similar fate. When the low hill upon which sat the palace of Knossos writhed and shuddered, Minos and his courtiers were trapped in the maze-like passageways. Not completely leveled, the palace was scorched beyond recognition. By some miracle, the royal family managed to escape, and the quick-witted Catreus swept Minos, Pasiphae, and the others off to the small town of Arkhanes. Before long, Catreus and Minos learned what condition the empire was in; they decided to flee Crete while they still could. After all, the king's authority was completely destroyed, his allegiances were worthless, and his inability to stem the tide of disaster that washed over the island made him the perfect scapegoat.

Catreus somehow pulled together a skeleton crew, found a seaworthy craft that had been spared at a nearby port and set sail with the rest of the royal family, fleeing the island of their birth in search of a refuge. Where they finally alighted or if they even made it across the vast sea, I haven't the faintest idea. Nor do I blame them for fleeing Crete.

What happened after they left was an unspeakable nightmare.

There were others who followed the lead of the royal family, setting sail as soon as they could. A few weeks after the earthquakes wrecked the island, no vessels, large or small, were to be found. Kydonia, Mallia, Gournia, Palaikastro, and Kato Zakro, cities already flattened by the great wave, were finished off by the quakes. Knossos, Gortyn, Phaistos, and other cities and towns in central and south Crete, all spared by the wave, did not escape the earth's wrath. Wherever the mighty Cretan palaces sat, the earth shook the most, it seemed, though the destruction touched every town, village, hamlet, and isolated farmstead. Without the well-placed palaces to administer food and supplies, the farmers simply hoarded whatever they already had, which was not very much. They feverishly tried to restore life to their fields, especially in the east part of the island. All to no avail. Every crop—grain, olive, vine, vegetable—had been crushed to death by the deposit of ash. When the provisions in the barns dwindled to nothing, work in the fields stopped: No one wields a shovel or a hoe when his stomach is cramped with hunger.

The shortage of water was a terrible problem. The quakes had snapped the long aqueducts that crisscrossed the island, and the cargo of precious water was soaked up by the thirsty ash layer, which acted like a great sponge. Since it was summer and the streams and rivers were already low, they became clogged with volcanic debris. Up in the foothills, there were lakes and good-sized ponds, but they were foul smelling and covered with a coating of green scum mixed with ash.

For a while, an occasional cloudburst kept us going. Frantically, we collected the sweet droplets in whatever containers we could find.

While the palaces stood, some repairs on north shore buildings that had been damaged by the wave were under way. Within time, new life would have been breathed into the flattened cities and towns. All relief and repair work stopped, however, when the royal residences succumbed to the quakes. Misery was added upon misery as more corpses lay rotting under the blistering sun, and the odor of putrefying flesh wafted over the island. As refugees roamed without food or water from one stricken city to the next, minor injuries became major. Before long the plague was upon us.

At Snow Crystal, as soon as some unfortunate was touched by the plague, we isolated him, then, when his agony was over, we swiftly buried him in a shallow grave. Isolation was not a problem because a well-fenced compound had sprung up next to the ruins of the tiny summer palace; the sick could easily be kept out of the compound and held within their restricted area. Within the compound, each family threw up a rough hut or lean-to and surrounded it with a crude fence made of branches, sticker bushes, briers, and all sorts of debris from the nearby palace. The compound was big enough to be called a village, except that no elders had authority and no bonds were forged from hut to hut. Each family was a unit unto itself.

Our daytime was spent hunting with bows and arrows and gathering grain, vegetables, and fruit. Since the Messara was generous we had little difficulty filling our cooking pots, even though some of us were unaccustomed to such chores. Brief showers had washed away the thin veil of ash that had settled on the valley floor, and the products of the earth, though bent and bruised, were there for the picking. Where one man's farm ended and another's began no longer mattered for we scrounged wherever and whatever we could.

The herds of the Messara, composed of sheep, cattle, and goats, blended into one enormous herd, which drifted over the valley floor disregarding everything in its way. From sunrise to sunset, the animals chomped incessantly at the browning grass and the rotting vegetables. When the herd moved on, the only thing which remained was a swath of brown dirt. The Messara, that great patchwork of plenty, was being eaten away by hungry animals, both beasts and humans.

Before disaster struck the empire, meat was taken only sparingly, fresh when sacrifices were made or smoked or salted when stowed aboard ships for long voyages. After the collapse, when half of Crete was going hungry, it was odd that we in the south had all the meat we could eat.

Much to our surprise, about a month and a half after the quakes, the grazing animals appeared to double in numbers. What had happened was that the half-starved herds from east Crete had eaten their way the length of the Messara and had finally arrived at Phaistos. Nobody cared that the scrubby beasts had eaten all of the vegetation that held the world-renowned soil in place. Nobody thought about the future. The patting of extended stomachs and the rubbing of greedy hands and the exchanging of knowing smiles were our only reactions to the arrival of the herds.

Alas, our visions of an endless banquet faded when, not long after the arrival of the new herds, people began swarming over the valley floor like locusts. They were refugees from the east who had been moving along with the animals. Though the animals in the valley may have doubled, the people increased tenfold. Shelters, compounds, and double compounds dotted the countryside.

While we gorged ourselves as if there were no tomorrow, the population of grazing animals plummeted. Some people tried to hoard smoked meat, but it was impossible in such living conditions. A few compounds built rough stockades and tried to keep small flocks of sheep and goats. Raiding became commonplace. And with raiding came reprisals. Every now and then, a red glow in the distance told of another compound being burned to the ground.

At the same time that the grazing beasts of the Messara were completely wiped out, the fields and grasslands died. That happened toward the end of summer. Those animals that survived the slaughter, mostly skin and bones by then, began to drift farther west, past where Timbaki once stood, and up into the mountains. We did not try to stop them, for that would have required teamwork and leadership. We had none. Instead, we slaughtered as many as we could, which seemed to make the survivors leave the valley more swiftly. Many huts and several compounds were abandoned as desperate people followed the beasts in the direction of the setting sun. Shelters were kicked over or set aflame by their departing owners, so that if newcomers arrived they would have to sweat and strain to build their own. Those who left the Messara took with them only a few meager possessions, such as knives, bows and arrows, skins, and the means for making fire.

Rhadamanthys had recovered and was as strong as ever, and Glaukus, although he missed his companion sages terribly, put on a stoic face. Ours must have been the oddest "family" on the hill, being made up as it was of two former princes and an ancient soothsayer. We were treated no differently, though, which simply means that we were ignored, left alone. Like the others, Rhadamanthys, Glaukus and I spent our days, and after the animals left the valley, part of our nights in search of food. Though he was still feisty, old Glaukus was too fragile to venture far away. He did his share by collecting berries, nuts, mushrooms, and whatever else he came upon on the outskirts of the compound. He also took his turn as cook. Rhadamanthys pulled his own weight, wandering farther afield than the old sage, bringing back vegetables, edible roots, and small creatures. Since I was the youngest, my job was to bring back as much meat as I could shoot with my bow and arrow.

At twilight, fires flickered across the valley like so many stars. The smell of cooking filled the air. It was a time to be on guard for visits from sly creatures—vermin, birds, and insects—all fully as hungry as we. Sometimes, if we were fast enough, those visitations worked in our favor as potential thieves wound up in our pot.

Mostly we roasted the meat of wild and domestic animals over an open fire. When we tired of that method and the resulting flavor, we soaked and cooked the meat in crude containers, which we fashioned out of wood or leaves. Resourceful Glaukus came up with the idea of steaming strips of meat in leaves, which made them very tender. It was a welcome change.

The seer instructed Rhadamanthys to gather up the seeds of cereal wherever he found them; Glaukus used them to prepare a hearty porridge. Bowls were needed for it, though, and one day I walked over to the charred skeleton of the palace of Phaistos on the other side of the hill. I didn't bother looking at Snow Crystal, because it had been picked clean the first few weeks after the collapse. Our only other pastime besides food gathering was scavenging.

After a few unsuccessful searches in the palace, I discovered where the pantry had stood and began to pick my way through the debris. I looked for a long time before I came upon four jars, miraculously spared. Since we were not expecting guests, we only needed three. I smashed the fourth and carried my booty back to the compound.

When the animals left the valley, we often talked of walking down to Timbaki or all the way to Matala to do some fishing. Always, we decided against it. "As long as we have something to eat, why bother?" was the phrase that usually closed the discussion. Besides, word had it that the people in the camps up and down the coast would beat any stranger caught fishing. Especially feared were the cave dwellers at Matala who would break the arms of those they caught.

We didn't need great stone circles, like those in the legends about the misty Green Isles, to read the skies. We read the sun, moon, and stars directly. The heavenly signs were the only ones marking the passage of time: there were no harvesting, no plowing, no festivals, and no games. The quest for food consumed our days, and it was only at night, around the open fire, that we spoke of the past, rekindling sparks of our former glory. With witty Glaukus and wise Rhadamanthys, the reminiscing nourished our troubled souls. The words, the dancing flames, the woody smoke, and Glaukus's mushrooms put us under a spell, during which we would forget our lamentable state.

Only the chore of fetching water broke the spell; it was a chore we never neglected. At Snow Crystal, we were lucky because on the north side of the hill there was a small spring, well-hidden by brush. Rhadamanthys and I took turns going to the spring, but, like the others in our compound, we went only at night. If anyone visited the spring in daylight, when outsiders might spy him or her, or if anyone divulged the spring's whereabouts, the penalty was expulsion. That law was the only thing our village of strangers agreed upon and swore to enforce.

The secret spring served us well, until the New Wine Moon, when Crete was hit by a severe drought. Mercilessly, it caught us when the valley's meat supply was depleted, and the plague was taking its toll. Somehow—we never found out how, though bitter accusations flew through the air—our spring was discovered by outsiders. We had to guard it day and night, driving away many interlopers and engaging in some bloody skirmishes. Nevertheless, the pilfering continued until the spring was dry. In retaliation, we raided our neighbors, stealing water, food, and whatever else they had. Eventually everyone was reduced to digging narrow holes, two or three feet deep, in which about a cupful of water would appear in the morning and at night. Soon the valley floor looked like one big strainer.

The days of drought wore on week after week. The island had experienced droughts before, but they had always ended when the cool season came. Not that last time. Some people knocked down their shelters and headed west, only to return a short time later with reports of similar conditions stretching all the way to Kydonia. Every so often, stragglers from the east, people who had clung to the mountains trying to wait out the disaster, stumbled into the Messara with worse tales of suffering and deprivation. Cruel famine had spread over that part of the island faster than any other because of the thick blanket of ash. From the east tip of the island to the Lasithi Plain, Cretans and Kallisteans were committing despicable acts in order to survive. Clans and families broke down. Individuals foraged madly on their own. When a morsel of food or a sip of water was found, thirsty and hungry grandparents and aged aunts and uncles were driven away by youths. Forced to scrounge whatever they could to stay alive, the elders went about hunched over or on hands and knees, searching for unripened berries, peels from rotten fruits and vegetables, charred bits of bone, hard roots, tough skins, anything.

On the other end of the scale, young children, four and five years of age, were being left to fend for themselves. For a while, they had received scraps from their parents, but when the scraps became too precious, the children were on their own. For the sake of survival, the little ones formed bands that prowled the countryside in search of food and water and resorted to violence to get what they needed. The aged and the sick were their targets.

How hard it was to believe the stories told by the stragglers from the east, so like horrible nightmares they were. Alas, before long, we discovered that such things could take place, not just in our sleepy minds late at night, but right on our valley floor in the brightness of day. In the morning when the sun showed its face, the compounds buzzed into action like so many beehives. Countless adults and bands of small children went their separate ways. Like bees, they went with the hope of tracking down sustenance. But bees, mere insects, bring their nectar back to the hive to be shared, whereas the humans who lived in the Messara stopped sharing when things got bad. If a person was fortunate enough to find a withered little bush with some shriveled berries, he gobbled down every one. Moving away quickly, so as not to be spotted, he would stealthily return later that day or the next in search of more bushes.

With a heavy heart, I remembered seeing people out in the valley, bolting down scraps of food instead of bringing it to their huts. Many of those people were husbands and fathers—providers—who should have brought life-sustaining food back to their starving wives and children.

How easy it was to despise those who lived in the valley then. But they were all half-crazed from hunger. Pity was not absent from my heart when I looked around me.

With the coming of fall, the drought was washed away, and the soil regained some of its strength. Nevertheless, gaunt grey trees and leafless bushes showed little signs of springing back to life. Food remained scarce. Rhadamanthys, Glaukus, and I shared what little we could find, but we were the exceptions; the other people had turned savage. Farther and farther into the hinterland and up the mountains, I went hunting. Sometimes I was gone for several days or for even a quarter moon at a time. Sometimes I was successful at bagging boar or wild goat. Then, under the cover of night, I would slip back to our hut. The beasts were scraggly, mostly loose skin, but they kept us going. In the morning, I put the remains of the carcass outside the hut, where in a flash they were reduced to white bones. There was always someone who did not get any; that person became our enemy from then on.

When winter came, deep snow shrouded the peaks, and every trek I made up the mountains was a failure. I returned with nothing but skinned knees and thorn wounds to show for my efforts. Our little family had to forage like every other, and we spent the winter hungry and cold, stripped of dignity and hope. All around us we saw mistrust and envy spring up between man and woman and between them and their children.

If there really is a Hades, as the barbarians say, could it be worse than Crete, once perfect and full of holiness, a paradise, now turned into a loveless barren wasteland? For all across the island, nothing mattered but mere survival. Friendship, family, and love had been cast out as useless and foolish ideas. Ideas which would only leave your belly empty and your mind clouded. Indeed, what good are high values when you're chewing bitter bark and sucking on round pebbles to stifle your hunger, while all around you, people with spindly arms and legs are dropping dead, though their stomachs are grossly swollen, as if they had gorged themselves at some enormous banquet.

Over Rhadamanthys's and Glaukus's vehement protests, I decided to try to find us some food along the coast. I fashioned a net out of some crude cord and, with my spear, headed out from our camp. From Timbaki all the way down to Matala, I skirted camps that dotted the shore; I saw many people fishing, but nobody catching anything.

Matala was deserted except for a few folks fishing offshore—I couldn't tell if they were men or women. Strange. No children. I climbed up the east slope of the hill and observed the scene for some time before deciding to check out the caves. Maybe there was a cache of salted fish in one, which I could steal, thus saving myself any work or possible detection. Stealthily picking my way across the west face of the hill, I examined the uppermost caves, finding little but the remains of old fires and charred bones. When I reached the groundlevel caves, I moved warily, spear at the ready.

Presently I came upon the reeking mouth of a large cave. I peered in. As my eyes slowly adjusted to the dim light, I saw a huge pile of what looked like tree branches. The floor-to-ceiling pile, however, was made of bones. Well, the ruffians of Matala got their share of the great herd, I thought to myself. My stomach churned at the prospect of such feasting. Why this concern for neatness, though? Why did they stack the bones together in this one cave?

Suddenly my whole being shivered. For staring out under the stack were eyes, or rather eye sockets, belonging to skulls. Human skulls. Don't tell me that the people of Matala didn't have the decency to bury their dead—at least in shallow graves—but, instead, tossed their bones into this stink hole, I thought. Though repulsed,

I approached the bone mound, dread clawing at my heart.

I got close enough to see that the bones were all short and thin, the skulls tiny. The bones were those of children. Not a shred of flesh or muscle was attached to the bones, as if they had been stripped. What? Though my feet didn't want to, I went closer. I stared carefully at a leg bone. It was scored with cuts and nicks. I looked at another bone, and it had the same marks. So did another. And another. All the bones had been hacked as…as if a butcher had been at work. My heart pounded; my head pounded; I was dizzy. I turned and ran out of hell, out of the cave, without a thought of being seen. I ran. And ran.

The next day I stumbled up the hill to Snow Crystal. "What on earth happened to you, Idomeneus?" asked Rhadamanthys.

"You look as though you've seen a ghost," said Glaukus.

"No fish. No fish," is all I muttered. Then I collapsed in the hut and slept for two days.

I never told my friends what I had seen in the horrid cave at Matala. Why should I? But from then on, I was never the same. I wondered how widespread the unspeakable practice was, if it had seeped beyond the Matalan caves. Later, when I had time alone, I wondered if everyone on Crete would have been reduced to cannibals if the ships had not arrived that spring.

TWENTY-SIX

"SHIPS! SHIPS!" The cry echoed across the broad valley not so much as an alert for others but, rather, as a pure paean of exaltation. Out of the west, furrowing the green-blue water, came a flotilla. The black fast-faring hulls and the shape of the sails told us at once who were aboard: Achaeans.

The ships hugged the coast until they neared Timbaki, then they moved farther out. Scores of people charged down our hill, heading for the port as fast as their skinny legs could carry them. On the valley floor, men, women, and children poured out of their compounds, running, limping, half crawling toward the remains of the port; thousands of feet thundered across the Messara, causing a great cloud of dust to swirl to the sky.

Hardly aware of what we were doing, Rhadamanthys, Glaukus and I began to race down the hill. Like children who see colts prancing across a meadow for the first time, we were thrown into a tizzy. Thinking back on it now, I don't know what we expected of the barbarians. All I know is that we felt elated, giddy to see that sleek ships still sailed, that canvas still flapped, that sailors still swaggered, that there was still a world beyond Crete.

Unlike all the others, however, my companions and I returned to our senses before we reached the shore; the wise prince brought us to. "My friends, stop, stop! Wait a moment," shouted Rhadamanthys, halting in his tracks, winded. Glaukus and I pulled up waiting for our friend to join us. "Listen to me," Rhadamanthys implored between gasps. "How do we know what these barbarians have in mind? They may have come here to slit our scrawny throats and to be done with us once and for all. Do you suppose they came to aid us in this time of woe?" he asked mockingly.

For the first time in months we forgot our hunger pains. Our minds raced over the possible reasons for the Achaeans' arrival; we could almost hear each other thinking.

After a few moments, Glaukus had an idea. "Let's hide in the remains of the warehouse across the road from the dock. That way we will be close enough to see everything, but away from danger."

"Sounds good," said Rhadamanthys. "Don't you agree, Idomeneus?"

"Yes, fine." I replied, glancing around at the clamorous horde rushing by us. "Shouldn't we try to warn some of these people," I asked. "We might be able to convince them to stop short of the dock and possible harm."

"Just look, Idomeneus, look into their eyes and their greedy faces," exclaimed Rhadamanthys. "Do you really think they'll listen to us if there's the slightest chance that those ships are carrying provisions? Ha! Step in front of them and you'll be trampled before you get a word out!" I nodded glumly for my friend was right; the only way we could have stopped our neighbors was by bow and arrow.

We broke out of the sea of people and headed for the dilapidated warehouse, which was once filled with stores owned by Rhadamanthys. When we reached it, we scrambled over the rubble and concealed ourselves behind a wall half destroyed by the earthquakes. From there we watched with an odd mixture of anticipation and dread.

People continued running at breakneck speed to the abandoned port. As they arrived, they elbowed their way to the edge of the dock. Stragglers, many of them crippled, eventually joined the others, until the whole valley was present. Except for us.

The vessels bobbed peacefully out in the Gulf of Messara. The sails were furled. There was no movement on the decks.

From the dock, shouts rose from the multitude.

"Food!"

"Give us food!"

"Help!"

"Save us!"

The pleas bounced over the calm water, but there was no reply. If they were wondering whether they would encounter opposition on Crete, the pitiful begging of those on the dock told the Achaeans otherwise.

Finally, we could hear noise aboard the ships, like scores of feet shuffling over the decks. Soon the creaking of wood pierced the air: oars were lowered, disturbing the tranquil sea. A sense of hopefulness hung over Timbaki.

Slowly, the flotilla began to move south. Cries of protestation rang out from the dock, "Don't leave!"

"You can't leave us!"

"Please, we're starving to death!"

The flotilla moved steadily away. Then, all of a sudden, as if in answer to the pitiable cries, the lead ship began to turn toward shore. A low-slung forty-footer, it was soon followed by the next ship, then the next, and so on. The dark-prowed vessels were brought alongside the dock but were not tied up. The vessels stayed ten or more feet away from the dock and the frenzied throng.

Straightaway the wisdom of the maneuver became clear, because people leapt from the dock, hoping to land on the ships. They failed miserably; every one fell short, plunging into the brine. But they did not give up. With arms and legs flailing wildly, they swam up to the ships. Unyielding oars were used to prod the swimmers away. All that took place amid savage screaming and gesturing — it was utter chaos.

After treading water for a while and being struck by the oars, the swimmers realized the futility of their actions. We couldn't make out what the Achaeans were shouting, but whatever it was, it caused those swimmers who could to return to the dock. They had to pull themselves up. There were no helping hands.

The entire port hummed like the string of a bow after the arrow is loosed.

A sack was hurled from the lead ship into the mob, and a deafening roar went up. The sack was followed in rapid succession by another, then another. From each and every vessel, bulging sacks were flung into grasping, clutching hands. My feet wanted to be off, flying across to the dock, but my mind kept them planted on the ground. People pushed and shoved to catch the sacks; several children fell into the water. As soon as a person caught a sack, he fought his way to the back of the mob, tore open the sack with his fingers and teeth, and yanked out the contents. Invariably, both hands shot up to the mouth and stuffed in life-sustaining food.

Like not-so-distant thunder, my stomach rumbled, then did somersaults. Rhadamanthys and Glaukus must have heard the commotion coming from inside me, but they said nothing; their attention was fixed on the bizarre scene. Though my friends must have been in the same boat as I, no one proposed that we slip over to the dock and beg for an Achaean handout.

As the sacks of food were cast over the sides, the waterline along the hulls slowly fell. How much food the barbarians had brought with them was anybody's guess, but the sacks kept coming.

Finally, all the food was distributed. It was an incredible amount, for it appeared that everybody was hungrily downing something. There was no more frantic shouting and shoving. On the hard planks of the dock, the half-starved Cretans, Kallisteans, and others sat or squatted, eating to their hearts' content.

My companions and I were seemingly the only ones to notice the oars quietly at work, inching the ships closer to the dock. Presently, wood bumped wood. The vessels were tied up and long gangplanks were slipped out. My heart raced. My throat was as parched as it had been during the drought. From each ship, a contingent of well-greaved warriors marched down the gangplank. All along the gunwales of the ships, bronze-shirted guards appeared, brandishing long sinister spears.

When those who were greedily stuffing their faces looked up and saw the soldiers among them, they cowered and slunk backward like frightened weasels. After a few tense moments, several bold people stepped forward and began parleying with the Achaean leaders, and before long, a number of men led the troops up the hill, heading directly for Snow Crystal. The majority of the people remained at the port, eyeing the formidable guards aboard the ships and gobbling the last morsels of food. They didn't think of saving any.

Without so much as a word between us, Rhadamanthys, Glaukus, and I withdrew from our hiding place, and, from a safe distance, trailed the foreigners and their escorts as they wound their way uphill. When they reached the ruin, the Achaean leader, a long-shanked man with a boar's tusk-decorated helmet, barked out some orders, and his troops swarmed through the debris-filled tiny palace, tapping walls and kicking over beams. The leader and his high-ranking officers talked and gestured during the inspection.

By and by, the officers called their men together, formed them up, and marched them toward the main palace of Phaistos. Upon reaching the palace, the Achaeans did the same kind of reconnoitering, which of course took much longer than at the summer palace. They also sent a detail down to the ravaged city.

By late afternoon, the detail returned just as the palace inspection was about completed. As they milled around the famous hill, the barbarians gazed across the wide Messara; I swear we saw them rubbing their greedy hands together. I glanced over at Rhadamanthys. His big brown eyes were flooded.

When the officers were satisfied, they gathered their men and marched them back toward the port. Once more we followed. As we passed our compound, I asked Rhadamanthys and Glaukus if they wanted to wait there for me; they both looked so weary I was starting to worry about them. Neither of them would have it, though, thus, the three of us continued on, veering off at the warehouse.

When the troops approached the dock, the buzzing throng formed a corridor so that the Achaeans could march through. The soldiers filed to their respective ships but did not go up the gangplanks. Leaping onto a mooring post, the leader of the expeditionary force began haranguing the people, but once again we could not make out his words. He talked with great gusto, though, for his arms never stopped moving. Even from where we crouched, the man put on a dazzling show. Clad in bronze from ankle to head, he posed before a glorious sunset and looked like some monstrous god capable of some supernatural feat. Timing it perfectly, the leader ended his speech just as the sun blinked out. Then he raised his arms high in the air, signaling for those aboard to toss out more sacks.

As the people grabbed for the handouts like so many monkeys, the troops swiftly slipped aboard their ships; the long-winded leader was the last one to leave the dock. Though the barrage of food-filled sacks was heavy, a few people ignored it and rushed the gangplanks—we assumed they were pleading to be taken to the inland, offering to pay for their passage with who knows what. Whatever they offered, the Achaeans weren't taking, for they flung the desperate people off the gangplanks into the water or onto the unforgiving dock.

The planks were drawn up, the oars dropped, the sails raised. The flotilla disappeared with the dusk. Being the wary sailors they were, the Achaeans probably did not make for home that night, but instead sailed beyond sight out into the Gulf of Messara, dropped anchors, and spent that night dreaming about their eventual rule of Crete.

Rhadamanthys, Glaukus, and I spent that night and the following days listening to people repeat the words of the Achaean leader. Hearing the dullards in our compound go on about the barbarians made us want to retch. How the Achaeans came as soon as the Sea God Poseidon had allowed them to cross The Deep Blue, for they were anxious to help their stricken neighbors. How, knowing we would need food, the Achaeans loaded their ships with as much as they could hold. How the Achaeans would return with even more. (That explained why the mob did not storm the flotilla and try to commandeer it: the barbarians had promised to return soon with even greater rations.) How the Achaeans had surveyed the palaces because they wanted to get a complete picture of the damage. When they returned, they would be sure to bring with them the proper materials for rebuilding.

Many times, we heard the same story, for the starving people of the Messara believed every lie that the Achaeans had told them. Eventually, the salty Glaukus could not hold back any longer and asked a talkative fool the obvious question. "Why on this Goddess-forsaken Earth do you suppose the barbarians would want to help us?"

The man, who had the hands of an artisan, threw back his big head and chuckled. "Why?" he hooted, mimicking Glaukus, "I'll tell you why. They want our goods to start flowing again! That's why! The inlanders love our well-turned pots, our golden jewelry, and our ivory carvings."

"Do you believe they want these things so badly they will rebuild our empire for us?" Glaukus broke in.

"No, not just these things," snapped the man. "The Achaeans need our wheat, barley, honey, vegetables, and other foodstuffs, too!"

"Right," shouted Glaukus, "and they'll make us do the back-breaking work to get them, while they lounge in the palaces. Aye, the barbarians will return. They'll rebuild the palaces and cities, sure. But that won't help us."

"What are you driving at, old goatbeard?"

"We're going to be enslaved, you fool," stormed Glaukus. "The barbarians are going to use every man, woman, and child on Crete as beasts of burden! No, the foreigners won't let us starve, just as a farmer won't let his mule starve. When Crete rises again, the Achaeans, not we, will be sitting on the thrones. We'll be groveling like mangy dogs—"

"Enough, Glaukus," Rhadamanthys interrupted, "you're howling in the wind. This jackass can't hear you."

"Yeh, that's right," boomed the man. "Take the old loon away with you. How do you like that? The inlanders come over the waves, feed us, promise to rebuild our homes, and this old codger can only accuse them of evil. Ha! Well, my belly's full and if these Achaeans keep it that way, you won't hear me saying a thing against 'em."

Glaukus stepped forward, wanting to shake some sense into the man, but Rhadamanthys and I intervened and dragged our friend away; there was no sense arguing with the man, for he had simply said what everyone else in the valley would have said. For a crust of bread, the people would have done the bidding of anyone: Egyptian, Hittite, or Achaean.

Though it mattered little, the Achaeans who had landed at Timbaki were from gold-rich Mycenae on the Peloponnesus. Later on, we learned that other inland cities had sent expeditionary parties to other parts of Crete: Pylosians had sailed to Kydonia, Tirynians to Mallia, Thebans to Kato Zakro, Athenians to Knossos. Whoever got to a city first must have laid claim to it. Even after all the destruction, there were so many prizes on broad Crete that the Achaeans never moved in on one another's territory. Around the island, all the Achaean visits were similar. The people were bought off with food, the cities and palaces were reconnoitered, and more food and the resurrection of Crete were promised.

The first promise was swiftly kept. Long flotillas soon arrived loaded with provisions for the hungry, building supplies, and herds of mules and oxen. And more battle-brave soldiers with more shining swords. The Achaeans swept across Crete. The crude compounds the people had built became thick-walled stockades, and the people became prisoners. A bevy of guards armed with bronze-pointed spears and oxhide shields controlled all movement in and out of the stockades. The downtrodden people of Crete lost the one thing they had always valued above all else: their freedom.

In return for the loss of their freedom, the people received nourishment and some meager clothing. At first, in order to keep the slave-force fed, the Achaeans made long trips between their Cretan cities and their homes. To Crete they brought grain from magazines filled the year before, doubtless grain from the Messara itself. No matter how many ships loaded to the yardarms they came with, the Achaeans knew that to feed their slaves they would have to force them back to the land.

After things were firmly in hand, every morning, bright and early, the people were awakened, fed, and marched off to the fields. Only in certain parts of east Crete was this routine absent: in these parts, the mantle of ash was still too heavy, which explained why a place like Palaikastro went unclaimed. The rest of Crete, however, was as fertile as always, and, strangely enough, the light dose of ash in certain regions seemed to improve the fertility of the soil. By late spring, Crete was once again carpeted with golden wheat fields and orchards heavy with fruit.

Rhadamanthys, Glaukus, and I were living by then in the foothills below Mount Ida. You see, when the Mycenaean sails had reappeared, we packed our meager belongings, left our compound, and headed out. From our vantage point, we watched the people scurry down to the port and become willing accomplices to their own enslavement.

Though we stole from the rich fields in the valley, things were still hard for us. But we never complained. We had each other. And we had our freedom. Every now and then, a Cretan or Kallistean would stumble upon our camp, and we would learn what was happening around the island. Every time our camp was discovered, though, we moved on, fearing that if our visitors thought for a moment that they could get an extra ration of food out of it, they would tell the Mycenaeans who we were and where we were.

The first part of summer passed with the three of us scratching out an existence while keeping a close eye on the activity around Phaistos. When the work in the fields was well underway, the Mycenaeans sent some slaves into the city and palace to begin cleaning up the debris.

It was at that time when the cicadas chirp the loudest, that our position below Mount Ida became impossible. Every few days, we were forced to move our camp; we kept being discovered. Not just by farmers who strayed from the fields, but by runaways. Glaukus had predicted it would happen sooner or later. The bonds of slavery were chafing, and the people wanted out, even if it meant no more free rations. The people were willing to go back to foraging and hunting. Every day, new runaways fled up the mountain. Some escaped to the barren east part of the island. Some never made it out of the Messara.

Those who found our camp wanted to join us, even though we had nothing to join. We were three powerless men who each day scrounged for sustenance. Besides, the more people in the camp, the more likely the fierce Mycenaeans would discover us. The first dozen or so runaways we fed and sent packing, but before long, there were just too many people fleeing their oppressors. Regardless of how far we moved our campsite up Mount Ida, we were constantly being found. Eventually, we had to decide whether to join the runaways and form a band or strike out for another part of Crete.

Packing our skins and bowls once more, Rhadamanthys, Glaukus, and I headed east up the wide Messara, hugging the mountains to the north. You see, we had no faith in the former slaves, Cretan or Kallistean, and did not want to throw in with them. We moved slowly, hanging around the outskirts of this town or that village. For a while, we foraged near the remains of Gortyn.

Before long, all across the island, bands were forming, composed of runaways from nearly every stockade. The bands raided the fields and the stockades and ambushed the Achaean patrols. Can you imagine the carnage with soldiers wielding well-cast swords and common people using crude homemade weapons? Nevertheless, the raids continued and, miraculously, some bands even had a few stunning victories.

As we continued to move eastward, my companions and I stayed out of the fray. We zigzagged north and eventually wound up at Arkhanes on the slopes of Mount Juktas. Just as in the south, we found bands of roughneck runaways plaguing the inlanders at every turn. Knossos itself, stronghold of a large Athenian force, was not exempt from thunderflash raids, usually executed under the cloak of night. Hateful war was spreading like wildfire, and it was becoming harder and harder for the three of us to stay out of it.

One morning during the New Wine Moon, while searching for water, we came upon a large band of especially nasty-looking rebels. To our surprise, the ringleader asked us to join him and his men for breakfast; there was more than enough to go around, it seemed.

"Aye, we've been holding our own against those inland bastards," growled the ringleader, chewing and talking at the same time. He was a brawny man who—I guessed by his accent—came from the east tip of Crete; he must have worked as a field hand somewhere. "Ambush is the only way to get 'em…eh, boys?"

The others snorted in agreement and went on eating.

"I'm telling you," the leader continued, "we have these Athenians looking over their shoulders."

"You mean," asked Rhadamanthys, "your weapons have stood up to their slashing swords?"

"Well, at first we just sniped at them with bows and arrows, then ran like deer if they charged us. But sometimes our shooting was deadly, and we routed the scum. Then we'd go down and pick up their fancy swords and spears." With a big toothy grin, the ringleader reached behind himself and produced an Athenian dagger with an ivory hilt. "Now," he said with a sneer, "we mix it up pretty good with them brave soldiers…right, boys?"

The others chortled in agreement, and from underneath the animal skins they wore, they pulled swords and daggers: a cache of fine spears was pointed out to us across the other side of camp.

"Yeh, we're on even terms with them, now, for they have their weapons, and we have their weapons," roared the leader, throwing his head back in laughter. His men joined him.

"Not quite even" I broke in.

The laughter came to an abrupt halt. The leader cocked his shaggy head my way. "How's that, stranger?" he snorted.

"Well, you men are Cretans, fighting for your homeland. They are but greedy usurpers, trying to fill their purses. Why they don't even know where all the hamlets and villages lie. No doubt, you and your men will make them rue the day they ever set foot on Crete."

Looking me up and down, the leader stroked his matted beard and said, "You speak smoothly, stranger. But you're not a Cretan."

"No. I come from the Cyclades."

"From Kalliste?" he asked.

I hesitated, looking around me, then replied, "Yes, from Kalliste, that accursed island."

The Cretan nodded his head, then stared at me coldly. "Aye," he said, "that bitch of an island caused us all this grief. But she got hers."

"How's that?" I asked.

"Ever since they took over Knossos, the Athenians have been going back and forth to Athens and sailing past Kalliste, and, according to them, the whole Goddess-forsaken island blew up! Or sank to the bottom of the sea. Who knows. There is no more volcano. There is no more great mountain. There is nothing but a few scraps of land, and they're covered with hundreds of feet of white soot. The place is one big ghost town now, not fit for man nor beast."

Though my mind was unable to conjure up a picture of what the ruffian was saying, somehow, I knew it was true. I don't think I felt either sorrow or despair. Just anger. I wanted to smash my fist into the man's face for telling me the news. Though the air around me fairly quivered, I checked myself for the sake of my companions.

I was sure the leader was enjoying my discomfort when he said something that made me believe he wasn't even aware of it. "I like you, stranger," he declared, looking me over carefully. "Looks like there's some fight in that body of yours. Why not join us? There's food to be stolen and plenty of Athenian blood to be spilt."

"Well, I thank you, but we—"

"We? Nay, I meant you, just you. Not these old scarecrows," he hooted, gesturing toward Glaukus and Rhadamanthys.

A moment before, I had to control my hot head: Suddenly, on either side, I had to block the way of a charging comrade. "Easy, friends, easy," I cautioned out of the corner of my mouth.

"Let the bags of bones come," taunted the bully, "I sharpened this blade last night, and I'd like to test it on their scrawny necks." The other runaways joined in a good laugh.

"Listen," I exclaimed, "a while back we left Phaistos because we didn't want to join a band. We feel safer going it alone."

"See, there's where you made a mistake," boomed the leader. "You should have joined one of those bands around Phaistos; they're growing like mad. The mountain bands are playing havoc with the barbarians, raiding the fields and storehouses, harassing the stockades, picking off troops on patrol. The rebuilding of the city and palace never got underway. If you ask me, I think the Mycenaeans will be packing before long. They've had it."

"How do you know all this?" demanded Rhadamanthys.

"Why word has spread across the island in leaps and bounds… where have you been? What has taken place in the Messara has given us hope. If only all the people on this island, Cretan and Kallistean alike, would unite, we could drive the Achaeans away in a hurry."

Feelings, feelings that I thought were long dead, began to rise up within me. Feelings for the rich land of Crete and her proud people. Feelings for the homeless Kallisteans and their woes. And what brought those feelings to a head and gave them direction was the presence of the barbarians. When the earth tortured us so, we had nobody to strike out at; we could only pray to the Goddess or curse Her. That morning we stood on Mount Juktas, an enemy made of flesh and bones was within striking distance: the swaggering Athenians could be seen and chased and killed.

When men have been together through as much as Rhadamanthys, Glaukus, and I had, they can read each other's minds. Looking deep into the eyes of my old friends, I read their thoughts and learned that they were the same as mine. And I knew they wanted me to do the talking. I stepped forward and spoke to the gruff leader. "Listen, uh…what's your name?"

"Hybrias."

"Well, Hybrias, how about if we promise to—"

"I just told you—"

"Hear me out, man! If we promise to carry our load and do our share, there should be no complaints. I'll do more than my share of the fighting. My friends here will secure the camp and stand watch. All three of us will help prepare the food and do whatever anybody else does. How's that sound?"

Glancing around the camp, Hybrias saw that his men approved of my proposal.

"You're a fast talker," he said, spitting on the ground. "I don't know what you did before, stranger, and I don't care, but you and your friends can join us. Just remember…blood and rank mean nothing to us. Strength. That's the only thing that counts now."

"Right," I muttered.

The ringleader quickly added, with a glint in his eye, "And we have a test of strength here, which newcomers, or regulars, can call for at anytime."

"A test of strength?" I asked.

"Yes. If you pass, you go right to the top and become boss of this band of cutthroats. That's the way I did it!"

I looked at my friends from the corner of my eye. They urged me on. "So, what's this test?"

"It's simple: To pass the test and become boss of this band, you have to beat the present boss at wrestling—no holds barred."

A little before noon, I led my band of runaways farther up the mountain and set up camp. Hybrias was angered and bitter after I had ground his face in the dirt and nearly twisted his head off. When we hiked up to the new campsite, he trailed behind like a beaten puppy. Once we ate, though, and began swigging some stolen wine, he came around. And when we planned the next raid, he offered his ideas. His ideas were not very sound—I was surprised that the band hadn't been wiped out long ago—but I listened, allowing Hybrias a measure of respect. I got the feeling that Hybrias was happy that the tiller had been handed over to me, for he must have known he did not have the makings of a leader. His rise to the top had nothing to do with being wise or brave, but had to do solely with strength. In the end, Hybrias was content to be one of the men. I never had a problem with him. Indeed, he turned out to be one of my best warriors, and he was with me until the end.

TWENTY-SEVEN

THE FIRST RAID with Rhadamanthys, Glaukus, and me aboard was considered a success by the others in the band. But what was considered a success then was strange, indeed. We had ambushed a small caravan halfway between Arkhanes and Knossos, and, after a brief but savage encounter close in with swords, the surviving Athenians hightailed it for the capital. They left behind three comrades who died in pools of blood. But we lost seven men, and seven more were badly wounded.

We came away with four cartloads of vegetables and some Cretans who had been forced to work on the caravan. The downtrodden men were eager to join us; our number increased by six. None of the new members, moreover, felt like challenging the leader.

Seeing me return triumphantly with the food and the new men, Rhadamanthys threw back his head in laughter and the old sage turned a quick jig. That night under the countless stars, we savored a tasty vegetable stew and told brave stories around the flickering fire.

It's impossible for me to recall all the battles we had with the barbarians. All I know is that from the end of summer, through the entire fall, and at the beginning of winter, my hands were bathed in blood. Sometimes we were successful. And still other times, there were gory deadlocks, when neither we nor the enemy could claim victory.

All around Crete, hundreds, maybe thousands, of lives were lost on both sides, though far and away more Cretans and Kallisteans died than Achaeans. But there were many more of us. We could lose five, ten, twenty times as many lives and still wage war; numbers and time were on our side. The usurpers from inland were constantly plagued by bands made up of former subjects of King Minos, which were constantly growing in size. New runaways were breaking their bonds and seeking methods to avenge the humiliations they had suffered.

As the weather became colder, the word flew around the island: the barbarians had had enough; they were packing up and fleeing. On the shortest day of the year, the Mycenaeans set sail for home, leaving Phaistos for good, relinquishing it to the original people of the Messara. When they heard the news, Rhadamanthys and Glaukus cheered wildly and got drunk for two days. Not long afterwards, the Pylosians left Kydonia and the Thebans left Kato Zakro. And so it went, until there was only one city left under Achaean rule: Knossos.

Under their proud officers, the Athenian soldiers proved as unyielding as the youths and maidens who had danced in the bull ring. Instead of throwing up their hands as the other inlanders had done, the men from Athens held tight to the shattered capital and fought as if it were their birthplace. More and more reinforcements came, until it seemed as if half the population of the City of the Rock was quartered at Knossos.

As winter wore on, our raids met little success. The enemy took greater precautions, guarding their caravans better and doggedly patrolling the area around the capital.

Each skirmish grew grimmer, more savage: my entire body was covered with ugly pale scars from those conflicts. In spite of the fact that the bands along the north shore increased in size, they could not pry the Athenians from the island. Indeed, we rebels were clearly losing the war. Life in our camps was miserable as snow and freezing weather kept us forever wet and shivering.

As the Snow Moon waxed, we were hard pressed to fend off the Athenian counterattacks, and, one by one, our bands were hunted down, trapped, and wiped out. One bitter cold morning after a raid, my men and I huddled around a puny fire in a gully, chewing on some stale hardtack. There were about fifty of us; Rhadamanthys, Glaukus, and five others were back at the base camp, which was situated at Vathypetro, south of Arkhanes.

"The enemy!" screamed our lookout just before an arrow pierced his throat. Before we could get to our feet, a company of Athenians was spilling into the draw, hurling spears on the run. Our backs were against a swirling stream, and, though it was swollen and ice-cold, we had to swim across or be annihilated.

The raging water, unfortunately, did not stop the Athenians. They swam across, too, and pursued us eastward, picking off several of my men who were acting as a rear guard.

The enemy stayed on our heels all morning, and, at noon, when we tried to outflank them and escape, our tormentors pushed us back reeling. They were determined to destroy us once and for all. We had one last ditch chance: to race across the Lasithi Plain and get lost in the foothills of Mount Dikte. We took it.

By late afternoon, we thought we had lost them and stopped in a ravine to catch our breath. We weren't there long before, without warning, the strong-willed Athenians appeared at the mouth of the ravine, trapping us. Like blood-thirsty hounds, they spilled over the steep walls and drove us back. My men and I knew that that day was our last; we were outnumbered at least three to one. But none of us threw his weapons to the ground. We fought valiantly, slashing with our swords and thrusting with our daggers. For all that, the foe, in their superior numbers, hacked through my band. Men who had spent every moment of the past few months at my side were butchered like sheep. At the end, there were only a few of my men left with me. Bristling like boars, we fought with our backs against the stony head of the ravine.

In the madness of battle, I somehow caught sight of one Athenian who was getting the best of every man he fought. In between his bloody triumphs, he signaled with his arms and barked out orders: He must be the officer in charge, I thought, though there was no way of telling from his breast plate and helmet. I'll take their leader with me, I said to myself.

Ferociously, I cut my way through the pack before me and headed for the rocky outcropping upon which the man stood. My feet moved without effort, for I seemed to skim over the boulder-strewn floor of the ravine.

The doughty Hybrias must have had the same thought, for he was dueling the officer as I approached. It looked like my comrade was holding his own, but as I got there, the Athenian faked a low thrust with his sword and Hybrias went for it, dropping his tattered shield to thwart the blade. Before you could blink an eye, the Athenian followed up with a backhand slash; Hybrias's head flew off, striking the rocks with a crack and rolling over the edge of the outcropping.

Screaming as I went like a high-soaring hawk, I leapt on the Athenian, and we locked up sword against sword, shield against shield. We fought for position, searching each other's body for the place likeliest to yield, then we jumped backward and began to duel.

The man was fleet-footed; I knew already that he could fake and feint. We thrust and slashed, blocked and sidestepped, both receiving cuts on our forearms. At that point minor wounds meant nothing.

From the corner of my eye, I saw a circle of men — like a noose closing in on us. They weren't mine. Immediately, I understood, for my mind was working faster than ever, that I was the last of the band.

"Stay back, damn it! He's mine!" screamed my adversary. His men taunted me, cursed and spit, but none of them lunged at me. How long the two of us dueled in the grim ravine I don't know, but it seemed like forever. My enemy could not get the upper hand. The more frustrated he got, the more vulnerable he became. Without so much as a fake, he charged me, paying for it by receiving a ringing blow on the helmet. That didn't stop him, for he charged again, managing to tie me up. At that moment of utter peril, one thought ran through my mind: I know the movements and body of this man. The jutting cheek pieces and low brim of his helmet hid most of his face…but the eyes. That's where I went wrong, staring into those eyes.

Before I knew it, my foe had slipped his leg behind mine and knocked me off balance. I fell backward, arms outstretched. Striking the unyielding rocks, my sword fell from my hand. I pulled my dagger from my belt, but it flew away, kicked by the Athenian. He straddled me; sword raised high.

Calls for my head filled the ravine. But the barbarian hesitated, standing over me like some stone statue; he was savoring his sweet victory. I looked up, staring into the dark hollow between the cheek pieces of his helmet. "At last I join my loved ones. Do it now, Theseus." Silhouetted against the sky, the blood-glistening sword descended slowly and was rammed into its sheath.

Moans and cries of disbelief filled the ravine. With one motion, Theseus tore off his helmet and flung it to the ground. "Idomeneus! Can it be you?"

"It is," I said. "You've won. Kill me and do it quickly!"

As he took a step backwards, Theseus grimaced, his eyes fixed on me as only they could.

"Kill the swine," someone shouted.

"Cut his throat!"

Theseus turned and yelled, "Silence! All of you!" He turned back and looked down at me and said, "You look like a different man. That hair. That beard. Those scars. Those rags. It looks like you've been to Hades and back!"

"Listen, I'm not going to beg for this miserable life of mine. Kill me and get it over with."

"The story of these last few years is etched deep into your once-fair face, Idomeneus. What horrors you must have seen," he said.

"Prince to prince, I say do what you must do!"

"It's King now, Idomeneus. King Theseus of Athens and Attica." He thought for a moment, then added with scorn, "And now, King of Crete." We stared at one another in silence. Then he sniggered and said, "That means dirt to you, doesn't it? You wouldn't beg whether I were pharaoh or king of the world or almighty Zeus Himself!"

I said nothing. My thoughts turned inward as I prepared to die.

But Theseus's sword remained sheathed. He turned to his men, saying, "This rebel and I have done battle before — in the arena. He could have broken my neck but didn't. Later he kept a secret, a dangerous secret, and, by so doing, spared my life a second time." Looking back down at me, Theseus proclaimed in a loud voice,

"Today, no one — not even I — will snuff out his life. But next time he and I meet, if there is a next time, each one of us will be free to destroy the other." He stepped back. "Rise, Idomeneus, man of unbearable sorrow. You are free to go."

Like a criminal pardoned just before the axe falls, I felt a surge of life rush through my body. Catlike, I moved warily, pushing myself up onto my feet.

"You have my word," Theseus said reassuringly, "none of these men will lift a hand against you."

"Your arrival on Crete was a well-kept secret, Theseus," I said. "How did you manage that?"

"Oh, I arrived" — He stopped and rephrased it — "I returned ten days ago, wanting to discover why it was taking my people so long to subdue homeless and long-suffering renegades. You see, Idomeneus, we aren't like the other *barbarians.*"

He said the last word with particular relish. "We Athenians aren't about to give up and retreat to the mainland like the others — though we're happy they did! Ha, that means all the more for us. The whole island, in fact!"

His men began to laugh and shout, but I cut them short. "Curse you and all your henchmen! You'll never see an end to this war!"

"Oh, we will," Theseus snapped. "True, it's a big task. But, one by one, we'll wipe out the bands. First those around Knossos, then those along the north shore, then those in the south and the west. Even if it takes a year or more, we'll do it."

"For every band you destroy, a new one will spring up."

"Maybe. But there's got to be an end to them. I'll be happy eliminating one at a time like I did today."

My hands were tightly clenched at my sides, my teeth, like millstones, ground the sand between them. Theseus took his eyes off me slowly and looked around at the bloody battleground. "No wonder this band plagued my people, causing them so much sorrow. You, Idomeneus, were at the helm."

"And now, you, Theseus, have massacred my band. I'm all alone, I have nothing."

"My troops back at Knossos will be safer for that. Go. Go up into the mountains, dwelling place of the Gods, and lick your wounds like some haughty lion, Idomeneus. For your sake, and mine, I hope I never see your proud face again."

Theseus brought his hand to his chest in salute. At first, I hesitated, wanting to strike out with my fist. But then, grudgingly, I returned his salute. As I turned and walked away, the ring of Athenians parted. There were no catcalls. No jeering. My mortal enemies simply gazed at me in silence as I left the hateful ravine.

Stumbling farther up the mountain, I had no thoughts of where to go. No plans. No hopes. I was utterly defeated. All I wanted was to crawl under some rock and die.

Without knowing how I got there or how long it took, I eventually found myself looking out over the Lasithi Plain. How different the mountain-ringed plain looked from that first time I had seen it over twenty years before with my father. The soft green carpet had vanished, replaced by a dull quilt of brown dirt and gray ash. The wind howled in my face, whipping around the great bowl and picking up dirt and ash and mixing them into a gritty haze. Through the macabre murk, I spied thin lifeless sentinels, the once leafy trees of Lasithi.

That long last day was drawing to a close. The creature within me pushed on to find some sort of shelter. At the end of a stoney path, the gaping mouth of the Diktean Cave was waiting for me, darker than night itself. Fanged bats clinging to the ceiling of the cave announced my arrival—to no one. If at the moment of birth, a soothsayer could see the future and know that he was to lead a life of pain and sorrow, he might try to crawl back into his mother. I was like such a man as I crawled on hands and knees into the reeking cave, tucked myself up in a dank corner and sleep overtook me.

EPILOGUE

NOW THE STORY of Kalliste and the empire of Minos has been told, scratched into these clay tablets by me, Idomeneus, son of Cretheus. I was once a well-respected prince. I once had the love of a tender mother and a radiant wife. I once walked in the most splendid palaces on earth and dressed in royal finery. Now I live in a dreary cave and wear stinking animal skins. Mouthwatering meals used to be brought to me. Now I'll eat anything, I'm starving. I used to pray and sacrifice to the Goddess. Now I believe in nothing.

Two months have passed since the battle in the ravine. And all that time I have remained in this hole in the ground; I venture out only to hunt with bow and arrow. How often I have thought of wise Glaukus and his dream about the cave, its bizarre inhabitants, and me. How prophetic that dream. I find myself in the same condition as those cave people: My body is covered with my own matted hair and I wrap hides tightly around me to stay warm. Those poor people in the dream lived many years ago, before man built cities and ruled the waves. I'm alive today—if you can call this living—but am no different from the shaggy people in Glaukus' dream.

Sometimes, though, I do have visitors down here. They're made not of flesh and bones, but of ethereal stuff. The spectre of my fair Aphaea brightens the gloom. My mother and father come hand in hand. There are Ta-ch'ih and Ananda. Two more I've been expecting haven't appeared: Rhadamanthys and Glaukus. Whether they are alive at this moment, I do not know. I left them safe at Vathypetro, but by now they may have been discovered and captured or killed. Why didn't I go back to Vathypetro to see if my only friends were alive? Because I was afraid, afraid to know the answer, I suppose. Afraid that I might learn that I was, in fact, the last of my line on earth.

Now that all the game in the Lasithi is gone, I'll have to head west anyway; before long I will know if Rhadamanthys and Glaukus have survived King Theseus, scourge of Crete.

If on the way I am overtaken by an Athenian patrol, it will matter little; my life means nothing. Nor the life of any Kallistean or Cretan. For this land now belongs to the barbarians. They are the only ones who matter. Though I spoke brave words to Theseus, I knew that he was right: he and his people will stamp out all resistance and rule Crete forevermore. The men of Minos are finished. The great empire lost. The long-lasting peace shattered. Our fine palaces and our lovely arts, our just laws and our gracious manners and customs are but misty memories. We had the perfect paradise. Did it ever exist at all? In a few short years, a way of life that had been refined over the past millennium and nurtured by some of the greatest minds on earth was irrevocably lost. And all because a beautiful little jewel of an island turned into a monster, spreading its deadly shadow across the entire empire.

What will these barbarians raise up in place of our institutions and achievements? Will they bring beauty and wisdom to the world with their cutting blades and sharp-tipped spears? No. Expect nothing for the betterment of man from these people or their offspring. They have finished off the greatest empire there ever was, and only for that will the world remember the men of Athens.

The End

AUTHOR'S NOTE

No other city in history has influenced mankind as profoundly as fifth century BC Athens. Today, most of the ideas we hold dear in philosophy, political theory, democracy, law, science, medicine, organized competitive athletics, lyric poetry, theater, and the visual arts originated with or were deeply clarified by the extraordinary people of the Athenian Golden Age. This was, however, a thousand years AFTER the events in *Kalliste*, which occurred over a three-year span sometime from 1615 to 1550 BC in the Late Bronze Age. The Athens of that bygone era may have produced gifted thinkers and impressive institutions, but what has come down to us is mostly legend, as in the case of Theseus and Jason and the Argonauts. Over the last century and a half, archaeology, aided by other disciplines, and the decipherment of texts written in Linear B have been greatly filling in the picture.

The Bronze Age people (called Achaeans in the book) who occupied Athens and all the other cities on mainland Greece are today collectively called Mycenaeans, after that formidable citadel in the Peloponnesus. Their counterparts were the Crete-and-Aegean-Island-dwelling Minoans, named by archaeologist Sir Arthur Evans after the legendary dynast Minos. The fortunes of the Minoans were on the rise for fifteen-hundred years, as they went about creating the first maritime empire in history, spanning the Mediterranean. Then things turned abruptly and decisively for the worse. Though the Mycenaeans were in their formative phase, they were able to take advantage of the rapid decline of the Minoans, caused by natural catastrophes on Crete and Kalliste, the island today known as Thera or Santorini.

By the Late Bronze Age, the volcano had not erupted in some twenty-two thousand years; it is likely that the Kallistean inhabitants did not even know that they were living on a quiescent volcano. During the eruption, huge amounts of magma were forced up the vent and exploded into the atmosphere in the form of gases, ash, and boulders. Then the great cone, possibly five-thousand feet high, caved in on itself, making the immense (some fifty square miles) caldera seen today. That collapse of the walls of the volcano, plus the earthquakes, no doubt generated huge tidal waves, by one estimate some of the waves may have reached hundreds of feet in height. The waves sped the short distance to Crete, devastating its north shore. The tidal waves, earthquakes, and sonic blasts may have stunned the Minoan world, but it was the fallout of ash which buried it. Mt. St. Helens produced a half cubic mile of ejecta, Vesuvius three-and-a-half cubic miles, and Krakatoa eleven. Kalliste may have produced over forty. A buildup of four inches of ash is enough to knock out a field for a year. Crete was probably blanketed with much more than that since the northwesterlies seemed to have been blowing during the final cataclysmic phase of the eruption. In the last century, ash from this volcano has been discovered in the eastern Mediterranean and the north shore of Egypt.

The volcanic ash deposited on Santorini itself reached in some places two-hundred feet in height. The ongoing excavation at the site called Akrotiri on the south shore is revealing more and more about a prosperous port city of possibly forty-five thousand people. Commonly referred to as the "Pompeii of the Aegean," Akrotiri had three-story buildings, many public squares, advanced plumbing, highly prized pottery, and wall paintings that rivaled any in the world. Going forward, new finds, no doubt, will help fill in the picture of this extraordinary Late Bronze Age city and its role in the Minoan Empire of thirty-five-hundred years ago.

Special thanks go to my dear friend the late Marjorie Livingston Valier for reading the manuscript and making important stylistic and textual suggestions. Over the time it took for this book to appear between covers, my son, Galen Dell, was a constant supporter and advisor. Special kudos are reserved for my daughter, Malia Dell, who encouraged me during slow periods, taught me everything I know about book production, and steadfastly believed in me and my story of Kalliste.

Finally, Kalliste could not have been written without the unwavering support of my wife, Nancy, who very early in the process typed and retyped the manuscript, suggested pivotal changes, and was my intrepid companion throughout our world travels. As always, she was and is the beacon for this wayfarer.

About the Author

Photo: © Sarah Szwajkos

Roger Dell is an art historian and an arts educator. He had a long career as the director of education at various American art museums, including the Honolulu Art Museum, the Museum of Contemporary Art in Chicago, and the Farnsworth Art Museum in Maine. He has written and lectured widely on the history of art, art appreciation, and art museums. Over the years, Roger Dell has taught in the capacity of adjunct instructor at many universities, including University of Hawai'i, University of Maine, Harvard Graduate School of Education, and the Harvard Extension School. Currently, he lives with his wife, Nancy, in Midcoast Maine. While doing research for the book, Roger and Nancy lived for a year in a traditional island cave on Santorini, which is the modern name for Kalliste.

CPSIA information can be obtained
at www.ICGtesting.com
Printed in the USA
FSHW010949240320
68426FS